DEVIL'S TRILL

DEVIL'S TRILL

A MYSTERY IN SONATA ALLEGRO FORM

GERALD ELIAS

Minotaur Books   New York

DEVIL'S TRILL. Copyright © 2009 by Gerald Elias. All rights reserved. Printed in the United States of America. For information, address St. Martin's Press, 175 Fifth Avenue, New York, N.Y. 10010.

www.minotaurbooks.com

The Library of Congress has cataloged the hardcover edition as follows:

Elias, Gerald.
    Devil's trill / Gerald Elias. — 1st ed.
        p. cm.
    ISBN 978-0-312-54181-1
    1. Violin teachers—Fiction.   2. Music—Competitions—Fiction.   3. Musical
fiction.   I. Title.
    PS3605.L389D48 2009
    813'.6—dc22

                                                            2009012722

ISBN 978-0-312-65350-7 (trade paperback)

First Minotaur Books Paperback Edition: August 2010

10 9 8 7 6 5 4 3 2 1

Dedicated to my father, Irving Albert Elias,

who loved to write and to listen to music

PROLOGUE

Other violins have been stolen. Great works of art have been plucked from their exalted perches in museums. But 1983 witnessed one sensational theft that, for its complexity and lethal repercussions, is unequaled. Some of you may have a distant recollection of a news item in your local press when a unique violin by Antonio Stradivari was stolen. The story made headlines for a short while, even reaching the desk of CNN, which reported it with great fanfare and modest accuracy. As leads in the investigation dried up, however, the story faded from front pages like last week's weather. As a result, few ever heard the tragic consequences of the whole affair, and almost no one, not even the official investigators, fully appreciated the depth and intricacy of motives and relationships that caused such a bizarre and unfortunate series of events.

It is worth briefly mentioning here the pivotal moment—well known within classical musical circles—in the life of violinist Daniel Jacobus, the central figure in this story, whose life, liberty, and unflinching pursuit of unhappiness were put in dire jeopardy. Like his hero, Beethoven, Jacobus was on the verge of a stellar career as a performer when he was afflicted by life-shattering illness. In Jacobus's case it was foveomacular dystrophy, a rare genetic mutation in which blood vessels in the eye grow too fast. The result is leakage of blood and fluid into the eye, which, if not promptly treated, can cause blindness within twenty-four hours.

Foveomacular dystrophy struck Jacobus on the eve of his audition for the concertmaster position of the Boston Symphony Orchestra. True to form, he eschewed medical attention, played his legendary audition from memory (since he couldn't see the music), and won it hands down against some of the finest orchestral violinists of his day. When his eyesight failed to return even after intensive treatment, the BSO had no choice but to award the concertmaster position to the runner-up. Jacobus spent months in seclusion, and when he eventually emerged from his self-imposed chrysalis he was transformed, declaring his intention to be a teacher. With a remarkably unorthodox teaching style, Jacobus produced students who over the years graced countless concert stages and teaching studios with their presence, or not, but in almost all cases ended up with a far more precious gift, an abiding love of classical music. Thus, as was the case with Beethoven, an individual's personal tragedy became the world's gain.

At the same time, *Devil's Trill* is about the psychological and physical abuse heaped upon children by a cutthroat world of unscrupulous teachers, managers, agents, and even parents. These children happen to have the rare natural gift (or, some would say, curse) of being able to move their fingers with amazing dexterity and to make a musical instrument sound astonishingly good, even though the children themselves may not have the vaguest idea what they're doing, or why. Thrown into grueling, merciless competitions against each other at an age when they are still emotionally vulnerable in order to satisfy some artificial standard of "perfection," these competitions are no less cruel to these children than cockfighting is to its bloody contestants. And cockfighting is illegal.

Finally, the book is about an often-shadowy netherworld of violin dealing, where dark currents of greed swirl quietly through the seemingly dignified white-tie-and-tail world of classical music. In the current market, where good violins are no longer affordable to the professional musicians who would play them, fragile masterpieces from the seventeenth and eighteenth centuries become a currency of obsession to dealers and collectors, and scruples are as rare as the instruments themselves.

He dreamed one night, in 1713, that he had made a compact with the Devil, who promised him to be at his service on all occasions; and during this vision everything succeeded according to his mind. In short, he imagined he gave the Devil his violin, in order to discover what kind of musician he was; when to his great astonishment, he heard him play a solo so singularly beautiful and executed with such superior taste and precision, that it surpassed all he had ever heard or conceived in his life.

So great was his surprise and so exquisite his delight upon this occasion that it deprived him of the power of breathing. He awoke with the violence of his sensation and instantly seized his fiddle in hopes of expressing what he had just heard, but in vain; he, however, then composed a piece, which is perhaps the best of all his works (he called it the "Devil's Sonata"), but it was so inferior to what his sleep had produced that he declared he should have broken his instrument and abandoned music forever, if he could have subsisted by any other means.

—As told to Joseph-Jérôme Lefrançais de Lalande by
Giuseppe Tartini in his "Voyage d'un Français en Italie,"
and translated by Dr. Charles Burney

The trill of the devil from the foot of the bed.

—Giuseppe Tartini, inscribed in his Sonata in G Minor, published 1798

INTRODUCTION

The Life and Death of Matteo Cherubino,

"Il Piccolino," by Lucca Pallottelli (ca. 1785),

translated by Jonathan Gardner (1846)

The wintry midday light, cold and unforgiving, passed through the stained-glass image of the Madonna high above, casting the bloodred of her velvet-covered bosom onto the sleeping face of Matteo Cherubino. The unnatural ray harshly highlighted its features—deep, worried furrows etched in his brow; darkened shadows of his unshaven cheek masking faint scars of youthful smallpox; the latent insolence of his protruding chin and its resultant underbite. Indolent dust particles floating in the chamber were momentarily radiated as they strayed without purpose into the column of pale crimson.

"Porca Madonna," muttered Cherubino. He turned his back on the Virgin's light and tugged the coverlet over his head. But was it this light or was it the distant sound of horses' hooves on cobblestones that had roused him? He was gripped by an undefined sense of doom. He felt suffocated by the dense mass of a feather pillow in which he had buried his head.

Awakening with his head on an unfamiliar pillow was not the specific cause of his anxiety or an altogether unusual circumstance for Matteo Cherubino. Nevertheless, or perhaps precisely for this reason, it took him a moment to recall whose lithe form was snoring contentedly beside him, still in the shadows.

"M—!" he said to himself in disgust.

That grave, intangible feeling of oppression increased in proportion to Cherubino's level of consciousness. Layers of heavy wool weighed down upon him. The Duchess's arm, which only a few hours before had been so magically graceful, now was a heavy iron chain across his chest, strapping him down like the Inquisitor's instrument of torture. Yet he was reluctant to move it, lest she wake.

From the cavernous fireplace, he was assailed by the acrid odor of damp ash. Those same ashes were the humble remains of the great flame that had blazed along with their ardor and had so recently cast their undulating silhouettes on the chamber's massive stone walls.

He turned his head toward an unlikely sound. A rat brazenly gnawed at the same pigeon carcass on which they themselves had feasted and then had carelessly tossed, between bouts of familiar intimacy, in the general direction of the hearth.

Paolina Barbino, Duchess of Padua, continued to sleep. Cherubino smelled her spittle, which had traced its way from the side of her mouth to his pillow. The scent of her quiet exhalations mingled the earthy black truffles and chestnuts with which the pigeons had been stuffed with Tuscan red wine.

Cherubino also smelled himself. He wanted to dress and leave.

"M—," he repeated to himself.

He, Matteo Cherubino, the great Piccolino, surrounded by such opulence—human and otherwise. Who would have believed it? Who would have imagined he would be repulsed by it?

Born in a cold, leaky hut on February 29, 1656, on the outskirts of the Umbrian hamlet of San Fatucchio, Matteo was the thirteenth and last child in a family of traveling entertainers—actors, acrobats, musicians. As he grew—or, more precisely, grew older—Matteo became aware of two things: the small stature of the family circus and of himself. Having been born on the one day that occurred only every fourth year, he seemed to have been cursed with a body that was growing at the same unnaturally slow rate. After a while Matteo stopped growing altogether. Siblings began calling him Piccolino, "Little One." With such a large family it was easier to remember this appellation than his Christian name.

Matteo's size disrupted the timing of the family's acrobatics routine, and any of his efforts at dramatic acting were inevitably received with howls of laughter. Matteo was given the jobs of providing background music and of passing the hat to collect meager offerings. Year after year the family wound its way along endless trails of San Fatucchios through the Umbrian hills, by and large following the same trail Hannibal forged thousands of years before in his victorious campaign against the Romans on the shore of Lake Trasimeno. The Cherubinos, however, were less in search of glory than in having enough food to evade their own enemy, starvation.

Thus they plodded from town to town—Castiglione del Lago, Tuoro, Passignano—on and on, day after day, through the malaria-infested swamps of the lowlands, setting up their little circus on whatever day the local market was held. And always they sought out the prime location next to the *porchetta* stall, where sweaty townspeople swarmed to feast on whole pig being roasted on a spit, stuffed with garlic, rosemary, fennel, the pig's own liver, and olive oil. At every opportunity, the Cherubino family would pilfer samples, especially the outer layer of crispy skin and thick fat, darting in while the vendor was serving paying customers. If they were caught, the Cherubinos would shout, "Hey, fair is fair! You watch our act for free! This makes things even!" The *porchetta* vendors, blackened by greasy smoke, would usually respond lustily with a hand gesture signifying more than a difference of opinion but rarely pursued it further.

Matteo began his musical career on plucked instruments—lutes, guitars, mandolins. They provided good accompaniment—quiet and unobtrusive. He could patter on for hours improvising lilting melodies or lively rhythms, depending on the drama at hand. However, after some time Matteo grew restless with these instruments. In his heart he heard music that was bigger, grander, and brilliant.

These lutes are fine for a dwarf, he thought. But that's all.

Matteo traded some of his collection for a few of the more popular bowed instruments—gambas and viols. There were all shapes and sizes of these, so he had little trouble finding ones suitable for his diminutive stature. He quickly taught himself how to be expert in the use of the bow, whether playing gambas between the legs or viols held on the shoulder.

These instruments opened up a whole new world of expressive possibilities. The family's tragedies seemed to become more tragic and the comedies more comic. More coins from the audiences began to be tossed in their direction, and as they multiplied, Matteo's newfound skill gained the appreciation of the Cherubinos, since feeding a family of fifteen was no easy task, even in the best of times.

Matteo, though, was not content. He wanted more sound. More brilliance. More power. More passion. More! More! Morose and defiant he became. His dissatisfaction was beginning to disrupt his family's equilibrium.

His siblings, with gathering annoyance, constantly scolded him. "Stop moping! Stop complaining!" they shouted, and threatened to expel him from their family troupe.

They don't understand, thought Matteo, and he came to despise their small minds and smaller vision.

"This song in my heart is just beginning to blossom, but now it is only a seedling. In my soul a majestic willow is growing!" he once confessed to a peasant girl who had rejected his amorous advances. He made an oath to himself that someday what he alone heard in his own heart would make another's break.

One day in November—a cold, cloudy day with a damp, relentless west wind at their backs—Piccolino and the family troupe reached the monumental Etruscan stone gates of the mighty Umbrian capital of Perugia. Their hearts chilled by the Pope's monolithic fortress of the Rocca Paolina, they wound their way up and up under its oppressive shadow, through a maze of cobbled lanes—lanes so steep they often required steps—in search of the town square.

By the time they arrived on the Corso, Piccolino's legs were aching; it was pitch-dark but for flickering torches held fast in the stone walls of buildings surrounding the square. One of these buildings was an inn from which exuded the savory aroma of stewing *cinghiale,* wild boar, so the "famiglia cherubini" decided to set up their gear right there for the next day's performance. Few people passed, and those who did scuttled by furtively, eyes downcast. Every hour or so a dark horseman cantered past. Piccolino protected his arms from the horse's hooves, which echoed ominously on the paved stones. No one bothered them, but as they bedded down the family wondered if their theater was doomed to fail within this atmosphere of dread.

The Cherubinos slept. From deep within Matteo's restless dreams, the sound of music—heavenly music—woke him in the dark. He shook his head in order to dispel the dream and return to his sleep on the cold stone, but the music persisted. The music was real. Matteo rose, standing perfectly still, his head slightly raised, using his ears to ascertain the origin of the sound as a dog would use its nose to seek out the source of the scent of stewing *cinghiale*.

Wandering off in the dark, he tripped along ever-narrowing alleyways turning this way and that, ancient alleyways that were already ancient when the Romans conquered this Etruscan city. Sometimes the music grew more distant as he turned in the wrong direction. He worked his way back, feeling his way with his hands on the walls of the connected stone buildings lining the way. He tripped in the stone gutters and stepped in cold effluent, but he hardly cared.

He turned a corner into a lane barely wide enough to walk through. Then, from inside a formidable stone house, Matteo heard the sound he had been searching for, the sound of his own heart. It was of a string instrument with a voice like a winged angel, soaring and swooping, luminescent as the light of heaven.

What was this sound? In frantic agitation, little Matteo jumped as high as he could, over and over again, in desperation to see into the window from which pale light beckoned. A lone passerby backed away, fearful that what appeared to be a demented dwarf was in the grip of some diabolical fit. She muttered, *"Gesù Cristo, salvemi,"* and gave him the hand sign to ward off evil contagion.

Matteo catapulted himself against the massive wooden front door with all his might. The pitiful thud of his body silenced the music. Matteo leaned against the stone wall, panting from his exertions. From inside the house came the sound of approaching footsteps.

A bolt slid. The door opened a crack. A shadowed face, momentarily perplexed at not seeing anyone or anything, finally looked down upon Matteo's heaving little frame.

"Sì? E che vuoi?" the face said, with cultivated disdain.

"You must tell me . . . You must tell me . . . That instrument . . . What is that instrument you are playing?" gasped Matteo.

"Why," said the face, smugly amused, "that instrument is a violin. Everyone's playing it these days. Didn't you know?"

A sound came from deep within the house—a woman's sound—and the rustling of sheets. The face turned away and then briefly back to Matteo, but without further effort at civility. The door to the house closed, but the door to Matteo's heart opened.

In Italy, the golden age of the violin had been blazing with blinding brilliance. Matteo sold all of his old lutes and gambas to get this new kind of instrument. He wasn't the only one either. Within just a few generations, the violin had swept across the musical world of Europe, overwhelming the traditional string instrument families like a tidal wave. Cascading along its uncharted currents came the great Italian makers—the Amati family, the Guarneris, Stradivari; and the virtuosi-composers—Tartini, Corelli, Vivaldi, Locatelli, Albinoni, Geminiani, Torelli. It was a period of musical virtuosity never equaled before or since. But among these giants, no one was greater—or smaller—than Piccolino.

Piccolino's talent blossomed into genius. With unfailing memory he could play the compositions of any of the other virtuosi after a single hearing, and he never had the need to write down a note of his own music. He had the ability to improvise the most dazzling, difficult, and beautiful music imaginable. No longer did he play in the background. Now it was the rest of his family that collected the money, the gifts, the jewels. Weighted pockets brought the return of their equilibrium, as is so often the case.

Cherubino's fame spread, particularly among the ladies. This surprised him at first. He knew that in part it was due to his playing. Another part was due to his enlarged male anatomy, the only physical asset Nature had endowed upon him. However, he knew that for the most part he was regarded as a plaything. He became their prize. It depressed him.

Piccolino, pierced by the chill of the bedchamber, gazed with sad affection at the sleeping Duchess. Distant footsteps from within the palace barely disturbed the surrounding silence.

If only I were a foot or two taller, he thought. If only I had been born to a family other than one of roving entertainers. If only! I would exchange all these secret trysts for one woman who truly loved me.

Would I exchange my musical genius for love?

A much more difficult question, he thought, as he tried to slip away undetected from the arm under whose weight he was still pinned. But as he did so the body beside him stirred, responding to his movement, perhaps even his thoughts. Her deep brown eyes fluttered open.

"*Porca Madonna,*" Piccolino muttered again. He hadn't even made it out of the bed.

"Ah, my little man." She smiled. With long white fingers she combed back her disheveled mane of black hair, which had settled over her eyes and thin delicate nose during her sleep.

Her movements, her sleepy wildness, stirred him against his better judgment.

"At your service, my Lady," replied Piccolino softly.

"Again? And so soon?" she cooed.

"Your wish is my command, my Lady."

"Ah! Then my command is"—she stifled a yawn—"Rise, *gran signor,* and prick my heartstrings with your divine instrument."

"That might be a bit impractical, at least for the moment, my Lady."

"You miss my point, Piccolino," said the Duchess, turning on her side to face him. As she propped herself upon her elbow, her cheek resting on her hand, the wool blanket slipped off her torso, exposing the curving line of her long neck, her exquisite collarbone, and her small, soft bosom, the deep crimson of the blanket emphasizing the pale whiteness of her skin.

Piccolino tried not to look at her.

Her tongue lightly traced the line of her upper lip. "I do miss your point dearly, but it is your violin I wish you to play for me."

"Ah. I see," said Piccolino, as his eyes followed the rising line of her hip under the blanket. "But even so, my Lady, the Duke . . . he may arrive any moment."

"Oh, yes, the Duke. He's probably still in Siena or Firenze plotting something revolting against Pisa. Don't worry, dear Piccolino. It needn't be long. This time."

"But my Lady," persisted Piccolino, increasingly anxious, "I haven't a stitch of clothing on. The fire is out—I could catch a cold from the draft."

"But Piccolino," said the Duchess, seductively batting her long eyelashes, "I will keep you warm. Besides, I have a very special present for your birthday today. Your thirteenth, isn't it?"

"Actually, my fifty-second, though I was born on leap day."

"Well, young man nevertheless, it's a very special present, one that you will hold very close to you."

"My Lady, you have already given me such a present."

"This one, I promise, you will love even more than me, until your last moment on earth," said the Duchess.

First the poverty of youth. Now the poverty of riches, thought Piccolino.

"Very well, my Lady."

Piccolino lowered himself from the bed until his feet touched the ground. Still feeling the effects of last night's wine, he stumbled across the cold stone tiles to the heavy wooden table along the side of the room. Only a few hours before he had put his violin down next to the remains of their stuffed pigeon, now being shared by a pair of flies luxuriating in the musty pungency of stale truffle. The flies ignored the empty bottles of wine, more bottles than Piccolino had remembered.

Piccolino picked up the cold violin and casually strummed its strings, gauging the acoustics of the chamber, trying to forget he was naked and shivering. The stone, brick, plaster, wood, and high ceilings alone would give the room a harsh echoey resonance. He squinted his eyes and gazed at the light coming through the figure of the Madonna in the stained-glass window, her loving gaze eternally fixed not upon him but upon the Infant at her teat. He looked approvingly at the immense tapestry hanging on one wall. Fortunately, the violin's sound would be dampened by it, eliminating the echo but not the luster. The subject of the huge tapestry, woven in rich greens, blues, reds, and golds, was the gruesome biblical tale of the Slaughter of the Innocents. Piccolino had never understood the popularity of the subject. To him, the portrayal of heavily armed soldiers massacring children still clinging desperately to their mothers' breasts was sickening and disconcerting.

"So here is my audience." He sighed. "My lover, the Virgin, dying babies, and," detecting movement at the hearth, "a rat. Well, I've had worse."

Consistent with his mood and his audience, Piccolino began to improvise a sad but sweet sarabanda.

Ah, the ladies always like a sarabanda, he mused, a dance the Roman Church, in its benevolent wisdom, had banned. Too sensual for public consumption. If only the Church heard this performance—let them see it too!—no doubt they'd ban it for eternity.

The seductive melody resonated softly off the frescoed walls and vaulted ceiling. The Duchess, enthralled, unconsciously twirled a strand of her hair around her forefinger, chewing on it with small white teeth.

Piccolino watched her as he played, watched her gaze with longing at his diminutive but stocky muscular physique.

Maybe I'm shorter and hairier than your past lovers, he thought, but I haven't heard you complain. He noted with approval and self-approval the deepening movement of her torso as she inhaled, her warm, moist breath condensing in the chamber's cold air.

"*Caro* Piccolino," the Duchess whispered throatily after the final, plaintive note died away. Only some distant commotion from within the palace walls disturbed the room's silence.

"And now you shall have my gift, Piccolino." With a graceful flourish, the Duchess reached under the bed. In her hand she held a violin.

But it was not just another violin, Piccolino immediately saw with widening eyes. It was a violin unlike any he had ever seen. The grain of the wood appeared to be in flame. The varnish was ablaze—now red, now orange, now golden.

As the Duchess placed the violin in his hands, he could see that the purfling—the fine inlay bordering the edge of the violin that was usually made of wood, straw, or even paper—was here made with pure gold. The pegs were gargoyles of engraved ivory. Breathing all this fire was a scroll in the shape of a dragon's head whose glowing ruby eyes stared defiantly into his.

"What man could create something such as this?" said Piccolino, staring. He could not move.

"Oh, I commissioned it from a handsome young man in Cremona. Antonio Stradivari," replied the Duchess. "Did he get the size right? I told him it must be built to your . . . dimensions."

"This is perfection. Perfection!" Piccolino suddenly shook himself from his reverie. "But, my Lady, the cost?"

"No, no. Antonio was very reasonable. He said, 'Someday I will be as famous as Signor Amati!' so he was very willing to make this one in order to enhance his reputation. Plus, he did owe me a little favor."

Without speculating on why he owed her a little favor, Piccolino raised the violin to his shoulder, shuddering with greater desire than he had ever felt. So overcome with emotion was he that for a moment he was physically unable to put the bow on the string. Then he was ready, ready to hear the ultimate song of his heart.

"Oh, one more thing," said the Duchess. "Look inside."

There inside the violin was a label bearing the statement: "To the great Piccolino on his 13th birthday, the only small violin I will ever make." It was signed "Antonio Stradivari, Cremona," and dated February 29, 1708.

"My Lady, I am forever in your debt."

As he said this, the heavy wooden door to the room was viciously kicked open, rebounding repeatedly against the stone wall, sounding in the cavernous room like the drumbeat of Death. It frightened even the rat, which skittered away from its bony breakfast. Enrico Barbino, Duke of Padua, brandished a long, glistening sword in his gloved hand.

"You!" he shouted, black of eye.

"*Ah, Dio! Ah, Dio!*" cried the Duchess. She pulled the blanket up to her neck to cover her nakedness.

"*Addio! Addio!*" bellowed the Duke.

"My Lord!" she wailed. "*Caro mio!* Forgive me! Forgive me for having lost my head."

"Thus you lose it twice!" he said, swinging the sword with deadly accuracy.

Piccolino gaped in horror as the Duchess's life ended with dazzling swiftness. Her brown eyes, more bewildered than pained, gazed vacantly from the floor only to see the rest of her supple body at some distance, still lying languorously upon the bed.

Piccolino, wearing no more than on the day he was born, stood frozen in terror.

"*Madonna,*" he whispered.

Then, gathering as much dignity as he could, he choked out an inaudible, "My Lord." Clearing his throat, he repeated in full voice, echoing through the chamber, "My Lord, I must apologize completely to you for losing my heart to the Duchess. It will never happen again."

He immediately realized the inflammatory truth of his remark, but it was too late in any case.

"Fool! Court jester!" shouted the Duke, as his sword thrust forward.

Piccolino raised his violin bow to parry the Duke's attack, but to no avail. With a single deft maneuver the Duke sliced the bow in half and pierced Piccolino's heart. Piccolino felt himself being lifted off the ground.

Piccolino's eyes widened with surprise. His life ebbing, Piccolino clutched at his violin. The Duke shook the skewered Piccolino to force him to drop the violin, to shatter it on the cold stone floor. Piccolino would not satisfy the Duke's revenge.

Finally, the Duke lowered Piccolino with grudging respect, but mainly so that Piccolino's weight wouldn't break his sword. As his knees buckled, Piccolino's final act was to place his beloved Stradivarius, yet un-played, gently upon the table. As his body crumpled just a small distance to the now red-puddled floor, a transient cloud passed between the sun and the stained-glass image of the impassive Madonna, blocking its light.

And thus ended the life of Matteo Cherubino, and began the life of the Piccolino Stradivarius, born in the blood of debauchery, lust, and death.

EXPOSITION

ONE

The third movement of Mozart's Symphony Number 39 in E-flat Major, with Herbert von Karajan conducting the Berlin Philharmonic, spun on the Victrola. The clarinetist was playing the solo in the minuet with simple if somewhat maudlin elegance. In midphrase, Jacobus wrenched the LP off the turntable, the stylus ripping nastily into the disc with a horrible screech, like car brakes before a fatal collision. He flung the record against the wall, shattering it. Jacobus collapsed back exhausted into his secondhand swivel chair, his frayed green plaid flannel shirt sticking to the torn brown Naugahyde seat back.

"Damn Krauts," he muttered, panting. "Think they own the sole rights to Mozart."

Jacobus had awoken that morning of July 8, 1983, drenched in sweat. Night had brought no relief to the relentless heat wave that had wilted New England, browning the leaves two months before their time, and though it was only dawn it was already searingly hot, hazy, and humid. But more than the heat, it was Jacobus's recurring ivy-and-eyes dream that had wrenched him from his uneasy sleep.

It wasn't that Jacobus enjoyed gardening. Actually, he hated it. He had planted the ivy—years ago, when he could still see—because Don at the garden center had told him how easy it was to grow, how little care it needed, how, trellised to the walls, it would make his house look so quaint, and, the clincher, how it would choke out all the weeds so he wouldn't have to do any yard work.

At first, everything Don had told him was true, and Jacobus was very pleased with his slyness. What he hadn't been told, though, was that once the ivy's roots started spreading, it would choke out not just the weeds but every other living thing, that its tenacious grip on the side of the house would loosen the mortar and rot the siding, that unless you cut it back, year after year after year, it would overwhelm the entire house in a deadly embrace. After Jacobus became blind, sitting in his personal darkness, he could feel—he swore he could even hear—the ivy making its slow, inexorable ascent around him, mocking him, consuming him. It was when the ivy had wrapped itself around him in the dream, pinning him down, suffocating him, that the eye appeared above him. A blazing ruby-red eye, it seared its gaze into Jacobus, immobilized by the ivy, burning his flesh. It was the same bejeweled eye that Stradivari had embedded in the dragon head of the violin he had made for Matteo Cherubino hundreds of years ago, the violin that had eluded Jacobus decades before and now taunted him without surcease. An eye that mocked him for his blindness and for his weakness.

Jacobus lay in his sweat. It was an understatement to say he didn't feel like teaching the violin on that July eighth. Nor had he felt like teaching on July sixth or seventh. The truth was he hadn't felt like teaching the violin for a long time. He was hot. He was tired. The prospect of having to communicate with another human—he hesitated to use that term in reference to a mere student—depressed him. In fact, it revolted him. Rummaging with fumbling fingers through the ashtray for a half-smoked Camel cigarette butt, he finally found one long enough and relit it. Why can't they leave me in peace? he thought. Peace. What's that? If being blind, friendless, and put out to pasture is peace, then I guess I've found it.

He dragged his way to his studio and collapsed into his chair. Would he go to Carnegie Hall that night for the coronation of the young girl he often referred to as the "Infanta," the child prodigy Kamryn Vander (formerly Vanderblick), student of Victoria Jablonski? *The* Victoria Jablonski. Jacobus felt the bile rise in his throat. His belief that great music was great enough to be played without conceit, without hype, without the dog and pony show was now considered old-fashioned, out of touch with modern lifestyle tastes. Why indeed should he go to this concert and witness the triumph of everything he had striven against his entire life? To torture himself? Was there another reason?

The silence surrounding Jacobus oppressed him. The sporadic gurgling of his antiquated refrigerator and an occasional car passing up the hill on Route 41, engines muffled by ever-encroaching woods, were the only white noises intruding upon his black, bleak solitude. Yet when somewhere out there a crow's shrill caw interjected itself, Jacobus cursed that too. He removed his violin from the case that he never bothered to close. The violin, like everything else, had been neglected. The fingerboard was caked with accumulated rosin, and the strings, unchanged for years, were blackened and frayed. He couldn't remember the last time he had his bow rehaired.

The next familiar sound was the knocking at the door—the student. Jacobus sat motionless in the silence, holding his violin on his knee. He sat long after the cigarette butt was cold, long after the knocking on the door had ceased, long after the student's footsteps had receded into the silence. Only gradually did he allow the sound of his own panting wheeze to resume.

That was how his day had begun. Now, nine hours later, the cab he was in lurched to a halt, propelling his forehead into the Plexiglas shield, knocking his dark glasses to the floor. "Coggy-ool," said the driver in an almost incomprehensible foreign accent.

"It's pronounced 'Carnegie Hall,' asshole," Jacobus croaked, groping to retrieve his glasses.

Jacobus got out of the car grudgingly, licking his dry lips, a condemned prisoner staggering to the guillotine. Stumbling from the cab into the sweltering July heat, he cursed the driver and slammed the door. He again asked himself why he had made this trip, but unaccustomed to introspection he received no clear answer. Was it only to hear this dexterous preadolescent pretend to be an artist? Was it to flagellate himself with cynical self-righteousness while everyone else rose to a standing ovation? After all, hadn't she just won the *prestigious* Grimsley Competition? What would he do when the smug New York intelligentsia fawned over this baby as if it knew the difference between show and artistry?

Dressed in his tattered gray tweed jacket, sleeves too short, which he had thrown over his flannel shirt, and stained wool pants with frayed cuffs, Jacobus was ignored by the tuxedos swirling around him. Just another street person—and a blind one at that—in a city of street people, as unseen to the gathering concert crowd as they were to him, he trudged toward the imposing brown brick walls of Carnegie Hall, his personal Bastille, awash in the evening's growing shadows. The vision of the ivy-and-eye dream returned. The vision of his own demise. He spat on the sidewalk.

TWO

The recital at Carnegie Hall had been one of Kamryn Vander's rewards for winning the Holbrooke Grimsley International Violin Competition. This competition, commonly referred to simply as the Grimsley, was unique in several ways. Held only once every thirteen years for violin prodigies no older than thirteen, the Grimsley not only guaranteed the winner a brilliant start to a concert career but also allowed the winner the cherished opportunity to perform on the legendary three-quarter-size "Piccolino" Strad. Considered by many to be the most perfect violin ever made, it was loaned to the winner of the Grimsley for his or her debut recital and concerto performance with a professional orchestra hired especially for the event. After that concert, the Piccolino was returned to the velvet-lined, climate-controlled vault of violin dealer Boris Dedubian for safekeeping, where it would sit for thirteen more years, waiting to bestow its largesse upon the next wunderkind.

Kamryn Vander's recital earlier that night had met everyone's expectations, to the delight of most, to the intense dismay of Daniel Jacobus. Those dilettantes! he thought. Those sheep! They listen with everything but their ears. A nine-year-old's life molded by a lie. The bile rose in his throat as he trailed the crowd to the gala reception being held in one of the two adjacent Green Rooms on the second floor of Carnegie Hall to celebrate her great accomplishment.

Few in the festive, glittering gathering knew who Jacobus was. To them, he appeared to be a destitute vagabond, and so they kept their distance. Those who did recognize him, those who knew him, kept an even greater distance. As a result he was left alone; essentially he was invisible.

Usually both of the interconnected Green Rooms were combined for receptions this size. Each had an entrance to the corridor as well as a connecting door between them. Tonight, however, the festivities were relegated to Green Room A. On this night the only special guest in Green Room B, which had been cordoned off, was the precious Stradivarius violin, still warm from Kamryn's performance. Both doors to Green Room B, one in the corridor and one that connected to Green Room A, were guarded by two of Carnegie Hall's 24/7 security personnel, who were very accustomed to protecting inconceivably valuable instruments at events like this. There had even been a special case made to protect the violin. The outer shell of the case was made of a lightweight epoxy compound designed by NASA for use on the space shuttle. Inside were coiled springs so that the violin was actually suspended inside. A truck could run over it and not cause any damage.

Another of Vander's rewards for winning the Grimsley was automatic representation by an organization officially called the Musical Arts Project Group, Inc., or MAP, which was a primary sponsor of the Grimsley and had footed the bill for the reception as well. MAP had been constituted as a nonprofit 501(c)-(3) charitable organization in 1971 with the novel mission of assisting gifted young violinists to establish solo careers in what is generally a hit-or-miss, highly capricious profession. The idea was to assemble a team of top professionals in all aspects of the classical music world—teachers, managers, violin dealers, even music critics—who would volunteer their time to nurture development of the best young talent, transforming the caterpillar into a butterfly without risk of it getting squashed. As the professional MAP team donated their time, they could also serve as its board, enabling the organization to run efficiently, and as it was a nonprofit, they could be the beneficiaries of substantial public and private philanthropic funds such as the National Endowment for the Arts and the Wallace–Reader's Digest Fund.

So well had the MAP concept worked that within a few years MAP had become a powerful force in the multimillion-dollar classical music industry, edging out many traditional for-profit concert agencies.

While Jacobus, slumped in the corner, was ignored by the swirling throngs, Martin Lilburn, longtime classical music critic of the *New York Times* and renowned wordsmith, was hard at work. Lilburn was one of those professionals who had volunteered for the MAP consortium, and now, at the reception, he fidgeted, trying to jump-start just the right tone for his review of Kamryn Vander's debut.

Lilburn stole another glance at his watch. There was still plenty of time—an hour and forty-eight minutes, to be precise—to get in his review of Vander's performance to the *Times*.

He removed his spiral notepad and monogrammed Waterman cartridge pen from his jacket pocket and began, as was his custom, to write down random thoughts. Later he would assemble them into a coherent whole.

"Time . . . Times . . . Best of times. Worst of times," he jotted down.

Lilburn sighed. Trevor Grimsley, heir to the Grimsley fortune and nominal chair of The Grimsley Competition founded by Grandpa Holbrooke, was in the midst of a prattling toast that showed no signs of abating.

He felt a nudge and turned to see Naomi Hess, his counterpart from the *Daily News,* a friendly rival. She was short, perky, and nicely dressed for the occasion. He put his notepad back in his pocket.

"Found your big story yet, Martin?" she asked.

"Ah, Naomi, what a pleasant unsurprise!" said Lilburn. "No. Not yet. Smell it, though."

"Well, keep sniffing. So what's your take on Grimsley?" She nodded her head in the toaster's direction.

"Trevor Grimsley! A Dickens name," Lilburn said. "Hmm. Grimsley—diminutively grim. Grimy. Yes, that is what he is— diminutively grimy, a half-developed caricature, an expedient whose existence neither precedes nor succeeds Dickens's book covers. When I write my novel . . . if I ever write my novel, there will be a Trevor Grimsley in it. I'd have to make him more believable than the real one. But Jesus! If Grimsley's a major character, what, oh what," Lilburn said, pressing the cold champagne flute to his aching forehead, "does that make me?"

They scanned the crowd of New York elite.

"Ah, the huddled masses yearning to be tax-free," said Hess.

"*Earning* to be tax-free," added Lilburn. "Perhaps I'll use that line in the piece."

"Hardly *earning*, though," Hess countered.

"Hmm. *Unearning* to be tax-free?" Lilburn tried.

"Too cumbersome, Martin. Too cynical for the politic *New York Times.* You'll offend the readers."

They observed the crowd's plastic smiles as they pretended to listen to Trevor Grimsley's monologue.

"In honoring Kamryn Vander on her special night," intoned Grimsley with practiced prep-school nasal monotony, glass in hand, *"I can't forget to recognize my fellow colleagues of the Musical Arts Project Group, without whose help this historic night would not have been possible."*

"I've sold my soul to the Devil," said Lilburn, "but to have to listen to this nincompoop—too usurious a price."

"What do you mean?" asked Hess.

"Never mind."

"As you all know," said Grimsley, *"the MAP Group started out as a dream . . ."*

Lilburn placed his thumb and forefinger to the bridge of his nose and pressed. He downed his champagne in one unpleasant gulp, unlike his usual self.

"Hey, Martin, take it easy," said Hess. "It can't be *that* bad a dream."

Lilburn lipped the mantra as Grimsley recited it: " 'a nonprofit consortium of respected professionals in the music industry who join together to build career opportunities for gifted young musicians.' I wrote those words, Naomi, in MAP's glossy brochure."

"Got a nice ring to it."

"But I absolutely refused to agree to 'Let Us Put You on the MAP.' "

"Definitely bad taste."

"Hold on a minute." Lilburn took out his notepad. "Include something positive about MAP in the review of Vander's performance," he wrote.

"To make a long story short . . ." The crowd's shoulders collectively sagged. Lilburn exchanged his empty glass for a fresh one that he plucked off a waiter's passing tray with enough virulence to create miniature foamy waves in the glass. His headache wasn't getting any better. He checked his watch again.

"So ladies first! Here's to Victoria Jablonski, diva extraordinaire of violin pedagogy"—all eyes sought Victoria, who, off in a corner, surrounded by a group of wide-eyed acolytes, momentarily suspended her extravagant

gesticulations—*"with whom every young aspiring Heifetz wants to study. Even at two hundred dollars a lesson"*—a frown from Jablonski—*"to say 'I'm a Miss J student' opens a world of concert doors. No one can prepare youngsters for a concert career—boy, can they play loud and fast!—better than Miss J."*

A smattering of applause.

"Just how 'Miss J' plays her life," said Hess, "loud and fast."

"Yes, taste seems to be out of taste these days" said Lilburn. "How in heavens will her tutelage affect the Vander child?"

Addressing the champagne glass he held before his eyes, Lilburn groggily asked it, "How much longer will this toast go on?"

Hess laughed.

"Let me take you away from all this," he continued. "Tell me your name again? Oh, yes. Bubbles. Pleased to meet you. Where is my story, Bubbles?"

"And to Anthony Strella, world-renowned concert agent and chairman of the MAP Group. Anthony Strella, at the top of the entrepreneurial ladder," continued Grimsley, *"whose long shadow wields more influence over symphony orchestras and concert presenters than their own managements."*

A few uncomfortable chuckles.

Lilburn scanned the crowd for Strella, a head taller than most, easily spotting the back of his silk Armani suit by the wet bar with others of his ilk, who continued to converse quietly to the accompaniment of clinking ice in cocktail glasses.

Hess followed Lilburn's gaze.

"A good-looking man," she said.

"Who makes me feel inexplicably inadequate," Lilburn added. "Here I am desperate to loosen my bow tie, but, looking at the gleaming Mr. Strella, the simple thought of doing so makes me feel guilty.

"I can imagine Strella coolly informing the band of concert presenters encircling him, 'Well, if you don't want to book my excellent young accordion player, Bubbles Pankevich, I certainly understand. But in that case don't expect to see Itzhak Perlman or Yo-Yo Ma in the next two hundred years.' "

"Hey, lookie here." Hess pointed at the other side of Green Room A through the crowd. "Isn't that old Daniel Jacobus?"

Lilburn spotted him, unmistakable with his dark glasses and shabby dress.

"What's Jacobus doing here?" Lilburn said under his breath. "He's always stayed away from these concerts like the plague! He detests us. And for him to come to the reception?"

As they observed Jacobus with these uncharitable thoughts, Jacobus suddenly raised his head so that it appeared he was staring directly at them.

"What the . . . ?" said Hess.

Lilburn actually stumbled backward; such was the power of Jacobus's blind eyes.

Suddenly sober and determined, Lilburn told Hess he would see her later—"He's all yours," she said—and started to make his way through the tuxedos to confront Jacobus—maybe this was his story—but after one step he was intercepted by a garish redhead with big teeth and bigger jewels inching toward him.

Damn, he thought as she caught his eye. Too late for escape.

"You're Martin Lilburn, aren't you?" she asked through a massive overbite, managing an extraordinary number of *f* sounds in a sentence devoid of *f*'s.

"Yes, madam," he whispered impatiently. It was more of a hiss.

"*The* Martin Lilburn?"

He put a cautionary index finger to his lips, as if he were listening to Grimsley. "Conceivably there is more than one. Now if you will . . ."

"I read your review in the Sunday *Times.*"

"Oh?"

"Michael Timmerman's Brahms Concerto?"

"Oh. Madam, I know what you are about to say. I also know that I am tired, hot, have drunk too much, and have a splitting headache, so if you'll please. . . ."

"That was very unkind what you wrote about Michael, you know," she said.

"Nor was Mr. Timmerman very kind to Mr. Brahms," Lilburn said, keeping his voice down while the endless toast meandered.

"But I *know* Michael. He's such a fine person."

"Yes, I'm sure he is, madam. But one must also consider the notes."

"At least his *friends* think he is."

"After the way he played I'm surprised the plural is still applicable."

Lilburn tried to move away, but she grabbed at his sleeve.

"Good God, madam. Please," he said in an angry whisper.

"So are you going to give Kamryn Vander a snow job too?" she persevered. "Or maybe you're here as a reporter. Or a MAP guy. Or something else?"

"Madam, as you may easily observe, I am here in my entirety." He yanked his sleeve from her grasp. "Now, if you will excuse me."

Lilburn turned his back on her and walked away, something he ordinarily disapproved of and rarely did.

He returned his gaze to where Jacobus had been only to find an empty space. He peered throughout the room. Jacobus had vanished.

"Damn," he said. He did spot the celebrity of the evening, Kamryn Vander, beginning to hold court at the corner of the room farthest away from Grimsley. He still had his review to write.

He swerved wobbily through the throng in her general direction, ears reluctantly returning to Grimsley's oration like a pedestrian trying not to listen to a jackhammer dislodge the trembling sidewalk.

Naomi Hess caught up with him.

"Why didn't God enable us to close our ears as well as our eyes?" she said.

"And of course, our dear friend Boris Dedubian, representing the third generation of Dedubian violin dealers, through whose storied shop passes virtually every great seventeenth-, eighteenth-, and nineteenth-century Italian violin. It goes without saying . . ."

"Then why say it?" said Lilburn. "Why waste words? Why? Without the right words the world would cease to exist!"

". . . that it is almost a prerequisite for concert soloists to perform on a million-dollar instrument, and having Bo provide our up-and-coming Groupies with one of them 'on favorable terms' is a benefit of untold value."

"Martin, where does Dedubian get all these instruments from?" asked Hess.

"I've asked him that question. He just says his family has had lots of personal contacts over the years. Other than that, he's pretty mum."

"A little bit of Svengali, don't you think?"

"Mr. Dedubian, I'm afraid, is unable to be with us tonight. He just called from a pay phone off the Long Island Expressway to say that he was hopelessly caught in traffic"— sympathetic moans and chortles from the crowd—*"on the way from his weekend place in Southampton and sends his regrets. But we're all indebted to Boris's granddaddy for helping my own granddaddy acquire the Piccolino Strad."*

"Indeed," said Lilburn, "that's the one and only reason he's here tonight."

"Or anywhere," added Hess.

"And to New York Times *critic Martin Lilburn"*—Lilburn almost gagged on his champagne—*"recipient of five Pulitzer Prizes for journalism."*

"Oh, God! Why?" said Lilburn.

"Isn't that correct, Martin? Five Pulitzers?"

Expectant eyes turned toward Lilburn.

"Actually, two, Trevor. Two."

Eyes, turning away, didn't see Lilburn's face redden.

"Ah! Recipient of two Pulitzer Prizes. His incisive and insightful reviews can make or break careers. With the stroke of his rapier pen he can stir his reading public into a frenzy of support for a new face as easily as he can disembowel the poor soul whose level of musical expression does not rise to his lofty standard. Fortunately for MAP's Groupies," Grimsley said with a self-congratulatory smile, *"he's usually on our side!"*

Lilburn squeezed out a smile of his own and added a self-deprecating little wave in Grimsley's direction, then turned away, hiding his face like an indicted CEO.

"And now, a toast! To our newest prodigy progeny," hailed Grimsley. Restless fake laughter from the crowded room as they followed his lead in raising their glasses yet again. *"Here's to Kamryn Vander, whose musicianship is earth moving, and whose career, we hope"*—pause for more chuckles—*"will be earth-shaking."*

"And here's to you, Martin," said Hess, holding her glass high. "May you find the story of your dreams."

Applause. "Hear! Hear!" "Bottoms up!" Formalities over, the hum of conversation and gossip resumed.

Lilburn went to the reception line for the nine-year-old earthmover. There were students in jeans and investment bankers in silk suits, musicians, Europeans, Asians, the whole New York concertgoing spectrum. No Jacobus.

Kamryn Vander sat at her throne sipping 7UP from a crystal champagne flute, imitating the adults. By her side was her mother and bodyguard, Cynthia Vander. As Lilburn was about to offer his congratulations, Kamryn lifted the unfamiliar champagne glass a little too high. The liquid, following the laws of gravity, first trickled down her chin and ended up staining her billowy pink concert dress between her legs.

"Kamryn, can't you even stay clean?" hissed Cynthia. Bending over her daughter, she wiped frantically at the barely visible stain with a red cocktail napkin that, for some untold reason, she spat upon. Her factory-made breasts threatened to shake themselves loose from her too-tight dress.

"You want to stay up late, you behave yourself. Hear me?" she added. "I said, do you hear me?"

If Kamryn heard her, she showed no sign of it and continued to swing her feet back and forth under the grown-up chair.

Lilburn cleared his throat. Cynthia Vander straightened up, wiped something imaginary from her cleavage, and instantly assembled a smile.

"Well, young lady . . ." Lilburn addressed the child but saw the mother flush. "Oh! I didn't mean . . . I meant . . ." So he just extended his hand. "You certainly put on an impressive performance tonight."

"Say thank you to Mr. Lilburn, Kamryn. He's a very important man," said Cynthia.

" 'Thank you to Mr. Lilburn, Kamryn. He's a very important man,' " Kamryn said, ignoring his hand suspended in the air.

"Well," said Lilburn.

A teenage girl barged in, violin case in hand, looking slightly dazed. "Like I can't believe how awesome you are! Like it was so fantastic!" she said through tears and braces.

"Thank you," said Kamryn, the quick learner, with a smile. And, as the older girl walked away, she added, "I play better than you."

Lilburn pulled his pen and notebook from his pocket. He wrote "stick to her playing," checked his watch once more, and began to head back to the office to write his review. He dodged the girl with braces and squeezed his way through the crowd of celebrants: professional musicians attacking the buffet table; a giggling gaggle of Juilliard students—almost all Asian girls these days; Mr. and Mrs. Rosenbaum—*the* Rosenbaums—schmoozing with who is that in that putrid gown; everyone conveying their respects, seeing how they could use the event to their own advantages. All were there. All seemed to be, at that moment, in Lilburn's way.

THREE

Lilburn received a sudden jolt from behind, causing him to spill his drink on the tuxedo jacket he had just picked up from the dry cleaner's that afternoon. "Philistines!" he cursed, but when he turned, his dour expression immediately brightened. A stocky man about his own age with brushed-back thinning hair and a short graying beard, wearing a brown wool herringbone suit (in July!), smoked salmon hors d'oeuvre in one hand, proffered napkin in the other, stood before him. It was Solomon Goldbloom, a well-known and highly respected violinist from the Boston Symphony.

"Mr. Goldbloom!"

"Sorry, Lilburn, didn't mean to shove you."

"No, no! You've suddenly made me feel like Diogenes rather than David!"

"That bad, huh?" said Goldbloom, chewing on his canapé.

"I'm afraid so," said Lilburn.

Trevor Grimsley approached, pink mixed drink, with cherry, in hand.

"Speak of the devil," said Goldbloom. Lilburn attempted to slip away, but Goldbloom grabbed his sleeve and held on, preventing his escape.

"Cute speech, Trevor," said Goldbloom.

"Ah! Sol!" said Trevor. "Sol Goldbloom! So good to see you. I didn't expect you'd make it."

"Well, I had a night off from the symphony tour, so I thought I'd stop and hear the kid. She plays pretty well, huh?"

"Pretty well? I'd say that's the understatement of the year!"

"Look, boychik," said Goldbloom, smiling as he swallowed his canapé. He let go of Lilburn's sleeve and gently grabbed hold of the lapels of Grimsley's tuxedo, pulling their faces close together. Though the chatter around him threatened to drown out his words, he spoke quietly.

"You're no jerk and I'm no jerk, and you know as well as I do that this kid has a long way to go before she should be put in front of a serious audience. If it wasn't for the Piccolino Strad she'd sound like a dozen other talented kids." He patted Grimsley gingerly on the cheek.

"Not sure what you mean, Sol," said Grimsley, clearly uncomfortable not only at Goldbloom's close presence but also the essence of what he was saying. He looked down nervously, staring at his maroon bow tie, then darted a glance at Lilburn for help—Lilburn returned only a shrug—trying to avoid Goldbloom's eye contact. "Everyone just loved her."

"They also loved the emperor's new clothes," said Goldbloom. "For the kid's own sake, give her some time. Okay, Trevor?"

"Well, I'll certainly convey that message to Victoria. I mean, it's really the teacher's decision."

"It certainly is. And I already have. See ya later," said Goldbloom as he wended his way through the throng back to the food table.

"You'll excuse me too, Trevor," Lilburn said, exploiting this sudden opportunity to pry himself from Grimsley, "but I need to follow up on Mr. Goldbloom's comments."

Without waiting for a reply he made his way in the same direction.

He caught up to Goldbloom, who seemed to have expected him.

Goldbloom said, "You know, Martin, you're a smart guy." Lilburn gave a small nod of thanks. "You MAP people had a good idea. When you started. Now, well, let's say, now it's a different animal."

"Oh? How so?"

"Well, you want to promote your own clients. Fine. Business is business. But what you guys are doing goes way past that. You guys drag the competition through the dirt. Don't forget, Groupies aren't the only talented young musicians on the block. But after you get through chewing up and spitting out your nonclients in the press, and with Strella's behind-the-scenes phone calls . . . Jesus Christ, no wonder their careers take these sudden nosedives. Fewer and fewer orchestras book them for engagements, and then, poof, they've disappeared, like this champagne I've been drinking. Hey, waiter!"

Lilburn began to protest, but Goldbloom went on. He grabbed two champagnes and handed one to Lilburn.

"Also—and Martin, I'm no kid, I know what you guys are up to—this 'volunteer' crap."

"Crap?"

"Yeah, crap. You know. Shit. I'm sure that over the years, seeing how competition is so stiff, it's got to require more and more business-related expenses—travel, meals, lodging, even time."

"Yes?"

"So, if your 'volunteer' work is essentially the same as the for-profit work you do in the normal course of business, what's the difference?"

Goldbloom left the question dangling as his hand shot out like a frog's tongue, latching on to a mini—egg roll as it passed by on a tray.

"Let's face it, they're essentially one and the same. Right, Martin?"

"I don't see what you're driving at."

"So the members of the MAP Group are pocketing, tax free, funds from public and private donations for doing exactly the same stuff you're already getting paid for. Further—"

"I think I need to go write my—"

"Hold on, Martin, I'm still answering your question. Further, as a nonprofit, it never looks good at the end of the year to be too much in the black, right? So you have to make sure that the millions you guys raise go somewhere—'somewhere' being your expenses and 'consulting fees.'"

"Mr. Goldbloom. You are welcome to check our books. We have the finest accounting firms go over them with a great deal of scrutiny and they assure us—"

"Martin. Look at me. Look who you're talking to. Sol Goldbloom. I'm no kid, like the Vander girl over there—sweet kid. I'm in the music business too. And I've got my own fine accountant scrutinizing me up the ass. But you guys take the cake. You guys are the board of MAP, and you're also independent contractors, at least as far as the IRS is concerned, right? That gives you 501(c)-(3) status as a charitable organization, right? Plus there's no oversight or accountability to speak of, no one to say what you can or can't do with the money, right? Boychik, you've got 'em coming and going. Mazel tov!"

"Ah, Mr. Goldbloom, what a pleasant surprise."

Lilburn had not even been aware of Strella's emergence from the crowd, but now that he had an ally, he looked heavenward in thanks.

"Hey, Strella," said Goldbloom, unperturbed, "you put on a nice party."

"An important occasion needs a little festivity. Martin, you're looking a little flushed. Are you feeling all right?"

"Mr. Goldbloom seems to believe we, at MAP, are somewhat unscrupulous in how we handle our affairs."

"Does he? Well, he's absolutely right. Can I offer you a drink, Mr. Goldbloom?"

"Excuse me?" said Lilburn. Could he have heard correctly? The room was noisy, after all. He was feeling suddenly woozy.

"I asked Mr. Goldbloom if he wants a drink."

"I'm referring to your prior statement. You agree with him?"

"Of course. Business is business. We do what we need to do to get ahead—short of breaking the law, of course—and we've been damned successful. Just look around you."

Strella waved his arm like the pope greeting the throng at St. Peter's Square on Easter Sunday, encompassing the room and all its occupants, but somehow his gesture suggested all of New York was in his grasp.

"Well, I'm looking around me," said Goldbloom, "but what *I* see is a little different from what *you* see. When you guys started MAP, you were working in the best interests of young musicians."

"And you think now it's different?"

"Strella, I hate to tell you this, but I've got some bad news for you. Now it's exactly the reverse. Your kids are fodder for your own interests—you just shoot them out, whoosh! Jettisoned like . . ."

"Flotsam?"

"Thank you, Martin. Like flotsam, only half prepared for the concert world—and you know very well that world can be pretty nasty—and you do it with a lot of slick PR.

"And here's the point. Now, you *have* to make sure your Groupies make it, whether they're capable or not. I really mean, you *have* to, or else you're going out of business because now you need the money. When you were little, you were respected. Now that you're big and powerful *machers*, you're just the most feared."

Lilburn was about to protest, "No, that's not the way it is," but his tongue was moving uncharacteristically slowly and Strella placed a restraining hand on Lilburn's arm, replying, "And the most sought after."

"Sought, shmought, you think all these people you're waving at are here because they like you? They'd just as soon toast your ass as toast your health."

"Well put, Mr. Goldbloom." Strella laughed, unfazed. "Don't you think so, Martin?"

Lilburn, for once, found himself at a loss for words.

"I'll see you characters later," said Goldbloom. "Thanks for the party."

He waved as he started making his way back to the buffet, Lilburn staring after him.

The only salaried employee of the MAP Group was Rachel Lewison. She wrote the grant proposals, set up appointments, arranged catering for events such as tonight's, and did anything else that was required of her. For her efforts in raising several million dollars a year she received a salary of fifty-thousand dollars, barely enough to survive in the city plus buy the evening gown that she was wearing tonight—chic bone white, low cut in the back. It helped Rachel in her job that she was also a violinist, but at this point she barely had the time or inclination to practice anymore. Her career as a performer never blossomed, though she once had been a student of both Daniel Jacobus and Victoria Jablonski. Being the business manager of MAP was her booby prize from Victoria.

This time it was Rachel Lewison carrying a glass of champagne whom Sol Goldbloom accidentally bumped into on his way to the caviar.

"Jesus Christ! Can't you watch where the hell you're going?" she screamed.

Lilburn, shell-shocked eyes still on Goldbloom, could hear her even from where he was standing.

Goldbloom looked amused and appeared to say something conciliatory.

"Asshole," sneered Rachel, turning her back and pushing people aside as she headed toward Lilburn and Strella.

Lilburn saw Goldbloom chuckle, then resume his beeline to the buffet.

"I can't stand that man," Rachel hissed into Strella's ear, ignoring Lilburn. "He could have ruined my dress."

"Don't worry, sweetheart," Strella said, putting his hand, consolingly, on the pale skin of Rachel's back. Lilburn tried to neither look nor listen.

"It could be worse," Strella continued. "It could have been that blind old goat, old—"

"Jacobus," interjected Lilburn.

Rachel's eyes turned to Lilburn, burning into him.

"What did I do?" he asked. "I only said his name."

"Jacobus. I loathe him," said Rachel.

"Yeah, old Jacobus," mused Strella. "Didn't I see him groping around here a little while ago?" His attention returned to Rachel. "Anyway, hon, just have a good time, okay? You've done a great job putting this shindig together, so put those old farts out of your mind."

His hand went lower down her back. Lilburn, unable to avert his eyes, noticed goose bumps blossom on her flesh.

"Mmm. You smell good tonight," Strella whispered into her ear.

Rachel looked directly into his eyes, a cryptic smile on her face, as she raised her glass to her mouth.

He sniffed her neck. "What's that perfume you've got on?" His hand slipped inside the back of the dress, migrating downward. She stood there, not moving, her champagne glass stationary on her lips, staring into the crowd. Lilburn quickly turned his head away.

Out of the corner of his eye Strella saw the look on Lilburn's face. "Rachel, honey, how about getting Martin and me a refill on our champagne? Atta girl."

As soon as she left Strella said, "What now?"

"Anthony, we need to have a meeting."

"Why? Are you worried about Goldbloom's pet theories? Or what?"

"Just schedule a meeting . . . please. I need some air."

Lilburn finally made it to the corridor, undoing his bow tie as soon as he was no longer on display.

Portly Harry Pizzi, not long for retirement, had sat in many a chair as a Carnegie Hall guard. Lilburn now found him sitting in yet another in the corridor outside the door to Green Room B—unoccupied but for the Piccolino Strad—where he diligently eyed passersby, paying extra attention to any suspicious-looking ones.

"Hey, Harry."

"Mr. Lilburn. How are we tonight? Hey, you're sweatin' up a storm! You want my handkerchief? Some coffee?"

Lilburn looked first at the wrinkled but relatively clean handkerchief in Harry's left hand and then at the Styrofoam cup in his right. The cup contained a light brown liquid in which floated what appeared to be the remains of a doughnut.

Lilburn chose the left hand and cautiously wiped his brow. "Thanks. I'll have this laundered for you. Maybe I'll take a rain check on the coffee."

"Hey, you got it. Have a seat."

Harry pulled up another folding chair. Lilburn sat down.

"Tough night in there?" asked Harry.

"Let's just say that working the crowd isn't all that it's cracked up to be. How about you? All quiet on the western front?"

"So far. So far. They've got two of us on security tonight."

"Really!"

"Yeah, Arnie Robison—he's a rookie—he's standing guard inside by the connecting door between A and B. No one's allowed to go into B without me or Arnie escorting them in and out. Strict instructions."

"Two guys for one violin, hmm? Sounds like you've got good odds."

"That's the idea. We have to check on it every fifteen minutes."

At that moment, a sulky young man, unshaven and shabbily dressed, tried to stalk into the party carrying a violin case.

"Excuse me, sir," said Pizzi. "Can I help you?"

"I am Victoria Jablonski student," said the young man in a questionable Eastern European accent. "He invite me here."

"I believe you mean 'she,' " said Lilburn.

" 'He,' 'she,' it is not your business."

"Let's see your ID," said Pizzi.

"I don't have ID. I am Victoria Jablonski student, okay?"

"Harry, I have an idea," said Lilburn. "Why don't you get Victoria to come out here and identify the young man, and I'll wait here with him. I'm sure he and I could have an interesting chat."

"Thanks but no thanks, Mr. Lilburn. If I leave this seat my ass is grass."

"Well . . . then how about I go and fetch Victoria and you entertain the young gentleman?" Lilburn was already retying his bow tie.

"I'd appreciate that, Mr. Lilburn. I'm sure he and I will hit it off just dandy."

Even in the crowd, Lilburn had no trouble tracking down Jablonski in her shimmering metallic blue sequined dress and interrupted a heated one-way conversation Jablonski was having with Anthony Strella. ". . . your goddam hands off of her" were her only words Lilburn actually could decipher.

"Excuse me, Victoria."

Victoria glared at him too.

"Sorry to interrupt your tête-à-tête, but there's a young man who claims to be a student of yours. The security guard would just like your confirmation. It'll only take a moment."

A moment later Jablonski hissed at Pizzi, "Of course he's my student! He's been coming here for lessons for the last three months. What kind of security guard are you? Why don't you keep your eyes open?" she said, turning her back on him.

"Sorry, Miss J. Just tryin' to do my job," Harry Pizzi said to Jablonski, already marching indignantly back to the party. Lilburn alone heard Harry's further description of Miss J.

Her student, in tow, gave Pizzi and Lilburn a look of triumphant disdain.

"I see what you mean, Mr. Lilburn. It takes all kinds, don't it?"

"Harry! Harry! It's Nick," squawked a voice from Pizzi's walkie-talkie.

"Jeez, what is it now?"

"When it rains it pours," said Lilburn, offering a sympathetic smile.

Nick Flores, the stage-door security guard, reported to Pizzi that someone had just hurled two rocks from the roof of the Joseph Patelson Music House, shattering the stage-door window. Patelson's was housed in a squat nineteenth-century brick landmark carriage house wedged between skyscrapers at 160 West 56th Street, just across from the Carnegie Hall stage entrance, and was a mecca for musicians searching for just about any music composed in the last three hundred years. Flores thought he had spotted a person on the roof and told Pizzi to come and guard the stage door while he tried to chase down the culprit. Flores logged in the time of the incident at 11:07 P.M.

"My story!" Lilburn exclaimed. He rubbed his hands together and rattled off ideas with machine-gun rapidity. "Rock slung from tiny Patelson's at monumental Carnegie Hall—David and Goliath theme—aesthetic purity smiting glossy bad taste. Headline: 'Vander and Vandal Knock Down Doors of Carnegie Hall!'" He looked again at his watch. Still almost an hour. Still time!

Pizzi turned off the walkie-talkie, muttering, and entered Green Room B. "They shoulda tore down that dump across the street years ago, just like they shoulda tore down this one when they had the chance in '60," he said as he looked in on the violin to make sure it was still safe, closed the door, and waddled as quickly as he was able to Green Room A. "This buildin's gonna kill me yet." With retirement around the corner, he didn't want to screw up and leave his post unprotected. Lilburn followed.

People were starting to depart the reception for home. He and Pizzi swam against the tide to get to Robison. The MAP people were getting ready to leave, as was "Victoria Jablonski student." A handful of Kamryn's admirers, some of them carrying violin cases, meandered about, soaking up her aura for as long as possible. The cleanup crew from Classical Taste catering was clearing off tables. No sign of Jacobus.

Pizzi found Robison at his station. "Arnie, there's some trouble down at the stage door," he said. "Some nutcase threw a couple of rocks through the window and Nick's going to check it out. Lock your door and take my place in the hall. I'll be back in a minute."

"Sure, Harry. Hey, the guy must be a real music lover. Ha!"

Robison locked the connecting door and went to take Pizzi's post. Before sitting down by the door, he switched on the light of Green Room B to double-check that the violin was still there. The case was exactly in its place, unopened.

Arnie sat down and folded his arms to wait as Lilburn, investigative reporter pursuing his scoop, dashed to catch up to Pizzi, who was already lumbering to the stage-door entrance. At the last moment his attention was caught by the sole person not in motion, a figure seated unobtrusively against the wall, seemingly unaware of the surrounding hubbub.

"Be right there," Lilburn shouted to Pizzi, slaloming his way through the exiting crowd to his quarry.

"The party's over, Mr. Jacobus," Lilburn said.

There was no response.

"I said the party's over."

Jacobus shook his head, as if waking himself. "And who might you be?" he asked.

"My apologies. Of course. Martin Lilburn. *New York Times.*"

"Lilburn." Jacobus made his name sound like an obscenity. "Looking for your big story, Lilburn?"

Lilburn was taken aback. "How did you know that?" he asked.

"If you had been listening, Lilburn, you would have heard that was a question, not a statement of fact. Now leave me alone."

Lilburn had had enough of the conversation. "As you wish, Mr. Jacobus," he said and raced off to catch up to Pizzi.

Green Room A soon emptied and the corridor was quiet. Swathed in the customary comfort of postconcert tranquillity, Arnie Robison, alert and relaxed, enjoyed the return of solitude after all the evening's clamor. A few minutes later, though, a blind man slowly approached him, his left hand gingerly touching the wall for guidance, the other groping in front to avoid collisions.

Arnie asked, "May I help you, sir?"

"Friend of the Vanders," the blind man lied. "Kam—that's what I call Kamryn—calls me Uncle Isaac, but I'm not really their uncle. You know what I mean."

"Sure, sure," said Arnie, graciously giving up his seat to sweet old blind Uncle Isaac.

The blind man continued to yack amiably until Arnie, waiting patiently for a respectful pause in their chat, told him he had to check on the violin. The blind man asked if he could accompany him. "Just to be in the same room with such an instrument," he said, "especially one that Kam played on . . . Well, you know what I mean."

Arnie, not wanting to insult a kind, old, bedraggled blind man, didn't see any harm in it. They entered Green Room B, Jacobus in tow, Arnie in the lead.

"Just keep your hand right here on my shoulder," Arnie said, "and you won't bump into a thing." Everything appeared in order, but just to make sure—Arnie later said it was just a hunch—he opened the case. When the blind man heard the spring-loaded clasps on the case snap open—one, two, then three—his body tensed, preparing to exorcise his lifetime of personal demons embodied by this violin, preparing to lurch forward past Robison and smash down on the evil eye of the Piccolino Strad with all his strength, hoping to bring an end to the nightmares of his life.

"Aw, jeez!" Arnie said, in a moan perhaps more profoundly disappointed than surprised.

Jacobus couldn't brake his forward momentum and collapsed into the opened case like a marionette with the strings cut. But neither did he feel the anticipated impact nor hear the *crack! crack!* of splintering wood under his weight as he landed.

The violin case was empty.

The New York Times, July 9, 1983
Diminutive Violinist Makes Big Impression
Valuable Violin Is Missing

By Martin Lilburn

Even the apparent theft of a violin did not overshadow the debut of the gifted nine-year-old violinist Kamryn Vander.

Winner of the prestigious Holbrooke Grimsley International Violin Competition, which is held only once every thirteen years, Miss Vander displayed not only the dazzling technique one has come to expect from today's wunderkinder, but a precocious musicality that belies her years.

Though slight in stature, Miss Vander offered up a heavy-weight program, one that would challenge the most veteran concert violinist. It included music by Wieniawski, Sarasate, Vieuxtemps, and Paganini, and ended with the virtuoso Sonata in G Minor by Tartini, known as the "Devil's Trill." Though these days a standing ovation is almost par for the course at any concert that has a rousing finish, it seemed that the audience was giving Miss Vander the ovation for a rousing beginning to an almost guaranteed headline career.

The famous three-quarter-sized Stradivarius violin on which Miss Vander performed was discovered missing after the concert when Carnegie Hall security guard Arnie Robison opened the case for inspection, shortly a pair of rocks were thrown at the stage-door window, breaking it. Famous violins are often referred to by the name of a previous owner. This particular Stradivarius is called "Il Piccolino" after a legendary, perhaps mythical, 17th-century violinist whose real name was Matteo Cherubino. Since prominent musicologists have uncovered no hard evidence to prove Cherubino's existence, however, fanciful stories surrounding the history of this violin can at this point be deemed nothing other than apocryphal.

Police are investigating the disappearance of the instrument and members of the Musical Arts Project Group, who are Miss Vander's sponsor and who were at the performance, have unanimously pledged their time and efforts to assist the authorities in retrieving the violin.

New York *Daily News,* July 9, 1983
Piccolino's Curse Strikes Again

By Naomi Hess

The ghost of "Il Piccolino" is at it again! After a concert by the budding prodigy violinist Kamryn Vander, the famous—or infamous—Piccolino Stradivarius violin was stolen from under the noses of security guards at Carnegie Hall after someone— or some *thing*—pitched two Tom Seaver fastball–sized rocks through the Hall's stage-door window. Matteo Cherubino, aka "Il Piccolino" because he was a midget, was a legendary 17th-century fiddler cut in half by the husband of his lover, a shapely Italian duchess, who had given him a 3/4-size Stradivarius violin (the most famous brand of all) for his birthday. Since then, anyone who has laid his—or her—hands on the violin has found misfortune or just plain bad luck. Even the greatest violinist, Paganini, who was allegedly no stranger to diabolical practices, lost his shirt when he owned the pint-sized instrument for a while.

When questioned, Carnegie Hall security guard Arnie Robison said, "The violin just kinda disappeared into thin air." When asked if the ghost of "Il Piccolino" might have had a hand in the theft of the violin, Robison responded, "Hey, anything's possible!" The violin is said to be worth $8,000,000—almost enough to buy front-row season tickets to the Knicks! The police have no leads at this point.

FOUR

Whether or not the stifling morning fog had lifted, Jacobus couldn't tell. Either way, nothing any more promising had been unveiled, as the air of the blind, gray sky remained torpid, damp, and unbearably close. The sweat had already started to drip down his back and it wasn't even ten o'clock. Jacobus was in his study.

The night before he had been momentarily stunned by his failure and by the empty case but had nevertheless extricated himself with little trouble from the tumult that had ensued after the Piccolino was discovered missing. After all, wasn't he just a clumsy old blind man who had only tripped onto a violin case? He had made sure Robison had witnessed what he referred to as his "blind man's shuffle" stumbling down the corridor, a ploy he shamelessly used from time to time to arouse sympathy.

Upon seeing the empty case, Robison called Pizzi, who immediately called the police. The police told them to sequester any remaining people in the building until they got there, so Jacobus was stuck with the petulant Classical Taste caterers and a few indignant personages—including the MAP dignitaries—who had attended the concert. The squad that finally showed up seemed more interested in going home than in investigating and, after some perfunctory note taking and question asking, let everyone go. The only potentially troublesome moment came when one of the cops asked him, "Why did you tell the security guard your name was 'Uncle Isaac'?" Before Jacobus came up with an answer, he was saved by another cop, who said, "Shut up, Malachi. Rookies don't ask questions. They listen. Now let's beat it out of here."

On his way out, the same cop, this Malachi, approached him.

"Where are you going now, Uncle Isaac? You told us you live hours from here."

"Bus. Two A.M.," said Jacobus.

"How about a ride to Port Authority? I'll drop you off there on my way home."

"Thanks for nothing," said Jacobus. "I'll take a cab."

The bitterness that enveloped him at Kamryn Vander's recital stayed with him all the way to his home and still choked him. Of all the things that were anathema to Jacobus, the most despicable was the use—he would say misuse—of music for the sole purpose of aggrandizing the performer. This is something he vowed never to permit or tolerate, neither from himself nor from his students.

Jacobus was even less in the mood to teach during the summer than the rest of the year, preferring to pawn off his violin students to music festivals or summer camps so he could get a break from them, and they from him. Inhaling his umpteenth Camel of this hot and muggy morning of July 9, he thought, Teaching more and enjoying it less.

Yet he had promised Max Furukawa, one of his few remaining friends, that he would listen to one of Max's students. A promise is a promise, he thought, though he found it peculiar and annoying to have to start this new student, this Yumi Shinagawa, in July. Furukawa, in a letter that he had translated into English, and which was subsequently read to Jacobus, explained that the girl and her mother had long planned to attend the Grimsley Competition performances in New York. He suggested it would be an opportune time for her to get started with Jacobus, but the family, especially the girl, had been resistant to the idea, which had surprised Furukawa. Perhaps she was fearful of being alone in a new country; perhaps she had heard of Jacobus's reputation for being a bit "creative" in his methods—Jacobus had chuckled when he read this description so politely put—but Furukawa had insisted, saying that no one had the ability to instill passion for the greatness of the music better than Jacobus.

When Jacobus heard Yumi's footsteps as she approached his studio for the first time, he noted that they were controlled, confident, purposeful. He flicked his cigarette butt into a toby jug of a blind pirate, his favorite coffee mug/ashtray, and, exhaling cigarette smoke through an overgrowth of nasal hair, said in his gravelly voice, "Don't bow when you come in." So began Miss Yumi Shinagawa's first lesson.

"Ah!" he said. "Irises, irises. Could use a pair. Ha! Smell like shit, but pretty. Purple ones, right? Put them on the sill over there."

Jacobus heard Yumi set the flowers on the sill, the soft clink of glass vase on wood.

So far, silent obedience. Typical. Nothing new there.

"Can you see out that window?" he asked. "Or is the ivy covering it?"

"There is a very pretty spiderweb covering most of it."

"Pretty?"

"Yes, the morning dew is on it. Like a string of pearls. A praying mantis hangs from a thread. Its wriggling makes the pearls shimmer."

"That's just lovely, Miss Shinagawa. May we get started now, or is this a haiku moment?"

Jacobus was an unkempt old man. He wore old plaid flannel shirts—the left collars frayed from years of rubbing against the upheld violin—which he rarely changed. His ashtray was usually overflowing. Spent

Camels and half-empty coffee cups lay strewn around the room, some sitting on piles of music scattered aimlessly about, one mug even on top of a makeshift coaster, the Toscanini recording of Beethoven's Ninth Symphony. A wooden chess game, long abandoned, white queen pinned in the corner at the mercy of two black rooks, lay on the floor in the corner, caked in grease and dust. Jacobus's patchy, curly graying hair was uncombed and he rarely shaved more than once a week. Well, here I am, he thought, easing back into his secondhand swivel chair. You want culture shock, honey, you've got it.

Yumi said, "I am wondering, sensei . . . I mean maestro . . ."

"Don't call me sensei. Or maestro either. Give me a swelled head. Swell enough as it is. And swelled enough," he muttered.

"Then what may I call you, please?"

"My few friends call me Jake. People who think I like them, or who pretend to like me, call me Daniel. You call me Mr. Jacobus. Someday, if you're real unlucky, maybe you'll call me Jake."

"Mr. Jacobus, then."

"So far so good."

"Mr. Jacobus . . ."

"Don't repeat yourself." His coarse voice was a low growl.

"You could tell that I had irises from the scent, perhaps, but how did you know they are purple?"

"Elementary, my dear Blossom. The only way you'd know to bring me irises is that Furukawa must've told you they were my favorite flower. Right? And if he told you that, he must've told you that purple ones were—had been—my color of choice."

"Mr. Jacobus?"

"What now, Iris?"

"Furukawa-sensei always tells his students to bow when they enter the room for their violin lessons. He says it is a sign of respect that the student must show to the teacher."

"I know that too."

"So why do you not permit me to bow, Mr. Jacobus?"

He wiped his sweat off his forehead with his sleeve and exhaled loudly, consciously conveying the impression he was dealing with this question with great patience. He wished it were true.

"Yumi, we agree that Furukawa is an excellent teacher?"

"Yes, Mr. Jacobus."

"Yes. If Furukawa is an excellent teacher, he must have a damn good reason to ask me to teach you, right?"

"Yes, Mr. Jacobus."

"Yes. So if Furukawa is such an excellent teacher and has a damn good reason for me to teach you, then don't you also agree that the reason must be that I do things differently from him?" He paused to catch his breath. "After all, why the hell should he want you to study with me if I did everything the same way he does? Yes?"

Silence.

"Yes yes. Yes yes yes," jabbed Jacobus, staccato. "So it is my firm belief that you show me respect when you show the music respect. Nothing more. Nothing less. So no ceremonies, no rituals. Okay?"

"I think so, but you are quite different from Furukawa-sensei, Mr. Jacobus."

"I'm sure Furukawa-sensei is thankful for that, honey. Now, what're you playing?"

"I will play the 'Devil's Trill' Sonata by Tartini," announced Yumi with a stiff formality that amused Jacobus.

"Ah, you will play the 'Devil's Trill' Sonata by Tartini," he mimicked. "I'm all ears. Ha!"

Yumi began the Larghetto, a slow, lilting Siciliana, with dark poignancy. It was immediately obvious to Jacobus that the girl had something. Furukawa's students were always tastefully well prepared, but this one was trying to say something. A little tight, a little imitative, maybe, but for a nineteen-year-old? Definitely something there.

Then the frenetic virtuosity of the second movement—during which the first distant rumble of thunder in the heavy overheated atmosphere rolled over the hills surrounding his house.

There was something else in her playing. He couldn't put his finger on it. Something different.

"Play the last movement," he said.

Yumi began the finale—impassioned operatic recitations alternating with a diabolically driven Allegro, replete with spectacularly gymnastic trills, for which the sonata was accurately named.

On the surface she's as hard and impersonal as steel, Jacobus thought. But underneath? Like she's trying to conceal something. Was this the typical Japanese reticence to expose one's feelings? Was it a teenager's self-consciousness to express adult emotion, especially in front of a stranger? Or was it simply what it sounded like to Jacobus, a determined effort to create a barrier?

By trying to conceal she had revealed to Jacobus a glimpse of her soul in that playing—a brief glimpse but, he thought with surprise, a striking one. Furukawa had sent Jacobus good students before. This one was different. Jacobus rubbed his hand over his grizzled whiskers.

"Okay, Yumi! Not bad."

" 'Not bad.' Does 'not bad' mean good?"

" 'Not bad' means 'not bad.' You have the tools to begin to learn. That's what 'not bad' means. Okay?"

Jacobus began to probe. "Are you sinister?" he asked.

"Sinister? I am confused."

"Well, it *is* the *'Devil's* Trill,' not the *'Angel's* Trill.' You think it's a coincidence Tartini focuses on the left hand to represent the Devil?"

"I'm afraid I still don't understand, Mr. Jacobus."

Confused? Am I confusing you? he thought. Still calm, though. Controlled. Let's see what I can do about that.

" 'Left' in Italian is *sinistra*. Don't you know that? One would not want to be a left-handed Italian. 'Hey, Lefty, I want ya should plug him full of holes.' "

"I'm sorry, I didn't know that."

"So now you know. Next time I want to hear sinister. You've got some sinister blood in you somewhere."

"Mr. Jacobus!"

Ah! Finally. A spontaneous response. A little shock? Confusion? Something more?

"Yes, my sinister Iris, there's left-handed deviltry in the music. And of course, you know the story of this piece."

Silence.

"Don't you?" Jacobus pursued.

"I'm sorry. No."

"You *don't* know!" His temper ignited like hot charcoals doused with lighter fluid. Jacobus bellowed, "Aren't you even curious? How many other pieces do you know are named 'Devil's Trill'? How do you expect to be a musician and not ask the most fundamental questions about the music you're playing? Do you think Tartini woke up in the middle of a cold night in his warm featherbed in eighteenth-century Italy and exclaimed, 'Hey, I think I'll call this sonata 'Devil's Trill'?"

"No."

"Yes!! Yes yes yes yes!!! He *did* wake up in the middle of the night! Probably in a cold sweat in the dark"—I've had enough of those cold sweats myself, Jacobus noted—"because the Devil himself was sitting at the foot of the bed. And he tells us that Mr. Devil commanded him to write down the music, including those infernal trills."

"Excuse me. I don't wish to sound impudent," said Yumi, sounding impudent, "but how do we know this?"

"We know this because Tartini wrote it in the music!" Jacobus jabbed his finger in the air in the direction of Yumi's music stand. "He wrote it there! There! There! In the last movement, right where it gets crazy, right in the music. Look! There at the bottom of the page, he wrote, *'Trillo del diavolo al pie del letto!'* 'The trill of the devil from the foot of the bed!' Don't you see it?"

"Yes, I see it now. It's in Italian. I didn't know what it meant. But surely it was just a story. Or a dream."

"You want the audience to think it was just a dream? Or real? Or that it doesn't matter? Or that you don't know? You want to tell a story, or just go through the motions?"

Silence ensued, except for Jacobus's panting as he tried to extinguish his temper.

"I'm sorry it wasn't perfect, Mr. Jacobus. I will work harder next time."

"Well, you know, at some point we'll have a nice long discussion of what 'perfection' means—if it means anything at all. For now I'll take you up on the issue of working hard."

"I will work harder next time," Yumi repeated.

"Hey, Yumi, you ever think maybe you're already working too hard? That tension and intensity are two different animals? That if you hold the bow, the violin, too tight, it makes it more difficult to play, and that, believe it or not, you can hear the difference?"

Jacobus thought, Number one, she's trying to figure out what the hell I'm talking about. Second, she's probably never felt so humiliated, being spoken to like this. She thinks I'm impolite and crude—tough shit—it'll make standing on a stage in front of a crowd a piece of cake.

A phone rang, a loud, brittle ring, breaking the silence. Jacobus let it ring. He had never bothered with an answering machine, so it rang for a long time before it stopped. Neither spoke in the ensuing silence.

Finally Jacobus said, "So why are you crying?"

"But I am not crying, Mr. Jacobus."

All the others would have been jelly by now, he thought to himself. Tough kid, this Yumi Shinagawa.

"Why should I be crying?"

How can I answer that?

More silence.

Jacobus cleared his throat. "Okay, okay. Let me put this in a way you may understand. My little Flower Blossom, even though playing the violin is one of the most unnatural acts ever devised in the history of the world, if we play the violin as relaxed and natural as possible, maybe we can have an outside shot at being successful. Now, I can show you how to solve this tension business in one minute."

"What is it you would like me to do?" she said with an edge to her voice.

"Hey, are you getting impatient with me already, Iris Eyes? Impatiens is not my strongest virtue. We can get you on the next flight back to Kagoshima if that's what you want," Jacobus said, standing up. "For now, just watch."

He put both arms out in front of him, somewhat bent at the elbow, wrists dangling limply. He looked, with his dark glasses slightly askew, more like the moribund praying mantis than a revered pedagogue.

"Try it," he ordered. After a moment of not hearing a response, he said, "Come on, be the obedient student."

"All right. I am trying," said Yumi.

"Now, I want you just to flip over your left wrist. One . . . two . . . three . . . flip. Still loose?"

"Yes, still loose."

"Good. That's exactly how it should be when you're playing. Even someone who doesn't play the violin can do that. Now, the beginning of the 'Devil's Trill.' Again."

She began again. This time the flow, the resonance, the ease that had been missing the first time around were there. Jacobus could hear the steel bend a little, and he smiled to himself.

"So?" asked Jacobus.

"Yes, thank you, Mr. Jacobus," replied Yumi.

"Don't get too excited. Now, ask Teacher a question."

"But Mr. Jacobus, would that not be rude?"

"What a fine, fine question that is, Yumi dearest! Let's see," he continued, as if rummaging mentally for the appropriate encyclopedia heading. " 'Would that not be rude?' 'Would that not be rude?' Ah, yes, here we are. It would be rude if I'm waxing poetic about Mozart and your question has to do with pepperoni pizza, but generally, no, it wouldn't be rude in the least. Never be afraid to ask questions. Never! Never! Never! In fact, I would hope that if you ever feel so moved, you will not only question me but argue with me!"

"Argue with you?" Yumi sounded genuinely astonished.

"Hey, there you go! Disagreeing with me already! Let me share a little-known secret with you, honey." Jacobus theatrically cupped his hand around his mouth and whispered with a theatrical rasp, "I don't know everything, and chances are I will learn something from *you* by the end of the year."

A wheeze whistled from his throat in appreciation of his own humor. The phone rang again.

"Goddammit," hollered Jacobus, his face turning red. "Why can't they goddam leave me alone when I'm teaching?"

He banged his hand repeatedly on the music table next to him, rattling the toby jug, spilling coffee and wet cigarette butts onto the music. Sweat streamed down his forehead from his matted gray hair.

"Mr. Jacobus?" Yumi asked after what she surmised was an appropriately long silence.

"Yeah? You've got a question?" Jacobus mumbled.

"When I first entered the room and bowed, how did you know I bowed?"

"You mean, how did I know *because I'm blind*?"

"I'm very sorry, Mr. Jacobus! I didn't mean . . . You said to ask questions and I only asked because you . . ."

"Don't be sorry, Miss Shinagawa. I'm not offended. Blindness is the least of my faults. Anyway, it's a very easy question to answer.

"I knew for two reasons. The first is, I heard you walk without hesitation all the way down the hall and into the room. Right? The sound was especially clear since you're obviously wearing those uncomfortable shoes with high heels, which, by the way, I don't recommend for the balance you need to play the violin, but I assume you do so because, judging from your short stride, you are not as tall as you would like to be. Right? No matter.

"At the door entrance your steps came to a halt—not with any sense of urgency or surprise, and only momentarily, as if by habit. You then resumed walking at your previous steady pace directly to the middle of the room where the music stand has stood for more years than I care to remember.

"So, what reason could there have been for you to stop in such a manner other than to bow in the time-honored Japanese tradition with which I am all too familiar?"

"And there is a second reason?" asked Yumi.

"Because you're Furukawa's student, of course!"

Yumi laughed. "Mr. Jacobus, Furukawa-sensei warned me that in some ways you see better than people with sight. I am beginning to understand what he meant."

"Miss Shinagawa, I don't intend to sit here in order to be flattered. But considering this is our first lesson on the 'Devil's Trill,' I'll forgive you. This time."

"Thank you, Mr. Jacobus."

Jacobus was beginning to be aware he was no longer the only one doing the manipulating. He cleared his throat, coughing up phlegm, spitting it into a yellowed handkerchief that he returned to his back pocket.

"Speaking of the devil," he said, feeling for the pack of Camels in his shirt pocket, "did you read Lilburn's story in the *Times* this morning? Seems the curse of the Piccolino Strad has struck again. Stolen from Carnegie Hall last night, right after Kamryn Vanderblick's so-called triumphant recital at the Grimsley Competition." He made an ugly giggle. "And not a clue who took it."

"Oh?" said Yumi.

Jacobus lit up the cigarette, inhaling deeply. Remarkable, he thought.

FIVE

The agenda alone would have been sufficient to raise the room temperature at the hastily assembled meeting, but with a power outage in the sweltering city triggered by record overnight air-conditioning use, the heat in the MAP conference room pushed toward the boiling point.

Rachel Lewison, who had spent half the night organizing the meeting, calling and recalling the parties involved, mediating between the early risers and late nighters in setting up the meeting time, neatly flattened out that morning's *Times* and began to read aloud Lilburn's article about the theft, her usual monotone even more pronounced in deference to the formal nature of the meeting.

"*New York Times,* July 9. 'Diminutive Violinist Makes Big Impression. Valuable Violin Is Missing. Even the apparent theft of a violin did not overshadow—' "

"I want him fired. Now!"

"And who is it you want fired, Victoria darling?" Strella asked.

"That schmuck Pizzi. For incompetence!"

"But Victoria, he was just doing his job," said Trevor Grimsley.

"Doing his job? *Doing his job?* You have your precious little eight-million-dollar Strad stolen right from under his nose because the idiot left the door unlocked, and you say 'he was just doing his job,' you overage queer?"

Grimsley averted his eyes, looking up at the ceiling.

Lilburn interceded. "Look, it was only a few seconds that the door was unlocked and unguarded. Who could have predicted it would be stolen in the blink of an eye? But in any event, Victoria, there's no need for this to become personal."

"You're defending Grimsley?" asked Jablonski. "What's the world coming to?"

"There's no need for us to fight each other, Victoria," said Boris Dedubian, a soothing voice of reason.

"Thank you, Boris," said Lilburn.

"Of course. We can certainly lodge a complaint with the proper authorities about Mr. Pizzi—"

"*Mister* Pizzi? *Mister* Pizzi? Now you're calling him *Mister* effing Pizzi?" cried Jablonski, unsoothed. "You know damn well his union is going to take your 'lodged complaint' and lodge it right up your—"

"Let's let Rachel just finish reading the article," Strella cajoled, "then we'll take it from there. Okay, Victoria?"

Jablonski simmered in silence, which Strella took for accession.

"Great. Go ahead, hon."

And so began the first-ever emergency meeting of the Musical Arts

Project Group. Duly called to order by Anthony Strella, chairman of the board, the meeting convened at ten in the morning at their impressive third-floor conference room of the newly renovated brownstone on Fifty-fifth Street, one block south of Carnegie Hall's stage entrance. Rachel Lewison had already taken 'notes' for the meeting—which had nothing to do with the subject at hand—in case anyone were to ask. Chewing her pencil, she sat in nervous idleness.

Rachel returned to the article, reading Lilburn's account of the recital and ensuing theft.

"Thanks, hon," said Strella when she finished. Rachel carefully folded the paper shut.

"But the fact is," said Dedubian, "as distressing as it is, especially to me, we have a much bigger problem than the loss of a violin, however valuable."

"We *could* have a problem, Bo. It has the potential to be a problem . . . but it isn't a problem yet," said Lilburn. "Is it?" He sat with his hands folded on the table, looking at them as he spoke.

"Must you always split hairs?" asked Jablonski.

"I'm not. Not really. In fact, if we play our cards right perhaps we could get some good press out of this. Potentially."

Trevor Grimsley interrupted. "Pardon me for sounding stupid, but could someone please fill me in? What precisely is a bigger problem than the loss of an eight-million-dollar violin?"

Strella said, "I'd be happy to, Trevor. Rachel, sweetheart, could you go down to the deli and see if you can find us some cold drinks? It's boiling in here. Just have them put it on the account. Thanks, babe."

Victoria Jablonski glared at Strella. Lilburn gazed out the window. Rachel Lewison quietly placed her pencil on the table, perpendicular to its edge, and left without a word.

"Okay," continued Strella as soon as the door closed, "now I can talk a little more freely, since all of us are in the same boat. Having a violin stolen is bad news, yeah, and of course we hope it'll be recovered and the authorities are doing everything they can and blah, blah, blah. But even if it's never seen again, we—all of us in this room—are none the worse for wear because it really has nothing to do with us."

"I still don't see your point," said Grimsley.

"Trevor," responded Dedubian, "the point is the police are asking us questions. We're all suspects. They think one of us might be the thief."

"They're schmucks!" said Jablonski. "If anyone stole it, it's that loser Jacobus. Didn't you see him there? Gave me an earful about 'integrity,' lecturing me about integrity. I told him where to go."

Lilburn related that he had seen Jacobus too and how unsettling his presence had been. Jacobus had been there when Robison had opened the case. Lilburn mused aloud whether the authorities had yet sought out Jacobus for further questioning. That thought was perhaps the single unifying one of the coterie's gathering. They agreed to promote Jacobus's name to the top of the list of people who had attended the reception when they were next confronted by the police.

"After all, why would any of us have stolen that violin?" Victoria continued, leering at her compatriots around the mahogany table. "It makes no sense at all. We've all got a good thing going. Why would any one of us ruin it?"

"They don't understand that yet, so they're looking," continued Dedubian. He pulled out a monogrammed handkerchief and wiped his glistening brow. "They don't know where to look; they don't even know how to look—"

"And that's precisely the problem," Strella continued. "That one officer—what was his name? Malachi—seemed something of a pit bull. If cops like him start turning over enough stones, even randomly— *especially* randomly—they might begin to ask questions about what we've been doing with MAP for lo these many years."

"As they sometimes say in the violin world," said Lilburn with a small puckered smile, "they'll 'leave no tone un-Sterned.' "

The hot silence that ensued strongly suggested his stale joke, and old spoonerism on the name of famed violinist Isaac Stern, was unsuccessful in relieving the tension. Lilburn resumed looking at his hands, immaculately clean and manicured but becoming moist with perspiration.

Dedubian resumed the discussion. "It is conceivable the authorities, the police, the insurance company—"

"The IRS," interjected Jablonski.

"Yes, even the IRS," acknowledged Dedubian, "could perhaps take exception to the way we've conducted some of our volunteer work. I would suggest that for now we cooperate with the authorities as much as possible to demonstrate our goodwill. Let us meet again, soon. Let us hope the violin will show up in the meantime. But remember, business-people can interpret numbers in different ways, and it is possible that if they get their hands on our numbers, they may have some concerns."

"And though we've done nothing wrong, that perception," said Lilburn, "could get us into much hotter water than this distressing heat."

Strella put both hands on the table, pushing himself to a standing position.

"Well, lady and gentlemen, it is now ten twenty-seven and Martin has provided us with two bad jokes in a row. We now all seem to be on the same page. We're all aware of the need to continue to live our lives and ply our trades, though, for the time being, we may wish to do so even more discreetly. I further suggest we adjourn if we're going to hit the greens by noon."

Lilburn adjourned to the men's room at the end of the hall. He washed his hands, with a wet comb arranged his egregiously thinning hair, and, as was his habit, wiped the sink dry with a paper towel. Returning to the corridor, he spied Rachel Lewison emerge from the stairwell next to the elevator carrying a cardboard tray of cold drinks. Outside the conference room door, she placed the tray on the floor, stood up, and attempted, unsuccessfully, to open the locked door.

She began to bend down to pick up the tray, and he began to pick up his pace to help her but, surprisingly, the door opened. Lilburn couldn't tell whose arm it was that emerged, wrapped itself around Rachel's waist, and pulled her—neither willingly nor unwillingly—into the room. The door clicked shut.

Lilburn walked to the door and briefly considered knocking. Instead he picked up the tray of drinks. The ice had already melted. After some searching he found a garbage can in the stairwell and disposed of the drinks before continuing on his way.

SIX

Yumi had a lesson the next day. She had just finished the Sarabanda from the Bach Partita in D Minor.

"Tell me about what you just played, Yumi," Jacobus said quietly. He felt himself ready to explode. He wasn't sure why, but he couldn't help himself. The iris blooms, unwatered, had wilted and smelled more like shit than ever. Yet he left them to wither in the vase. Maybe, he thought, it was the relentless heat that was igniting him.

"It's a kind of dance. Isn't it?" Yumi asked.

"Yes, it is a kind of dance. So are the hokeypokey and the bossa nova. Isn't there anything you can add that might enlighten us a bit further?"

"I really don't know, Mr. Jacobus. As my teacher I trust you to tell me all I need to know."

"Well, isn't that awfully kind of you? Let me tell you something, Yumi, that I regularly inform my students," said Jacobus. "If there is one thing I hate more than bullshit, it's sugar-coated bullshit. Now, would I really be doing my job if I just told you everything?"

"Aren't I supposed to learn from you?"

"I should hope so, but as a teacher *my* goal is for my students not to need me anymore. I knead your brain—you don't need me. You don't get that? Never mind. That means, number one: I have to teach you not only physical skills to play the instrument, but more important, number two: I have to teach you how to think on your own. If that is at all possible. So when Bach, arguably the greatest musical genius who ever lived, writes a sarabanda, as opposed to a minuet, *giga*, or even a sarabande with an *e* at the end, don't you think he must have had a damn good reason? If he's willing to go to that much trouble for us, don't you think the least we can do—*the least we can do* if we consider ourselves serious musicians—is to try to understand the basic characteristics of that dance form? Once we do that, then maybe we can start playing music. Now, yeah, you play in tune and your sound is just dandy, but lots of people can do that. Musically it was as much of a sarabanda as

I'm Mickey Mantle, and, surprise! Guess what? I'm not Mickey Mantle! I suggest, Yumi dear, you do a little sleuthing and bring this back next time.

"And one more thing." Jacobus was almost shouting. "You remember when we spoke about bowing as a symbol of respect? Remember that? Yeah? Well, maybe bowing is a symbol of respect and maybe it isn't, but it is never any more or less than that: a symbol. The real respect, the true respect, not the symbol, is in what goes on up there!" At which point Jacobus (with uncanny accuracy) suddenly pointed his violin bow, like a rapier, directly at Yumi's temple.

His crescendo broke off with a sudden, jagged silence. The only sound was the indifferent drone of Jacobus's old oscillating table fan, bringing little relief to the heat and none to the tension. Time seemed to be suspended, as in the climax of a great symphonic finale—Beethoven's Third or Tchaikovsky's Fifth—when the audience has been given no choice by the composer but to hold its collective breath to the limit of endurance, waiting for an unknown denouement after the grand pause.

Finally, "Sermon over. What else do you have for today?"

"Mendelssohn Concerto," choked Yumi, hardly able to speak.

"What?" he hollered.

"Mendelssohn Concerto!" she hollered back reflexively.

Good, Jacobus said to himself, I've got her yelling at me already. Starting to break through. Starting to free her from a lifetime of ingrained behavior. And only the second lesson.

"Play it," he muttered.

He heard Yumi take a deep breath.

See if she can focus now!

She managed to make her way through the first page of the concerto relatively unscathed, Jacobus stopping her at the point the orchestra takes over.

"Yumi," he said, almost in a whisper, "I ask this question, which I ask of all my new students, not out of anger, but only to know you better, and perhaps so you will know yourself better.

"Yumi, you play the violin very well, no doubt. But let me ask you this. *Why* do you play the violin?"

She took some moments before responding.

Jacobus wondered why she was taking so long. It wasn't such a hard question. Was she afraid of another lecture—she didn't seem to be afraid of anything—or was she trying to come up with a reasonable answer? Or part of an answer?

"Your question, Mr. Jacobus, is so basic and simple, but I truly had never thought about why."

Hearing Jacobus's incipient growl, she quickly added, "But I think there are several reasons."

He said nothing, only leaned back and cocked his head to hear better.

"First, because my mother and her mother played the violin. In fact, it was my grandmother who was my first teacher and sent me to Furukawa-sensei when I was ten. So it really was not my choice."

She paused suddenly, in a way that to Jacobus seemed almost as if she had said more than she wanted. So many kinds of silence, he thought. This one puzzled him. Hers was a common enough story.

"Anything else?" he asked, breaking through her contemplation.

"Yes. I love music. When I was young . . . younger," she corrected as Jacobus quickly stifled a smile, "I listened to music all the time. Not because it was forced on me but because I always wanted to hear more. It is as much part of our life as eating."

"Our?"

"My family."

Another pause.

"Is that the correct answer?" asked Yumi, without sarcasm.

"Correct? Is there a right or wrong answer to that question? I don't know, but your answer is as good as most. I once had a student, Rachel Lewison, who had only one reason for playing the violin: to win competitions! I asked, 'How about the beauty of the music? How about the pleasure of playing?' Blank. How about 'Isn't it fun for you to get together with other young musicians?' Didn't register. Zilch. For her, music was a means to win a prize. A goddam prize!" He shook his head, muttering, "You'd think the music would be prize enough."

"And did she?" asked Yumi

"Did she? Did she what? Oh, did she win? Afraid not. In the long run I don't know whether that's fortunate or unfortunate for her. I *am* sure that one reason she always came in third or fourth, if that, was that she had no conception of beauty, let alone her ability to create it. Maybe you've got it in you, Yumi. She didn't. It was all manufactured, a phys-ical skill honed only to win a contest. Put a finger here, put a finger

there. A finger here, a finger there. Press the buttons. Paint by numbers. Tried for a couple years to get through to her that there really was
more to music—and life—but then I threw in the towel. Yeah, I gave up.
I sent Rachel over to Victoria Jablonski, figuring she'd fit right in at that
factory."

"Isn't Miss Jablonski Kamryn Vander's teacher? Her students always win competitions!" Yumi stopped suddenly, almost choking on
her last words.

Jacobus laughed bitterly.

"Ah! We've made a faux pas, have we! The truth comes out! Good,
good, good!

"No, my students haven't won as many competitions as Victoria's,
but then again look what happens to her students and mine over a
whole career. Hers go up like rockets, *Fshhhh!* Fame and fortune before
they can shave! Pretty good, huh?

"But then just as quickly back down to earth. *Splat!* Chronic physical
problems—tendinitis from overpracticing the wrong way before they're
fully developed. Or worse, nutcases from being pushed too hard, way
too hard—produce, produce, produce! Or under the control of some
well-intentioned adults—some not well-intentioned adults, yeah, some
real assholes who don't allow the poor kids to have a childhood—agents,
managers, recording companies. Parents! Or sometimes they burn themselves out just when they're reaching a point in their lives when they
should only be beginning to put the whole ball of wax together.

"One of the greatest violin talents of the century, Michael Rabin,
gave his Carnegie Hall debut when he was thirteen and died at the age
of thirty-five. There were rumors of emotional problems, drug use,
unstable personal life. He developed a fear of falling off the stage. One
day he fell on a parquet floor, struck his head, and died. So much for
prodigies, huh!"

"And *your* students?"

The phone rang. Jacobus let it ring, this time waiting patiently for it
to stop.

"My students," continued Jacobus. "A lot of my students don't even
become performing musicians, I'm proud to say . . ."

As Jacobus talked he heard something. Something very quiet and
furtive. It took him a moment—Yumi quietly slipping out of her shoes?
Gliding on her bare feet?

Ah, a little experiment! Jacobus thought. So you want to try your luck, huh?

Jacobus calmly picked up rosin from the coffee table next to him as if he were about to engage in the routine task of rosining his bow, when suddenly in one motion he hurled it at Yumi, hitting her squarely on the shoulder.

"What the hell are you doing?" he screamed. "Are you testing me? Are you testing me?"

Yumi froze.

"You think this is a game? You think music is a game?" the rasping voice shot at her. "Are you testing me? Fool the blind man! Blindman's buff?"

His face distorted in anger.

"Get out of here! Get out!"

"I'm so sorry! I'm . . ."

"There. Is. No. Such. Thing. As. Sorry!"

Sudden silence descended upon them, broken only by the fan and Jacobus's panting. He clearly heard her walk toward the door.

"And don't come back!"

SEVEN

But she did come back, the next day, to Jacobus's surprise and grudging admiration. Of course, Jacobus didn't express that sentiment to her. His only explicit acknowledgment of her courage and tenacity was to tell Yumi that she must be "even more meshuga" than he was.

"Some of my students became doctors, some teachers," Jacobus continued, as if neither his rage nor the intervening twenty-four hours had ever transpired. "One of my students was a great physicist and another an equally great floor-covering installer. But for the most part they got jobs in symphony orchestras or played in string quartets . . . or taught. Often had nice long careers, and if I could, I tried to instill a love—believe it or not—for what they do, for whatever they do, that will last longer than the next competition.

"Some of them did very well in competitions, though I never encouraged them too much. I've had prize winners in the Naumberg, Montreal, Queen Elizabeth, among others, though I don't broadcast it as well as Victoria. No, not nearly as well. But I never, ever, allowed one to enter that despicable Grimsley Competition. The people who run that menagerie—the whole bunch of them—should be locked up."

Jacobus seemed ready to explode again, so Yumi quickly responded, "But do you not think it important to succeed in the beginning? I am already nineteen and I've not yet won anything. It seems so many younger students are better than I am."

Jacobus cackled, but it was more jeering than joyful.

"You think Isaac Stern worried if he was as great as Heifetz? Or Perlman if he's as great as Stern? Who do you think you are? You think you're different? You think you're special? Either you're dedicated to making something beautiful or you're not. Period! Not comma! Not comma! Period! If you love it, that's the reward. Who's better than who! So please don't give me this 'I'm so terrible' victim bullshit. Okay?"

Before Yumi could reply, Jacobus changed the topic. He was still trying to figure out this kid. There was something about her, something different. The way she talked. The way she reacted. He liked it. And he didn't like it.

"Question. *Why* do you play the Mendelssohn Concerto? After all, everyone and his uncle has either played it or heard it."

"You change subjects so fast for me, Mr. Jacobus."

Don't want prepared answers, he thought. That's why.

"Tell me why you play the Mendelssohn."

"Well, it is a beautiful piece and it gives me pleasure to play it," said Yumi. "Is that not enough?"

"Maybe. But is it enough reason for two thousand people in the audience to want to listen to *your* performance? There are dozens of great performances already recorded. Do you intend to give pleasure only to yourself? There's a name for that, I think."

Blushing, Yumi? he thought. Tired of being embarrassed and bullied? Maybe now I'll get some gut answers. I want to see your *mind* work, not just your training.

"I suppose for someone to want to listen to my performance, I need to understand that there is something special about the music I'm playing, so that whoever is listening is hearing it in a way that is different from other performances."

"And what might that be?" asked Jacobus, guiding her.

"Perhaps," said Yumi, "perhaps that would be the way that I think the composer wanted it to be heard."

"Which time?" Jacobus pursued.

"Which time?" asked Yumi.

"Are you deaf or something? Which time?"

"Which time? I don't . . . Yes, of course! Which time? Of course, the first time!"

"And why the first time?"

"Because, I think, the first performance is when the music is full of surprises for the listener, when only the composer and the performer know which way the music will go. Yes, if I can play it that way, then even the Mendelssohn Concerto can be new!"

"Tell me some things that are special about the beginning of the Mendelssohn Concerto, Yumi."

"I'm not quite sure I know what you mean, Mr. Jacobus."

"Hey, philosophy's fine, but you gotta back it up. Mendelssohn may not be Mozart or Beethoven. But this concerto, this Mendelssohn violin concerto, is a masterpiece. No surprise it's played so often . . . too often. It's so damn familiar"—don't overlook the familiar, Jacobus thought in a flash of perception—"that if you haven't done your music history homework, you don't realize this concerto begins unlike any violin concerto before it and in a way that many composers after him copied. Tell me what's different."

"I don't know."

"Tell me!"

"I don't know!"

"Of course you know!" Jacobus yelled, losing his patience. She's smart but she's damn stubborn, he thought. Not as stubborn as I am, though.

"It's just never registered with you. You've just never thought about it. Why not? You said you love music. Tell me. Now, how do all the violin concertos of Mozart, Beethoven, and Brahms begin? With a little tweety birdie?"

"No, they all begin with the orchestra first."

"So, you *do* know! You *do* know! Why do you say you *don't* know when you *do* know? You just had to ask yourself the right question."

"I don't understand."

Come on, Yumi, Jacobus thought. It's in there. Just puke it up.

"Yes, you do. Tell me. How does the orchestra begin in those other concertos?"

"With a long introduction."

"And what's in the introduction?"

"All the melodies. It's almost like an entire exposition."

"And the Mendelssohn?" asked Jacobus, now perched on the edge of his seat.

"Yes! I see," Yumi said slowly, then with increasing animation. "All those details I've worked on without seeing it. Yes, I see what you mean."

"I don't see anything. I hear. Tell me what you hear."

"Yes," she pondered aloud, "the Mendelssohn has *no* introduction. Rather, just two measures, only soft but turbulent."

Ah! She knows the answer now.

"Yeah, and what's so special about that?" Jacobus prodded.

"Because the violin comes in after only those two measures, which no violin concerto had ever done before. It's a surprise. It means that the music needs to sound urgent, almost as if the violinist *can't* wait for a whole introduction. Mendelssohn indicates it to be played soft—"

"But he writes '*Molto appassionato*'!"

"—so it wouldn't be right to just barge in."

"And the key!"

"E minor. It's dark and brooding."

"And the melody!"

"It reaches up over and over again but never seems to reach high enough to be able to grasp what it's reaching for. It makes sense now. It's incredible"—Jacobus heard Yumi's voice break—"and I had never seen it."

"Better late than never. After all, you're already nineteen," said Jacobus, sitting back in his chair. "But aren't you leaving a little something out?"

"Something out?" asked Yumi. "Yes, I suppose so. But I don't know. There is so much to think about now, isn't there?"

"Just the small matter of *how* to play it the way you now hear it in your head."

At that moment, the phone rang again on the small table next to Jacobus. Finally, he answered it after first mistakenly grabbing the cup of day-old coffee sitting next to it.

"Yeah," he said into the receiver.

"Jake!"

"Nathaniel!" said Jacobus, immediately recognizing the voice. Another of his few remaining friends, Nathaniel Williams had once been a colleague but changed in midstream to pursue a more lucrative career in the insurance industry.

"What's it been, three years?" Jacobus continued. "Good to hear your ugly voice again. And I'm not going to help you find the Piccolino Strad. Good-bye."

Jacobus began to hang up.

Nathaniel stammered just in time, "Well, Mercy Circe, Jake, how could you possibly know that's why I called?"

"Hold on a second." Jacobus covered the receiver with his hand. "Yumi, that's enough for today. Put your fiddle away but stick around for a minute. My friend wants to badger me about the Piccolino. You may be interested."

Jacobus returned to the phone. "Okay, Nathaniel. Nathaniel, are you there?"

"Yeah, I'm here. I think."

"So you think you can fool me after all these years? You don't think I know how to put two and two together? My only surprise was you didn't call sooner."

"I did call sooner. You just never answered the phone. So what two and two have you put together?"

"Why do I always have to spell things out for everyone? For you, though, I will try to be patient."

"Okay, big shot, let's hear."

"First of all, you'd have to be deaf and blind to miss the stories in the papers and TV. Then, the same day the Strad was stolen from Carnegie, there were two murders in New York and one of those sicko Central Park beatings, all in the same precinct. Since Hizzoner the Mayor is making violent crime his number-one reelection campaign issue, do you really think the police will put the theft of a violin at the top of its ever-growing crime docket? And a violin—valuable as it may be—is generally considered a plaything for sissy rich kids. Where do you think your average man on the street wants his hard-earned tax money going?"

"Well? So?"

"So, if the police aren't going to bother pursuing a case that doesn't seem to have any leads anyway, who's most interested in seeing an eight-million-dollar violin found? Of course, the insurance company. Which one is it this time?"

"Intercontinental Insurance Associates," offered Nathaniel.

Nathaniel sounded deflated. Not a small accomplishment for someone of his girth, Jacobus thought.

"Okay, so Intercontinental whatever whatever doesn't want to pay out eight million to the Holbrooke Grimsley Family Trust, which owns the fiddle and sponsors the damned competition. When they realize that New York's Finest, who don't know about and don't care about art theft anyway, aren't going to do a damn thing to find it, they naturally get nervous."

"And?"

"And, so they, Intercontinental, decide to hire someone to try to recover the violin. And why not hire the person who for some reason is considered the best such agent of that kind and also claims to be highly conversant in the language of the music world? Someone who also is enough of a professional that his ego isn't too big to ask an old friend for, let's say, special consultation?"

"So, Jake, are you going to help me or what?" asked Nathaniel. "I'm hardly assuaged by the flattery."

"Sorry, Nathaniel. Not a chance."

"But Jake, why not?"

"Are you sitting down, Nathaniel?"

"Yeah, why?"

"Because I stole it." Jacobus let out a hideous cackle.

"You stole it!? Come on, Jake. Get serious."

"Who's not serious? I stole it, chopped it in eentsy-weentsy pieces, and burned it in the fireplace."

"In this heat? In July? Right."

"Look," said Jacobus, "I detest that competition. I detest the people surrounding it. The Piccolino Strad symbolizes everything I detest about the music business. Detest. Detest. Detest. So, do I pass de-test?"

"Very funny. You going to help me or not?"

Even as Jacobus joked, an idea began to occur to him. Maybe he could be persuaded. Maybe it would be worth his while. Maybe there was a bigger prize than the recovery of the Piccolino Strad. Maybe.

"Or not. Look, I've got better things to do. First, I have a shitload of highly deserving overachieving students." This was a lie. Nathaniel knew it and Jacobus knew he knew it. The number of Jacobus's students had dwindled in inverse proportion to the growth of ivy on his house. "In fact," he continued, "there's one standing in front of me as we speak.

"Second, a wild-goose chase is not in my best interests, and anyway, most stolen violins never again see the light of day. Third, as stunning as that Piccolino Strad seems to be to everyone, it's ruined anyone who's ever put his hands on it. Good riddance, as far as I'm concerned. Eight million is a small price to pay. And, as I mentioned, I stole it."

"Jake, I'm going to make you an offer."

"Go ahead, but there's nothing you could offer that would change my mind," Jacobus said, but in fact his mind had already changed. It was one of those impulsive split-second decisions that Jacobus was prone to make that altered the course of his life.

He reasoned that the Piccolino Strad was tied to the Grimsley Competition, which was joined at the hip to the Musical Arts Project. He hated all three. Everything they stood for was repugnant to him. His discussion of it with Yumi had opened up old wounds. Maybe this would be his chance to heal them. He had already failed to destroy the Piccolino Strad, but that had been a stupid idea concocted in the depths of his depression. Perhaps that failure was a reprieve. Would he ever have another opportunity to bring the walls down? What would he be willing to sacrifice to do it? How would he do it?

Williams then made Jacobus an offer of half the twenty percent commission he would receive for the safe recovery of the violin. At an insured value of eight million dollars, Jacobus would pocket eight hundred thousand.

Jacobus responded to Williams's offer, saying he was insulted that someone who he thought was his friend would try to bribe him. Williams, flabbergasted, asked him what it would take.

Jacobus said, "Nathaniel, if you expect me to leave the peace and quiet of my house in the country to go traipsing around New York City and who knows where else to try to find something that I want to stay lost, just to avoid incriminating myself, I expect you to provide me with a pastrami and corned beef combo at the Carnegie Deli. Extra lean."

"What?" asked Williams, bewildered.

"And with one Dr. Brown's Cel-Ray Tonic."

There was a momentary silence on the line.

"I'm not really authorized to spend this much, Jake, but I'll swing it . . . somehow."

"Nathaniel, you've twisted my arm," Jacobus said. "If you're willing to go out on a limb like that just to get me to pretend to track down a heinous thief when I've already told you that I did the dastardly deed, who am I to stand in the way of justice? Why don't I take the five eighteen bus into the city? I'd be there by nine."

"Um, Jake?"

"What now?"

"Well, I'm not calling from the city. I had this weird feeling you might decide to help me out, so at the moment I'm at the Main Street Doughnut Shoppe, you know, the place you warned me never to go in because 'Shop' is spelled with *pe* at the end. You were right. Now the sign even says, 'Purveyors of Fine Fried Pastries.' If this coffee I'm drinking doesn't burn a hole in my stomach first, I can be at your place in fifteen minutes."

Jacobus was amused and, as always, had to remind himself that Nathaniel had more of a head on his shoulders than he usually gave people credit for.

"Nathaniel, I suppose you know me almost as well as I know you."

"I suppose so, Jake."

"See you in fifteen minutes or when you finish your first dozen doughnuts, whichever is sooner."

Jacobus hung up. He called out, "Yumi, you like pastrami?"

EIGHT

Though it was indeed true that Jacobus had not seen his good friend Nathaniel for several years, it didn't take long for his initial exhilaration to turn to irritation. Jacobus's behind was getting sore sitting next to Yumi as they waited on the stone stoop outside his front door. With each passing car his annoyance increased.

He was, as usual, disheveled. Sweating in the heat, he ineffectually slapped at mosquitoes feeding on his neck. The stoop was narrow so Jacobus felt Yumi's body against his. With the intense heat the contact was merely an additionally chafing and clammy irritant.

As the minutes passed, Jacobus mulled. Yumi had been far from enthusiastic about going to New York with him. Maybe she was uncomfortable going to the big city with strangers, he thought. He suggested she might have a chance to play on the stage at Carnegie Hall. Her reaction was at first negative, but a moment later she precipitously changed her tune. She said it would be a thrill for her, but to Jacobus's ear, there was no thrill in her voice when she said it.

It crossed Jacobus's mind that he didn't know what Yumi looked like. After so many years of blindness, the concept of a visual world threatened to become more and more of a vague memory. It would have been easy for his world to become an endless series of voices—a series of invisible talking heads. He could learn a lot about a person from a voice, but to know who someone really was, he wanted to know more.

Jacobus had taught himself to learn not only from the way people sounded but also from the way they felt, smelled, even tasted. There had not been much tasting lately.

Jacobus heard the distant but distinct sound of tires on gravel. Nathaniel, finally, and an opportunity to find out more about Yumi.

"Here's the car now," Jacobus said. He suddenly turned toward the sound, brushing heavily against Yumi in so doing—the clumsy blind man act. He hated it, but it always worked.

"I hear nothing," said Yumi.

"Coming down the driveway. Listen. Trees block the sound a little. Same old '74 red Rabbit, if I'm not mistaken."

He had felt the coarse fabric of jeans—seemed to him fashionably tight. Billowy blouse, silk maybe, loose-fitting for the heat. No perfume—didn't really need it; she smelled clean, even in this weather! Likely no makeup either, if she's consistent. She had earlier asked for a rubber band for her hair so he was guessing ponytail.

Not a bad picture for starters.

As the car rounded the final bend, careening, it clanged into a pot-hole.

"You heard that, I imagine," said Jacobus.

"Yes."

"Probably was brushing the remains of his French cruller off his ample girth. At least he missed the tree."

The car shuddered to a halt in front of Jacobus's house, which in the hot, hazy dusk looked disembodied. Jacobus heard the car door open and close, and rose immediately to greet Nathaniel, noticing that Yumi's footsteps on the gravel behind him were initially tentative but then more rapid. He noted to himself that she was probably at first surprised and taken aback that he had an extralarge, bearded African-American friend, no doubt wearing one of his favorite bright-patterned dashikis. He also noted how quickly she regained her self-control.

"Well, if it ain't Beauty and the Beast!" said Nathaniel. Jacobus was engulfed by a smothering bear hug.

"Jake, you and the house haven't changed a bit. Unkempt as ever! When are you going to get a little TLC?"

Jake extricated himself from Nathaniel's suffocating embrace and readjusted his glasses.

"Great to see you too," he said. "Let's go." He hurriedly introduced Yumi and Nathaniel. They packed their violins and bags in the back of the car.

They were soon on the winding Taconic Parkway, heading south. As the heavy sky darkened, the haze transformed into patches of dense fog. Nathaniel had to drive slowly.

Yumi asked how Nathaniel and Jacobus had met.

Nathaniel said to Jacobus, "So you haven't even explained our in-famous relationship yet?"

Jacobus grunted, indicating he wanted Nathaniel to do the talking. Nathaniel explained that the two of them had gone to Oberlin College together, when Nathaniel had still been a cellist, and that after graduating they formed a trio with a pianist who later went successfully into what was then the computer industry in its infancy. After the trio broke up, Nathaniel followed in the footsteps of his idol, the iconoclastic early twentieth-century American composer Charles Ives, who went into the insurance business where he could make a lot more money and be freer to pursue whatever direction he wanted in music.

"Except," Nathaniel said, "insurance was b-o-r-i-n-g. Everyone sittin' around in a gray suit acting truly concerned for their clients' well-being. The only part I liked was the dirt—fraudulent claims, stolen property, contested wills. The real low-down,. and the lower down the better, honey."

The car was suddenly engulfed by fog on the unlit parkway. Jacobus felt Nathaniel overcorrect his steering. The car swerved. Nathaniel corrected again. Jacobus bounced uncomfortably off the door as Nathaniel finally brought the car under control.

"Hey, asshole, you wanna get me killed? Keep your eyes on the road."

"You wanna drive, Jake?"

"It might be safer."

"Real sweetheart," muttered Nathaniel.

"Sorry, Miss Shinagawa," he continued. "You're probably trying to figure out how you got to be in this situation with such strange and unpleasant people. Don't worry. We're not so bad."

"Speak for yourself," said Jacobus. "And slow down."

Nathaniel returned to his subject. After working for a single insurance company for a few years, he decided to freelance, where he wouldn't have a boss or have to wear a fancy suit or work nine to five. Since Nathaniel's real genius in music was his encyclopedic knowledge of the field—composers, repertoire, recordings, performers—he was in great demand any time an instrument of value was stolen. Insurance companies would hire Williams to recover the instruments, greatly preferring to pay him a commission of twenty percent of its insured value than to reimburse one hundred percent of the owner's claim.

"So," said Yumi after a moment, "if the Piccolino Strad is insured for eight million dollars, and you find it, that means you will receive . . . one and one half million dollars!"

"One point six, honey!" said Nathaniel. "Whoa, mama! You don't think I'd want to be with ol' Jake here for a walk in the park? Even when Jake starts gettin' ornery we make a great team."

"Yes, that must be very exciting," said Yumi.

"I have two questions," said Jacobus.

"Mercy Circe, Jake, why you always talkin' in pairs? 'I got two questions.' 'Just two points.' 'First and second.'"

Jacobus folded his hands and said quietly, "Sometimes, Nathaniel my friend, things cannot be explained as simply as one would like. My first question is, since you're so intent on becoming a millionaire, I suppose you'd like me to question people? Maybe those MAP bastards who were at the reception?"

"Yes, for starters I'd like you to talk to 'those MAP bastards,' and also the Vanders. I've made the appointments for you, and I'll check out the invitation list and do some research on the Carnegie Hall Corporation and the Grimsley Competition itself." Jacobus had had dealings with most of the MAP people he would be interviewing, and the others he knew enough about. There was not one he particularly cared for, and he was confident the feelings were mutual.

"Quite an entourage for a nine-year-old," said Jacobus. "Haven't the police already interviewed everyone?"

"Yeah," said Nathaniel. "But they hardly know anything about art theft like this. They treated everyone at the reception—at least everyone they could find—like a two-bit breaking-and-entering suspect. You know how flippy these arts folks are, with their fragile egos and all. They all just clammed right up. Probably the only way you could ever get them to shut up." Nathaniel chuckled. "Anyway, the cops also dusted everywhere for prints—walls, doors, violin case—nothing suspicious. Likely the thief wore gloves."

"Now, if you don't mind, here's my second question."

"Actually, your third."

"No, the last one was merely an elaboration of the first. It doesn't count."

"My, you always must win, Herr Profesor Jacobus, mustn't you?" said Nathaniel. "All right, what's your second question?"

"Just think about this one for now. Why would any of them want to steal the violin? Any more than me, for example. Let's talk about that when we get to the deli. When do you want me to start with the interviews? First thing tomorrow?" asked Jacobus.

"Actually," answered Nathaniel, "Martin Lilburn said he needs to see you tonight. He said the next few days are all booked up."

"Prissy ass," said Jacobus.

"By the way, Jake," said Nathaniel, "it's none of my business, but how come Miss Shinagawa here is coming to New York with us? I mean, she's certainly welcome, but, you know, sometimes these jobs can get . . ."

Jacobus had anticipated Nathaniel would ask this question. He was, in fact, intrigued by Miss Shinagawa but, at this point, anyway, did not want to admit as much to Nathaniel and of course not in front of Yumi.

"Two reasons, Nathaniel. First, she's living on Long Island at the moment. Westbury, isn't it? So why the hell should she have to take a shitty bus back? Second, I need someone to be my pair of eyes, and how better to get Yumi into the swing of things—"

"Really!" said Nathaniel. "But Jake—"

"Why the hell not?" said Jacobus. "Nathaniel, do you still have that Heifetz tape of the Mendelssohn Concerto that used to be in that jungle you call your glove compartment?"

"Does a bear do his thing in the woods?" Williams replied.

"If there is a thing a bear does in the woods that means 'of course,'" said Yumi, "I would like to add it to my list of American idioms; for example, 'You ain't just whistlin' Dixie.'"

"Let's save the English lesson for later," Jacobus said as he inserted a tape into the cassette player. Unfortunately, it was the wrong tape. Instead of Heifetz playing Mendelssohn, it was Tom Jones singing "What's New, Pussycat." Before trying the next cassette, he confirmed its identity with Williams.

The three drove along silently. The car windows were rolled down to cool them in the muggy summer night, but with the volume turned all the way up, even the combined noise of the road and the Rabbit's venerable engine failed to intrude upon the magical collaboration between Felix Mendelssohn, a great German composer of the nineteenth century, and Jascha Heifetz, the greatest violinist of the twentieth.

After listening to the few minutes of music that Yumi had played earlier, Jacobus told Nathaniel to stop the tape.

"So, Yumi, what do you think?"

There ensued a long technical discussion of how Heifetz was able to play not only with great accuracy but also with great ease, allowing the music to flow both naturally and with great drama.

Finally Nathaniel said, "It's fine to dissect how Mr. Heifetz plays, but the plain fact is, the man's got soul, and either you've got soul or you ain't got soul. If you ain't got soul, and you want to try to get it, you better spend some time listening to those that do."

"Somehow, Nathaniel, you always manage to come around to having us listen to your Ella tape."

Jacobus reached back into the glove compartment and rummaged around for the tape, removing it and a small booklet as well, a booklet with a moldy feel and earthy odor. Williams had an uncanny knack for getting his hands on one-of-a-kind recordings of ancient live concerts, out-of-print tomes, autographed manuscripts. If the Library of Congress didn't have it, Nathaniel Williams did.

"Ella?" asked Yumi.

"Ella Fitzgerald, honey," said Nathaniel.

"Is she a famous violinist?" guessed Yumi.

"Ella Fitzgerald," answered Jacobus, "was a jazz singer."

"The greatest," added Williams.

"Mr. Williams seems to believe you'll hear a lot of what you hear in Heifetz's playing in terms of intonation and rhythm, tone, and—"

"Soul," Nathaniel finished. "Heifetz had it. Ella had it. Jake, hand me the tape. Yep, you got the one this time. It's got a song with your name on it: 'Mr. Paganini.' "

"Before I do that," asked Jacobus, "what's this book? All I can tell is that it's only about twenty pages and the cover's frayed almost all the way through."

"Something I found for our investigation. I'll tell you about it in a minute. Let's listen to this first."

Nathaniel pushed Play on the tape deck. The number was upbeat, a big-band dance tune with Fitzgerald at her jazziest. Within moments Nathaniel was beating the jaunty rhythm on the steering wheel and singing scat with his idol. Yumi chimed in on the second verse, humming the melody, making up words. Jacobus almost found himself tapping his toes until the lyric, "*Mr. Paganini, now don't you be a meanie, what have you up your sleeve*?" brought him back to reality. Try as he might to stem the tide of his obsession with the Piccolino Strad, everything, even this innocuous, decades-old jazz tune, conspired to harass his tortured mind.

"Jascha or Ella, it doesn't matter to me," Nathaniel said when the song ended, "as long as it gets to you."

"I think we've paid due homage to Lady Ella," said Jacobus. "Now tell me about this book."

"*La Vita e la Morte di Piccolino*," responded Nathaniel. "*The Life and Death of Matteo Cherubino*, by Lucca Pallottelli."

"You must be kidding!" said Jacobus.

"Nope," said Nathaniel, triumphantly. "The one and only biography, and the baby you're holding's a rare first edition of the English translation by Jonathan Gardner in 1846. Pallottelli's original—the Italian version—is from about 1785. Pretty colorful stuff, but I have to admit I'm not sure how he got some of his information, since the only two people present to provide it at the end were both murdered. I guess you could call it 'fanciful.'"

Jacobus heard Yumi shift her weight.

"I guess you could call it bullshit," said Jacobus. Why should a writer of soap operas like Pallottelli be of value? A nineteenth-century romanticized translation of eighteenth-century fiction of a seventeenth-century phantom midget violinist? You must be kidding."

"But as you know, Jake," said Nathaniel, "Pallottelli wrote a whole series of pamphlets about the great Italian Baroque violinist-composers: *I Maestri del Barocco*. Corelli, Locatelli, Tartini, Geminiani, and some others. They all turned out accurate, even if he did get a little flowery."

"Because they've been corroborated. Piccolino's hasn't."

"But Pallottelli's *Vita di Vivaldi* wasn't corroborated either. Vivaldi had been totally forgotten, but based on the information in his book they rediscovered all of Vivaldi's music and his whole life."

"Bah," said Jacobus, his final argument. He tossed it into the backseat. "Here, Yumi, why don't you read us a fairy tale to pass the time?"

Yumi picked up the booklet and read out loud.

"*The wintry midday light, cold and unforgiving, passed through the stained-glass image of the Madonna high above, casting the bloodred of her velvet-covered bosom onto the sleeping face of Matteo Cherubino. The unnatural ray harshly highlighted its features— deep, worried furrows etched in his brow; darkened shadows of his unshaven cheek masking faint scars of youthful smallpox; the latent insolence of his protruding chin and its resultant underbite. Indolent dust particles floating in the chamber were momentarily radiated as they strayed without purpose into the column of pale crimson.*

"'Porca Madonna,' *muttered Cheurbino.*"

NINE

Phones rang. Computers hummed. Even though the press office was air-conditioned, reporters sweated as they rushed around to meet deadlines. Daily life. Martin Lilburn was insulated from the tumult by a Plexiglas wall, one of his perks from his employer, the *New York Times*.

It was through this wall that his gaze found Jacobus wending his way toward him through a maze of desks, avoiding collisions as adroitly as if he could see. Jacobus even somehow dodged a couple of reporters with copy in hand darting to the editor's desk, following his ears toward the recording Lilburn was playing of the Adagio from Beethoven's Third Piano Concerto, faintly audible through the wall. Lilburn pressed Record on the cassette player in his desk drawer.

"Welcome, Mr. Jacobus. Good to see you again."

"Martin."

"Have a seat. Please. I'm sorry this Plexiglas doesn't keep all the racket out, but it's the best I could do to keep my sanity around here. Coffee?"

"Thanks."

"Cream? Sugar?"

"Black's fine."

"Mr. Jacobus, I don't mean to sound inquisitive . . ."

"Why not? It's your job. Mind if I smoke?"

"Sorry. Company rules."

"Shit. So?"

"I was wondering how you managed to evade those two reporters just now. And without a cane!"

Jacobus barked out a laugh.

"No cane. Able! And on a day as hot as this you can smell a reporter on a deadline a mile away."

"I know what you mean," Lilburn chuckled as he poured coffee for each of them in delicate porcelain cups. He placed one in front of Jacobus, deliberately clicking on the glass-covered wooden desk louder than necessary so that Jacobus would know precisely where it was placed.

" '*Porca Madonna*,' my ass," said Jacobus. "That's enough. Yumi, turn off the overhead light, if you don't mind."

"But how did you know I had that light on?" she asked.

"Must we always play this game?" Jacobus was tired. "You tell me. How did I know?"

"Did you feel me lean against the back of your seat to reach the light?" asked Yumi after a pause.

"That's number one."

"Did you hear the sound of the light switch when I turned it on?"

"Number two."

"There's more?"

"Three and four."

"I know! I read the old print too fast for it to have been dark."

"Good!"

"But I can't think of another."

"Well, as soon as you started reading, Nathaniel slowed down from his normal breakneck speed. I concluded that the overhead light was impairing his night vision. That's really why I told you to turn it off."

"Thanks," said Nathaniel.

"You're welcome," Jacobus said to Nathaniel, but what he was thinking was that Yumi was passing all of his tests.

When they eventually exited the Cross County Parkway, Nathaniel said, "We're almost in the city. Here's one more Ella for the road. 'Angel Eyes.' This one's somethin' else."

The song began, a slow, sad bluesy ballad of mistakes made and loves lost. The purity of Fitzgerald's voice, transparent as air, cast a spell in the night.

Jacobus said, "Yumi, you might have heard how she—"

"Shush your mouth, Jake!" said Nathaniel. "Ella's still singin'."

The trio listened in dark silence. Nathaniel quietly hummed the tune "*Angel Eyes, that old devil sent, they glow unbearably bright.*"

A few hours earlier, when they had begun the drive, there had been a moment when Jacobus felt his life returning, the prospect of redemption a fragile flame beginning to glow inside him. Now, as the approaching lights of Manhattan undoubtedly became brighter and the scope of his task loomed ominously larger, Jacobus wondered whether he could possibly feel any blacker.

Jacobus picked up the cup without spilling a drop. He said, "Thanks, Lilburn, but no need to coddle me."

Lilburn sat back down, unnecessarily combing back his carefully managed but thinning gray hair with his fingers, revealing even more of his increasingly furrowed forehead. He adjusted the jacket of his poorly fitting blue suit. Jacobus, in his threadbare corduroy pants and tattered flannel shirt, looked much more at ease in Lilburn's own office than Lilburn himself.

"Well, then, Mr. Jacobus," said Lilburn, clearing his throat, "what is it I can do for you?"

"Brendel?" asked Jacobus.

"Good ear, Mr. Jacobus. Yes, it's Alfred Brendel's Beethoven recording from 1968. Good ear for a good year."

"A fine pianist and a fine musician, Alfred Brendel. Very fine. If I remember correctly, you also gave a convincing performance of the same concerto."

"You do? How kind of you to remember! You flatter me. Those were the days before the anxiety of performing—of being onstage alone, without music, with thousands of notes to play, hundreds of ticket-paying customers awaiting a perfect performance—made it impossible for me to keep going. But that was another lifetime ago."

"No," said Jacobus, sipping his coffee, "it's the same lifetime, Lilburn. Only one lifetime."

"I would love nothing better than to discuss philosophy with you, Mr. Jacobus, but I understand you're here to discuss . . ."

"Those kids."

"Those kids?"

"Yeah, those kids that MAP foists on the public. The Grimsley Competition. All it is is musical child porn for weak-of-heart yuppies. Why would someone like you be a part of it?"

"Mr. Jacobus." Lilburn stood up, his chair screeching as he pushed it back. "I see now that your compliment was only a setup. It was my understanding from Mr. Williams that you were here to discuss the disappearance of the Piccolino Strad. If I am mistaken in that understanding, then I must ask you to leave."

Jacobus sat there. The warm glow of muted strings continued in the background.

"Mr. Jacobus, I said—"

"Sorry," said Jacobus. "I was listening to the music.

"You know, Lilburn, you're the best music critic I've ever read," he continued.

"I don't see what that—"

"Most critics know nothing about music or writing. Some know a little about music but can't write. Others write with a certain style, but what they write about is pure bullshit."

"That may be, but—"

"You know more about music than most musicians, and you write as well as any journalist on the *Times*. Better."

"That's very kind," said Lilburn, sitting down, "but—"

"What concerns me," continued Jacobus, "is that someone of your intellect should pander to commercial interests.

"What is the essence of music, Lilburn? It's subjective. The skill of the performer—that's secondary. If the music doesn't get you in the gut, it's simply not music but a glorified carnival act."

Lilburn tried to interrupt.

"Please, Lilburn, let me finish. When you listen to a truly great violinist—Milstein, Oistrakh, Szigeti, the list goes on—behind every phrase, every nuance there's an intent, an affinity, a *meaning* to the music. It goes far beyond 'happy music' and 'sad music.' In fact, most of the time there are no words to define music's meaning. Yet when it's performed properly it's very clear to every listener exactly what the meaning is, and the greater the performance the more powerful the meaning."

"Mr. Jacobus, I could not agree with you more, and I applaud the sincerity and dedication with which you have conducted your entire career," said Lilburn. "I'm sure you richly deserve all the kudos you have received. However, you must agree that people who may totally share your philosophy of music, myself included, while listening to exactly the same performance, may have a different reaction. Some may love it, others may be thoroughly disgusted, even though they've all been listening to the exact same notes."

"And it's precisely because of that, Lilburn, that it's so important your reviews make the distinction between different perceptions of a truly great musician's performance versus glossy theatrics of highly skilled, well-meaning, but essentially ignorant toddlers who ultimately are communicating nothing."

"Mr. Jacobus, you are a nuisance, but it is rare for me to find some-one with whom to have an intelligent conversation, so I will bear with your bullish style a little longer. More coffee?"

"Thanks."

"But I don't see that that's a particularly significant distinction."

"That's where you're wrong, Lilburn. That's where you're wrong. Because if we, as a culture, start listening to musicians who have noth-ing to say—"

"Then in the long run the music itself will become meaningless? Is that what you're saying?"

"And we will have lost some of the greatest achievements in human history. Even worse, they will have become irrelevant."

"You're afraid we're losing the connection," said Lilburn.

"That is why I'm concerned, for instance, that since MAP started, you've given highly positive reviews to its clients more than ninety per-cent of the time—including toddlers like Vanderblick—but less than forty percent to non-MAP musicians."

"You've been counting?" asked Lilburn. "I must say I am astonished."

"Yes."

"Well, then," said Lilburn, "I will be happy to explain, because there is a very good reason."

"Go on," said Jacobus, sipping his coffee, the piano's meditative ca-denza in the background.

"It is quite plainly evident," said Lilburn, clearing his throat again, folding his manicured hands on the desk. "MAP is so highly selective in choosing its artists, its standards set so high before taking on the se-rious obligation of assembling a new career—don't smirk, Mr. Jacobus—that it is almost a fait accompli that the performances of MAP artists will be on a level far superior to those of your ordinary concert artists. And please understand, I use the term 'ordinary' in no disparaging way. In my sincere opinion, MAP artists do have the ability to convey the meaning of the music, as you say, to the listener."

"Ah, yes," said Jacobus. "I seem to recall a quote from your review of a recital by Yung Cheng in 1979? Or was it 1980?"

"My God," said Lilburn, "the one review of them all that I would most like to forget, and you've remembered it! Mr. Jacobus, certainly you can't expect me to accurately predict *every* artist's future! I'm not a fortune-teller."

" 'Mr. Cheng,' recited Jacobus, " 'if not the embodiment of the young Yehudi Menuhin, is no doubt his spiritual equivalent, if not his superior.' "

"Verbatim!".

"Martin, where is Mr. Cheng now?"

"I can't help it if—"

"And the other concert agencies?"

"Meaning?"

"Meaning, why your predisposition for negative criticism of other agencies' artists, other than because of your association with MAP?"

Lilburn took off his glasses and began cleaning them with a handkerchief.

"I can't speak for other agencies," he said "but apparently they're not so discriminating in the selection of their artists, to the dismay of the public as well as to me as a critic. Their philosophies, perhaps, may tend toward win some, lose some in determining whom their clients will be. Any negative reviews on my part simply reflect the results of *their* philosophy."

He put his glasses back on and picked up his cup of coffee, accidentally dripping some onto his white shirt.

"Damn."

"Do I hear contrition?" asked Jacobus.

Lilburn laughed. "It will take more than spilling coffee on my shirt to solicit absolution from you, Mr. Jacobus."

"So those reviews have nothing to do with the philosophy of knowing where your bread is buttered?" asked Jacobus. "After all, it is speculated that you and your MAP cohorts receive—"

"That's enough," said Lilburn. "I've tried to be civil throughout your bullying, but you've just crossed the line. Mr. Jacobus, even though as a journalist I'm trained to let people talk, I'm going to cut you off right there. We have a standard of ethics in this profession—"

"Is that so?" interrupted Jacobus. "Well, Mr. Lilburn, let me tell you something about the ethics of your profession. Last year, Mr. Lilburn, a colleague of mine who shall remain nameless for reasons you'll understand in a moment gave a recital in San Francisco. A major critic there wrote a negative review based upon the program that my colleague had submitted to the paper. Only problem, Mr. Lilburn, was that the music on the program had been changed at the last minute. The fucking critic hadn't even gone to the concert! So what were you saying about the standard of ethics, Mr. Lilburn?"

"If that truly happened, then it's an exception."

"And you're not an exception, I take it. Why, for instance, does the *Times* keep you on when there is so clearly a conflict of interest? What about those ethics?"

"You're giving me a headache, Mr. Jacobus. I don't have to answer you."

"But you will, won't you?"

"Yes, and only to put a stop to your insinuations—which are beneath contempt—in their tracks. The *Times,* and its readers, have apparently determined, year after year, that my opinions are unbiased, fair, and—all things considered in a very subjective field—accurate. I've made no secret of my association with MAP to my employers and they have determined, after great soul-searching on their part, that my volunteer efforts are sufficiently detached from individual MAP clients so as not to pose the conflict that seems so obvious to you. If they had determined otherwise, you may be certain I wouldn't be sitting in this office today."

"I don't suppose your employers would ever think of bragging about the literary awards of its staff writers in order to charge their advertisers more?"

"Mr. Jacobus, are you or are you not interested in the stolen violin? That's what your friend Mr. Williams said you wanted to see me about. Yet you've avoided the subject entirely."

"I'm interested in the truth," said Jacobus.

"Well, here's a truth for you," said Lilburn. "I happen to be a reporter as well as a critic, and I've had the opportunity to do a little investigating of my own. I have in front of me as we speak a photograph. It was taken in 1931. Friday, July 13, to be exact. You would have been, oh, about ten years old at the time, Mr. Jacobus."

Jacobus was silent.

"Let me describe this photo to you, Mr. Jacobus. It is a group picture from the 1931 Grimsley Competition. On two back risers stand the taller boys, crammed together, austere in stiff black suits. In two front rows the photo shows the ranks of younger and smaller boys with pink dimpled knees, dressed in sailor suits with short pants to make them appear even younger. Seventy-eight out of the eighty contestants—all but one of them

boys—form a semicircle around the three judges, world-famous peda-
gogues, who are in front. Two of the judges are Sir Owen Davis, beloved
violinist of the United Kingdom and the London Conservatorium of
Music and Art, and the flamboyant mustachioed Italian virtuoso Silvio
Signorelli. In dead center of the photo sits a fat little man with a shiny
liver-spotted head. That would be the infamous Feodor Malinkovsky of
St. Petersburg, Russia—wouldn't it, Mr. Jacobus—whose success inspired
awe and whose methods inspired fear. The one girl in the photo sits stiffly
on the prominent paunch of Professor Malinkovsky. In the proper musical tradition of obeisance, both Davis and Signorelli stand a half step
behind Malinkovsky, each with a hand on one of the maestro's portly
shoulders. In the photo they make their best efforts to look down endear-
ingly upon the greasy pate of the elder colleague who, away from the cam-
era lens, they in reality despised.

"Mr. Jacobus," said Lilburn, "what interests me about this photo is
that it appears the only contestant absent from it is yourself."

"Give me the photo," Jacobus said.

Lilburn ignored him.

"By all accounts you were doing very well in the Grimsley, Mr.
Jacobus. You passed the first round with flying colors—you played two
movements of the Bach G-Minor Sonata, Paganini Caprices numbers
two, nine, and twenty-one, the first movement of the Mozart G-Major
Violin Concerto, and the last movement of the Mendelssohn Concerto, if my information is correct."

"Give me the photo."

"You even made it past the semifinal round. Very grueling, I'm sure!
Debussy Sonata, Prokofiev D-Major Concerto, and—my! my!—both
Wieniawski Polonaises. Bravo, Mr. Jacobus! And all from memory!

"But then, after the second round," Lilburn continued, "you were
'invited' to meet privately with the renowned—or should I say notorious—
Maestro Malinkovsky. I don't know what happened between him and
you behind closed doors, Mr. Jacobus, but I do know that the day after
that meeting, you were dismissed from the Grimsley with no reason
given, and right after the Competition Mr. Malinkovsky was deported
under a cloud of accusations that he had been molesting little boys for
years. It seems he was as much a pedophile as a pedagogue. Would you
care to elaborate to this reporter what transpired in your private meeting with the maestro? Did he help you with your vibrato, perhaps? Or

did he offer you a prize in the Grimsley in exchange for 'favors'? Come, come, Mr. Jacobus. You must remember something about it? Or has time dulled your memory of what must have been a truly enlightening experience?"

Again there was silence, a long silence, but for the return of the heartrending melody of the Adagio of the Beethoven Concerto.

"Here, Mr. Jacobus, here is your photo, though as you can't see it I don't know what good it will do you. In any event, I have plenty of copies."

Lilburn slid the photo across his desk. It went too far and fell on the floor.

"It's all yours, Mr. Jacobus," Lilburn said. "And if you agree to terminate your ill-considered investigation, I will refrain from sending a copy to the police, who no doubt would be highly interested in anyone who had attended the reception with a possible motive to harm the Grimsley Competition. And now I would suggest that this interview is over. I have a deadline to meet."

Jacobus groped for the photo and picked it up. "I'll make my way out."

Lilburn opened the Plexiglas door. Jacobus left.

Lilburn pressed Stop on the recorder. He dialed Anthony Strella's number to convey the message that even though he may have shaken Jacobus, this crazed but highly intelligent man might be on a rampage, that it was quite possible Jacobus had stolen the Piccolino Stradivarius, but only in order to achieve his ultimate goal to destroy MAP.

He heard the phone ring on Strella's end with a strident out-of-tune G-sharp, jarring Lilburn's ears as it conflicted with the last chord of Beethoven's Adagio, a reaffirming E Major. Lilburn quickly hung up the phone until the resonance of the chord faded. Then he dialed again.

TEN

Jacobus arrived at the Carnegie Deli to claim his pound of fleisch. Williams and Yumi were there waiting for him, already in line to get a table amid the posttheater and concert crowd. They were eventually seated in one of the rear rooms, sharing a table with tourists from Salt Lake City who had come all the way from Utah to see the Broadway production of *Les Miz.* Because of the close quarters, Jacobus, Williams, and Yumi kept their conversation light, concentrating on eating, until the customers started to filter out.

Jacobus described his meeting with Lilburn, though he did not dwell on his attack on MAP. He did not want Williams to think he was usurping the theft investigation for his own purposes, though he knew that sooner or later the issue would come to a head between the two of them. He would do what he could to make it as later as possible. Jacobus gave the photo he had received from Lilburn to Williams, telling him it might or might not be helpful. He didn't really know at that point, though something about Lilburn's verbal attack was gnawing at him.

Yumi looked exhausted. She had gotten up that morning before dawn in order to catch the early bus to the Berkshires for her lesson with Jacobus. Now she was back in the city and it was after midnight. She reluctantly accepted an offer from Williams to stay overnight at his spacious apartment on East Ninety-sixth Street. Jacobus insisted on her accompanying him on his round of interviews the next day, which would begin early in the morning, so going out to Long Island was not a viable option. Jacobus promised Yumi that before twenty-four hours passed she would learn more about the music profession than most people would in a lifetime.

"Sylvia, where's my Cel-Ray Tonic already?" shouted Jacobus. "Doesn't anyone do any work around here?"

A sudden crash on the table in front of him caught Jacobus off guard. He jerked his arms protectively in front of his face.

"Here's your Cel-Ray Tonic," Sylvia, the waitress, said. "You think you're my only customer?"

"It's one in the morning. We *are* your only customers! The last ones left a half hour ago."

"So what's the matter? Who d'ya think you are, anyway? Prince Charles or someone?" To Yumi she said, "What's the matter, dear, you didn't like the pastrami or sometin'? You hardly touched it."

"Excuse me?" asked Yumi.

"Don't ya speaka da English, dear?"

"Oh! Yes, the pastrami. It was delicious," said Yumi. "It's just that the sandwich was so big. It could feed my entire family."

"First time in New York and already a comedian!" Sylvia wailed.

Jesus, who's she yelling at? thought Jacobus. The empty restaurant?

Sylvia had been annoying Jacobus for decades. Though he never admitted it, he loved it.

Nathaniel ordered coffee, cheese danishes, strudel, and babka for the three of them as Sylvia removed their empty plates, and their talk turned to the Piccolino Strad.

"Miss Shinagawa, you're lookin' a little pale. Too much pastrami, honey?"

"Oh, thank you, Nathaniel," said Yumi politely. "Excuse me, it is just so disturbing to hear about such a beautiful violin stolen like this. Kamryn Vander must be so upset. I was shocked when I heard about it."

"Yes," mused Jacobus, "things like this rarely happen in Japan. But if you remember," he continued, "I asked in the car why someone would want to steal the Piccolino, anyway. Any takers?"

Yumi responded first. "Well, Mr. Jacobus, isn't it worth so much money? It could make someone very rich."

"No kidding," Jacobus said.

"Only if it can be sold," reasoned Nathaniel. "And this violin most likely can't be sold. It's one of a kind. Anyone who sold it would be nabbed right away."

Nathaniel explained that other violins, even other Strads, can be stolen and get new forged pedigrees. "Under the best of circumstances, a violin's provenance could be traced all the way back to the maker himself using bills of sale and certification by recognized dealers, but with stolen goods, sometimes the documents are counterfeits. Sometimes original labels signed by the maker inside the instrument are removed and replaced. Some violins even get cannibalized, disassembled with their parts reattached to lesser instruments. A scroll here, a back there. A good old Italian fiddle by an anonymous maker is worth tens of thousands of dollars, but with a Strad scroll, it's worth hundreds of thousands. A smart thief could steal a single Strad, bastardize a bunch of other violins to increase his profit margin, and cover his tracks in the process."

"It's been done," said Jacobus. "But probably not in this case."

"Why not, Mr. Jacobus?" asked Yumi.

"For two reasons," said Jacobus. "First, because this is the one and only three-quarter-size violin Stradivari ever made. Anyone in possession of any piece of it would incriminate himself, as at least an accomplice. Second, there aren't any other valuable three-quarter-size violins you could you use to enhance profit margins. Three-quarter-size violins are played by kids for no more than two or three years until they get big enough for a full-size, so parents aren't going to spend more than a few hundred bucks for them. Good makers simply don't invest their time and energy into making them."

Another point that Jacobus and Williams agreed upon was that it was hard to think of a reason one of the MAP "bastards" would risk such a long shot as to steal a one-of-a-kind Stradivarius for any reason whatsoever. All of them were already preeminent in their respective fields, with incomes to match. Why would one, or all, of them be involved in a scheme that could ruin them permanently?

As they mulled over this question, Sylvia returned with coffee and dessert.

"Well, if it ain't the three monkeys!" said Sylvia.

"What are you talking about?" said Jacobus. Sometimes he found her incomprehensible. And annoying.

"See no evil—that's you, Jake—speak no evil, hear no evil."

"Ah, Nikko!" said Yumi brightly.

"Sorry, dear," said Sylvia. *"Aquí no se habla español."*

"Nikko is a beautiful place in Japan," said Yumi. "A famous shrine in the mountains where those three monkeys are carved."

"The mysteries of human nature," Jacobus mumbled, almost to himself.

"Okay, okay," said Sylvia, dropping their food onto the table. "Forget the three monkeys. Moe, Larry, and Curly, then." She lumbered away.

Since a motive for the theft still eluded them, Jacobus suggested that analyzing the theft itself might help them. To this end he had a novel approach, likening the task of the investigator to a musician, the thief to a composer, and the actual theft to a piece of music.

He described a musician looking at a new piece that he had never heard, and the process of practicing it, living with it, growing with it, trying to understand the composer's intent, the composer's message. What was the composer trying to say about the world? Why did he write it the way he did? What makes it unique from all other compositions? If the musician can't answer those questions, Jacobus reasoned, then he has failed to learn the music.

He went on to say that a crime, strangely enough, bears marked similarities to a symphony. An inspired thief develops an overarching structure for his composition, planning his moves with extreme care and carrying them out smoothly and efficiently. The theft of the Piccolino Strad, for example, had been laid out in front of them, in all its detail. Perhaps examining those details with the trained skill of a musician would give them some insight.

"F'rinstance?" asked Nathaniel.

Jacobus replied by noting the artistic simplicity of the plan. More Mozart than Mahler. The theft took place at Carnegie Hall, not in the street or at the Vanders' place or at Dedubian's shop. So the thief must know something about Carnegie Hall, or at least have an affinity for it. There was no thuggery or violence involved. No weapons, no intent to harm.

The theft occurred *after* the concert, not before. Why after? Maybe the thief had sympathy for the performer—let her play the concert first. Maybe the thief wanted to hear the music. Another consideration: If the apparent decoy of the rock through the window hadn't worked, what would the thief have done? That question suggested that the thief, who planned this out so carefully, had the ability to pass for someone going to the reception in the event plans went awry. Someone who went to the performance, sat through it, appreciated it, then walked—well dressed or at least dressed inconspicuously—quickly but casually to Green Room A, milling with the crowd, maybe carrying a violin case that was empty but which, upon the success of the decoy, soon contained a very valuable violin.

"And what about the decoy?" asked Nathaniel.

Jacobus observed that the decoy must have been someone who not only could scramble quickly up and down from Patelson's roof but also had a strong and accurate enough arm to throw rocks across Fifty-sixth Street and through a reinforced plate-glass window. The angle from the roof would have helped the force of the throw, but still, someone must have had a pretty good fastball. A younger person, probably; the thief himself, probably older. But with the timing so important, the accomplice also had to be dependable and trustworthy.

Jacobus concluded by saying that in reality, even though they didn't know the identity of the composer of this crime, they did know quite a bit about his personality. All they had to do was continue to examine and explore the crime in the same way that he taught his students to learn a new concerto, and surely once they derived why the crime was committed, they would be able to figure out who did it.

"Then you can decide what you want to do about it," said Jacobus.

"Then why bother with the rest of these interviews we've scheduled for tomorrow?" asked Nathaniel, looking at his watch and seeing that it was almost two in the morning. "I mean today."

"Because, Nathaniel," continued Jacobus, "each of these crooks who have been involved with the Piccolino Strad is like a performer, is like us. Each of them views this crime from a different perspective, with his own interpretation, maybe with his own involvement. What a boring world it would be for every great violinist to play the Brahms Concerto the same way.

"By getting to know different interpretations, which is what every good musician should do anyway—and, by the way, let me just say that this is one more reason this damn Competition is unfair to these children; for all intents and purposes it isolates the winners from all the wonderful ideas they should be absorbing—"

"Save the sermon for later, hon," interrupted Sylvia, bringing the bill. "Or should we watch the sunrise together?"

Jacobus grumbled his usual profanities but noted to himself that all through this discussion Yumi's silence had been deafening. He sniffed the air.

"Nathaniel," he said, "not another damn book!"

"How'd you know I brought a book with me? Yumi tell you?"

"Old books have a unique odor, didn't I tell you in the car? What else would it be, unless they overcooked the brisket? Except this book has better leather than the Pallottelli. Cared for too. I can smell the polish. Not moldy."

Jacobus heard the thud of a book dropped onto the table.

"Leather bound, ornately handwritten, good-quality paper, used often," said Nathaniel. "The real thing."

"What's this you got?" asked Sylvia. "The Gospel according to Saint Nathaniel?"

"Sister," said Nathaniel, "if it was, it wouldn't help you anyway. This just happens to be the personal diary of Matthilda Barrington Grimsley, wife of Holbrooke Grimsley, the millionaire who bought the Piccolino Strad at the turn of the century and who founded the Competition in his name."

Jacobus asked, "How the hell did you get your hands on that?"

"I have a friend who shall remain nameless," Nathaniel said, "who works for one of the big auction houses in the city. Last year, when the Sneeden Piermont estate went to auction—Sneeden Piermont being the nephew of Harrison Grimsley—my friend gave me a call to let me know this little baby was in one of the lots and asked if I was interested. So I made my own personal bid on it, and since there weren't any other bidders there at the time—"

"Well, now that you've stolen it, what good do you think this diary is going to do for us?" asked Jacobus.

"It's not just any old diary. It's the diary she wrote on her trip to Europe in the summer of 1904, the trip the Grimsleys went on with Henry Lee Higginson when Holbrooke Grimsley bought the Strad."

Nathaniel explained that Higginson was a Civil War veteran whose major claim to fame was as the founder of the Boston Symphony, which he single-handedly financed and nurtured for almost forty years. Though Higginson didn't have the same vast resources as Andrew Carnegie, he was one of the greatest and most dedicated patrons of the arts the country had known, and a well-trained musician himself.

"Lovely," said Sylvia. "Maybe before Yumi here falls asleep you'll care to share with us some of Matthilda's words of wisdom."

"Don't mind if I do," said Nathaniel. "Here we go.

"*'August Twenty-four,'*" he began. "*'H'*—that must be Holbrooke—*'and HL'*—Henry Lee Higginson—*'had a row at dinner tonight. It was terribly embar-*

rassing. Fortunately the help spoke no English or we surely would have been thought little of by those in no position to think such things.' "

Matthilda Barrington's text, in the quaintly chatty style of the time, followed with a description of a dinner that the Grimsleys and Higginson were having at a restaurant in Tuscany. She then reflected upon the envy Grimsley bore toward Higginson, especially of the high esteem in which Higginson, the philanthropist, was regarded. " *'I must admit H has been a bit jealous of HL over the years. HL has become so famous with his Boston orchestra, but hardly anyone outside our circle knows poor H, even though he has lots more money than HL and, fortunately, has never had to work for a living.' "*

She spoke of the circumstances around which Grimsley accidentally came across the Piccolino Stradivarus, which had been lost for generations, in a dusty corner of a curio shop in Italy and bought it as a present for his wife, not knowing its true value; and how, on a lark, he had taken it to Aram Dedubian (Boris's grandfather) at his violin shop in Rome. " ' *"That Dedubian," said H, "is a sleazy looking fellow, but they say he knows his business, and I say if a man knows his business it doesn't matter what he looks like or where he comes from."' "*

After a thorough inspection, Aram had said, " ' *"Mr. Grimsley, I don't know where you found this violin, but in my opinion this is the violin made by Antonio Stradivari for Piccolino Cherubino in 1708, and purportedly owned for a time by Niccolò Paganini."' "*

Grimsley then told Higginson, " ' *"I didn't want Dedubian to wheedle his way out of what he just said, so I told him to put it in writing along with what it was worth. He did so but suggested I leave the violin with him so that his restorer—a curious Neapolitan named Bartolini or Bardolino or something like that—could shine it up. He said though the violin was in mint condition, this swarthy little fellow was the finest restorer in Italy—though from the look of him I found that hard to be believed—and would make the appearance of the instrument 'worthy of the name Stradivari,' as Dedubian put it.*

" ' *"At first I didn't want him to put his peasantlike hands on it, but then, after thinking about the situation with the cold logic of an American businessman, I decided there was good reason to leave the violin with him. In any event, today, several weeks later, I walked out of his shop with a Stradivarius worth five thousand dollars! Mind you, in New York one can obtain a perfectly decent German violin for twenty dollars. And all because my little Matthilda wanted a souvenir!"' "*

Grimsley had heard the legend of Matteo Cherubino, aka Il Piccolino, which included the tale that he had been born on leap day and so technically died at the age of thirteen (indeed, Stradivari's label to Cherubino inside the violin seemed to corroborate this). Now, having the three-quarter-sized Stradivarius himself gave Grimsley the idea to establish a trust fund for a violin competition " *'to be held only for child prodigies up to the age of thirteen, and which will be held only every thirteen years so that we don't saturate the market with little toddlers in knickers.'* " Grimsley went on to describe the prizes and perks that would be associated with the Competition: " ' *"a Carnegie Hall recital, a concerto performance with a great orchestra"* (H winked *slyly at HL to make his intent clear), "and the use of my little Stradivarius for the recital and concerto."* ' "

Higginson thought it was a horrendous plan. Grimsley, dumbfounded by Higginson's response, asked why. " *'Well, Henry stood up, right there in the middle of the restaurant for everyone to see, and actually pointed his finger at my Holbrooke and said, so slowly that I'll never forget his exact words, "Because you're condemning the winner to a life of misery and the runner-up, no matter how brilliant, to a life of obscurity. You can't simply harvest talent, bottle it, package it, market it, and claim a profit. If I hired children, no matter how talented, for the Boston Symphony, I'd first be laughed off the stage, and then, no doubt, I would be locked up."* ' "

The two men almost got into a fistfight—" *'The scene reminded me of that nasty baseball player, Tyrus Cobb, arguing with an umpire'* "—but Higginson walked out of the restaurant before they came to blows.

"Well, anyway," said Nathaniel, slapping the book shut, "it kind of meanders from there."

Jacobus expressed appreciation of Higginson's scruples but suggested that as entertaining as Nathaniel's growing book collection might be, their time might be better spent talking to people who were still alive.

"Maybe. Maybe," said Nathaniel, "but somethin's buggin' me and I can't put my finger on it. Hey, Jake," he whispered. "Yumi here's fast asleep. She's using her arms for a pillow."

"Well, just hoist her up in those big arms of yours and get her to bed. Let's get the hell out of here."

As Jacobus stood up to leave, he felt Sylvia entwine her flabby arm through his.

"I don't need your help," protested Jacobus, attempting to disengage her.

"I know you don't, Jake," said Sylvia, holding on tighter. "It's just that I thought if I were nice to you, you'd give me a bigger tip, that's all."

Jacobus relaxed. "How long have I known you, Sylvia? 1960?"

"Nope. I'll never forget when we first met. February 12, 1958—chopped liver on dark rye with extra onions. Lincoln Birthday Special. Why?"

"Are you still as good-looking as you said you were then?" asked Jacobus, smiling.

"Haven't changed a bit, Jake."

ELEVEN

Jacobus walked to the nearby Stuyvesant Hotel, where he had booked a room, having refused Nathaniel's invitation to stay at his place. Jacobus's years of solitude had made it almost impossible for him to endure more than small doses of human contact.

The night was quiet and as cool as it would get. He strolled along the nearly vacant sidewalk, head down, musing deeply. What should he do about MAP? And the recovery of the Piccolino? How could he tie them together? Should he? What did he know for sure? What was he guessing at? What were the unsupported hunches of an old man?

He heard the wet hiss of car tires cross his path on the damp street in front of him, and after taking a few more steps, confidently extended his toe to feel for the curb at the corner. That's the beauty of Manhattan, he thought. Eighty-six steps, every block, as long as he walked in a straight line. Once he had been asked how he was able to walk in a straight line without being able to see. He had replied, "Same way you know where your dick is when the lights are out."

The sound of the traffic patterns told him when the light was green or red, though at this hour traffic consisted only of an occasional taxi or delivery truck. He crossed the street.

As far as the first question, what to do about MAP, Jacobus felt strongly that none of the coterie stole the Piccolino. He was almost certain, though the *almost* bothered him. It just seemed too much of a risk, even for a fast eight million dollars, compared to the danger of being exposed for all the wrongdoing they were covering up. Why risk their fame and fortune? But regardless of whether or not one or more of them stole the violin, he would use the theft as a wedge, use it to get through the door. He would get under their skin—he knew he was good at that—

unsettle them, create suspicion, fear of exposure, turn one against the other. He had already set the wheels in motion with Lilburn.

Eighty-three, eighty-four, eighty-five, eighty-six. Fifty-third Street. Jacobus stepped into the street. Almost halfway across, he heard a car to his left speeding westbound, crossing Seventh Avenue. A horn blared. Jacobus whirled and jumped back to the corner. "You *momzer!*" he shouted. The car hadn't even slowed down.

His second try crossing the street was uneventful.

Who *could* have stolen the Piccolino? he asked himself, putting the car out of his mind. Answer: Anyone had the opportunity. Trying to guess who *could* have gone in and out that door was a waste of time. Let the cops interview everyone who was there.

Jacobus felt wet. Whether he was sweating from his close call, or it was just the smelly, dank city humidity, the hot dampness clung to him uncomfortably.

Who had the means? Answer again: anyone. All someone needed were two rocks and a violin case. No other traces. Dead end.

Motive? Now there's the intriguing part.

He smelled the stale beer of a cheap bar as he passed Fifty-second Street, which almost made him throw up. Overdid it on the pastrami, he thought, which made him want to throw up even more. Not too many blocks to go, he consoled himself, swallowing bile.

Money and greed were out as far as he could tell. If Nathaniel and he could both agree on that, it was probably true. Probably.

Other motive? A sicko who gets off on the thrill of stealing little violins? Well, the world was full of sickos, and he couldn't totally rule it out, but there was nowhere to go with that.

Then what? What other motive?

Somewhere between Fiftieth Street and Forty-ninth, a voice said, "Hey, mister, want a flower?"

Hmm, thought Jacobus, Asian inflection? One of those Hari Krishna bums. Money-grubbing fruits.

"Beat it," Jacobus said.

Suddenly he was grabbed by his collar and yanked forward so hard he was pulled off his feet.

"Jesus!" shouted Jacobus. "What the hell have I got you could want?" He was not afraid, but he felt helpless.

The voice had bad breath to go along with it. It was in his ear.

"My boss says to tell you to drop your investigation," it said, then added what sounded like an effort of improvisation, "or you're going to lose your own piccolino."

"Tell your boss to go fuck himself," said Jacobus, and he spat at his attacker.

The voice let out a mean, semistifled laugh as it shoved Jacobus backward.

Jacobus careened into a garbage can, knocking it over. The can rolled down the street, sounding like firecrackers on Chinese New Year, echoing in the otherwise silent night. By the time Jacobus recovered his balance and cursed at his bruised hip there were no footsteps to be heard, and midtown Manhattan was again eerily quiet.

Prick! Goddam prick! Jacobus was seething; wondering too—but not really caring—whether the car had also been meant to scare him. One night in New York City and he had been threatened with being reported to the police, almost run over, and now mugged. He wiped molding ketchupy french fries off his shirt with his snotty handkerchief, vowing revenge. He resumed walking to the hotel, now with a slight limp. His ears stayed alert, but no echo followed him.

He stopped in his tracks. Revenge! Could that have been the motive for stealing the Piccolino? Revenge against whom? Against the owner of the violin, against Grimsley? Why? No information to decide one way or the other.

Revenge against the Grimsley *Competition?* Why? Personal reasons? What reasons? Ruined career? He himself had suffered unspoken humiliation at the 1931 Grimsley—more than anyone would ever know—that had gnawed on him his entire life. Could there be another out there like him?

Jacobus began to walk faster, limp forgotten.

Ruined career! Whose was ruined? Winners? Unlikely—they won. Losers? Maybe. Last-place finishers? Unlikely. Last-placers may bitch, but to steal the Piccolino? Too extreme. Nope, not last-place finishers.

Jacobus smelled the hot dogs and heard the salsa music seeping out the open door of the all-night restaurant (or so it called itself) on the same block as his hotel. Salsa did nothing for him, but a hot dog! Maybe tomorrow. Very close to the hotel now.

Very. Close. *Second-place* finishers!—Higginson's prediction! "Because you are condemning the winner to a life of misery and the runner-up, no matter how brilliant, to a life of obscurity."

Runners-up! Very close, runners-up. Not *ruined* careers. Worse. *Stillborn* careers. So close! So close! Lifetimes of frustration, creative voices silenced. Lives ruined. What might have been but for one capricious decision. The Piccolino as metaphor for gross manipulation of art. So remove it. Destroy it. And destroy the Grimsley Competition.

Jacobus's thoughts were racing. He stopped just to breathe, steadying himself with a hand against the wall of a building. He thought maybe his reasoning was just a way to rationalize a hunch. Maybe it was the product of his own bitter experience. Probably. Nevertheless, he had an assignment for Nathaniel—trace the lives of second-place finishers of the Grimsley Competition. Can't be too many. Only every thirteen years. Lilburn's photo. Find out who in the photo came in second. Lilburn might have given him the clue he needed.

Jacobus sat alone in his room at the Stuyvesant dressed only in his boxers and wife-beater under-shirt. He sat with his hands on the arms of a desk chair, his chin on his chest, a position in which he was accustomed to spending many hours at a time though it never brought him respite. A half-empty pint of Jack Daniel's was on the desk next to a half-empty pack of Camels. When he had arrived, the bellhop had insisted on walking him to the room and had made the unpardonable gaffe of asking, "May I turn the lights on for you, sir?" Jacobus had said, "What are you, an idiot?" before tipping him.

It was quiet in the middle of the night, with few distractions. A toilet flushing from room 321. A fleeting splash of a soccer game on a Spanish TV station as a door opened and closed. Otherwise, only the intermittent churning of the outdated air conditioner intruded upon the silence, and that too had given out sometime earlier.

Jacobus was organizing his thoughts. With the attack tonight the situation was becoming increasingly complicated. The jerk had tried not to laugh when Jacobus told him to tell his boss to go fuck *himself*. Was Jacobus merely being taunted? Or did the laugh mean his boss was not male? If so, the boss could have been Victoria Jablonski, Cynthia Vander, Rachel Lewison. Or Yumi. No other females knew of his involvement. If not a female boss, then what about homosexual? Grimsley?

Maybe Lilburn? Or did it mean nothing? Maybe the thug's accent wasn't really Asian. If it was, would that tie him to Yumi, or, again, was it just a meaningless detail? It wasn't even clear that the only people who knew about his involvement in this investigation were Nathaniel, Yumi, and the handful associated with MAP whom Nathaniel had contacted for interviews. At this point there was nothing to be concluded and little more to be conjectured.

Jacobus sat for a long time—an hour, maybe two or three—before he felt satisfied that his thoughts were in order. More questions than answers but at least an infrastructure. Sometimes Jacobus's thoughts came as slowly as the constipated grandeur of a Bruckner adagio. At other times they rushed forward in complex cascades with the intriguing potential of a Debussy chord progression.

Jacobus found the room telephone and pressed 0.

"Front Desk," answered the night manager.

"I'm suffocating in here."

"Sir?"

"The air conditioner's broken. Send someone up to fix it."

"It's very late, sir. Have you tried opening the window?"

"The air conditioner is mounted in the window. If I open the window, the air conditioner will fall very fast onto someone's head and kill them. You want me to do that?"

"I'll send someone up right away."

As he waited for the maintenance person, he went over once more what had become his most convincing scenario. It surprised him, but he couldn't deny it added up better than anything else.

Am I sure? An educated guess? Just coincidences? Don't overlook what's right in front of your face, he had cautioned Yumi about the Mendelssohn Concerto. Good advice for himself.

There was a knock at the door.

"It's unlocked."

"May I turn on the lights, sir?"

"We going to play that game again? What's your name, anyway?"

"Salvador, sir."

"Well, Salvador sir, just fix the damn air conditioner with or without the lights on, sir."

As Salvador noisily disassembled the unit, Jacobus tried but was unable to regain his train of thought. He poured himself another drink and said, "Sir Salvador, you want a drink?"

"Thank you, sir, but I can't on duty. But I think I've got your problem solved here. The filter was packed with crud and was overheating the compressor, which automatically shut itself off. I think if I just clean out the filter it should work fine."

"Hmm," said Jacobus. "You always good at solving problems?"

"I do my best."

Jacobus decided he needed to hear his thoughts out loud, and get a response, in order to make sense of them. And, at this point, better a stranger than Nathaniel, especially a stranger who had half a brain. Jacobus outlined the whole situation in as coherent a nutshell as he could, only leaving out names, while Salvador finished his repairs.

"I say you're now off duty. Sit down and pour yourself a drink, Salvador."

"So what was it about the Japanese chick that makes you think she's in on it?" asked Salvador, sipping his unexpected Jack Daniel's.

"First, silently obedient. Second, showing up for her first lesson in July—unusual—and the day after the theft. Third, the quality of her footsteps."

"Hey, that's stretching it, man."

"All by itself, maybe. But what about her fascination with the spiderweb? The steel in her playing, and the passion underneath. Her shock at being tagged 'sinister.' She didn't bat an eyelash when I laid into her—and then to play the Mendelssohn flawlessly!"

"Nerves of steel, man. What do cops call it? The psychological profile. She got it."

"She said her teacher 'warned' her about me. I don't know much Japanese, but I do know her teacher and I'd bet a thousand yen that 'warn' is not the translation of what he said."

"So you want to know what's Japanese for 'Freudian slip.' "

"Hey, Salvador, you shouldn't be a bellhop. You should be a psychiatrist."

"Tell that to my girlfriend. So, is that it?"

"No, there's some more, Herr Doctor Salvador. Her curious response when I first mentioned the theft. 'Oh?' she said. Now, you might think 'Oh?' is just a useless little tidbit. But think about this. Every violinist in the world knows the legend of the Piccolino Strad. Every violinist knows what it represents and what it would mean to play on it. Let me ask you this, what would you think of someone who said 'Oh?' when asked if he had heard that JFK was shot?

"Then there was that 'total trust in teacher' BS she handed me and then that little game of fool the blind man I told you about. Her lack of enthusiasm to go to New York and then the phony excitement at the chance to play in Carnegie Hall, the scene of the crime. Her silence when Nathaniel asked me why I was bringing her with me and again when we were discussing a possible motive."

"So you think this chick's tied to the runner-up—the planner. You have to find the planner, man. If you're right about the motive and if she's involved, she'll be loyal to the planner and'll never agree to return this violin, even if you nail her. That's more than a hunch, man."

"Pour me a drink, Salvador. And pour yourself another."

"Think she could have planned it herself?" asked Salvador, handing Jacobus his whiskey.

"Doubtful," said Jacobus.

"Could someone at that agency have planned it? The chick might steal a violin for one of them. Maybe she's doin' one of those guys on the side. The boss, he sounds like a real ladies' man. Hold on a second. I think the AC is ready to go." Within seconds Jacobus heard a gentle whirring and a cool breeze wafting in his direction.

"You've been a real problem solver, Sir Salvador," said Jacobus. "But I still put my money on Mr. Second Place. Maybe we'll be lucky and there'll be a Japanese runner-up somewhere in the checkered annals of the Grimsley Competition." Jacobus drained his glass. "Salvador," he said, "I think I've gone as far as I'm going to get tonight. You've been a true help. My wallet's on the night table. Take whatever you want."

"It's all right, man," said Salvador, going out the door. "As you say, I was off duty. I'll just turn these lights out for you. It has been my pleasure being your temporary . . . amanuensis."

"Amanuensis, eh?" said Jacobus. "Sporty vocabulary for a bellhop."

"Well, I was going to say 'factotum,' but I think amanuensis is a little closer."

"What do you do during the day? Go to NYU?"

"Columbia, sir. Working my way through college, you know. Psychology major. Good night, sir. And may I say, sir . . ."

"Yeah?"

"You can trust me to keep this confidential. But I have to tell you, I think the reason you asked me here tonight was only in part to organize your thoughts. You didn't really need me to organize your thoughts. I think the main reason is that you feel alone and need people more than you admit to yourself."

"Thank you for telling me nothing. I'm sure you'll do well on your Psych 101 exam."

Jesus, thought Jacobus as he heard the door close, can't even take a bellhop at face value.

Alone again, Jacobus turned to new questions. How was he going to find Mr. Second Place? And where? Japan? Would Yumi return to Japan? Why would she? She just got *here*. Steal a Strad, study with sensei, get a career. Bing-bang-boom. No one finds out. Why go back? Need to give you a reason. What reason?

Jacobus heard the wail of someone's alarm clock. Time to rest.

TWELVE

Just a few hours after Jacobus dozed off, the second emergency meeting of the Musical Arts Project began. It was Tuesday, July 12, and the meeting convened at 7:30 A.M. in order for the attendees to be at their regular desks by 9. On one side of the mahogany table was Victoria Jablonski, with Lilburn and Trevor Grimsley serving as her bookends. Facing them were Anthony Strella and Boris Dedubian serving the same function, with Rachel Lewison, chewing on a pencil, as the book.

Two contentious subjects of discussion had arisen overnight. One was Jacobus's frontal assault on MAP and Lilburn's counteroffensive. The second was the article Lilburn had written in that morning's *Times,* attempting to defame Jacobus by innuendo. The atmosphere in the room was filled with nervous tension. As usual, Victoria tried to draw first blood. Rising from her chair, she jabbed her *New York Times* in Lilburn's face.

"Are you crazy, Martin? How could you have written this?"

Lilburn, who had opened his notepad to take notes, said without looking up, "WordPerfect."

"I actually think it was a stroke of genius, Jablonski," said Strella.

"Then you're crazy too." Jablonski pointed the paper at Strella.

Grimsley, who never read the paper until after his late morning breakfast, had no idea what the current fuss was about.

"I'll be happy to read it to you," said Jablonski with venom.

"Ah, the belligerent fervor of the righteous," Lilburn wrote on his pad. He took a sidelong glance at her. She was still standing, and he could not avoid a sidelong glance at her breasts. "Heaving bosom," he penciled. "How ' Victorian.' "

" 'Mr. Daniel Jacobus,' " Jablonski read, " 'onetime concert violinist, has been assisting Mr. Nathaniel Williams, an agent hired by Intercontinental Insurance Associates, in its search to retrieve the Stradivarius violin that has been missing and presumed stolen from Carnegie Hall on July 8. Though Mr. Jacobus has not stated his motives for his efforts, it is fairly common practice for insurance companies to pay a sizable reward for the recovery of stolen property that it insures.*

" 'In a discussion of the violin with this reporter on July 11, Mr. Jacobus was reluctant to discuss details of his investigation but was more than forthcoming in his opinion of the Musical Arts Project Group, which sponsors the young violin prodigy Kamryn Vander, and the Grimsley Violin Competition, of which she was the recent winner.' "

Jablonski raised her voice for effect. " 'His reference to the Competition as "musical child porn for weak-of-heart yuppies—" ' "

"What?" shrieked Grimsley. "Martin, how—"

"Calm down, calm down," said Strella. "As I said, I think it was a stroke of genius. Let me read you another little excerpt. " 'Mr. Anthony Strella, president of Zenith Concert Artists and spokesman for MAP, by which name the Musical Arts Project Group is often called, commented upon Mr. Jacobus's observations. Mr. Strella said, "While I admire the contribution Mr. Jacobus once made to classical music, I am also proud of MAP's achievements over the years, providing young artists with the opportunity and the means to bring great music to an appreciative public." ' "

"You see," Strella pointed out, "what Martin has done is to paint Jacobus as a fanatic, fortune-hunting has-been, and MAP as the voice of reason. If, as we expect, Mr. Jacobus is out to scandalize MAP, it appears that Martin has effectively turned the tables using Jacobus's own words. Bravo, Martin."

Lilburn looked down at his hands folded on the table.

"You don't know Jake like I do," persisted Jablonski.

"How could I?" countered Strella with a nasty smirk.

"I'll ignore that. For now. Jake is dangerous. Once he starts some-thing, he doesn't let go. He's a pit bull. He's—"

"Is that why you sicced your lackey on him last night, Victoria?"

The entire group suddenly wrenched to attention.

"What are you talking about?" asked Grimsley.

Strella continued calmly, ignoring Jablonski's withering stare.

"Victoria decided, unilaterally, I might add, to persuade her most testosterone-enhanced student to try to bully Jacobus into submission."

"Without consulting us?" asked Dedubian. "What if he was to figure out you were behind that stunt? That kind of thing could make us, *all* of us, and not Jacobus, look like we had something to do with stealing the violin and him look like the hero who was getting too close."

"Right now," retorted Jablonski, "you, all of you, look like you don't know your ass from your elbow. And just how did you know, An-thony, that I had anything to do with Jacobus getting a taste of what he deserves?"

"We have no secrets here, Victoria. You should know that by now."

"You know," Lilburn the mediator said tentatively, looking up from his hands. "On one hand, it's quite plausible that Jacobus was indeed involved with the theft."

"Of course he was," chimed Grimsley. "Didn't the police say he might've crushed the violin? That is, if it had still been there?"

"Why would he have crushed it if he had already stolen it?" asked Dedubian.

Grimsley fell silent, but Strella conjectured, "Perhaps as a pretense of innocence. He took the violin, hid it, and returned in the guise of the troubled but clumsily unsuccessful amateur."

"Possible," Lilburn agreed. "But at this point all we know definitely is that he was there and, as I pointed out to him, he had as compelling a motive as can be imagined. If it's proved that he did it, then he certainly should be tried, convicted, and locked up, with due consideration given to his motive, of course.

"That being said, not everything Jacobus had to say about MAP was so over the edge. Perhaps some of our efforts have been too merce-nary. I'm just being devil's advocate, you see."

"Why, of course," cajoled Strella. "But there's really nothing to worry about."

He maintained that all they had to do was just keep their cards close to their vests. Dedubian and Grimsley admitted that if they were living too high off the hog feeding from their MAP trough, it might not be such a bad idea to cut back, at least for the interim. After all, their own professions were certainly lucrative.

Rachel urged cancellation of all the interviews that had been scheduled by Nathaniel for Jacobus. She already had a backlog of appointments for all the members, and this was getting them even more behind schedule.

"I've got a fund-raising luncheon for Trevor with B'nai B'rith that's already been postponed twice. Boris is supposed to do a violin-making workshop at Juilliard. Anthony's supposed to meet with the American Symphony Orchestra League to talk about 'saving the Symphony.' Victoria's got her master class at Carnegie coming up, and then she and I'll be going to Oregon for a one-week residency at the U of O. So why are we bothering with Jacobus? Why should we play his game when it didn't even look like he was interested in finding the violin?"

Jablonski noted that no one even knew yet if her or Lilburn's attempts to frighten Jacobus had succeeded. Maybe Jacobus wouldn't show up for the interviews at all.

Ultimately two things were decided. One, that if Jacobus did show up, Lilburn would be notified and he would immediately send the photograph of the 1931 Grimsley Competition to the police—who were in desperate need of a suspect—along with his dossier on Jacobus. Two, that since Jacobus was working for Williams, who was working for Intercontinental Insurance Associates, MAP would cooperate in the interviews—they didn't want to risk losing their potential eight-million-dollar insurance claim—but only so far as proclaiming their innocence.

Jablonski didn't care for the plan. "Why don't we just kill him?" she said matter-of-factly.

"Aha! Yes, let's kill him," said Lilburn. "A fine idea. I can see my headline now. 'Blind Violinist Meets Unsightly End.' 'Once-famous musician Daniel Jacobus, disconsolate over a career that went down a blind alley, apparently has committed suicide by flinging himself down a flight of stairs and landing on his own violin bow.' "

"Hoist on his own Peccatte?" said Dedubian with a humorless chortle, making a pun on the name of a famous Parisian bow maker.

"Blinded by fame!" piped up Grimsley.

"Daniel in the lion's den," mumbled Rachel, eyes fixed upon her overflowing appointment calendar.

"What was that you said, Rachel?" asked Lilburn.

"Nothing important, I'm sure," said Rachel.

"All right, let's get serious for a moment," said Strella, wiping an imaginary tear of laughter from his eye.

Dedubian spoke up. "Excuse me. Joking aside, Jake could never have stolen that violin—it's just not possible."

"And why not?" asked Strella.

"Yes, why not?" Lilburn echoed. "After all, there seems to be a growing consensus among the assemblage here that all leads are starting to roam toward him."

Dedubian, sitting next to Jablonski, offered his response without looking her in the eye.

"One thing I must say in Jake's defense is he's honest, maybe to a fault," said Dedubian. "Can you believe that in all the years I've known him he's the only teacher who has not once accepted a commission for instruments I've sold his students!"

Jablonski gave Dedubian a withering stare, but Dedubian ignored it by fussing with his gold cuff link.

"But that's not the point, Boris," said Grimsley. "Whether he did it or not, the point is just to create a distraction. To get the authorities off our backs. Isn't it?"

"Exactly," said Strella. "Our job when we meet with him is to turn the tables. Don't let him badger you about MAP. After all, we *are* legitimate. We *have* done good. We *do* abide by the rules. And if Jacobus or anyone else thinks otherwise, they would have a harder time proving it than we would proving that he stole the Strad. As I said, we have nothing to worry about."

Strella admonished Victoria from resorting to any more violence, instructed Rachel to contact Cynthia Vander about their strategy to deal with Jacobus, and adjourned the meeting.

THIRTEEN

The same refreshing early morning sea breeze that was repelled by the sealed windows of MAP's conference room managed to curl its way through the open window of Yumi's bedroom in Nathaniel's apartment a couple miles uptown. Distant sounds gently pressed against the dark envelope of sleep's comforting silence—a bus engine far below, water flowing through a pipe in a wall, an elevator humming. City sounds.

Yumi's eyes opened, closed, opened again, not yet entirely willing to surrender her darkness. Through half-opened lids she saw the countryside, green fields in the distance; above, a pale blue summer sky with thin fair-weather clouds. Warmth. She closed her eyes, intent upon returning to her soothing cocoon. Sometime thereafter, the small part of her awareness that had not been asleep acknowledged the discrepancy between what she had heard and what she had seen.

Yumi sat bolt upright in a panic of disorientation. Where was she? Then a flood of recognition rushed in, accompanied by all the anxieties of the past few days.

Yumi looked around the unfamiliar room. What she had taken to be distant fields were an impression created by green texture-painted walls, the upper half lighter than the lower. The ceiling was a mural of a summer sky—convincing but unmoving.

On the opposite wall from her bed was a rustic old pine dresser, nicked with age. Leaning against it was her violin case. Beside her bed was a simple wooden night table with spindle legs on which stood a framed photo, her purse, and a wind-up alarm clock. An oak rocking chair in the corner, sitting on a braided rug, shone in the morning sun. It was still early. She picked up the photo to examine it.

The vintage frame was of unfinished wood, with dust on top and in the corners where it met the glass. The glass, with a little crack in the lower right-hand corner, protected a photo of an African-American couple. Nathaniel's parents? The photo appeared brittle and cracking—one of those that were not quite color and not quite black and white, the kind she had seen in antique shops and on old people's dressers.

The couple in this picture was photographed from midtorso up and at a slight angle. The woman was wearing a dress with broad and square shoulders; the man had on a suit jacket with very wide lapels. Their hair was wavy and stylish. They were both smiling. The man's lips were slightly parted as if he were about to say something in the midst of being photographed.

Yumi was drawn to the photo. Why, she couldn't say. She wanted to say something back but didn't know what.

Yumi replaced the photo where it had stood. Next to it was a half-melted thick candle sitting in a chipped ceramic candle holder. Under the candle holder was a piece of paper. The paper had words scrawled in pencil. Yumi picked it up.

> Dear Yumi,
> Welcome to my guest room. I call it my old Kentucky home, which is where I grew up. I hope you slept comfortably, because if I know Jake, you have a busy day ahead.
>
> I'm out doing some research but I'll pick you up at about 9:30 and will drop you off at the Vanders'. Jake still insists you'll be his best helper.
>
> In the meantime enjoy yourself in the apartment. Use any room you want and help yourself to the fridge. (Most of your pastrami sandwich is in there.)
>
> > Yours,
> > Nathaniel

Yumi reached for her purse, removing the booklet she had begun reading in the car. Nathaniel's guest room was so peaceful. All she knew about the Piccolino Strad was in relation to its tie to the Grimsley Competition. She had never even seen it. Now she had an opportunity to learn more about Matteo Chrerubino, Il Piccolino himself, the first owner of the Stradivarius. She moved to the rocker and started the book a second time.

She read Pallottelli's quasi-erotic, sometimes humorous, almost always lurid tale of Matteo Cherubino, a midget who rose miraculously from humble peasant beginnings in the Italian region of Umbria to become one of the most celebrated musicians in seventeenth-century Europe. How he became a favorite of princes, and even more so, if

Pallottelli is to be believed, the princes' wives. How his amazing combination of virtuosity and seductive musicality brought him fame, fortune (including the gift of the Stradivarius that bears his name on the label), and finally his violent death at the hands of a cuckold husband.

Legend said that even the skills of the most renowned violinists of his day, like Corelli in Rome or Vivaldi in Venice, didn't compare to the brilliance of Matteo Cherubino. His persona expanded to mythical proportions, in part because Cherubino, by reputation a highly secretive, untrusting individual, never wrote down a note of his music in order to jealously guard his musical secrets from his rivals. Everything he performed was either improvised or played from memory. It was said his improvisations could stir an audience into fits of emotional ecstasy or distress. However, because there is not a single verifiable note of his music (purported "findings" of his music have all been thoroughly disproved by Baroque music scholars), or one painting of him (reportedly so self-conscious was he of his dwarfish physique and allegedly brutish countenance), the very existence of Matteo Cherubino has never been convincingly proved.

The booklet's print was old-fashioned and the ink had blurred from age into the pithy paper, so Yumi read and reread slowly. She was intrigued and amused at Pallottelli's effort to be didactic, incorporating Cherubino's explanations of violin technique to his lover, using puns and double entendres. It almost made Cherubino sound like Mr. Jacobus from an earlier century, Yumi thought.

When she came to the description of the violin that Stradivari made for Cherubino, the very violin being sought after by Jacobus and Nathaniel, it took her breath away.

It was not just another violin, Piccolino immediately saw with widening eyes. It was a violin unlike any he had ever seen. The grain of the wood appeared to be in flame. The varnish was ablaze—now red, now orange, now golden.

As the Duchess placed the violin in his hands, he could see that the purfling—the fine inlay bordering the edge of the violin that was usually made of wood, straw, or even paper—was here made with pure gold. The pegs were gargoyles of engraved ivory. Breathing all this fire was a scroll in the shape of a dragon's head whose glowing ruby eyes stared defiantly into his.

"What man could create something such as this?" said Piccolino, staring.

Yumi stopped rocking in her chair and put her head in her hands. She heard a knock on the door.

"Yes?" she asked.

"It's me."

"I'm sorry to have kept you waiting, Nathaniel," said Yumi, opening the door. "It was so quiet. I forgot all about the time."

"That's okay, but we better go or we'll be late meeting Jake at the Vanders' apartment. He really has a bee in his bonnet this morning."

Yumi dressed quickly. They took the elevator to the lobby and hurried to Williams's car double-parked on the north side of Ninety-sixth Street. Williams made a U-turn, nearly hitting a tree planted on the opposite curb, in order to head east.

Almost immediately Nathaniel slowed from eight miles per hour to six in order to let a cab cut in front of him and avoid having the front hood of his car demolished. The lady in the car behind sat on her horn to offer her opinion of Nathaniel's driving. Yumi reflexively gripped the door handle as if it would provide protection and cautiously turned around in order to see whether the lady was truly honking at them. The lady gave her the finger, confirming her suspicions.

Perhaps she's a relation of Mr. Jacobus, she thought.

They turned right onto Lexington Avenue to head downtown to the Vanders' apartment. Traffic was at a standstill.

"Hope we're not late for Jake or we'll have hell to pay," said Williams.

"Mr. Williams, while we're waiting here, may I ask you a question?"

"Shoot."

"Shoot?" Yumi was taken aback.

"That means, 'Go ahead and ask.' "

"Thank you. The photo in my room. Were they your parents?"

"Yeah. Elna and Robert Williams."

"They look like nice people."

"I suppose they were. That photo is one of the few things I can remember them by."

"I'm sorry."

"It's okay. It's not a secret. My mother, she had a peacetime job with the American armed forces in the '40s. Cleaning clothes. My pop was a jazz musician and my first music teacher when I was a shrimp. Mom was doing laundry for the naval officers on the USS *Arizona* when it was bombed and sunk at Pearl Harbor. Pop just couldn't get over it. He needed to get back, or so my grandmother told me. He enlisted in an all-Negro regiment in the army. He died of malaria in a prisoner-of-war camp in Malaysia in 1943. I never saw him again."

"I'm so sorry!" said Yumi.

"It's okay. Certainly not your fault. Nothing against you, though I'm telling you I'm not planning any trips to Japan in the near future."

After an uncomfortable silence, Yumi sought to change the subject.

"Mr. Williams, I am trying to understand Mr. Jacobus a little more. The two of you seem so different. Yet it is obvious you're such good friends, even when he . . . when he . . ."

"Gets ornery?"

"Yes, I suppose that is the word I was looking for."

"Well, it looks like we'll be stuck here for a while, so at least I don't have to give you the *Reader's Digest* version." Williams laughed his carpenter saw laugh. "I'm just gonna drop you off when we get there, anyway."

Williams explained that after he and Jacobus had met as students at the Oberlin Conservatory in Ohio, the two of them decided to form a trio along with pianist and fellow student Helen Kaufman. "When we graduated we began touring, first locally, then nationwide," said Nathaniel. "We called ourselves the Dumky Trio."

"After the piece by Dvořák?" asked Yumi.

"Sort of. Dvořák actually named the piece after a Czech dance called the dumka, which is characterized by contrasting moods and tempos. Since our trio had a Jew, a woman, and me, the name Dumky Trio made a good fit, don't you think?

"One time, a few years after the war, we were touring the Midwest and had a concert scheduled in the town of West Aberdeen, Ohio, not too far south of Cincinnati. Since most of the places we played were small towns, we tried to do music we knew the audience would like . . . not too much avant-garde stuff like Elliott Carter or the politically charged stuff."

"Like Shostakovich?"

"Yeah, you get the idea. I can't remember exactly what was on that West Aberdeen program—probably Haydn or Beethoven or Mendelssohn.

"So anyway, we arrived at the high school auditorium about an hour before the concert—our transportation was one of those old-fashioned station wagons with wooden sides. All the ushers were arriving—just a bunch of teenage girls with big puffy pink dresses and big puffy hair and acne cream, getting things all spiffed up. Chairs were set up, flowers were arranged. They even had the piano tuned!" Williams laughed.

"Jake was sort of the business leader of our trio, so he asks this one girl, 'Honey, where's Mr. Drake?' Orin Drake was the director of the Greater Aberdeen Concert Society. Anyway, when this itty-bitty girl looks at the three of us, she turns even whiter than her carnation, and without saying a word just points over to a dinky little office off the side of the stage, behind some brooms and old desks and sand bags.

"By the way people were lookin' at us, we had a feeling what was up, but anyway Jake puts on his best smile when he finds Drake, a big guy in a small suit. Drake's gut was just poppin' out and his tie wasn't even coverin' it! Jake's smile was the first thing Drake saw, so he started to kinda smile back, but when he saw me, honey, Jesse Owens couldn't have been faster than the speed that smile disappeared!

"He says, 'Ohhhhhh. Oooooh. No, no, no. I'm sorry. Ohhhhhhhh. Ooooooh. We can't have this. No, we can't have this.'

"Jake says, still with the smile on his face, 'Mr. Drake, is there a problem?' as if he had no idea what was goin' on.

"Drake told Jake that the presenters of their concert series do not permit Negroes in the auditorium. 'Mainly for his safety,' Drake said, pointing at me.

"Jake pointed out that as they were in a public school, the laws of the state of Ohio would permit persons of any color access to its premises.

"Drake insisted that since the concert was being presented by a private organization, the Greater Aberdeen Concert Society, it had the right to decide who may and who may not perform.

"Well, Yumi, they went around in circles for a while. . . . Whoops." Williams had been stopped at a red light at Eighty-sixth Street and it had been green for about two seconds. Several impatient drivers behind him were reminding him of the fact.

"Where was I?"

"You had just said, 'They went around in circles.'" Yumi, who had maintained her steel grip on the door handle, wondered whether she would live to hear the end of the story.

"Oh, yeah. Thanks. At that point I would have expected Jake to tell the man off and we would have driven away, minus our $250 fee, of course, which was a lot of money for us in those days. That would have been fine with me. I didn't need to be surrounded by a bunch of white folk lookin' for a black boy like me to lynch."

"Mr. Williams," said Yumi, "certainly you must be exaggerating. Those people were music lovers. They were there to hear a concert!"

"Well, maybe I am, and maybe I'm not. But I didn't feel like waitin' around to find out, honey!"

Yumi considered that if Americans were as belligerent as their driving habits suggested, perhaps Nathaniel wasn't exaggerating.

"What did Mr. Jacobus say?"

"He says, 'Well, Mr. Drake, it appears we have a problem. What do you suggest?'

"I'm tellin' you, I was just dumbfounded and felt like lynching *Jake* for dealing with this guy. But Drake, he says, 'Would it be possible, Mr. Jacobus, for you and Miss Kaufman here to play a violin and piano recital?'

"Jake thinks for a minute and says, 'Well, Mr. Drake, it's such a last-minute thing, you see. I couldn't give a standard type of recital with a lot of Beethoven and Brahms. But what I could do is play some traditional favorites, some Americana, some popular encores. Helen and I often play together as a duo, and we keep some of our encore-type music in the back of the station wagon. Would that suit?'

"I'll never forget how he said, 'Would that suit?'" Nathaniel laughed. "I don't think Jake ever said 'Would that suit?' before or since. 'Would that suit!' It was at that point when I knew somethin' was up, so I just kept my mouth shut.

"Drake obviously didn't want to have to cancel the concert and disappoint the people who were already filling up the auditorium, let alone return all their money, so he swallowed Jake's proposal hook, line, and sinker. When Jake asked Drake to please announce to the audience at the beginning of the concert that Daniel Jacobus was going to play a traditional Americana program and that Mr. Jacobus would announce the individual pieces as he played them, Drake was only too relieved to agree.

"You followin' me so far?"

"I think so."

"Good, because that was just the preamble. This here's the juicy part. As Jake and Helen and I were walking back to the station wagon to get his violin, Jake says, 'Nathaniel, wait here in the station wagon, lock the doors, and as soon as the concert's over, get the engine running.' "

Williams rolled up the window of his red Rabbit as the exhaust and noise from the bus in front of them made it impossible to continue the story. But since the air-conditioning in the Rabbit wasn't working, the result was hardly more bearable.

"Now, you've got to realize that I got the rest of the story secondhand because I was lyin' down in the backseat of that old station wagon with the windows rolled up and sweatin' up a storm just like we are here, except it wasn't the heat so much that was makin' me sweat, it was the fear. It wasn't until it was all over that Helen told me what had happened inside the auditorium." Nathaniel chuckled conspiratorially.

"So anyway, Orin Drake announces to the audience that because of 'technical difficulties' the Dumky Trio would be replaced by a violin and piano recital by Daniel Jacobus and Helen Kaufman. The audience hems and haws a bit but applauds when Jake walks on stage and bows. Then he announces, 'For my first number I would like to play the spiritual "Deep River," so beautifully sung by the great Negro opera singer, Marian Anderson.'

"When he finishes 'Deep River,' he announces that he would like to play 'a transcription of 'Ol' Man River,' composed by the Jew Jerome Kern and made famous by the Negro Communist Paul Robeson. After that he says, 'Next I'd like to play the Second Prelude by another Jewish composer, George Gershwin, which is based on the Negro blues style, and arranged by the Russian-Jewish violinist Jascha Heifetz.' Then, 'Next, the slow movement of the Violin Sonata by Aaron Copland, who is not only Jewish, but I think he's homosexual as well.' Finally, 'Speaking of homosexuals, for my final number I'd like to perform 'Sérénade Mélancolique' by Peter Tchaikovsky, perhaps the greatest homosexual composer of all, the man who wrote the *1812 Overture,* the *Nutcracker,* and *Romeo and Juliet.*'

"Well, Yumi," Williams said, "by the time Jake finished the Tchaikovsky there were about six people left in the audience and they only stayed in order to boo. But after each piece, Jake just bowed and smiled as if he were playing at Carnegie Hall.

"After Jake walked off the stage and was putting his violin back in the case, ol' Drake went up to him, fit to be tied. He said, 'Mr. Jacobus, I have two things to tell you. The first is, neither you nor your friends are welcome in West Aberdeen. We hope, no, we strongly suggest, that you never return here again.'

" 'Oh?' said Jake. 'And the second thing?'

" 'The second thing is, since your contract with the Greater Aberdeen Concert Society required you to perform a trio concert, not a violin and piano recital, we feel we are under no obligation to pay your fee.'

" 'Well, that's fine,' Jake said.

"Drake said, 'That's fine?' I guess he expected Jake to make a fuss.

"And Jake said, 'Yeah, that's fine, because I would rather kiss Jackie Robinson's ass than take one cent from you.'

"And that's why I will always love Daniel Jacobus, Yumi," Nathaniel said as he double-parked in front of the Vanders' apartment building. As Yumi got out of the car, he called out, "Even when he's ornery."

FOURTEEN

Jacobus, who had fallen asleep on his feet in front of the Vanders' apartment building, felt someone touch his arm. Thinking it was the doorman again, he swung wildly, trying to hit him with whatever little strength he felt. He missed, and when Yumi said, "Mr. Jacobus, it's me," he replied, "About time. Let's go."

Jacobus had arrived early and waited for Yumi under the building's green awning, shielding himself from the city's sullen heat. He looked more haggard than ever, having barely slept the previous night, wearing the same shoddy clothes as yesterday. The doorman had told him not to stand in front of the upscale building and had threatened to call the cops on him for loitering, taking him for a blind beggar. Jacobus asked him. "So where's my tin cup?"

Jacobus knew he was living on borrowed time. He knew that as soon as he stepped inside the Vanders' opulent residence, the call would go out to Lilburn that he hadn't dropped his investigation. Lilburn would then undoubtedly raise the hue and cry, and with Lilburn's powers of persuasion it would be only a matter of time before the cops got interested enough to pick him up. With no other suspects, why not?

Jacobus saw his task, as he usually saw things, in two parts. The first was to turn the MAP principals on each other like a pack of wild dogs, using the Piccolino Strad as meat. Second, he hoped to recover the Piccolino Strad. What complicated matters was that he didn't think the MAP people had anything to do with the theft. He thought, on the other hand, that Yumi did. Yet the more he considered the possible motivation for Yumi and whomever she might have worked with, the more sympathetic he became. He knew he couldn't confront Yumi with his suspicions because she would just put up a brick wall of denial, which would lead to a quick dead end. Rather, he had to flush her out of her current role and see where it took her but without allowing anyone to realize he *didn't* think MAP was involved. How he would reconcile his commitment to Williams to recover the violin with his growing sentiment not to see the actual thief punished was still up in the air.

At the same time, he knew that he himself was a suspect, that he would probably be attacked as such by the MAP people, and that if he didn't recover the violin he might well end up being the one in jail. It intrigued him to think how Yumi might react if he were to be accused. He decided he would let MAP rant and assess Yumi's reaction. He was guessing that if she was culpable she would maintain her silence, willing to let him take his lumps. If she wasn't she would probably jump to his aid. However, there were no guarantees to these assumptions either.

In any event he had to maintain the posture that he suspected the MAP people because of his obligation to Williams, whose one and only objective was the recovery of the violin. If Williams found out that he had co-opted that objective for his own purposes, their friendship, one of the few things Jacobus valued, would be severely jeopardized.

Jacobus decided his only chance to win the day with his head still intact was to do what he had always done—tell the truth, though perhaps "with a little extra mustard," fully aware of his seemingly limitless ability to disturb people.

He and Yumi entered the lobby of the new East Side high-rise. Echoing from its marble walls rang the overtly sentimental refrain of "Zigeunerweisen," or "Gypsy Airs," the nineteenth-century composer-violinist Pablo Sarasate's universal crowd pleaser.

"Help you, bud?" asked the security guard.

"Appointment. Vanderblick," said Jacobus.

"Vanderblick? Oh! You mean Mrs. Vander? Hey, you're one lucky guy."

"Really."

"You don't know her? What a lady! I mean, a real . . . lady." The guard grinned.

"Right."

"You said it, she got real class. That's the only word for it. Class. Always smilin'. Always saying, 'Hi, Mike, how're you doing?'

"You hear that music, bud? That's her kid playing. Sweet kid. Mrs. Vander, she gave me the CD. She *gave* me the CD. Free. Just like that. Said I should play it in the lobby every day and share it with all the people that come in and out. Real thoughtful. I don't know nothin' about classical music, but Mrs. Vander tells me the kid is a 'prodigy.' You know anything about classical music, bud?"

"A little."

"Well, here, take a look at the CD. It says right here on the back she's a prodigy. Oh, you can't see. Sorry. How 'bout you, young lady, want to see the CD?"

"Thank you," said Yumi.

The title of the CD was *Roller Coasters: The Virtuosity of Kamryn Vander.* The cover had a picture of a little girl on a roller coaster, head back, smiling with excitement. Her hair was blowing in the wind, and she had one arm around a large stuffed koala. The recording, the first of three similar ones that Vander would make in the following five years, contained a dozen or so flashy warhorses to go with "Zigeunerweisen."

"Very nice," said Jacobus to Mike. "I'll be sure to add it to my collection."

"Yeah," said Mike. "I know where you can buy 'em too. You wanna know?"

"Maybe you can tell us after our appointment," said Jacobus.

"Oh, yeah, good idea. Let me ring Mrs. Vander. I'll tell her you're on your way up. She expecting you?"

"I'm afraid so."

They arrived at the top-floor apartment, rang the bell, and waited. Jacobus heard the sound of wrestling with the locks for a considerable time. Finally, the door opened but was almost immediately slammed shut. Jacobus heard a child's footsteps running away from the door and then a little girl yelping, "Mommy, it's a blind man and a Chinese lady." A few minutes later the door was yanked open.

So, we're not hiding our hostility today, are we? thought Jacobus. A sudden waft of perfume made his useless eyes immediately begin to tear.

"Of all the nerve!" Cynthia Vander said. "Why can't you just let the police do their job and go away? Don't you think she's been traumatized enough? How is she going to play at the gala next week without that violin? If she blows it, she could lose half her bookings for next year. I don't know why Anthony said I should talk to you."

"Mrs. Vanderblick, if we could just come in," Jacobus said quietly.

"Suit yourself." She turned her back on her guests and stomped back into the apartment. "And the name is Vander."

Yumi led Jacobus to a couch. He sank into an overstuffed cushion with a protective plastic cover.

Yumi sat next to him. Mrs. Vander disappeared, but Jacobus soon heard her voice in another room.

"Three more hours, Princess," she shouted.

"But Mommy, I'm tired," came the whiny reply.

"It doesn't matter. Miss J said eight hours a day, and you still have 'Poème,' 'Meditation,' and 'Perpetual Motion.' So get going."

She reentered the living room. "What do you want?"

"I want to find the Piccolino. For your daughter."

"Give me a break. You're the one who stole it!"

"Ha!" said Jacobus. "And tell me why I did that?"

"Don't give me 'Ha.' Victoria said you've been jealous of all her students who've made it big, and who is it that's been ranting for years about the Grimsley Competition? She said only someone like you would be devious enough to steal it right from under their noses."

"And who threw the rock through the window? Yumi?" asked Jacobus.

"No!" shouted Yumi.

"Who cares?" Mrs. Vander said. "I ought to call the police right now to pick you up."

"So the cops would put me away, but Kamryn still wouldn't have her violin back. Is that what you want? What's she playing on now, anyway?"

"Some piece of crap Dedubian is trying to sell us," Mrs. Vander said. "He keeps whining that there aren't any good three-quarter violins around."

Jacobus saw an opportunity to divide and conquer and plunged in, saying truthfully that in his experience, Dedubian, though sporting a highly gentlemanly exterior, was nevertheless a shrewd if not ruthless trader, and that if anyone could find what she was looking for it was Dedubian. By saying something positive about Dedubian he hoped that Vander would subscribe to a variation of the old axiom "The friend of my enemy is my enemy."

Mrs. Vander dismissed Jacobus's assessment. "I told him to just do his job and find one, because if he doesn't, we're screwed," she said.

"I'm sure your approach will produce results," said Jacobus.

"Look, Mr. Jacobus, you're wasting my time," said Mrs. Vander. "You have some questions for me. Ask them, then go."

"You want the violin back in time for your daughter's performance? We think it's conceivable that someone you know might have been involved with the theft. That with your cooperation we can find that person. Right, Yumi?"

Before Yumi could reply, Cynthia interrupted.

"You're saying that you, a blind man, that friend of yours, and this girl, whoever she is, the three of you are going to find a stolen violin that the police can't even get a clue on? You're a very funny little man, you know that?"

"Well, if I stole it as you suggest, it shouldn't be too hard for me to find it, should it, Mrs. Vander?"

"I think this has gone on long enough. You can just let yourselves out."

"M-o-m-m-y!" hollered Kamryn from another room. "My hand hurts."

"Keep practicing," Mrs. Vander hollered back.

"But it hurts worse!"

"Princess, Miss J said you'll just have to play through the pain. How many times do I have to tell you? It'll go away."

"But it's not! It hurts!"

"What the hell am I going to do with her?" Mrs. Vander asked. "Ever since she got that damned new violin her hand's been hurting."

"No surprise," Jacobus volunteered, spotting an opening. "You want some help?"

"You? What could you do? She already has a *good* teacher."

"Does her hand hurt or doesn't it?"

Mrs. Vander was silent.

"Okay, Mrs. Vander, I know what you're thinking. On one hand you've got your loyalty to Victoria, on the other are the engagements Kamryn'll lose if she isn't able to perform in just a few days. It's up to you. Makes no difference to me."

Mrs. Vander thought for a moment.

"Kamryn," she hollered, "get in here."

Jacobus heard Kamryn, sniffling, enter the room.

"Mr. Jacobus is going to try to help you. I'll be here. I won't let him hurt you."

"Kamryn," Jacobus said gently, "I'd like you to play something for me, and maybe I can hear what the problem is."

"What should I play?"

"How about 'Meditation'?"

" 'Meditation'? That's the easy one."

"Maybe for notes, but not so easy to play beautifully."

"I don't get it."

"Well, you know," said Jacobus, "that 'Meditation' is an interlude from a beautiful opera called *Thaïs* by the nineteenth-century composer Jules Massenet, about an ancient Egyptian courtesan who became a saint. Even though Massenet was a fine composer, 'Meditation' is the one piece he's still remembered for, because it has such a lovingly evocative melody. Does that help?"

"What's an opera?" asked Kamryn.

"Never mind. Let's just give it a try, okay?"

Kamryn started to play. As she had said, the notes were easy, almost perfectly in tune and in time. But the sound was very forced and harsh. After a few moments she stopped.

"It hurts! It hurts! I can't play anymore!"

"There, you see?" said Mrs. Vander. "She can't even play 'Meditation.' I think she's just spoiled."

Jacobus said, "Well, I can't help you with that one, Mrs. Vander, but

I can suggest some things that will help her playing. Since I'm not Kamryn's teacher, she can take them or leave them. I don't particularly care one way or the other."

"At least you're honest about that," said Mrs. Vander.

"First of all, Kamryn," said Jacobus, "as much as you want it to, this violin will never sound like the Piccolino. No matter how hard you try it's almost impossible to change the basic character of a violin . . . like with some people. So you just have to accept it for what it is until we get the Piccolino back. Don't try to force the sound out of it. Just let it be itself, okay?"

She mumbled something unintelligible. At least she didn't run away.

"I assume it's your left hand that's the one that hurts. Am I right?" Another mumble. "Good. So, once you stop squeezing the bow and pressing with your *right* hand, your left hand should already start to feel more relaxed."

"How did you know it was her left hand that was hurting? How can you tell if you can't see?" asked Mrs. Vander accusingly.

"That's easy. There were two ways, and I'll give her a little exercise for each."

Jacobus then explained a few things about mechanics fundamental to good violin playing that he explained to all his students, consistent with his philosophy of trying to make the very unnatural motions of playing the violin feel as comfortable and relaxed as possible. He used images like "seaweed at the bottom of the ocean with an easy current swaying it back and forth" for the motion of the left arm; or "like skating on ice" for shifting, which is the sliding motion of the left hand from one position to another. To help her visualize why it was so important to keep all the joints of one's fingers, hand, and arm flexible when playing with vibrato, Jacobus jumped up and started to walk around like Frankenstein's monster until he bumped into the glass table by the couch, almost knocking over the interior design magazines on it. Kamryn's attempt to suppress a giggle was not totally successful and did not go unnoticed by Jacobus. He described a certain simple exercise to loosen her vibrato and asked her to try it.

"It feels weird," Kamryn said

"I'm sure it does. But, tell me, does it hurt?"

Shrug.

"Well, assuming your silence means it doesn't, let me suggest that you practice your vibrato just like that. Once you're comfortable with that, try connecting the vibrato from one finger to the next. It all should take about five minutes a day and give you plenty of time left over for *Sesame Street.*"

This time it was Yumi's unsuccessful attempt to totally suppress *her* giggle that did not go unnoticed. Jacobus heard Kamryn march out of the room.

"Okay, how much do I owe you, Mr. Jacobus?" asked Mrs. Vander. He heard the click of her wallet as impatience returned to her voice. She no doubt would be dialing Lilburn's number the minute they left.

"Owe me?" asked Jacobus. "I offered to help. You owe me nothing."

"Miss J says the amount a teacher is paid is a sign of how much she's respected. That's why she charges two hundred dollars an hour."

"In that case, Mrs. Vander, you can pay me three hundred . . . but let's wait until I return the Piccolino, shall we?"

FIFTEEN

Nathaniel thought Jacobus's theory that the thief might be a second-place finisher in the Grimsley Competition was far-fetched, but Jake's hunches—based upon a logic that defied normal analysis—had been correct in the past, so he decided that he would at least use it as a starting point for his research.

The first and easiest part of his strategy had been to eliminate the dead runners-up. He had begun his legwork with the archives—or so the pair of oak file cabinets was called—in the basement of the Grimsley Competition offices. An indifferent part-time employee whose mumbled name he didn't understand handed him a key and told him to help himself. Rummaging didn't take long, and soon he had a complete list of all the contestants and how they had placed, assembled from programs and rosters elegantly handwritten in fountain-pen ink on yellowed paper in the Competition's inaugural year of 1905, moving up to distinct Underwood type in 1944, and finally on an IBM printout from the previous Competition in 1970. What disappointed him was that the Grimsley people seemed uninterested in what happened to the contestants—including the winners—*after* the Competition. There were a few random manila files about individual contestants, but other than uninformative yellowed press clippings, many of which were undated, there was little of value to be gleaned.

List in hand, along with a thermos of black coffee and bag of Hole-In-The-Middle frosted chocolate cake doughnuts, Nathaniel visited the *New York Times*, where he researched the obituary files. When those proved inconclusive, he followed up with a computer search of the records of the genealogy library of the Church of Jesus Christ of Latter-day Saints. The Mormons, in their desire to give all of humanity—current and past— a free pass to heaven, had assembled heaven on earth for genealogy researchers, with the most extensive birth and death records in the world.

When Nathaniel was finished, the runners-up list had shrunk considerably: 1905 was dead, as were 1918 and '44; 1931 was still alive. So were 1957 and 1970.

Nathaniel started with the most recent, 1970, an Israeli, Daniel Lenzner. Nathaniel vaguely remembered the name. He thought he recalled that Lenzner had studied in New York, so he dialed the most likely place, the Juilliard School of Music. They put him on hold long enough for him to hear a recording of almost the entire Beethoven opus 59#3 String Quartet, interrupting his listening just as the last-movement fugue was reaching its climax. They told him Lenzner had studied with the famed pedagogue Ivan Galamian. Word had been that Lenzner would be the next Perlman or Zuckerman, but after taking second in the Grimsley his career petered out. Juilliard had a phone number for him in Tel Aviv but it was several years old.

Nathaniel checked his watch, hoping it wouldn't be too late in Israel, dialed the number, and waited while the connection was made. The phone rang several times.

"Nu? Don't you know what time it is?" said a gruff voice.

"Is this Daniel Lenzner?" asked Williams.

"Who is asking?"

Nathaniel introduced himself and explained that he was compiling updates on Grimsley Competition finalists for a future publication.

"You can tell them two things," said Lezner.

"Yes?"

"Number one. You can tell them I am a professor of violin at the Tel Aviv Conservatory of Music. And number two, you can tell them to go to hell."

Nathaniel thought that maybe he had hit the jackpot on the first try—here was an angry runner-up—and that Jacobus had been correct in his theory.

"Have you been in New York City recently, Mr. Lenzner?"

"Why should I? The bagels are better here." Lenzner hung up.

Nathaniel wrote a note to himself to double-check Lenzner's contention that he wasn't in New York; that would be easy enough—he could just call the Tel Aviv Conservatory and find out if Lenzner had been fulfilling his teaching schedule and other commitments. Nathaniel then went on to 1957, a French violinist named Jean-Marc Robert. According to the scant Grimsley file, Robert was born in Strasbourg, France, in 1945. There was a home address and phone number. He tried the phone number but was informed by the international operator that no such number existed. In fact, current phone numbers for Strasbourg had two additional digits. No, there is no current number for a Jean-Marc Robert at that address. Nathaniel asked the operator for any number for anyone with the name of Jean-Marc Robert in Strasbourg. The operator said she wasn't paid to be a detective. Nathaniel thanked her, hung up, and put 1957 on hold.

He had similar luck with 1931, an English girl named Kate Padgett, and was about to call it a day when he had a thought. Of the three judges at the 1931 Grimsley, he knew that two were dead. The great and infamous Malinkovsky had returned to Russia and survived World War II, but one day vanished into thin air during one of Stalin's purges of the 1950s. Silvio Signorelli, the flamboyant Italian virtuoso, had perished in 1948 in a plane crash over the Atlantic with his beloved Stradivarius on his way home to Milan after a concert tour.

Only Sir Owen Davis, now ninety-one, was still alive. His ninetieth birthday the year before had been cause for great international celebration. Though he was too frail to attend any of the galas held in his honor, it did not take Nathaniel long to find the story that the *New York Times* had written. Martin Lilburn had been sent to interview Davis at the Alden Grove Convalescent Home in Bournemouth.

"Hello, Alden Grove, Rebecca speaking."

Nathaniel explained that he was compiling a history of the Grimsley Competition and asked if it would be possible to have a minute with Maestro Davis.

"Marvelous!" said Rebecca. Did Nathaniel perceive a giggle? "He has such little company these days compared to all the hoopla last year, aside from Mr. Giles."

"Mr. Giles?"

"Yes, Sir Owen shares his room with Mr. Giles. Mr. Giles is his constant companion."

"Well, I wouldn't want to disturb anyone at this hour."

"Don't worry, Mr. Williams. Sir Owen and Mr. Giles always love company. Let me put you through."

Nathaniel spent the next hour listening to an encyclopedic first-hand oral history of classical music of the twentieth century from Sir Owen. His voice raspy and high-pitched by age, Owens waxed nostalgic over the waning of the Victorian Elgar era but offered an uncensored opinion of the new music of Philip Glass—"I wouldn't wipe my arse with it, would I, Mr. Giles?" Nathaniel heard high-pitched "yip yip" barking in the background. "You see, Mr. Williams? Mr. Giles is in agreement."

Davis had performed virtually every major concerto with every major orchestra until his retirement from the stage only a decade earlier, leaving a legacy as both an artist and a humanitarian. He seemed to remember every performance and was not hesitant describing each one in blazing detail, from Sir Thomas Beecham's droll one-liners—"Owen, perhaps your Brahms could benefit from a bit more sauerbraten"—to Toscanini's fiery rants. Nathaniel wished he had thought of taping this conversation—monologue, really—for his personal archives but satisfied himself with furious note taking. Finally Nathaniel brought the subject around to, "Whatever happened to that little girl, Kate Padgett, who finished second in the 1931 Grimsley?"

"Padgett, Padgett? Can't say I recall the name. So many years ago . . ." There was silence. Davis must have exhausted himself. He had been talking nonstop and it was well into night in England.

"Piddle?" he said.

"Say what?" asked Nathaniel.

"Piddle? No. Plush. No, Piddle. Yes, not Plush. Piddle it is."

"It must be late, Sir Owen."

"Aha, you think I'm daft! Senile! Is that it? It is Piddle. In Dorset, next to Plush. That's it."

"That's what, Sir?"

"Her hometown. Padgett's hometown. Check the *Piddletown Herald*—goes back to the 1600s. They must have something. Wonderful talent. Should have won. Bad lot, that Grimsley. Good luck, sir. Off to bed now, Mr. Giles! Good-bye, sir."

SIXTEEN

The Dedubian et Fils violin showroom was on the twelfth and top floor of the elegant Bonderman Building, a grand turn-of-the-twentieth-century edifice. The Bonderman had one of those old-fashioned elevators, wood paneled with a well-oiled brass grate inner door that had to be closed by hand. That hand was provided by the white-gloved, uniformed elevator operator Sigmund Gottfried, a small old German who had been working the elevator since Jacobus was a student. They first met when Jacobus went to the Dedubian shop, at that time run by Boris's father, to get a new bridge for his violin. In those days Jacobus knew very little about violins. The elder Dedubian used to tease Jacobus in his sardonic Armenian accent, chiding him that he couldn't tell the difference between a Tononi (a highly regarded Italian violin maker) and a "No-Tone-y."

As Jacobus entered the elevator with Yumi, Gottfried said, "Ah! Mr. Jacobus. It has been a long time. Has it not?"

"Not long enough, Ziggy," said Jacobus.

Gottfried chuckled. "Ja," he said. "The violin business. It never changes."

Gottfried had a little battery-operated fan running in the elevator, which, along with the dim light, provided a modest oasis from the blinding heat and sun outside.

The elevator was of the vintage variety that would brake sharply about a foot or so before reaching its destination, and would then slowly coast the remaining distance until perfectly even with the floor. Jacobus was well prepared for this, but Yumi, whose only elevator experience had been with high-tech Japanese designs, was not, so when Gottfried began his maneuvers in order to admit a passenger on the fifth floor, she lost her balance and would have stumbled but for Jacobus, around whom she instinctively wrapped her arms.

Gottfried apologized profusely to Yumi, and Yumi to Jacobus. Though Jacobus did not respond aloud to Yumi's apology other than to grunt, that simple human contact—Yumi's arms momentarily around his shoulders—was enough to give Jacobus a sense that maybe there was a shred of purpose to his life, but rather than being buoyed by this thought he felt it only destabilizing. For the first time he began to doubt the assuredness of his instincts. In the cold light of day, he thought, what, really, do I know about this young lady to even speculate that she was involved with such a brazen plot to steal a violin? Why *couldn't* one of the MAP coterie have done something so patently ridiculous? After all, the same confidence they had mustered to attain their position of dominance of the music world could easily serve them as well to execute a theft. And why couldn't it have been anyone, someone else entirely out of the blue, who stole the Piccolino? What compounded Jacobus's distress was that he knew the most likely out-of-the-blue candidate was himself.

Jacobus's ardor for dismantling the Musical Arts Project was also ebbing. Yes, he despised them, but if the rest of the world could live with their bullying tactics, why should it be upon his shoulders to do the dirty work? Jacobus did not suffer zealots gladly, and his own actions were beginning to smack of that which he loathed. After talking to Dedubian and Grimsley, and then Strella, Rachel Lewison, and Victoria Jablonski the next day, he would simply report his findings to Nathaniel and go back to his cloister in the Berkshires. Why had he agreed to help Nathaniel, anyway? Was it to destroy MAP, as he had so confidently boasted to himself, or was it due to something far more difficult to admit? Was it, as Salvador had insinuated, only to distract an old man from his loneliness?

The elevator doors slid open to reveal the Dedubian showroom, which contained hundreds of the world's greatest violins. Gottfried said, "Good to see you again, Mr. Jacobus. And good luck."

Jacobus offered Yumi words of caution as they entered a world of nineteenth-century opulence.

"Just remember," he said, "even though Dedubian and I have been friendly for what, thirty-five, forty years, he's got violin dealer in his genes."

Jacobus recollected Dedubian's shop from long before he was blind. Over the years the sounds and smells had remained the same, so he assumed that the sights hadn't changed much either. The cavernous main hall still extended from the front to the back of the gray stone building, which when it was erected commanded a sweeping view of midtown Manhattan, including Carnegie Hall just a few blocks away. Faded Persian rugs sprawled across polished oak parquet floors. Through curved glass windows with wrought-iron balconies, the city's hazy light cast shadows on dark, elaborately carved woodwork ascending twenty feet to the ceiling with its turreted skylights. Precise temperature and humidity controls kept out the oppressive heat and protected the instruments that hung in glass cases everywhere. Violins sitting on silk-covered tables awaited inspection by discerning hands, eyes, and ears.

Jacobus felt Yumi tug at his sleeve. "Mr. Jacobus, there is a man trotting toward us."

"Face kinda like a horse with a smile? Fancy gray suit?"

Before Yumi could reply, a voice with an elegant Eastern European accent intervened. "Jake, my old friend! It has been too long."

"Bo," said Jacobus. "Forty years in America and your accent is worse than ever. Must help sell the fiddles, huh?"

"You make me blush, Jake. And who is this attractive young lady on your arm?"

"New student, Yumi Shinagawa," said Jacobus.

"A new student! Ah! Miss Shinagawa, is it? Yes? *Konnichiwa,* Shinagawa-chan. So very pleased to meet you. If only Jake could see what a beauty he has! And those eyes! Tell me the truth, either they're made of pure jade or you're part Irish leprechaun."

Jacobus was amused by Dedubian's salesmanship much more than he admired it. At least the suckers go away smiling, he thought.

"You know," Dedubian said, now in a confidential tone, "a student of Daniel Jacobus must play on only the best instrument. I happen to have just received a perfect, *perfect* J. B. Vuillaume—mint condition!— but I will only sell it to the person who is the right fit."

"Like Cinderella?" asked Jacobus.

"Just so, Jake. Just so. You put it so well. Shinagawa-chan, you, dear, may be that person. Beautiful, sensitive, but with strength! Would you allow me to show it to you, Miss Shinagawa? I have it on consignment for eighty thousand dollars, but if you leave it to me, I think I could get the owner to come down on the price, but only if you really love it."

"What about lowering your commission also, Bo?" chided Jacobus.

"Let's let the young lady—"

"Bo, I'm sure Miss Shinagawa would be happy to try it, but she's not going to buy anything without her mother seeing it first."

"Of course, of course, by all means. And did your mother come with you today, dear?"

"She is in Japan, Mr. Dedubian," said Yumi.

"Oh. I see. I see. Well. In the meantime, you wanted to talk to me, Jake?" said Dedubian. Jacobus felt a polite push as Dedubian guided him and Yumi into his private office.

"About the Piccolino," said Jacobus.

"Yes, the Piccolino."

Dedubian hesitated. Jacobus wondered if Dedubian was about to make something up. Maybe MAP did have something to do with it.

"Jake," said Dedubian, "you and I have known each other for a very long time. I have never, never been so humiliated in my life. You see how this has affected me—see, I haven't even offered you a seat yet. Please, please," he said. Jacobus felt Dedubian bodily corral him into a very comfortable leather easy chair.

But he hasn't denied anything, has he?

"Cognac?" he asked Jacobus.

"Coffee," he replied.

"Mrs. King," he announced to his secretary over the intercom, "espresso for Mr. Jacobus."

· "Mind if I smoke?" asked Jacobus.

"Sorry, Jake, my insurance for all these instruments is exorbitant enough as it is, and that's without permitting smoking. If I let anyone smoke, do you know what—"

"Screw that. Forget it."

"*O-cha*, Miss Shinagawa?" Dedubian asked.

"Thank you."

"And make that tea for Miss Shinagawa," he added into the intercom.

"Jake, my grandfather, Aram, fled the Turks and set up a shop in

Rome. My father, Ashot, who expanded the business to Paris, fled the Nazis for New York. Now, here, in America—*in America!*—your Gestapo police barge into my business and interrogate me about this damned violin right in front of my clients. It's unbelievable!"

"Don't worry too much about that, Bo," said Jacobus, smiling. "Most of your customers already think you're a crook, anyway."

Jacobus heard Yumi gasp at this blatant insult of the world's foremost violin dealer. *She* might never have heard worse, Jacobus thought, but Dedubian has . . . and from me too.

Dedubian chuckled but didn't disagree.

"What am I to do, Jake? What am I to do? I am just a businessman. I *like* musicians. But some of them think I'm cheating them because I have to make a little profit when I sell a fiddle. Yet at the same time they think I am being unfair when I say no when they try to sell me their fiddle at such a high a price even I would be embarrassed!

"Then they ask for inflated insurance appraisals from me. They want me to put in writing that their piece-of-shit instrument is worth fifty percent more than it really is, giving me the excuse 'just so I won't have to get it appraised again for another three years.' Then they go and try to sell it two weeks later for the value I appraised it, using the piece of paper with my name on it as justification. Who is fooling who, Jake?"

"That may be," said Jacobus, "but you have to admit that the price of a good old violin has gone through the roof. Most working musicians can't even afford them anymore. A Gagliano that was going for ten thousand dollars in '75 now goes for a hundred, and the Strad that Joe Lefkowitz bought from you for twenty thousand in 1960 is now worth a million."

"But that is because of the collectors, Jake. Not me. If someone offers me top dollar for a violin I'm selling, what am I supposed to do, interview him to find out if his purpose is noble enough? Jake, I just want to save enough in the next few years so I can retire to my condo in Montreux."

"Come on, Bo," said Jacobus. "Don't give me that line. You could have retired to your condo ten years ago and thrown in all your girl-friends in the bargain. If you sold only the inventory Grandpa left you at just half market value, you could probably own Montreux itself."

"A slight exaggeration. A slight exaggeration," said Dedubian. "You flatter me. But let's come back to the issue at hand. Why would I ruin all that by stealing a violin that everyone would know I stole as soon as I sold it? I wasn't even there when it was stolen, for God's sake. I was stuck on that damned Long Island Expressway. Jake, between you and me, as old friends, you must believe me when I tell you I have very good reasons I could never do such a thing. You know and I know, only a crazy person would steal that fiddle. Why can't the police understand that?"

Jacobus did believe him, more or less. Rather, he had no reason not to believe him, though there was that protest-too-much tone in his voice. Something was being left out.

"Any ideas specifically who might have done it, Bo? Anyone of your MAP buddies who were at the reception capable of arranging it? Make believe you're taking this seriously and mull it over for a minute."

"Well, Jake, I'll be honest with you. We all know no one's perfect. Strella, maybe he's conniving and greedy enough to want it. Vander's mother is ambitious enough. Grimsley, he's got money problems, but he already owns the Strad, so why would he steal his own violin? Victoria's ambitious too, but she's got great violins coming out of her tight little you know what; and as for Rachel . . . well, she just does not have the nerve, period.

"No, Jake, I do not think any of my MAP colleagues would have done it. I *know* they didn't do it. Though the question I ask myself is not who, but why? Why, Jake? It just does not make sense. Unless, of course . . ."

"What, Bo?" asked Jacobus, sipping his espresso. "You have a theory?"

"Unless," Dedubian continued cautiously. "I have known some collectors—whose names I cannot reveal—who have no desire ever to resell their instruments. They buy them, put them in a vault for safekeeping, and every once in a while take them out to look at them, touch them, talk to them. It makes them feel good to be able to say, 'I own a Stradivarius.' You know the sort, Jake."

"Yes. Morons."

"Well," said Dedubian, "I did not want to say that word because they are my clients; I have to call them connoisseurs. But I think you have captured the essence."

"Would any of these 'connoisseurs' have stolen this violin, Bo?"

"That is the trouble with my theory, Jake. They might buy a violin way above market cost with no questions asked, but basically they want anonymity, so they stay as far away from trouble as possible."

"So how strongly do you think the Piccolino's in the hands of a collector and will never see the light of day again?" asked Jacobus.

"It is possible, of course," said Dedubian, "and believe me I have made some discreet inquiries. But I doubt it. I sincerely doubt it."

At that moment, Mrs. King's voice blared over the intercom.

"Mr. Dedubian, Ms. Jablonski's on line one. She—"

Dedubian cut her off. "I'll call her back," he said hastily.

Jacobus sensed embarrassment in Dedubian's voice.

A relationship? Jacobus pondered to himself, continuing to sip his coffee. Or something else?

Jacobus's own fling with Victoria happened too long ago for him to be jealous of Dedubian now, but he felt a twinge nevertheless. Affairs with students had always been ethical anathema to him, but Victoria had clearly turned the tables. Young and lusty and full of herself, Victoria had made Jacobus the first big notch on her gun. When she ended the relationship in search of younger, more adventurous fare, his relief had been only mildly tinged with regret.

"And you, Miss Shinagawa," said Dedubian, "you have been so polite and quiet. What's your point of view?"

Dedubian and Victoria, thought Jacobus. Is there an angle there? Is that why he's changing the subject?

"Me?" asked Yumi.

"Why not? A student of Daniel Jacobus must by definition be highly intelligent and perceptive as well as talented."

"Certainly I am not able to understand this business if you and Mr. Jacobus—"

"Not at all," said Dedubian. "We would consider any theory you might have most seriously and respectfully. Wouldn't we, Jake?"

Jacobus nodded. He had planned on asking her the same question at some point, but better someone else be the first to do it. He put his coffee down, sat back, and pretended not to be overly interested.

"Well," started Yumi tentatively, "I am reminded of a story my grandmother told me when I was a little child."

"Yes, go on," encouraged Dedubian.

Jacobus heard Yumi gently place her teacup in its porcelain saucer as she began her story.

She told a tale of a famous wood-carver named Ichiro Noda who had lived in her small village centuries ago. The village managed to get by from scratching crops out of the rocky mountainside. Noda-san, however, became very rich and famous and came to be referred to as Noda-sama. Master Noda.

"One day he decided he wanted to help the poor villagers, so he built a shrine outside the village, actually carving the trees that were literally still growing in the earth. It took him years to finish, but at last the shrine attracted the attention of people from all over the land, as Noda-sama predicted it would, and they traveled hundreds of miles to the shrine as a religious pilgrimage. They would come to the shrine by the hundreds, and then by the thousands, to pray for good fortune, and of course they would spend their money in the village, as Noda-sama had also predicted. In a few years the villagers grew comfortable, and then even prosperous. But as their fortunes grew they gradually forgot to tend their land, which became useless. After a time they also became greedy and began to fight each other. One day, Noda-sama, who had seen what his shrine had done to his village, decided it was his responsibility to set things right, so he cut down the trees that formed the shrine and burned them to ashes. Instead of being appreciative of this act, which for an artist like Noda-sama was an act of supreme sacrifice, the villagers were horrified that the source of their wealth had been destroyed. They were so angry at Noda-sama that they chased him with sticks and torches out of the village into the mountains, where he spent the rest of his life as a poor hermit."

Yumi paused. There was silence. Jacobus thought the story was over and didn't really see much of a connection. The shrine was the violin, the village was MAP, the Grimsley Competition, and everyone affected by it. Big deal. Piccolino's thief would have to be a masochist to want to be Noda-sama.

But Yumi continued. "One would think Noda-sama would have been heartbroken that he lost his shrine and that his friends turned against him in this way. But he was not sad. He was joyful because he understood that what he had done would in time return the proper balance to the village, and although the villagers would once again be poor, they would be happier, and one day they would appreciate what he had done for them. That is my theory, Mr. Dedubian."

"A lovely, lovely story," said Dedubian. "Lovely and well told. And worth thinking about, certainly. However, it does not quite fit our current situation."

"No? How not?" asked Jacobus, interested.

"First of all, the person who stole the violin was certainly not the creator of it, so there is not nearly as much justification, shall we say?"

"Anything else?"

"Yes. It seems this Mr. Noda sacrificed something, essentially his life, to help his village. The person who stole the violin got away scot-free, and now someone else, the insurance company, I suppose, will have to reimburse the Grimsley family eight million dollars . . . unless it's recovered."

"No, Miss Shinagawa," Dedubian continued, "I believe the person who stole the Piccolino is a thief. Intelligent, well motivated perhaps, but a thief nevertheless."

"Bo," asked Jacobus, "let's say you knew it was me who stole the violin, but that I was motivated with the same altruism as this guy Noda. What would you do? Two choices—send me up the river or keep your mouth shut?"

"Jake, that's such a tough question. After all, we've known each other for—"

"Go ahead, no hard feelings."

"Well, Jake, what would happen to my business if I let people steal violins from each other? It wouldn't be right, would it?"

"Fair enough, Bo. And how about you, Yumi? Do you protect old Mr. Noda-sama-sensei because he has a good heart, or does he go into the slammer?"

"I would protect Noda-sama. I would protect you," Yumi said.

"Thanks for your hospitality, Bo," said Jacobus, standing up. "I must admit our thief is damn remarkable. Bo, I've got to make a phone call. Do you think Yumi could try that Vuillaume now? Not to buy. Just to try."

"Certainly. Of course. Just follow me. I will find you a private room so you will be undisturbed. I also have some wonderful French bows I think you will like, Miss Shinagawa. Peccatte, Voirin—beautiful, gold-mounted, I am told it gets a lovely sound from the Vuillaume violin—Pageot, Sartory. Well, you will see."

Jacobus stayed in Dedubian's office, shut the door, and called Williams, anxious to find out if he had gotten the names of Grimsley Competition second-place finishers. Williams reported he had compiled the names of all the contestants, including all the prizewinners. Jacobus eagerly asked for the names. He was not going to divulge his suspicions at this point, but his hopes were dashed when the list, which included Russians—of course—Germans, English, French, an Israeli, and one American, contained not a single Japanese entrant among any of the hundreds of Grimsley competitors over the years, let alone a prizewinner. Williams had meanwhile corroborated Lenzner's whereabouts. He had been in Tel Aviv at the time of the theft, performing a series of Baroque music concerts on original instruments. As for the Frenchman, Robert, it turned out he now owned a small but growing chain of crêperies in Paris and Los Angeles, and it seemed unlikely he was the type to have been involved in the crime.

Williams said he was still trying to track down entrants from the 1931 photo Jacobus had given him, but it would take time. He had made some progress, however. He reported that one of the older contestants in the back row, a thin, pale boy with serious eyes named Nikolas Kolkowski from Poland, had won first place, displaying searing technical skill and Paganini-like intensity. Kolkowski died at a tragically young age, a victim of the Nazi invasion of Poland. Williams told Jacobus about his conversation with Sir Owen and suggested that Jacobus have a conversation sometime with Mr. Giles about contemporary music. From what Sir Owen had said, and from the bits of information he gathered in the file, he concluded that the girl in the photo was a ten-year-old from England, Kate Padgett, who came in second. After being deadlocked with Kolkowski in the early rounds, she had finished her recital with a performance of a technically simple little tune, the rarely heard "Sicilienne" by the eighteenth-century composer Maria Theresia von Paradis. Padgett's exquisite tone and poise had won over many in the audience, but the judges ultimately opted for Kolkowski's fiery virtuosity in a close decision.

"You sure you don't remember any of this, Jake?" asked Nathaniel. "After all, you were there."

"If I remembered, why would I ask you?" Jacobus answered testily. "Hey, I was a kid. A little hurt kid who was trying his best to forget, not to remember. The only thing I wanted to do after that competition was die. Anyway, they wouldn't let us associate with the other contestants and I was long gone before the winners were served up on a silver platter."

The next blow to Jacobus's plans was Williams's gentle warning to

Jacobus that the Piccolino investigation was off-limits to his MAP prejudices. After Jacobus's meeting with the Vanders, Cynthia Vander had called Lilburn, who in turn called not only the police but Nathaniel as well, accusing Jacobus of being more intent on harassing MAP than finding the violin, and that if Williams didn't call off Jacobus he would file an official complaint against both of them and the insurance company that had hired him. Williams, whose bond to Jacobus was virtually unbreakable, nevertheless admonished his friend to stick to the issue of retrieving the Piccolino.

"Don't go on a crusade. Please, Jake," Nathaniel pleaded.

"Yeah, yeah," said Jacobus, preoccupied with names *not* on the list, and put the issue in the back of his mind.

Who, then? thought Jacobus after hanging up. Who planned the theft? It still could be just about anyone. Second-place-finisher theory—disappointing so far. Square one? More and more Jacobus was coming to the conclusion that the theory he had developed the previous night with Salvador was just the rambling of an old man with too much time on his hands.

SEVENTEEN

Dedubian escorted Yumi through the alluring ambience of the showroom to one of the several small adjoining tryout rooms for prospective instrument buyers. Quiet violin playing and even quieter conversation, given a hushed mellow resonance by the wooden surroundings and the Persian rugs, created an esoteric atmosphere, conducive to making the customer feel privileged. Conducive to buying.

Against one wall of the small room was an antique cabinet with no fewer than ten drawers, each drawer only about three inches in height. Dedubian opened the top one, which displayed a dozen beautifully cared-for violin bows arranged side by side in individual compartments laid out on a plush velvet lining.

"Here you are," said Dedubian, admiring one of the bows. "This is the Voirin I was telling you about. Hold on to this while I get the Vuillaume violin down for you. Don't drop it, though. It's worth ten thousand."

Yumi clutched the bow. If this one bow was worth that much, and there were a dozen in one drawer, and there were ten drawers, and in this room there were two cabinets, and there were—how many?—at least eight rooms. The value of the bows alone staggered Yumi.

Dedubian unlocked a glass-covered display case above the other cabinet on the other side of the room that contained a row of violins arranged on hooks, like soldiers in formation. They all looked stunning. He lifted one from a hook. "Here we are," he said, handing it to Yumi. "Take your time. Enjoy." He smiled and exited with a diffident bow, closing the door behind him.

Yumi played a few listless notes of Mendelssohn, Tartini, and Bach, but soon placed the violin and bow on a counter and sat down in an overstuffed Victorian chair. She was overwhelmed. This was a far different world from the one she had known or had even imagined. Music had always been just music. A sound. An ideal. Certainly she had seen one or two beautiful violins in her small hometown, but only one at a time, lovingly held by their owners as if they were family members. But what she was now being exposed to—music as a commodity, violins hanging on racks like so many umbrellas in a department store—was shattering her understanding and her faith. It was too much. She closed her eyes, dizzy with doubt.

The door opened.

"Sorry!" said the man. "I thought the room was empty." He began to back out, then said, "Excuse me again, are you okay, young lady?"

Yumi attempted to smile. "Thank you. I'm just very confused."

The man smiled. "I know just how you feel. Maybe I can help?"

Yumi said, "All these bows. All these violins. I just don't know where to start."

The man laughed. "Let's start by introducing ourselves. My name's Goldbloom. Sol Goldbloom."

Yumi introduced herself, repeating her need for guidance.

Goldbloom gently took the Voirin from her hand and began to explain about bows, that in a way they are like any other commodities—violins, cars, or houses. A bow is worth what people pay for it. The number-one consideration is supply and demand. Older French bows from the early nineteenth century, the greatest bows, are increasingly difficult to find. They break. They can wear out and become limp as overcooked spaghetti. Number two is the way the bow looks and its condition.

"A beautiful bow can really stand out in a case with a dozen schlocky ones," said Goldbloom, admiring the Voirin.

"Schlocky?" asked Yumi.

"Schlocky means shitty," explained Goldbloom.

"Thank you," said Yumi.

Third is the way it handles—strength, balance, control, and weight. What a professional musician, as opposed to a collector, would look for.

"On the other hand," said Goldbloom, "I once had this gorgeous gold-mounted bow made by the German maker Ludwig Bausch that played as well as any French bow, but because it was a German bow it was 'worth' only fifteen hundred bucks. But listen to this, if that bow had been stamped 'Kittel,' who was a famous dealer and maker who Bausch worked for for a while, and whose bows are extremely rare, the bow would have been 'worth' fifteen thousand. Don't tell anyone," he said, in a softer voice, "but I was tempted to have Bausch's stamp sanded off the bow. It was almost worn off anyway from having been held for so many years.

"Now, a Dominique Peccatte bow is 'worth' twenty or thirty thousand these days because they're rare, beautiful, old, and play marvelously. But why should a bow that isn't quite as good, but almost as good, be 'worth' only two thousand, simply because it was made last year in . . . Utah?"

Goldbloom answered his own question. "Because that's what people will pay for it. You take a house and move it from Scarsdale to Yonkers and it's worth half as much. Same house. Or gold! You have an ounce of gold. Today it's worth three hundred bucks, tomorrow it's two fifty. The same identical piece of yellow metal. You can't even play it! It's just what people will pay for it."

Yumi asked how someone decides what he's willing to pay for a bow.

Goldbloom explained that many bows are clearly the work of a given maker, with distinct identifying characteristics, particularly in the way the frog—the end of the bow gripped by the violinist—and tip of the bow are crafted. If the maker stamps his name at the base of the stick, so much the better. If the bow looks like a Simon and is stamped Simon it's probably a Simon. Once that is known, it is also known where a Simon fits within the cosmology of the universe of makers.

"But," continued Goldbloom, "Simon also worked in the shop of Vuillaume for a while, as did a lot of the other great nineteenth-century French makers: Peccatte, Pageot, Henry. And when they worked for Vuillaume, who also made bows, by the way, they were all stamped 'Vuillaume à Paris.'

"Generally an expert can spot the differences. But the fact is, when makers work in the same shop, they also trade ideas with each other, like how much to grade the curve of the stick, how big to make the screws or pins inside the frog. Hundreds of minute details like that. The result is that there are a lot of bows whose maker can't be definitively authenticated. That's why, when an unstamped bow is presented to a reputable dealer, he might say, 'This is French' or 'This is German,' but will rarely name a specific maker. If the same bow is taken to five different dealers, one of them might know or guess something that the others won't and the owner might get lucky."

About twenty years before, Goldbloom had tried a seemingly nondescript, unstamped bow from Dedubian, but the price was low so Goldbloom bought it. There was just something about it, he said. The next time the Symphony went on a concert tour to Europe, Goldbloom took the bow to some of the big shops in Paris and London and ended up with papers for the bow certifying it as a rare example of Adam, the Elder, made in Paris in the early nineteenth century. Simply having established provenance by obtaining a reputable certificate for a few hundred dollars, the bow was converted from a worthless piece of junk to a collector's item valued at thousands of dollars.

"How was it," asked Yumi, "that all the other dealers knew it was an Adam but not Mr. Dedubian?"

"I took that bow to five different shops—reputable shops—and got five different opinions, four of which were noncommittal. But the guy in London said it was an Adam. So I had him write up the papers. Now, if I decide to sell it, it's an Adam.

"My God! You should have seen Dedubian. He pretended not to be, but was he furious. He claimed he knew it was an Adam all along and that he was just being nice to me. He also offered to buy it back from me at any time. Gonif!"

Yumi thanked Goldbloom for his seminar on bows, and asked whether the same was true for violins as well. She still had the Vuillaume in her hands. Goldbloom handed her back the Voirin bow and said, "Play something. And listen."

Yumi began to play the Siciliene from the "Devil's Trill" Sonata by Tartini that she had played for Jacobus at her lesson. As Goldbloom had asked, she listened, closing her eyes to help her concentrate, but was not sure what she should be listening for. All she knew was that this instrument was so much easier to play and so much more resonant than her own. After less than a minute, Goldbloom stopped her. He was holding another violin in his hands.

"Here." He handed her the violin. "Now try this one. Play the same thing."

The beauty of the sound of this violin put the Vuillaume to shame. It exceeded by far her own degree of effort, as if the violin had been waiting for someone to play it in order to sing. In just a few moments she felt her being had been transformed.

"Ah! You like the Amati!" said Goldbloom.

Looking inside this magical instrument, she saw a label indicating the maker to be Nicolo Amati, from Cremona, Italy, and the year 1664.

"A fine, fine violin," said Goldbloom. "One of the great original Cremonese makers. Just before Stradivari. I almost bought this one once. I should have, but I also needed a house at the time. Now it goes for almost a million."

Yumi sat down, cradling the violin in her lap.

"If only I had a million dollars!" she said. "I would buy this violin."

"Yeah. Well, listen to this one," Goldbloom said as he removed another violin from its perch.

He started to play the same thing Yumi had just been playing. To her ear, the sound was only slightly different from the Amati. Not better, not necessarily worse. Just different. Beautiful in its own way.

"Is that another Amati?" she asked.

"No. In fact, it's probably not even Italian. It looks like it was made about the same time, but probably in Tyrolea, not too far from Cremona as the crow flies. So, no pedigree, no definite date, not Italian. Pretty good condition, nice looking. What would you give me for it?"

"Five hundred thousand dollars, perhaps?" Yumi guessed.

"How about thirty thousand?" said Goldbloom.

Yumi was taken aback. She had thought she was beginning to understand the violin business.

"But they both sound so beautiful! Shouldn't they be worth approximately the same?"

"Yeah, well, unfortunately in this business, a rose by any other name isn't as good an investment. On one hand, you could spend a million for a beat-up Strad that sounds crummy; on the other hand you can get a perfectly beautiful-sounding, affordable instrument for a hundredth of the price, but it won't add much to your retirement portfolio. If you put blindfolds on these so-called violin experts who say they can tell one violin from another and played both of these fiddles, I'll bet you they'd be in for a real shock."

Yumi thought about all the different kinds of people associated with violins. Musicians, of course, but also the dealers, the repairers, the insurers, the collectors, the makers, each with a different definition of value, but all stemming from one source.

"Mr. Goldbloom, what is it about violins that makes people want them so much?"

"Well, there's the value, which is always going up, the sound quality, the—"

"No. I'm sorry to interrupt. I think I understand all of that now. But there's more. It's almost as if people lose their minds about violins."

"If I told you what I think, you'd think I was meshuga. Crazy."

"I've come here to learn. I don't think you're . . . meshuga."

"Well, okay, then. I think you're old enough. Sex."

"Sex?"

"See, I told you."

"Could you explain more, please?"

"Well, first of all, look at how we've named the parts of the violin. And as I describe this, just run your fingers along that Amati you just happen to be cuddling in your lap and then tell me if I'm crazy.

"At the top, what's usually referred to as the 'scroll' is also sometimes called the 'head.' People say they can look and feel either masculine or feminine, depends on your inclinations, I suppose. Attaching the head to the body of the violin is what we call the 'neck.' When we play we gently slide our left hand back and forth along the neck—that in itself is

suggestive—and what do we come to? Those beautifully curved 'shoulders.' Along the sides we have 'ribs,' which are contoured to have a slender waist in the middle. That contour enables us to play on the outer
strings without hitting the instrument, but it gives the violin a very, very
attractive waistline.

"Of course, the back of the violin is called the 'back,' made of maple,
which is hard and strong. The top of the violin people often call the
'belly'; it's softer, made from spruce, and it's got the same kind of curves
as the people we sometimes like to . . . 'think' about. Not to mention
those two sensuous 'f-holes.' "

Yumi reddened and quickly removed her fingers from the f-holes.

"Am I embarrassing you?" asked Goldbloom.

"Go on, please."

"Well, this is the X-rated part."

"Go on, please."

"Okay. Now, what do we do when we play the violin? First, we take
the bow—a long hard shaft. Just before we play we tighten it, which
makes it even more erect. We then gently embrace the violin, holding it
by the neck and drawing it to our body. We lower this erect shaft on the
belly of the violin, pressing down and moving it back and forth so that
the coarse hairs of the bow make the strings vibrate. Those vibrations
go from the string down into the very core of the instrument, making
the whole thing vibrate. When you're playing the violin you actually
feel the vibrations enter your body; you feel the instrument responding to your touch, how you're touching it."

Yumi felt her chest constricting, her breath shorten. Whether or
not he was meshuga, he was a convincing storyteller.

"And not every bow goes with every violin. You have to find the perfect match. Even with great instruments the violin and bow have to com-
plement each other. So, between you, the violin, and the bow, it becomes
a threesome.

"Now, here's the clincher. When you play the violin—when you play
Bach, Mozart, Beethoven, for example—these are the most intimate,
the most personal thoughts musicians have. That's our soul. That's the
essence of our being. When we touch the violin the right way, it recip-
rocates. It responds. If we play angrily, it will sound rough. Some people
like that. If we play lovingly, it will love back. It gives us as much as we
give it—sometimes more, depending on the violin. With a great violin,

the sound is more than just a reflection of our feelings—it almost has a life of its own. It's almost like the violin is playing us!

"Now, Yumi, tell me I'm crazy."

Yumi was thinking about Jacobus, about his passion. She realized that it was his passion, even when he was chastising her, that drove him. She couldn't immediately think of anything to say to Goldbloom but found that she was hugging the Amati. She loosened her grip on the violin and it almost slid off her lap. Goldbloom reacted with catlike quickness, catching it well before any damage would have been done.

"So you do see what I mean," he said, returning the instrument safely to its hook.

"I have never thought about playing the violin in this way before. Do you really think this is true?"

"Who knows?" Goldbloom laughed. "Maybe it's just a coincidence that the Italians and French were the best violin and bow makers. Maybe not, but it's the only theory I could come up with that might explain some pretty meshuga behavior."

Yumi was glad to hear Goldbloom laugh. His humor broke the spell and her tension. She smiled.

"Yeah," said Goldbloom. "It's bad enough when people get obsessed buying and selling and playing violins. But then you read about people stealing and killing for them, and you begin to wonder."

"Killing?" asked Yumi, no longer smiling.

"Sure," said Goldbloom. "You reminded me of it."

"Did I?"

"Uh-huh. The 'Devil's Trill' you just played. You know the story?"

"Yes," said Yumi, once again relieved. "My teacher told me about it. How the devil played for Tartini in a dream, and how Tartini tried to write down what he had heard—"

"That's the story that most people know. He told it to a French author, Lalande, who wrote a book about his travels to Italy. Tartini said that the devil's playing was so much better than what Tartini himself wrote that he would have broken his violin and given up music if only he could've duplicated it."

"Yes," said Yumi.

"But that's only a small part of the story I'm talking about. You see, Yumi, Giuseppe Tartini was a wild, rootless kid who tried his hand at everything from fencing to being a priest, but succeeded in nothing. When he was nineteen he had a fling with a young girl named Elisabetta Premazone, who happened to be the niece of Cardinal Giorgio Cornaro, the archbishop of Padua. The two lovers eloped, and guess what? The cardinal charged Tartini with kidnapping. So poor little Giuseppe fled, hiding in a monastery in Assisi for two years. But in those two years Tartini supposedly not only decided to play the violin, he became an overnight virtuoso who played so magnificently that the cardinal, who finally found out where Tartini had gone, forgave him and allowed him to return to Padua and Elisabetta. The rest, as they say, is history, and Tartini became the most renowned violinist of his time."

"That sounds like a happy ending to me," said Yumi.

"It does, except for one thing. Do you really think someone—anyone—can become a violin virtuoso in two years? It's hard enough to play a C-Major scale in tune after two years!"

"You have another theory, Mr. Goldbloom?" asked Yumi.

"Call me Sol. My theory is this. Tartini was pretty old when he told Lalande about his dream about the devil, sometime in the 1740s. He said the dream was in 1713, so he was carrying that dream around him for a lifetime. The year 1713 was right at the beginning of his hiding in Assisi. But just before he fled Padua a curious thing happened. His sweetheart's older sister, Paola, was married, but she also had a lover. Both Paola and her boyfriend were killed by her husband, the son-in-law of the cardinal's brother, who was enraged when he found them in a compromising position. The lover was also a violinist, but when they went to find his violin, there was no trace of it! I think Tartini informed on Paola and her boyfriend, not considering the possibility they'd lose their lives. He probably thought the reward for ratting was Elisabetta's hand, but then when it became apparent he was in hot water, he ditched it out of Padua with the violin. Think about having a dream—in a monastery, of all places—of making a pact with the devil himself. I think Tartini's devil dream was not only about diabolical music. I think the dream was about the violin. And about guilt."

"But why couldn't Tartini have just gotten another violin?" Yumi argued. "After all, Padua is right near Cremona, isn't it? Isn't that where that Amati was made, the one you showed me?"

"Well, Yumi, this particular missing violin happened to be an extraspecial one. Maybe the only violin in the world that could have enabled Tartini to become such a great virtuoso in such a short time. That violin was—"

"The Piccolino Stradivarius," said Jacobus, standing in the doorway.

Yumi, bombarded by three almost instantaneous shocks, closed her eyes and clutched the arm of her chair to keep herself from falling for the second time in an hour. The first shock was hearing that the Piccolino Strad was yet again the focal point in a murderous tragedy. The second shock was hearing it from the mouth of Jacobus who, like an apparition, had been among them, unseen, for who knew how long? The third shock was . . .

"Jake, you old fart! Look what you've done to the poor kid."

Yumi opened her eyes in time to see Goldbloom embrace Jacobus.

"You know each other?" she asked.

"You know each other?" asked Goldbloom.

Yumi explained that Jacobus was her teacher. Goldbloom explained that he and Jacobus had sat next to each other during the two years that Jacobus had been in the Boston Symphony, after his Dumky Trio had disbanded and before his blindness. It was Goldbloom who had driven Jacobus to his audition for concertmaster despite Goldbloom's protestations that he should take him to the hospital first. Goldbloom had considered Jacobus's achievement brash but heroic. Jacobus himself had felt only humiliation.

After Jacobus left the Symphony, the two had remained friends, but because of his bitterness Jacobus vowed never to go to another symphony concert, so he and Goldbloom drifted apart, rarely communicating.

Goldbloom asked Jacobus what he was doing in New York and Jacobus explained his task assisting Nathaniel in the recovery of the missing violin. Goldbloom also knew Nathaniel Williams, whom he felt was meshuga for having given up music to go into the insurance business.

Jacobus invited Goldbloom to meet them at the Carnegie Deli, along with Nathaniel, after his and Yumi's meeting with Trevor Grimsley. Goldbloom couldn't because of his concert at Carnegie Hall that night, where the Boston Symphony was playing Berlioz's *Damnation of Faust*, so he invited them to the concert. Jacobus, as expected, declined, but Yumi was eager to go. Goldbloom suggested they all meet after the concert at the deli, which was agreed upon.

The three walked out of Dedubian's together. Sigmund Gottfried had the elevator door open and welcomed them into his domain, politely expressing his wish that they had had a successful visit with Mr. Dedubian. Goldbloom commented to Yumi on what a fine teacher she had found in Jacobus.

Yumi, preoccupied, asked, "Do you think they can possibly find who took the Piccolino?"

"Nathaniel alone, I don't think he could do it," said Goldbloom, as the brass lattice door of the elevator slid closed silently in front of them. "But with Jake, yeah. Of that I have no doubt. Take us down, Ziggy."

EIGHTEEN

Just before Jacobus and Yumi were greeted by Trevor Grimsley in the dark coolness of his study smelling of oak, books, and expensive cigars, Yumi quietly expressed hope that the comforting environment would provide them relief from the city's withering summer heat.

"Don't count your chickens," Jacobus whispered back.

"Drink?" asked Grimsley. "Looks like you could use one."

"Single-malt?" asked Jacobus.

"Name your poison."

"Lagavulin. Sixteen years?"

"Coming right up. Rocks?"

"Straight up."

"And for you, Miss Shinagawa?"

"Tea, please."

Grimsley poured the scotch, mixed himself a margarita, and had his housekeeper bring the tea.

"Bottoms up," he said. "As you know, Grandfather initiated the Competition in 1905. To tell you the truth, I think he did it mainly to impress Grandmother. Just between you and me, he really didn't have an artistic bone in his body. Just between you and me."

"Grandmother and Grandfather, huh?" said Jacobus, and took a sip of scotch, thoughtfully letting it sit on his tongue before swallowing. I wonder what Grandmother and Grandfather would think of their sixty-year-old dandy grandson. The taunting laugh of his mugger returned.

"It's quite a grueling ordeal," Grimsley continued, "and I'm not quite sure just how those youngsters manage to get through it all. I've got to hand it to them"—Jacobus heard Trevor sloshing the crushed ice in his drink—"they really do go at each other's throats," he chuckled, "especially in the final round. But I suppose it's worth it to them. There *is* the ten-thousand-dollar first prize, of course. But mainly it's the chance for a career. For stardom. Frankly, I don't think the children know what it all means. It's for the parents and, to a lesser extent, I suppose, the teachers. I shouldn't tell you this next bit, but it's true. Would you believe that some of the less scrupulous parents even plan for their children to be born not quite thirteen years before upcoming Competitions, so that they'll be at the maximum qualifying age? What a way to get an edge! Seems a bit perverse, doesn't it? Well, I suppose that's what makes the world go round."

Jacobus nursed his scotch, listening with half an ear. Grimsley was doing a poor job of containing his anxiety with his spouting. At least when you're blind you don't have to look interested, Jacobus thought.

"But they all say it's worth it. And then, of course, there's the Carnegie Hall recital we provide them. That in itself costs us a bundle. Renting Carnegie, paying for the security—some security!—printing programs, advertising in the *Times.* You'd be surprised at some of the hidden costs, no doubt. Grand old hall, anyway.

"There are two things, though, that make this Competition unique. Unique! The first is the gala. The winner gets to play a concerto at Carnegie Hall with an orchestra of a hundred musicians who are hand-picked from all the great orchestras of the world. Just between you and me, it costs a fortune, but Grandfather stipulated it in his will, so there you have it. You wouldn't believe how much it costs to pay these musicians! We have to fly them from all over the world, pay for their food and lodging. The fee for the rehearsal is three hundred dollars per musician and the performance is twice that. I don't know why they need so much money—they're only musicians—but thank God I can afford it."

"Yes, thank God," murmured Jacobus, lifting his glass.

"Yes, I suppose so," continued Grimsley. "And of course the jewel in the crown is the Piccolino, one of the greatest and certainly the most beautiful violin ever made. The contestants kill—absolutely kill—to have a chance to play on that violin. It's as if it plays itself, they tell me. I'm no musician. Like Grandfather, I suppose. But you knew that. They tell me all they have to do is put the bow on the string of that violin, and voilà! 'I'm a virtuoso!' Pity it's missing. Do you believe in magic, Mr. Jacobus? Oh, I suppose not. You've seen how much practicing it takes. Fortunately, I've never really had to work a day in my life, though I must say that managing this competition is no mean feat. These children practice from sunup to sundown, and beyond, for the chance to play on that violin."

Jacobus put down his empty glass and stood up.

"Thanks for the scotch, Trevor."

"What, are you leaving? Already?"

"Doesn't sound like there's anything you want to tell me that I don't already know."

"Well . . . what about the Piccolino?"

"What about it?"

"I'm quite fond of the Piccolino. If I do say so myself. We desperately do want to get that violin back."

"We?" asked Jacobus.

"Well, yes, the family," said Grimsley. "All of us. Why?"

"I understand the family underwent some financial setbacks recently."

Jacobus sat back down. It was now his turn to do some mudslinging.

"Pardon?"

"Don't I remember the *Times* reporting last year that some members of the family lost quite a bit of money on junk bonds and stock options? As I recall, there was also some talk of insider trading."

"That's all been cleared up. Eons ago."

Jacobus heard Grimsley place his glass on a table with a distinct clack. Must have just drained it.

"What's that got to do with anything, anyway?" asked Grimsley.

"Only that since you're not allowed to sell the violin—because of Grandfather's will—an eight-million-dollar insurance claim would go a long way to restoring one's checking account."

"Are you insinuating . . . ?"

"And to be rid of the fiddle means to be rid of the Competition and its expenses. You yourself were saying just now how exorbitant the costs are. And I would imagine the trust fund that Grandfather initially set up ninety years ago doesn't come close to covering today's costs. I would guess a lot of it comes right out of your pocket. Paying someone ten, twenty thousand dollars under the table to abscond with a violin is a small price to pay for an eight-million-dollar return, plus ridding yourself of all those headaches in the bargain."

"Mr. Jacobus, you're suggesting that I stole my own violin for my own profit? How dare you! You're the one who's supposed to have stolen it. You, not me."

Trevor Grimsley, Jacobus thought derisively, is trying to bully me?

"I'm merely suggesting that it's a reasonable angle, Mr. Grimsley. One I'm sure the police would be interested in pursuing if presented in the right way. Maybe last year's investigation needs a little follow-up."

"This is preposterous. Absolutely preposterous. I had nothing to do with that theft, and the money business has all been cleared up. You're trying to blackmail me, Jacobus. You're threatening to expose me to public ridicule. But for what reason? What would your price be?"

"Terminate the Competition."

"Terminate? The Competition?"

Jacobus had taken a page from Lilburn's textbook. "You heard me. Assure me, in writing, that after this year there will be no further Grimsley Violin Competition and I won't take my suspicions to the authorities."

Jacobus was almost enjoying himself now.

"But I can't, can't, do that. It's in the will. Impossible!"

"It's that or the headlines, Trevs. I'm sure you can afford a good lawyer to get out of the will. You're a very resourceful person."

"Mr. Jacobus," said Grimsley.

There was a distinct change in Grimsley's tone. Ah! thought Jacobus, a new tack?

"I think you've got us all wrong. What we're doing, or at least trying to do, with the Competition, with MAP, is create opportunity. Yes! Create opportunity! Give the kids a chance. A chance for a career! Isn't that good?"

"Mr. Grimsley, let me ask you a question." Jacobus waited, intentionally exacerbating Grimsley's anxiety. "How many Grimsley Competition winners have had lifelong, fulfilling careers?"

"How should I know?"

"Well, I'll tell you, because that's one of the things my associate, Mr. Williams, has been researching. It turns out that since the Grimsley began in 1905 *none* of the winners were able to sustain their careers at a high level to the age of thirty. One made it to twenty-seven. Do you want to know why, Trevs?"

"That's none of my business, now, is it?"

"Do you want to know why?"

"Oh, I suppose you'll tell me whether I want to or not."

"Hey, that's one thing you're right about. Without naming names, we have left-hand paralysis, severe depression, drug use, suicide, and, can you believe this, 'I just don't care about music anymore.' Quite a track record your Competition has."

"But that's not the fault of the Competition. It's the system. It's the system that comes afterward."

This guy's a born victim, thought Jacobus.

"Mr. Grimsley, do you know what spiccato is?"

"No, I don't know what spacado is. I've never heard of spacado. What has that got to do with anything?"

"Spiccato is a kind of bow stroke in which the bow bounces, or appears to bounce, off the string."

"So what?"

"To play spiccato, the violinist needs to grip the bow so lightly that it almost feels as if it's falling out of his hand and at the same time keep his wrist as loose as possible. It appears as if the violinist is *causing* the bow to bounce. But that's not really the case. It's really that the violinist is *allowing* the bow to bounce on its own. Dr. Krovney, whom I studied with as a youngster, used to call this an optical illusion. 'You don't get what you see!' he used to say. I think it's more accurate to say that it's a misperception of cause and effect."

"Just why are you telling me this, Mr. Jacobus?"

"Because you are under a misperception of cause and effect. You're under the impression that your beloved Competition was created out of some kind of need of the musical world to find talented musicians. It's an artificial need. In fact, if anything, your Competition casts a shadow on any potentially great musician who *doesn't win* or chooses not even to enter. What you've done is perpetrate a false cult of child worship that ultimately has nothing whatsoever to do with music."

"Are you finished with your . . . your spiel, Mr. Jacobus?"

"Yes, except to repeat my offer to drop any further investigation of your involvement with the theft if you agree to terminate the Grimsley."

"Then I think our meeting is finished. You'll please see yourselves out."

"One more thing Trevs," Jacobus said, standing up.

"Yes?"

"Never try to lie to a blind man."

"What are you talking about now?"

"The scotch. You said it was sixteen years old. What you gave me was only eight. Just between you and me."

Back in a taxi, Yumi asked Jacobus, "Do you really think Mr. Grimsley was involved in stealing the Piccolino?"

"Grimsley? That dufus?" Jacobus said. "Who knows? You wouldn't think he has the brains or the balls. So you're wondering, why did I threaten him with public embarrassment if I'm not sure?"

"Yes."

"Well, two reasons. One was the outside chance that he'd fall for it."

"And the other?"

Jacobus snarled, "It feels good to make him sweat."

As soon as Jacobus left, Grimsley picked up the phone to call Lilburn. He wanted Lilburn to call the police and have Jacobus arrested for harassment. But there was no answer at Lilburn's so he next called Rachel Lewison, asking her to find someone to call the police.

"What do you mean, 'someone'?" Rachel responded.

"Anyone. Anthony, Victoria, Martin. Anyone!"

"I'm not your servant," Rachel said. "Why don't you call the police yourself? I've got enough to do."

"But I'm not good with words," said Grimsley. "And calling the police! I'd . . . I'd just get the jitters. They might end up arresting *me*!"

"Well, that's not my problem, is it?" said Rachel. "I'm not going to bug Anthony or Victoria about this. I *take* orders from them. I don't give them."

"Please, Rachel. What about Martin? Martin can be so persuasive."

"So?" said Rachel.

"He'd be much better convincing the police to put a stop to Jacobus, don't you think?" Grimsley said.

Rachel thought for a moment. Putting a stop to Jacobus. "All right. You've persuaded me he's more persuasive." She said she would try to contact Lilburn and hung up.

She called Lilburn's *New York Times* office number and the answering service told her that he was planning on attending a Guarneri Quartet concert that evening. She tried his apartment, but apparently he had already left. She was about to leave a message on his machine, but hung up.

Instead, she called the police department herself and was connected to that rookie detective, Al Malachi.

Malachi had the distinction of being the only graduate of Yeshiva University in the New York Police Department, a distinction of which he was personally proud but one that brought great dismay to his parents, who had dreamed of their only son becoming a rabbi, or at worst, a violinist. He was also the only one in his precinct who cared for classical music; his listening to WNCN at his desk was met with derision and an occasional spitball. Perhaps due to his musical tastes, he had just been assigned to handle the Piccolino investigation when it was determined by his superior to be too cold a case to bother with himself. A depressingly thin file had been dropped on his desk accompanied by a snide chuckle. "Here you go, sport," the lieutenant had said. "Right up your alley."

"Malachi," Malachi said, answering the phone.

"This is Rachel Lewison. From the Musical Arts Project." Rachel told Malachi that she wanted to report Jacobus's recent behavior.

"No need," said Malachi.

"Why not?" asked Rachel

"Because I got a call from your compatriot, what's his name, hold on a minute, here it is, Martin Lilburn, last night, suggesting that Jacobus might have been involved in the theft of that kid's violin."

"This is different," said Rachel. "This isn't about the theft. I want a restraining order issued on Jacobus."

"A restraining order?" asked Malachi. "For what?"

"The man has been a pit bull in his behavior toward members of the Musical Arts Project. He has intimidated, threatened, and tried to extort them. He is vindictive, irrational, and has the potential to commit violence," said Rachel.

"Forgive me if I sound a little incredulous," said Malachi. "But are you saying that you guys are afraid of a blind geriatric? Also, not to get too nitpicky, but restraining orders come from the judge, not from the police."

"I'm not concerned with the process," said Rachel. "I just want him to leave us alone. And if you don't cooperate, maybe you should connect me with your superior."

"Look, lady," said Malachi, "threats aren't going to get *you* anywhere either. If you insist, I'll talk to the guy and explain to him, nicely, your concerns. But other than that, there's nothing I can do, or frankly, want to do."

"Fine," said Rachel. "Please come to Carnegie Hall tomorrow at six o'clock. Jacobus will have finished his interviews with Mr. Strella, Ms. Jablonski, and myself, and I assure you that by that time you'll have ample grounds to warn him off."

Rachel hung up, organized her work for the next day, and cleared her desk. She was almost out the door when she returned to make one more call. This one was to Victoria Jablonski. Rachel told her about the calls she had just made and suggested that Victoria might help move their plan along by provoking Jacobus into rash behavior.

"I'll run it by Anthony," said Jablonski, still smarting from being admonished by Strella for her rash decision to intimidate Jacobus.

"No," said Rachel.

"Why not?" asked Jablonski.

After a brief pause, Rachel said, "All right, tell Anthony."

Another pause. "Never mind," said Jablonski. "Consider it done."

NINETEEN

"What is chicken soup with kreplach?" asked Yumi, perusing the Carnegie Deli menu.

"Jewish gyoza," Jacobus answered tersely. Yumi had been invigorated by the *Faust* performance at Carnegie Hall from which she and Goldbloom had just arrived, but Jacobus was not in the mood for conversation. He was on a low simmer from the meeting with Grimsley and from being chastised earlier by Nathaniel, plus he was still gnawing on scattered and seemingly inconclusive information.

"I'll try it," Yumi said to Sylvia, who had been standing by.

Nathaniel ordered the blintzes—one blueberry, one cheese—smothered with sour cream. Goldbloom ordered a liverwurst on pumpernickel.

Jacobus wanted something to calm himself down.

"I'll have the cold borscht," he said.

"You want the hot," said Sylvia.

"No, I want the cold."

"I'll get you the hot. You want that," Sylvia snapped.

He heard her shuffle off. Jesus Christ, he thought.

As they waited for the food to arrive, the four speculated randomly on possible motives for the theft of the violin. Were Rachel and Strella having an affair, as Goldbloom gathered from his contact with them at the Carnegie reception? What about Dedubian and Victoria, as Jacobus sensed from Dedubian's reaction to her phone call? Considering that the Piccolino Strad was on public view only briefly every thirteen years, was this the last opportunity for one of the older MAP clients to carry out a long-simmering plan? Would Rachel, a onetime precocious violinist and current MAP underling, harbor resentment against the Competition or Grimsley strong enough to want to steal the violin? After the day's events Jacobus was less convinced that Yumi was involved with the Piccolino theft. Was there any tie-in whatsoever with a Grimsley second-place finisher? The question was, what to do next?

Sylvia arrived noisily, slamming the silverware and plates of food down on the table. She must have sensed the tension that Jacobus was disinclined to dispel.

Jacobus took a sip of the borscht.

"Goddamit!" he hollered. "I said I wanted cold—I almost burned my fucking tongue off!"

"I told you that's what you were getting," Sylvia hollered back. "And why is it you always gotta come here after midnight on *my* shift?"

"Because it's the only time we thought we'd get decent service at this place."

"Oh! May I take that as a compliment, kind sir?"

"You may take it however you want, though it was intended more as an indictment."

"You know what, Jake? You remind me of that big old horse that goes into the bar."

"What are you talking about?"

"Yeah, this big ugly old horse goes up to the bar. And you know what the bartender says?"

"No. What does the bartender say?"

"He says, 'So why the long face?' " Sylvia waddled away.

Yumi burst out laughing. When Jacobus asked, "What's so funny?" her guffaw became even more raucous.

Jacobus was not amused, but he did note that Yumi's laugh—halfway between a chortle and a whoop—was most un-Japanese.

"Maybe we should change the subject," said Nathaniel, "while I can still keep my own lips zipped."

"Jake," said Goldbloom, jumping into the void, "tell me about your meeting with the Vanders. You think the kid's as good as all the hype she's been getting for winning the Grimsley? I'm thinking the person who stole the Piccolino maybe had it in for the kid. Maybe it was personal."

"Let's put it this way," said Jacobus. "First, I think little Miss Vanderblick was just an innocent bystander. Second, she's about the most talented nine-year-old I've heard."

That comment not only reflected his true opinion, it was a retaliatory low blow aimed at Yumi for having laughed at his expense.

"And if you feel bad about that, Yumi, well, don't," he added. He acutely recalled his own feelings of humiliation when he had been eliminated from contention in the 1931 Grimsley Competition—the same year that the intense boy Kolkowski had won. His conviction that the world scorned him for supposing he had talent had never totally died, nor did his certainty that he had disappointed his parents. And then too there had been Malinkovsky.

"The Infanta may have some hard times coming," Jacobus continued.

"How can that be? She's so far ahead of everyone else," Yumi said.

Jacobus was convinced that, like other gifted children, Kamryn had been pushed hard by MAP, the agents, record companies, even her own mother. Too hard. That MAP's grandly advertised plans for her to record the Tchaikovsky and Sibelius concertos, two of the most taxing works in the violin literature, at age nine, was insane. With so many other recordings of the same pieces, he also questioned the need for yet another.

Goldbloom shared his opinion that a talented child should be playing music—sonatas, Baroque music, short concert pieces, smaller concertos—that would help her grow gradually as an artist. "Chamber music—God forbid—so she can learn how to be a musician and not a trained monkey."

As far as Jacobus was concerned, the slower a student went, the faster the student progressed.

"If the Infanta doesn't watch out, she may end up the same way a lot of other prodigies do—forgotten," he concluded

"But why do you think that, Mr. Jacobus?" asked Yumi. "The reviews of her recital were so wonderful."

"Let me tell you something, Yumi. I went to the recital, okay? First of all, the *Times* review was written by Martin Lilburn, who happens to be a MAP stooge, so you can forget about objectivity.

"Second, I was there, sitting in the back of the Hall, listening. All the people there wanted that kid to be the next Heifetz mainly because they want to be part of history. They want to be able to say, 'I was at Vander's Grimsley recital,' with an emphasis on the 'I.' That's why it's difficult to criticize, especially for me. They'll say, 'Oh, it's just poor old blind Jacobus. He's just jealous.' Assholes.

"On the other hand, she's been pushed far too hard for someone her age. Trying to play too loud, too fast, too big, and far too schmaltzy for anyone's good taste."

"Schmaltzy?" asked Yumi.

"Yiddish, honey," said Goldbloom. "Means 'chicken fat' in real life. In music, it means 'heavily expressive.' At the Carnegie Deli it means 'health food.' "

As a result, Jacobus explained, fundamental mechanics were being sacrificed just to enable her to play louder. "Her fingers were spread too far apart on the bow so she could press down harder with her first finger. Her right elbow was much too high in order to squeeze down on the bow with all her might to play loud enough, rather than using her arm weight to build the sound naturally. She pressed far too hard with her left hand, squeezing the neck of the violin with her left thumb, and vibrating only with her arm with an inflexible wrist. All that to compensate for small size and undeveloped strength.

"What do you expect a little kid to—"

"Now hold on a second, Jake," interrupted Nathaniel, "but if I'm not mistaken, by last account you were a blind man. You might've been there, but you didn't actually see it."

"Did Beethoven hear his music?" asked Jacobus, his voice rising.

"Oh, please, Jake. Now you're bein' Beethoven?" said Nathaniel.

"Hey," shouted Sylvia. "Keep the shoutin' down. I told you yesterday, you're gonna disturb the customers."

Why does she keep talking about customers? thought Jacobus. He didn't hear any other customers. All he heard were fluorescent lights.

Fluorescent lights! He knew what fluorescent lights sounded like, but what the light itself looked like had almost completely faded from memory.

"Sorry, Sylvia," said Jacobus quietly. "We wouldn't want to do that."

"So, Ludwig, you were sayin'?"

"I was saying, Immortal Beloved," said Jacobus, his voice returning to gravelly normalcy, "that I didn't need to see, because I heard. The rest of the audience saw but obviously heard very little. Kamryn Vander's playing was loud, bright, and ostentatious, but she sacrificed tone quality, which was metallic; color, which was uniformly bright and glossy; and any kind of refined phrasing because of her jerking the bow changes in an effort to play loud.

"You wouldn't want to pay a hundred bucks to hear that kind of singer at the Met, Nathaniel. Or Ella." He smirked. "And without a violin like the Piccolino Strad, it would've sounded entirely too rough and coarse. In fact, even the Piccolino didn't help all that much, which surprised me. The only way to play what I heard was in the way I just described. Period. End of discussion."

Sometimes self-righteous indignation does wonders for the soul, thought Jacobus, if not for peace of mind.

"What would make a violin worth stealing, Sol?" he asked. "Let's say I stole the fiddle. You know me better than I know myself. Why would I have done it? What would've motivated me?"

"Obviously, the violin would have to be very important to you for some reason."

"I'm sorry I asked," said Jacobus. "Is that all?"

"Of course."

"Sol, I used to think I understood you. Maybe it's been too long."

"Think about it for a second, Jake."

Jacobus felt Goldbloom's hands pulling on the collar of his shirt, talking intimately.

What does he want me to do, read his lips? thought Jacobus.

"You couldn't do it for money, right?" said Goldbloom. "Not *this* violin, because you couldn't resell it. Any schmuck would know that. So greed is out. So that particular violin would have to be very, very important to you, and not because it was worth a lot."

Jacobus felt Sol brush some nonexistent lint off his shirt.

"Just give me a 'for instance,' Solomon," Jacobus asked impatiently.

"Okay, Jake. Here's what's important. Family, music. Doing the right thing. Good food."

"In that order?" asked Jacobus.

"It depends on what's on the menu. Now, let's pay the bill and get out of here."

TWENTY

Jacobus said good night to Nathaniel, who drove Yumi uptown to his apartment. Goldbloom offered to walk Jacobus to the Stuyvesant. Jacobus dismissed the invitation with a perfunctory no, but as he began to walk away felt a hand on his shoulder.

"What?" he said.

"Jake," said Goldbloom, "remember when we sat together in the orchestra and they used to call us Tweedledum and Tweedledee?"

"Yeah. Though I've tried to forget. So what?"

"It's because we knew each other inside out. Look, I can tell this Piccolino business is eating you up. It's killing you. I don't know why, but I've got to tell you that sometimes the world is going to be the way it is no matter what you think it should be and no matter what you do to try to fix it."

"Is that all?"

"Only one more thing. Sometimes a violin is just a violin. Good night, Jake."

Goldbloom headed to his room at the Wellington Hotel across the street from the Carnegie Deli. Jacobus began walking south down

Seventh Avenue. He eschewed a taxi, the night's hot, misty drizzle and the previous night's mugging notwithstanding, again preferring the sound of his footsteps in the nearly dormant city. Recollections of the Grimsley Competition, *his* Grimsley Competition, which he spent all his waking hours trying to suppress, had flooded back into his gut at the deli. Now it nearly doubled him over. Getting roughed up by a two-bit thug was nothing compared to what he had to endure day after day. Being pushed around was almost a welcome relief to the endless blackness of his existence.

As Jacobus crossed Fifty-third Street he felt a gust of air coming from his right, from the west. Strangely enough, Jacobus thought, even though it was coming from the Hudson River and beyond that, New Jersey, the breeze smelled fresh. Go figure.

Halfway back to his hotel, Jacobus began to regret his decision to walk. Gradually, what had been a drizzle when he left the sanctuary of the Carnegie Deli had turned to what could modestly be termed a downpour. Jacobus had no hat, no coat. No umbrella, dammit. Rain pelting against the pavement ricocheted up inside his trouser legs. In seconds his shoes were waterlogged, squishing spongelike between his sock and insole.

Staggering along, he extended his right hand, searching for a wall for guidance. The wall was closer than he estimated, and his palm caught on a piece of metal or glass—he couldn't tell—slicing it open. Oily water cascaded down the side of the wall, stinging his wound. His heavy clothing was soaked through. The rain slamming on the pavement was deafening, making it impossible for him to hear crossing traffic. He lost count of his steps and as a result was unsure whether he was approaching a corner. Disoriented and trapped between Forty-ninth and Forty-eighth streets, Jacobus groped for shelter. His bloody hand found a large cardboard box, something that had once contained a television or a microwave oven and had been discarded on the curb. He broke the back of the heavy, soggy carton to form a makeshift roof and held it over his head until it soon became too heavy and his arms gave way. He leaned his head against a brick wall, exhausted, water streaming over him. He was so tired, so ready to give up. The puddled pavement beckoned to him: *Don't struggle anymore. Come lie down. Sleep.* The rain kept falling. Why did he continue to stand up? he asked himself.

A hand grabbed his sleeve.

"Hey, mister," a voice said, barely audible above the din of the rain's hiss.

Goddammit. Not a mugger. Not again.

"Get the hell out of here," said Jacobus.

"Sir, I'm the priest of this church," the voice hollered back. "I just thought you might want to come in and dry off until the rain stops."

"Ah, why the hell not?" Jacobus allowed himself to be hoisted up and ushered into the church by his elbow.

"I'm not a bum," said Jacobus.

"We're all equal in the eyes of God," said the priest.

"I'm not a bum," Jacobus repeated.

The priest sat him down on a wooden pew and said, "I'll try to find you a towel. And a bandage for that wound on your hand. It's bleeding pretty bad. I'll be back in a minute. Or would you prefer a blanket? Or maybe a bucket."

"Just a towel."

The priest's footsteps receded, the sharp clack of heels against the stone floor, a diminuendoing echo into the church's resonant ambience. The rain's relentless battering waves on the roof high above were remote, seemingly kept at bay by old ladies' whispered prayers, scattered about like the last dry leaves of autumn. Funereal organ music somewhere in the background meandered like flotsam in the East River.

The hard pew made Jacobus's back hurt and his drenched clothes were making him cold. His saturated flannel shirt emitted an odor reminiscent of New York City during the garbage workers' strike of the 1960s—just about the same time he had bought it.

The scented adorational candles flickering by the altar brought some relief, but they didn't prevent Jacobus from shivering uncontrollably. He should have swallowed his pride and accepted the blanket, he thought, cursing himself.

He closed his eyes, fighting delirium and fighting himself, but even his blindness could not block out his own stink, rancid from wet filth and sweat. He vowed he would not die a bum. His consciousness ebbed and flowed. The ivy returned, surrounding him. The eye of the Piccolino Strad mocked him. He forced himself to exert his internal will to survive the onslaught. He ripped at the ivy around his neck. Suddenly there came a momentary blaze of intense mental lucidity, as if his sight had returned. His mind raced faster than his comprehension. Family fame infamy fem do the right thing English-English Noda-sama granny grinny greeny I dream of Yumi with the leprechaun eyes have it. . . .

By the time the priest returned with the towel and bandage, Jacobus felt an unaccustomed sense of repose, especially in what was for him an alien environment.

"Thanks, Padre," Jacobus whispered.

"The name's McCawley, Father McCawley. And you?"

"Jacobus. Daniel Jacobus. Padre, think you could lead me to the confessional?"

Once seated in the confessional, Jacobus had no idea what to do. Am I supposed to push a button, or what? he thought. Some apparatus? He felt around the walls in vain. Claustrophobia for a blind man?

Just as he was about to abscond, a voice said, "Yes, my son."

Jacobus sat back down.

"I'm not your son, McCawley. I'm an atheist, and I'm not converting. I just wanted you to know that right off the bat."

"We're all children of God."

"Tell that to my parents in Auschwitz."

Jacobus was not by nature ecclesiastically inclined. His only concession to the possibility of a deity had been an acknowledgment that perhaps there was no other way to explain the genius of Mozart.

After a pause, the voice continued, "You take a jaundiced view of the church. You appear to be harboring a certain hostility . . . yet you've come to confess."

"I'm not here for absolution."

"Then what?"

"Actually, I just wanted to bounce a few ideas off you. This is all confidential, right?"

"Whatever you say here will be heard only by me and God."

"Fine. It's a deal, then. Even if there were a God, I don't suppose It would spill the beans."

Jacobus proceeded to explain the entire situation, how he suspected Yumi of being an accomplice in the theft of the Piccolino Stradivarius. How he was out to expose the "gonifs" at MAP. Jacobus finished with how he had been accosted the night before in almost the same spot that Father McCawley had encountered him tonight. That maybe the thug had been sent by the thief or, more likely, by someone at MAP.

"Why haven't you reported your assailant to the authorities?" asked the priest. "Maybe they could help you track down the bigger culprits you seek."

"You really think the cops will put out an all points bulletin to nab a voice?"

"But you drew such a comprehensive description of him from your brief contact. You've guessed his height, weight, age, possible ethnic background, level of education. Even his diet! I'd say the police had a lot to go on."

"As you just said, I *guessed* those things, and even if I'm right that reduces the number of suspects to about two million. Anyway, as I said, I don't want the cops involved at all.

"You see, Padre, I hadn't been sure about Yumi until, sitting there in the pew, I put two and two together. How everything with her had been slightly out of joint. And how something Dedubian had said didn't seem right. And the way Yumi talked. And what Goldbloom had said about family, doing the right thing, and music. About my theory of second-place Grimsley finishers."

The priest didn't interrupt, commenting only with an occasional *hmm* or *yes* or *ah*.

"Then it hit me that Dedubian had said something about Yumi's 'jade eyes, like a leprechaun,' or something like that. Japanese almost never have green eyes. Leprechauns, though, are from the British Isles. You see, Yumi's English is fluent, but I could tell from day one it was not American English. I didn't know what to make of it, I just thought it quaintly entertaining, until it dawned on me that it was English English. Yet English English hasn't been taught in Japanese schools for decades. So who could have taught her English English? Maybe the grandmother who had also first taught her the violin? Who was that grandmother who played the violin? Maybe the English girl who had won the silver medal at the 1931 Grimsley Competition? She didn't necessarily have to be a Shinagawa by blood if she had married a Japanese man. Maybe she could be scrawny little Kate Padgett. Maybe maybe maybe maybe."

"Ah, yes," said Father McCawley, "and so you wish to protect this Miss Shinagawa and this Padgett because you sympathize with them. But how certain are you? Are you sure your sympathies aren't swaying your judgment, my son?"

"How certain is your own faith?" asked Jacobus.

"Absolute and unshakable," said Father McCawley.

"Well, maybe I'm not as certain as that," said Jacobus. "But I'd be willing to lay you pretty good odds."

"That being the case, what's left? You understand why they've done what they've done. Like Mr. Noda-sama, they wish to make the world right again."

"That's more or less it, McCawley, and that's the same reason I'm out to screw MAP. But first, I've got to get Yumi back to Japan. Number one, if she stays here, she'll slip up and get caught."

"Inevitable. Also, if you yourself confront her here with your suspicions, she'll never betray her loyalty to her grandmother and you'll be stalemated."

"Good thinking, Padre. Hey, am I taking up too much of your time?"

"It's okay. I don't have too many customers at two in the morning."

"Good. Number two, then. If I follow her back to her home, I have an easier job convincing Grandma to return the violin, since Yumi will no longer be in a position of risk."

"And three," said Father McCawley, "if she's not in jail it sounds like she may turn out to be a hell of a fiddle player—just a figure of speech, my son. But what of this MAP business? I'd say you're on high moral ground in trying to save Miss Shinagawa from her fate, though legally . . . but fortunately I'm not required to speak legally. MAP, on the other hand . . ."

"McCawley, this is my one and only opportunity to disrupt MAP, to expose them for what they are—opportunistic, greedy, power-hungry child predators. My question is, can I do that once the irritant of the missing Strad is no longer part of the equation? I have to find other means to shatter their alliance, to turn them on each other. And I have to do it fast. I've got Grimsley and Lilburn rattled. Vander's no longer sure of Jablonski's teaching methods. Dedubian's not so easily shaken—as a violin dealer he's used to the abuse, plus he's got more of a conscience than the others. Rachel, Strella, Jablonski—they're still on the list. Those last two are the toughest nuts to crack. And I'll soon be the number-one suspect as far as the cops are concerned.

"So I've planted the seeds. Now I need the Miracle-Gro. Got any miracles up your sleeve, Padre?"

"Have you considered blackmail, perhaps?" asked Father McCawley.

Jacobus was floored. From the mouths of babes!

"Not that I condone such a thing, of course, but Mr. Grimsley, I think it was, didn't he mention that?"

"Yes, Padre, I think you've hit upon something."

"Maybe we should call it a night, then."

"Yeah, sure." Jacobus began to stand up to leave, but then he sat back down. "There's just one more thing . . . if you've got the time."

"What is it, my son?"

Jacobus struggled for words he never would have expected to utter.

"Don't worry," said the priest. "Go on."

"You see, Padre, I'm used to blackness on the outside. But at the moment. At the moment, it's blackness on the inside that . . . that . . ." No, he wouldn't go on. He couldn't. This wasn't for another human's knowledge. He closed his eyes.

"Anyone seeking the truth deserves to see the light at the end of the tunnel," said the priest, finally.

"Even an atheist, Padre?"

"Anyone."

"Well, thank you for this little convocation. I think I'll go now," said Jacobus.

"Do you need help to the door?"

"No. Thanks." He paused. "Er, does one leave a tip for this sort of thing?"

"There's a donation box by the exit. Good night."

Jacobus was almost dry as he left the church, and the rain had almost stopped. Within a few blocks, though, the downpour resumed, and by the time he arrived at his hotel he was again waterlogged.

As he sat in his chair, the dampness on his skin chilled him to the bone and made him feel like a moldy potato. He reached for his pack of Camels in his pocket, but they had the consistency of day-old oatmeal. Damn, there's so much I have to accomplish, he thought. So much at cross-purposes. Is it possible?

Jacobus spent the endless hours of the night thinking and brooding. The more he understood, the more his despondence returned.

How to persuade—coerce?—Yumi to bolt for Japan. That's essential, he thought. If she knows for certain that I suspect her, she'll never flee, because she'll know that she's just leading me back to Grandma.

But if she's *not* sure, though, if she's only *guessing*, she might just haul her ass out of here in order to escape further suspicion. But she needs an alibi. What alibi can I give her as a cover to pack up and leave?

An idea had occurred to Jacobus that sickened him, and though he spent a long time in the dark trying to think of a better one, he couldn't. It made sense, more than any other.

Jacobus heard the bed in the next room start to squeak rhythmically. Soon he could hear its headboard banging on the other side of the wall. He reached into the drawer of his bed table and pulled out a Gideon Bible. He flung it against the wall. The banging stopped.

His idea would protect Yumi, get her out of harm's way, encourage her to beat it out of here, and lead him to Grandma.

I'll give you a week or two head start, he thought. I won't make it look too obvious or you'll guess what I'm doing and stay here. Then I'll follow your tracks. And to convince you to go back to Japan all I have to do is just be myself—more or less.

I'll only have to be a bum a little while longer.

You'll go back if you hate me.

TWENTY-ONE

Yumi called out Nathaniel's name, and called it a second time, both without reply. He must have left the apartment before dawn. She looked at the clock. Still almost two hours before he would return to take her to Jacobus, but it was already hot.

The apartment's one bathroom, unlike the *furo* in her home in Japan, was a sorry substitute for soul-cleansing. The floor and walls were graying hexagonal tiles, smaller on the floor, larger on the walls. Grout was missing here and there, replaced by mildew. The one small window had been painted over, most recently with white paint, some of which had dripped down the tiled wall before drying. As the window was unopenable, the paint on the ceiling had bubbled and peeled from years of accumulated moisture. There was an old stained porcelain tub that had once been white. The toilet ran and the sink dripped. The one light fixture in the room, a high-watt bulb hanging from the ceiling, cast a glaring yellow light and managed to make everything even more vulgar. In other words, a typical New York City bathroom.

How can they live like this? Yumi asked herself. How can they ever be clean?

But I need a bath, Yumi said to herself. It was more than a need. It was a compulsion, a necessity. She needed to clean the filth off her. The filth from the sweltering city, from the turmoil, from her soul. She had awoken licking perspiration off her upper lip, the early morning sun streaming in on her face. Like the infernal presence of the Piccolino Stradivarius, the oppressive heat hovered relentlessly over her.

Repulsed by the tub, she decided on a shower. However, the showerhead, which looked like the end of an old tin watering can, only intermittently vomited forth bursts of scalding hot water. Developing a new plan, she soaped her body while the shower dripped, then frantically scrubbed and rinsed herself whenever a spasm of water attacked her.

After becoming relatively clean, Yumi scrubbed the tub as well as she could, using powdered cleanser and a brush she found behind the toilet. She couldn't totally remove the rust-and-green bruise of a stain around the drain, but when the tub looked decent enough she turned on the tap as hot as possible. The faucet acquiesced only spittingly, so she wrapped herself in Nathaniel's robin's-egg blue terry cloth robe that was hanging on a hook and walked down the hallway with the hem of the huge robe trailing behind her like the train on a wedding gown. The corridor's old runner was almost threadbare in the middle and hadn't been vacuumed for a long time. She could hardly distinguish the edges of the wooden molding on the walls for all the coats of paint that covered them.

The kitchen was small but well equipped, designed by someone who knew how to cook: lots of gadgets, marble counters, and very neat and clean. Yumi opened the refrigerator. It was filled to capacity with glass jars and bottles, food in plastic containers or wrap. Food from every country in the world, it seemed: tandoori paste, Spanish capers, tofu, Vietnamese fish sauce, Tabasco sauce, a wedge of Camembert, a chunk of Gorgonzola, her congealing pastrami sandwich, kiwi fruit.

She removed the tofu from the culinary United Nations. Finding an appropriate knife among a large selection neatly arrayed in a wooden rack, she cut the tofu into small cubes on the butcher block table, and then, pleasantly surprised to find a wok among the assortment of pans hanging on the wall, quickly sautéed the tofu in a little peanut oil, which she found among many other varieties in a cupboard. While it cooked, a more thorough investigation of the refrigerator revealed soy sauce, rice vinegar, and a scallion. She added those ingredients in familiar proportions to the tofu, which was by this time turning an appealing golden brown.

Her breakfast satisfied not only what little hunger she had—her stomach still hadn't forgotten its meal at the deli—but also her growing need to feel reconnected to her home, her family in Japan, herself. Her sense of uneasiness began to dissipate.

Yumi returned to the bath, finding the tub still not yet full but full enough. The room was dense with steam, fogging the mirror opposite the tub. She took off the robe, hung it back on the hook, and stepped into the tub, immersing herself into the steaming water slowly but without hesitation. Slender though she was, water nonetheless lapped over the sides onto the floor, at which point she remembered that Western bathrooms don't have a floor drain. She would mop up later but decided not to worry about it for the moment.

She would not allow herself to be overwhelmed by anxiety. She must not. If she were to succeed for her family she had to be the master of her feelings. She needed to arrange her thoughts and prepare for challenges. Thankfully, Grandmother has taught me how to live with gaijin, she thought, though to understand Westerners seemed impossible. She slid down farther into the tub so that the water came all the way up to her chin, cranking her neck to avoid the obtrusive faucet. Other than her head, only the very top of her knees broke the surface. She would not think about the past or the future. She would concentrate only on the moment.

She massaged her arms and legs, pressing her fingers and thumbs deeply into taut muscles to loosen the tension. Grandmother had always encouraged her athleticism. Grandmother herself had been deprived of games as a little girl long ago in order to practice the violin.

Yumi was pleased that her body was both feminine and athletic. She was a little less than average height for Americans but was taller than the few friends she had at home in Japan, and her breasts, cupping them in her hands, were somewhat larger than the other girls'. Grandmother's genes, she thought. As Grandmother had said to her when she had begun to develop, "Never be embarrassed about your body. After all, it would be difficult to play the violin without one."

Yumi closed her eyes and allowed her thoughts to float as randomly as her long black hair, which spread in intricate patterns on the surface of the water. As her skin reddened from the heat, tension and anxiety slipped away from her body, permitting her mind to wander freely. She thought about the simple pleasures of her home in Nishiyama—a real bath, the quietness, the sounds of birds and rain, the music.

The music. From the day she was born she was part of the music. It had always been so natural. First her studies with Grandmother and Mother. Then, Furukawa-sensei. Now Mr. Jacobus. But, she wondered, was it truly a natural progression? Had her training always and only been part of a larger purpose?

The stress of the past week had been enormous. Jacobus loomed in her thoughts. He frightened her with his erratic, almost violent behavior. More so with his perception. She sensed that he knew her with the absolute thoroughness he knew music.

She recalled the moment she had lost her balance and fell on him in the elevator. Though embarrassed at her own clumsiness, her physical contact with him seemed to loosen a barrier that she had considered impenetrable. Only hours before she had touched him for the first time outside the Vanders' apartment building. That touch had been tentative. Except for the wild swing he took at her, mistaking her for the doorman, which had come disconcertingly close to her nose, he had seemed so vulnerable.

The story Nathaniel had told her about their trio certainly moved her, but what affected her most was how Jacobus had made Kamryn Vander smile. The smile, she had seen, was not just Kamryn's reaction to Jacobus being funny—a revelation in itself—but of Kamryn having learned something about playing the violin in a few short moments that until then had been unattainable. Jacobus had made Yumi smile too, and it made her ponder what suffering he had endured to have buried his joy so deeply.

Were his outbursts intended to disguise the vulnerability she had fleetingly glimpsed? Yumi wondered what might have been the cause. What was Jacobus like when he was young? When he was nineteen, like her? She closed her eyes to imagine it. His unkempt hair once black and curly. His skin, white. Muscular? No, probably skinny, but eager, enthusiastic. She smiled. She never thought about Furukawa-sensei this way. He had always been old, and though he thought he knew her, he could not see into her like Jacobus. Other students had told her they had "secret thoughts" about their teachers, but she couldn't imagine such a thing with Furukawa-sensei. She had related this to Grandmother—she would never have discussed such a thing with Mother. Grandmother had smiled and told her she was free to think however she wanted but to understand there was a difference between thoughts and behavior. Yumi turned her thoughts back to her new teacher.

And what about his eyes? She couldn't see them through his dark glasses. Brown? Gray? Blue? No. They would be green. Unusual, penetrating. She was sure that his eyes were green, like hers. In Japan, they had teased her because of the green eyes she had inherited from Grandmother. They would imitate the whine of a cat and run away, laughing—but she felt power in her green eyes.

Yumi arched her head and back so that she was almost floating in the hot water. Young Daniel Jacobus. Yes—curly hair, white skin, skinny. Green eyes. The young Daniel Jacobus could see her with his green eyes. For a moment his eyes smiled. Then they changed. Vulnerable. Penetrating.

As the image began to coalesce—to become whole with nose, mouth, arms, legs—Yumi slid her hand from her breast, placing it gently between her thighs, indulging herself in her fantasy. The image began to have its own energy, responding to her. She gazed through half-open eyelids through the fog at the mirror, dripping with condensation. She could barely make out the blurred reflection of her own form; the second one, the imagined one, seemed almost as real.

She heard a delicate click in the water next to her cheek. Turning her head, she saw it was a cockroach that had fallen from the ceiling. Its legs flailed futilely as it struggled to swim on its back.

Yumi watched with fascination, not moving. Would her new bath partner survive this hot water? Would it sink and die?

Sitting up to get a better view created turbulence in the water, enabling the cockroach to right itself. Now it swam with a coordinated effort toward the side of the tub, negotiating the streams of water cascading from Yumi's torso. She observed the cockroach's unsuccessful attempts to climb the two inches from the water level to the top of the tub, not interfering as it slid back down, over and over.

Finally the cockroach stopped moving. Yumi cupped her hand under it and lifted it out of the tub, placing it in a small puddle on the bathroom floor, leaving it to its own fate.

She took a black washcloth off the chrome towel rack, soaked it in the hot water, and covered her face with it. Its warmth comforted her as she pressed it against her closed eyes, leaning back again in the tub.

What a mystery Jacobus was, Yumi thought. On the surface so hard, so dominating. But underneath, something so giving. Obviously Furukawa and Nathaniel sensed that as well. And Goldbloom. And even the waitress last night, whose words to Jacobus were so harsh, had eyes filled with affection for him.

Yumi tried unsuccessfully to coax her fantasy to return.

The bath wasn't relaxing her anymore and the now tepid water was reclaiming its heat from her body. Yumi stood up, slowly, to avoid dizziness. Even after having washed the tub, the water hadn't been clean enough. So she pulled the rubber plug on the rusty chain, let the water choke its way down the drain, and took another shower, this time scrubbing her entire body so vigorously with the washcloth that her skin was streaked with red. She rinsed herself one last time.

Trying to dry herself in the steamy bathroom, compounded by the city's humid summer heat, proved to be uncomfortable and futile, so she took a fresh towel and returned, naked, to the airy bedroom. On the way out she noticed that the cockroach had disappeared from its puddle.

Yumi dressed, ready to explore the rest of the apartment now, opening doors as she wandered. The first room she entered took her by surprise. It was literally a library of recordings, floor to ceiling, all four walls covered, highly organized. On one wall were records—LPs, 45s, 78s, even ancient wax cylinders. On another wall were tapes—cassettes, reel-to-reels of all sizes, even, as she examined them, something called eight-track cartridges, which she had never seen before. A third wall, the neatest for its uniformity, had shelves of CDs, the most recent technological breakthrough. She slid her finger along the CDs, alphabetically labeled with every imaginable category of music—Australian Aboriginal,

Blues, Broadway, Classical, Folk, Gamelan, Gospel, Jazz, Medieval, Renaissance, on and on.

Arranged on the fourth wall was the listening equipment—receivers, amplifiers, speakers, disc changers, tape recorders, equipment she couldn't identify, all looking very highly advanced. In one corner, as if ostracized, on a mahogany cabinet stood an ancient acoustic RCA turntable with a crank and huge horn.

The next room Yumi entered was equally surprising. Obviously Nathaniel's bedroom, as the huge unmade bed unmistakably advertised, this room was as messy as the others were neat. Magazines and books lay opened and unopened on the bed, the floor, the dresser, all intermingled with assorted items of clothing.

A large bowl of what appeared to be the remains of strawberry ice cream sat on the night table, along with an empty bag of cheese puffs and a remote control device. At the foot of the bed was a television with a screen as big as some of those she had seen at the Akihabara electronics shops in Tokyo.

But the striking feature of the room was the photographs of famous musicians from every point on the compass of the world of music, signed, framed, and lining the walls. As she wandered around the room, trying to avoid tripping on the scattered landscape, Yumi recognized some of the faces and names immediately: Isaac Stern, Leonard Bernstein, Jascha Heifetz, Slava Rostropovich, Vladimir Horowitz, Aaron Copland. There were many faces, and names too, that she didn't recognize—Aretha Franklin, Oscar Peterson, Joe Venuti, Richard Rodgers, Gheorghe Zamfir. One photo said: *Hey, Nate. Stay cool. The Velvet Fog, Mel Tormé.*

What was a velvet fog? Yumi wondered. A line from haiku, perhaps.

One more room to go. Yumi tentatively turned the knob. This room was similar to the record library, except instead of recordings there were books. Music theory and composition, music history, biography, reference books, music dictionaries, music textbooks, a complete *Grove's Dictionary.* New books, ancient books, leather-bound and paperback, in English, German, French, Italian.

In the middle of the room was a pine desk, actually a plain table like the one in her bedroom. On the table was a clear glass paperweight on a stack of papers.

Yumi went to the table to inspect further. On top of the pile was another note from Nathaniel.

Dear Yumi,
Thought you might find this. You know how you were asking me yesterday about Jake? This book isn't just about violin playing. Hope you find it interesting.

Nathaniel

Yumi picked up the typed manuscript. The cover page read "Violin Lessons: A Practical Guide to Violin Playing" by Daniel Jacobus, as told to Nathaniel Williams. It was dated 1966. Yumi sat down at the table, turned over the stapled page, and began to read. It was only a few hand-written pages long.

Music, of all the arts, has the greatest power to elevate the soul and the mind. This may sound like a rash statement, but consider this: One may stand before a great painting, a Rembrandt or Picasso, and admire the skill of the artist, the inspiration and beauty of the work itself.

But when was the last time you stood before a painting and were moved to tears, anger, excitement, depression, sadness, or exaltation beyond reasonable expectation? When has a painting received a standing ovation?

Music has this power, greater, I believe, than do the visual arts. Why? I don't know. Why, or how, certain combinations of frequencies, made audible at certain volume, with certain tone quality, resonate within the human psyche to create such a moving effect is a mystery. That they have this effect, however, is undeniable and is one reason why armies, kings, and churches have used music for their formidable purposes for thousands of years.

Perhaps the power of music is greatest because it is temporal rather than spatial, meaning that once it is heard it is gone forever. The sense of gain from the experience of having heard the music is accompanied by a sense of loss. It is over, never to return. Perhaps that reminds us of our own mortality. Perhaps not.

Nevertheless, when I listen to a late Beethoven string quartet or Stravinsky's Rites of Spring *I am struck to the core of my being where resides something more elemental than I myself can comprehend. When I listen to the Bach B-Minor Mass I am moved to contemplate the Infinite not because of the religious text but simply because the combination of frequencies, which Bach indicated as a series of dots on lined paper two hundred fifty years ago in a country thousands of miles away, compels me to do so. It finds something in me I cannot find myself. Obviously, I have not been alone in this experience.*

The manuscript went on to ask basic questions about interpretation and offer a fundamental approach to violin playing: "... there are nevertheless common traits that all great violinists seem to share, which might be summarized with the statement: Ultimate technical control leads to ultimate musical freedom."

It ended with the following statement: "Expressive communication is the goal of playing the violin. It is something that must be learned but cannot really be taught. It must be learned using the same tool, though utilized in an infinitely more trained and sophisticated way, with which the listener is able to assimilate these unique vibrations: one's ears. If a musician listens carefully enough, the fingers will find a way."

Yumi turned to the next page. It was headed "Lesson One" but was otherwise blank, as were the remaining pages.

Closing the manuscript, Yumi contemplated with eyes shut, hands folded on her lap, in the peaceful silence of the room. Mr. Jacobus was not, after all, what Americans harshly referred to as a bum. That was his façade, she could see now. His short tome was inspirational. After some minutes, she inspected Nathaniel's biographies wall. Scanning for *B*, she selected the thickest biography of Johann Sebastian Bach, returned to the table, and began to search for sarabanda, with an *a*. After that, she went back to her bedroom and her violin, and began to practice.

TWENTY-TWO

"We should've walked. We could've spit from the hotel to Strella's office," Jacobus muttered to Yumi. Nathaniel had dropped Yumi off at Jacobus's hotel a half hour earlier. Now he and Yumi nudged through a hot, becalmed sea of traffic, cars honking like a herd of rutting walruses.

"Shit! This cab isn't even air-conditioned! It's stifling in here!" Jacobus ranted. "At least roll down the windows!" he yelled through the Plexiglas barrier to the driver.

"Hey, buddy, they *are* rolled down," hollered the cabbie. "If you don't like it, why don't you and your fucking Oriental Seeing Eye dog get out and fucking walk?"

Yumi put her hand on Jacobus's arm. "It's all right," she said. "Perhaps if you're too hot I can help you take off your jacket."

"No! Jesus, why did I agree to do this?" said Jacobus.

Yumi looked out the window, away from Jacobus.

"Shit," he finally said in a more reasonable tone.

"Perhaps you can tell me about Anthony Strella," said Yumi. She needed to get him out of his funk, wherever it had originated.

"I was only introduced to him once," Jacobus said, "very briefly, at some crap wine and cheese reception. Years ago. We shook hands, or I should say I shook his hand. No strength in his handshake—none—and he pulled his hand away very quickly, too quickly, so either he was repulsed by the fact that I'm blind—oh, yes, that does happen—or he was afraid his hand would get bruised. Either way, definite weakness of character. Expensive cologne, far too much, trying too hard to impress people, maybe, probably got some real insecurities somewhere. Pretty tall—self-conscious about it."

"You could tell his height from his handshake?" asked Yumi.

"Downward angle of his hand when we shook, if you could call it that. Easy to figure—six three or four, but from the smell of his breath—mouthwashed—hitting my forehead I also could tell he was slouched over. Seems to need to show off, prove to himself he's worth the space he occupies on this earth, but maybe insecure. Deep down insecure. Overly cool and collected. Maybe that's why, as an agent, he surrounds himself with people more talented than himself—showing off his jewelry."

The taxi came to an abrupt stop.

"Thank God we're here," said Jacobus.

"You heard his emergency brake?" asked Yumi.

"Trying to think like me, huh?"

"Four seventy-five," said the driver.

Jacobus pulled five bills from his wallet, all singles.

"And that is so you know how much you are paying the driver," said Yumi.

"No shit."

As they got out, he handed the bills to the driver. "Thanks for nothing."

"Fuck you, buddy." The cab screeched away.

Yumi took Jacobus's arm and entered the new office tower. They took the elevator to the twenty-first floor and entered the overly air-conditioned outer office of Zenith Concert Artists, the address of Anthony Strella's "nine-to-five" job. The bright white and metallic office space was chic and expensive with large works of ostentatious contemporary art adorning the walls. It was entirely unappealing to Yumi. The receptionist, just one more matching accessory, smiled.

Before she could say hello, however, the door to Zenith's inner office opened and out whooshed Cynthia Vander. Looking straight ahead with a pretense of a smile, she ignored Yumi and the others as she swept out of the outer office.

"Good-bye, Mrs. Vander. Have a nice day," said the receptionist.

"Oh, dear!" Yumi said quietly to Jacobus. "Kamryn's mother!"

Jacobus chuckled. He whispered, "Yumi, would you say Mrs. Vander's hairdo is slightly disheveled, her makeup is smudged, and her dress needs some adjusting?"

"Yes," said Yumi. "How do you know?"

"Because under that scent of cheap perfume and hair spray, I do detect a trace of male cologne, sweat, and, how shall we say, adult relations."

"Have a seat, please," said the receptionist to Jacobus and Yumi. "Mr. Strella will see you . . . momentarily."

Momentarily they were buzzed in to Strella's office.

"Ah! Mr. Jacobus. So good to see you again." As he shook Jacobus's hand, Yumi noticed, as Mr. Jacobus had related, that contact was quickly made and broken. Yumi had no trouble smelling the cologne.

"And is this your new student, Miss Shinagawa, who Mr. Williams mentioned?"

As Yumi extended her hand, Jacobus said, "Yeah, this is Miss Shinagawa. Now tell me about these fish, Strella."

"Surely you can't *smell* them!"

"No, Strella Fella, I'm not talking about Cynthia Vander. That's another kinda fisha smella."

Strella guffawed. "Then how *can* you know, if I may ask?"

In a wall-sized aquarium behind Strella's desk hundreds of brightly colored tropical fish darted in all directions through fake sunken pirate ships, plastic seaweed, and ceramic rock caves, ignorant of the artificial world in which they were manipulated and displayed.

"Whirring of the pump. Bubbling of the water. Didn't think your cappuccino foamer would be running on 'continuous.'"

"Marvelous, Mr. Jacobus. Marvelous. But I must say the foamer *is* indispensable."

"Don't insult me, Strella. There's nothing marvelous about it. Anybody with his eyes closed knows what a fish tank motor sounds like. I'd think even you would be able to figure that one out, Strella . . . from your lofty perch."

"Clever, Mr. Jacobus. And how do *you* like my little aquarium, Miss Shinagawa?"

She had indeed become mesmerized by the continuous and unpredictable flashes of color.

"I don't imagine fish feel happiness, Mr. Strella, but they seem to survive harmoniously."

"They do create quite a kaleidoscope, don't they? But harmony, I'm not so sure. Watch this."

Strella turned his back to her and sprinkled a small handful of food into the tank. As the flakes touched the water, a blur of color simultaneously swarmed to one spot, gorging on whatever food each fish could rip away from its competitors.

Seconds later they began to disperse. Strella turned to face Yumi and Jacobus, wearing a bright white smile. This was the first time Yumi had met Anthony Strella, though like every classical musician she had heard stories of his domination of the industry. He was indeed tall, as Jacobus had guessed—not guessed, determined—and once was thin as well, but success had begun to go to his stomach. His coiffed hair—glossy, silvery-tinted around the ears, combed straight back—combined with facial features congregating right in the middle of his face to give him a rodentlike appearance that was incongruous for someone so tall.

To Yumi, he looked like someone who had mastered the appearance of power. She wondered, though, whether all the trappings were a manifestation of strength, or were they just camouflage? The opposite of Mr. Jacobus, whose appearance was inconspicuous at best, but whose power seemed limitless.

"As sorry as I am to have kept you waiting, it's worse if I keep *them* waiting," Strella said, nodding to the tank. "If I'm a minute late for feeding time, they start eating each other." He chuckled.

"But enough about fish," said Strella, sitting in his CEO swivel chair behind his teak desk. "Tell me more about Miss Shinagawa, Jacobus. She's cute. Very cute. Plays well?"

"She plays very well, Mr. Strella."

"Anthony, please. We're all friends here."

"Yes, Anthony. In fact, she plays quite a bit better than some of the elementary school children you manage that MAP calls 'artists.'"

Strella put both hands up in surrender. "No argument there. No argument there, Mr. Jacobus. May I call you Daniel?"

"Mr. Jacobus is fine for now, thank you."

"Well, Mr. Jacobus, I'm sure Miss Shinagawa here is every bit the musician you say she is, but these days youth is in. Not my decision. Really it isn't."

Yumi felt like a commodity up for barter. Gazing at the aquarium, she recalled the tuna auction she had witnessed as a little girl at the Tsukiji fish market in Tokyo. She now felt like a chunk of frozen tuna being carted around on a motorized dolly. Choice sushi grade! Two thousand yen a kilo! I'll bid three!

"You mean to tell me—Anthony—that nineteen is no longer youth?"

"I'm afraid that's the long and short of it—or the young and old of it. These days the public wants cute, especially girls, as long as they can play, of course. I get calls from the symphony orchestra managers every day, *every day,* asking for the youngest artists on my roster. They tell me those kids are the biggest draw, and they're right. They're the only ones who'll pack the houses, except for Perlman or Yo-Yo. And since the younger ones have smaller fees, let's say five or six thousand for a pair of weekend performances, the orchestras net out a lot better. Bigger house, smaller fee, orchestra stays in business. Simple equation. I'm just trying to do my share. Nothing wrong with that, is there?"

"No, no. Nothing wrong with that. Anthony. Except that, number one, finer artists who might be a little older get shut out of careers. Number two, audiences are deprived of *truly* great performances. Number three, those poor kids are burned out physically and emotionally by the time they're twenty. Number four, orchestras are using a false premise to justify their existence. Number five—"

"Okay, okay, Mr. Jacobus. I'll concede there are two sides to this coin. But let me assure you that MAP's intentions are only the best."

"What's your percentage, then?"

"I take no fee for my work with MAP. MAP, as you may know, is a nonprofit and the work my colleagues and I do for it is strictly voluntary."

"So MAP's books are a matter of public record?" asked Jacobus.

A bottom-feeding catfishlike creature attached its suction-cupped mouth to the tank and vacuumed its whiskered way along a random route up the glass. Another fish with bulging eyes and a big mouth poked its head out of a sunken blue pirate ship.

"That's for the accountants to determine," Strella replied. "My job is to use my estimable talents as an agent to enable MAP's artists to be able to compete in a very tough market."

"Well, that's very interesting. Because in this year's *Musical America Directory,* I read—yes, I read, it comes in Braille—MAP's artist roster. It seems MAP has a corner on the market for cuddly instrumentalists under fifteen, who you say are being lusted after by all these orchestras. If this were a business other than music—"

"Mr. Jacobus, you're not the first one who's ever tried to insult my integrity, but—"

"I'm just pointing out what I've observed. Anthony. We're still friends, right? I can still call you Anthony, right?"

"Of course."

"So, Anthony, you dress the little kids up in cute red dresses, put their smiling face and a teddy bear on a CD, push 'em out onto a stage and make the audience think they're part of some 'historic' event. Use them until they're over the hill at twenty, then dump them in favor of the next litter of puppies from the puppy farm, already spayed, complete with shots, ready for the Christmas tree."

"Mr. Jacobus," said Strella. "Mr. Jacobus, it just so happens that we—yes, we, that means you too—are in a cutthroat business. If you think you can rattle me, you are quite mistaken. Let me tell you some facts. Not opinion. Facts."

The phone rang.

"Do you mind?" he asked Jacobus.

"Go right ahead. Anthony."

"Strella," he said into the phone.

Except for the whirring and bubbling from the aquarium, and an occasional car honking from far, far below, there were several minutes of silence in the office while the person at the other end of the line talked. Yumi felt trapped, like a fish in the tank. Her presence here seemed purposeless.

Finally Strella said into the phone, "No, he's not over the hill. He may not be at his peak, but he's still a major artist, and yes, he can still play the Brahms D Minor. He's played it more times than you've jerked off, believe it or not."

More silence, but not as long. Strella said, "I don't care what Maestro thinks. Zenith's contract is with the Symphony, not with Maestro. You want your pick from the A-list for your orchestra's pension fund concert, you take Kristof now, and you tell Maestro what to do with his baton. Understood?" He hung up.

"You see, Mr. Jacobus, it's not just puppies I protect. Sometimes it's the toothless old mongrels as well."

"You were going to tell me some 'facts.' "

"Thank you for reminding me. Fact number one, Mr. Jacobus: Classical record sales were down last year twenty percent. Twenty percent. Nevertheless, recordings of artists under age twenty doubled their market share of those recordings in that period.

"Fact number two: Symphony orchestras, which are in the red year after year, would go out of business if they couldn't book less expensive, ticket-selling, hall-filling, good-looking young artists.

"Fact number three: Without those recordings and those concerts, you older orchestra musician types would be out of a job. As it is, you guys make a fraction of what MAP can get for its teenage clients, so who's fooling who, Mr. Jacobus? And a lot of recording engineers would be out of work too and, for that matter, so would a lot of you high-powered teachers."

"And a concert agent or two, perhaps," added Jacobus.

"I'm simply stating facts, Mr. Jacobus. Fact number four is, I'm not forcing these youngsters to take the money. Their parents want them to have the opportunity. Most of the young artists on my roster are quite happy with the chance of being paid over a hundred grand a year to perform with major orchestras, which is something, I understand, you never had the opportunity to do."

Yumi tried to concentrate on a pair of yellow-and-black-striped fish whose large heads didn't seem to have any bodies. They were sucking something off a ceramic deep-sea diver that had bubbles coming out of it. She yearned for their oblivion.

"Now, what exactly was it you came here to talk to me about?" asked Strella. "The police have already interrogated me and, as you can hear, my phone rings quite often."

"You were in the Green Room after Kamryn Vander's recital."

"I was. I've never denied it."

"Thank you, Anthony. You are certainly an honest man. Did the police ask if you noticed anyone go from the reception into the room with the Piccolino Strad during the course of the evening?"

"Of course they did."

"And did you?"

"I did not," Strella said. "It was extremely crowded. People were coming and going. I'm not a gatekeeper."

"Was there any point during the reception," asked Jacobus, "when your back might have been turned from the door leading to the adjoining room, making it possible for someone to have gone into that room without you noticing?"

"Of course it's possible. In fact it's highly likely that's exactly what happened. What are you driving at?"

"Well, Anthony," Jacobus said, folding his hands, "to be successful in your line of business you've got to be a serious student of human nature, right? And whether we agree on things or not—and you have brought up some interesting points—there's no doubt that you're considered tops in your field, right?"

Strella put his elbows on the teak desk and leaned forward.

"So," continued Jacobus, "if there was anyone in the Green Room astute enough to have an inkling of who might have been involved in stealing that violin, it's you.

"Tell me, Anthony, of all the people—let's just say people you know well—in the Green Room, what one person might have been capable of doing it? Not necessarily the one who actually removed the violin, but the one who may be the mastermind behind it."

Yumi looked carefully at Jacobus, recalling his initial belief that nobody from MAP was involved with the theft. She said, "But Mr. Jacobus, weren't you saying—"

"Please don't interrupt, Yumi."

Strella sat back in his chair.

"I'm sorry to disappoint you, Mr. Jacobus," he said in a bored and dismissive tone, "but as far as I'm concerned it's highly unlikely that anyone, anyone I know, had anything whatsoever to do with the theft."

"Well put, Anthony. Well put. Highly unlikely. Highly unlikely perhaps, but not impossible! After all, how many convicted murderers do you read about in the papers where the neighbors say they just couldn't believe good old Billy Bob could do such a thing?"

"True. True."

"So let's say, pure conjecture, for a moment that someone you know did the dastardly deed. If you *had* to choose one person, which one would it have been? Surely at some point someone must have seemed suspicious to you. Dedubian, perhaps? Jablonski? Rachel Lewison?"

Strella drummed his fingers on the desk. Suddenly he smacked it with both palms, startling the fish, which silently exploded from their monotonous, conditioned paths.

"You!"

"Me?" asked Jacobus.

"Yeah, you! Lilburn saw you there. Victoria saw you there. I saw you there! Robison even escorted you into the room with the Strad. Are you telling me that was your twin brother?"

"No, Anthony," said Jacobus. "I have to confess. It wasn't my twin brother."

"Aha! So it was you!"

"No. It was my twin sister. I'll be sure to notify the authorities to slap the cuffs on her—by the way, is she under contract with Zenith also?"

"Touché, Mr. Jacobus!"

"Now where were we in our hypothetical discussion?" pursued Jacobus.

"Are we still playing that game? Okay, Vander, I suppose," said Strella, calmly inspecting his manicured fingernails.

"Really? Kamryn Vander?" asked Jacobus. "My, my. She *is* precocious for a nine-year-old, but—"

"Not Kamryn, Jacobus. The mother, Cynthia. Jesus, what a bitch," he said with a chuckle.

"Ah, yes! Cynthia Vander!" said Jacobus. "But didn't she just flop out of your fish tank a few minutes ago?"

"So what? I have a lot of clients' mothers come for . . . consultations."

"You know," Jacobus exclaimed, "I hadn't even considered her as a possibility. So you think Mrs. Vander had something to do with the theft. Hmm. And why is that?"

"Don't put words into my mouth, Mr. Jacobus. You want to play a little game and you ask who could have, *could* have. All hypothetical, but you should see her around that kid. She treats me like I'm the enemy, some sort of child molester. But she's the one who treats the kid like shit. All I want to do is make some money for them. Okay, okay. For me too. And I *have* made money for them. Lots of it. You think she would let me make a suggestion once in a while, since I like to believe I know this business pretty well—like what dress she should wear when she performs. Stop laughing, those things are important. This is the entertainment industry, Mr. Jacobus. Music is nice, but it's secondary. Success is what's important and MAP has made that kid into a success, but you'd never know it by the way I'm treated. Vander the Viper. Only listens to what that other serpent has to say."

"Other serpent?" asked Jacobus.

"Jablonski. Miss J. I tell you, between the two of them it's a snake pit."

Strella chuckled at his own little joke.

"You should've heard Miss J's language when the violin was stolen! Would've made a longshoreman blush."

Yumi was astonished that Strella would talk about these people with such loathing in front of her, a stranger.

Strella continued. "Mr. Jacobus, you want a scenario? Try this on for size. The two of them are in on it together. Yeah, now wouldn't that be something?" He had become animated, snapping his fingers.

"They arrange to have the violin stolen so that the kid could get her hands on it after the Grimsley business is over, and that way Jablonski is in good with Vander, whose husband—ex-husband, I should say—has had to fork over millions in alimony. Maybe the two of them even get it on together. Who knows?"

"Ingenious, Anthony. I never would have suspected either one of them," said Jacobus. "I'll have to check out that angle."

Yumi began to say something but then stopped. Mr. Jacobus's behavior was too alien. She was lost.

"Hey, I told you it was a snake pit," Strella said. "And just between you and me, I've heard better playing than that kid's too."

"Really?" asked Jacobus.

"Yeah, especially from the Asian kids these days. They have an unbelievable work ethic, you know. When you and I were kids it was Jewish boys, right? Where have *they* gone now, huh? But these Asians! Yo-Yo Ma, Jimmy Lin, Midori. Those are *really* great artists. And good people.

"Take your student here. Japanese. Beautiful. Green eyes too! Probably has the work ethic, right? A little too old for MAP, but if you play well enough, maybe Zenith . . . Hey, think you could play something for me?"

"I don't think so, thank you," said Yumi, trying to smile politely. I would rather remain invisible, and inaudible, until I understand where I am, she thought.

Jacobus spoke up. "As your teacher, Yumi, I think it would be an important step in your career for Mr. Strella to hear you play, and he is always looking for new talent. I'm sure Anthony understands that you haven't prepared for this as an audition or have had a chance to warm up."

"Certainly, certainly. Exactly," Strella chimed in. "Just a chance to hear you. Informal. Break the ice, so to speak."

"But Mr. Jacobus," Yumi began to protest. Could it be conceivable the two of them had actually planned this scenario?

"Yumi, the last movement of the 'Devil's Trill.'" Jacobus's voice was harsh and threatening. "Unless you need the Piccolino to play on."

Yumi looked at Jacobus for a long time. Nothing that entered her mind was positive. Finally she opened her case, rosined her bow, and tuned her violin.

"Don't worry," said Jacobus. For that one moment his voice was almost gentle.

With currents of doubt and uncertainty swirling around her, Yumi sought stability and direction in the fixed star of her music. She began to play. Though revolted by the circumstances, she tried to focus on performing with conviction and skill but was not particularly pleased with the result.

"Brava! Brava!" said Strella, who stood up, applauding, as Yumi finished.

"What a find! Brava! Miss Shinagawa, may I call you Yumi? Yumi, I want you to think about this very seriously. I can't promise you anything this year because the Zenith roster is already full, but if you agree to allow me to represent you . . ."

Is this why Mr. Jacobus told me to bring my violin? Yumi wondered. Has he been trying to get Strella to help me begin a career? Is this how it's done?

"Anthony," said Jacobus, "I don't know about this."

"Okay, okay. I'll try to get you ten concertos this year. No promises. You play Paganini?"

"Anthony, Anthony," said Jacobus. "I mean, don't you think you're being a little premature? After all, Yumi has studied with me for only a very short time. She's only nineteen."

Yumi was momentarily comforted. Mr. Jacobus was being her buffer, protecting her. He knew how to talk to these people. She had no idea how to respond. The suddenness of Strella's offer, this entire situation, was surreal. But then again, why had the tone of Mr. Jacobus's voice been so dismissive of Strella's offer?

She began to think, Why not? Why not consider his offer? After all, isn't this what I've been working for all my life? To have a solo career and be on the roster of the world's most influential concert agent? Is Mr. Jacobus truly speaking in my best interest by turning down the offer? Or is he somehow using me in his war against MAP? I won't be his pawn. I'd rather return to Japan than lower myself to that level, career or not.

"Only nineteen?" Strella laughed. "That's almost over the hill. Sorry, just joking. We'll give her the mature look. Sexy. Strapless gown. Slit up the side. The whole package. She's certainly got the figure for it. I'll bump her up the list over some of the other kids—"

"That all sounds very promising, Anthony," said Jacobus, not allowing Yumi the chance to say anything, "and we'll seriously consider your kind offer. But we really need to be leaving now."

Jacobus grabbed Yumi's arm with an uncomfortably tight grip, and it was he who ushered Yumi, almost pushing her, out of the office. Jacobus said over his shoulder, "We'll be in touch, Anthony. You've been a big help."

"Nothing at all, Mr. Jacobus," said Strella, loudly enough to be heard through the closing door. "And to tell you the truth, I'd much rather work with you than with the serpents."

Back in a taxi, Jacobus was growling. "Let him feed his fucking fish. That pimp will be out of business in a year."

Yumi asked, "Then you don't want him to be my agent?"

"I wouldn't let you be his client if he paid you a million dollars."

"Then why . . . ?"

"Because after Cynthia Vander née Vanderblick and Victoria

Jablonski hear Strella's ridiculous theory of them stealing the violin, what he said about their wonderful personalities, and that he wants to represent one of *my* students, they'll dump him in a minute. Once they drop him, it's only a matter of time before all his other clients do the same, especially since a lot of them are Victoria's students."

"But how will they know what he said?"

"I've got it on tape." Jacobus patted the pocket of his jacket, the jacket he had refused to take off earlier. "As Strella said, it's a cutthroat business."

TWENTY-THREE

Jacobus rolled down the window of the cab to get some air. "We've certainly made some lifelong friends the past couple days. Haven't we?" he asked.

Is he truly trying to make conversation? Yumi thought. Does he think I can forget what just happened? Should she ask the cab to stop and let her out?

"Have we?" responded Yumi. She was in no mood to discuss anything with him. She had been humiliated. Yes, she was indeed a pawn in his warped game. How could she continue studying with him now? She couldn't even say his name to herself anymore. From now on Jacobus was "him." Let him fight his own battles—she had fought hers. She should return to Japan.

The conversation ended. She left it at that.

The cab crawled toward the MAP business office, Rachel's office, on West Fifty-fifth Street, one block from Carnegie Hall. Again stuck in crosstown rush-hour traffic, the cab moved at a snail's pace on the narrow one-way street, delivery trucks and double-parked cars stifling its progress. The retching smell of fetid garbage smoldered as blistering heat reflected off the pavement, creating mirages that reduced the lower bodies of the pedestrians to ghostly insubstantiality. Above the office towers, outlines of dense clouds began to define themselves in hazy overcast.

"I've heard Rachel's given up the violin for good," said Jacobus.

Yumi did not respond. Amid the hot stench surrounding her, the idea of returning to Japan gained in appeal.

"Last that I heard, anyway," Jacobus continued.

His nonchalance was infuriating Yumi.

"Probably for the better," Jacobus pattered. "When she made it abundantly clear I wasn't getting through to her, I arranged for her to study with Victoria. For some reason things didn't gel there either. Surprised me. Thought it would have been a good match. Go figure."

Yumi watched a group of teenage skateboarders flaunting their way in and around the stalled traffic. Horns blared at them as if they were to blame for the traffic's inertia.

"Rachel's role just kind of evolved to where she became Victoria's manager. Organizing her lesson schedule and auditions for new students, making her travel arrangements to do master classes, even taking care of her banking needs. Which are considerable. That kind of stuff. Then, MAP manager. Anyway, Rachel seems to have found her niche."

"I think we are here," said Yumi.

"About time."

The cab pulled up in front of the MAP office. Emerging from the taxi, they made their tortuous way between double-parked cars and hordes of pedestrians on the sidewalk. Yumi cynically considered their New York–style egalitarianism—the swarm didn't break its stride even for a blind man.

A young lady in a short skirt and long heels accidentally stepped on the back of Jacobus's shoe. Losing her balance, she stumbled into Jacobus. Both of them fell to the ground.

The embarrassed woman apologized profusely, trying to assist Jacobus to his feet. Jacobus, on his back, flailed wildly with his arms and legs. Yumi watched impassively.

"Aaahh!" screamed Jacobus. "Get away from me, dammit! Dammit, leave me alone! Get off of me! Aahh! Do it myself!"

The woman backed away. Everyone else pretended to ignore the spectacle, forming a widening buffer zone as they continued on their way. The woman who had tripped Jacobus melted back into the crowd and disappeared.

After a few minutes, Jacobus, panting in the heat of the pavement, rolled over onto his stomach and gradually pushed himself up to his hands and knees. Yumi let him do it on his own. Straightening his sunglasses, he finally rose to his feet and brushed himself off.

"Bitch can't even watch where she's going," he muttered.

Yumi wordlessly offered her arm. Jacobus didn't refuse it. They managed the final ten feet to the office without further incident and walked down the street-level steps to the small but tidy air-conditioned basement office. Closing the soundproof glass door behind them, Yumi was suddenly disconnected from the chaotic energy outside.

A pale young woman, lining up her pencils on her white desk, looked up at them. Behind her were sentries of white file cabinets. Everything in the office was white. No pictures hung on the white walls. Parallel vacuum cleaner lines partitioned white wall-to-wall carpet into a sanitized gridiron. White chairs, white leather couch.

"Well, aren't we a mess?" she said to Jacobus.

"Hello, Rachel." Jacobus was still short of breath. "Been a long time. Introduce you to my new student. Yumi Shinagawa."

"How do you do, Rachel?" said Yumi. "Mr. Jacobus has told me all about you."

"And what has he told you?" asked Rachel in a low voice.

"He told me that you are a talented violinist and are doing a fine job working for MAP."

"Did he tell you he didn't want to teach me anymore?"

Rachel went back to straightening her pencils, though they already were perfectly aligned.

"Rachel, is it necessary to go into this again?" Jacobus asked.

"That's all right," said Yumi, curious to hear the story of another Jacobus student. *Does he manipulate all of them?* "I'm interested in knowing, Rachel."

"You are?" asked Rachel. "Why?" She stopped straightening her pencils but didn't look up.

"Just today I have found that I can learn a great deal from others' experiences, and I know from Mr. Jacobus that you especially liked to play in competitions. I admire that."

"Do you?"

"Yes. I find it extremely difficult to play when people are listening to me in such a critical way. For instance, today Mr. Jacobus had me play for Anthony Strella. I didn't want to and I was very nervous—"

"You played for Strella?" Rachel's attention was now riveted on Yumi. "I can't believe it!"

Yumi was taken aback by Rachel's intensity. By challenging Jacobus's assessment of Rachel her objective had been retaliation for the way he had treated her at Strella's. But she expected the response to come from him, not from Rachel. Now she wondered if she had gone too far.

"I begged him for years to let me play for Strella," Rachel said, twitching her head in Jacobus's direction. "He never would."

"As I told you many times in the past," Jacobus responded, "first of all, you weren't ready. And second, even if he had accepted you he would have given you all the worst engagements. That's the way he is with new clients. You would have been miserable."

"And that would have made life any different?" asked Rachel. "Why did you have Yumi play for him? She likes misery?"

"For the experience."

The experience! Yumi decided she had not gone far enough. Perhaps it was a mistake and she would have to return to Japan, but she could not continue with Jacobus like this.

"Rachel," she said, "Mr. Jacobus had me do it in order to get Miss Jablonski angry at Strella so that she would discontinue having him represent her students."

"Yumi!" shouted Jacobus.

"I'm sorry, but haven't you tried to teach me that the truth is important?" Yumi asked. "Or is it only when it serves your own purpose?"

"Shit."

"Well, aren't we all one big happy family?" said Rachel, gazing down at her hands on the desk. "I suppose I should ask you if you want to sit down."

They sat on the couch and Rachel continued. "So, as I understand it, you've come here today because you think I stole the violin."

"I didn't say that, Rachel," said Jacobus. "I just promised Nathaniel I would talk to everyone who was in the Green Room the night of the theft."

"Ah, Nathaniel! How is the overstuffed teddy bear? Still eating his soul food, listening to his soul music, and making his soul money?"

"Nathaniel is a very kind man," said Yumi.

"Whose side are you on, anyway?" asked Rachel.

"Side? I don't understand."

"Is it so difficult?" said Rachel. "You're either on my side or his. Right or wrong. Win or lose. That's the way the world works, though Jake might try to convince you otherwise."

"Do you think whoever stole the violin was a winner or a loser?" asked Jacobus.

"It's none of your business," Rachel said flatly. "That violin should have been for me to play, but you wouldn't let me enter the Grimsley."

"I've never let *anyone* enter the Grimsley, Rachel. You know that."

"I don't care about 'anyone.' I care about me. I *should* have stolen it. For the years of work I put in I deserve to have it."

"Is that why you left Mr. Jacobus to study with Miss Jablonski, Rachel?" asked Yumi. "Because Jake wouldn't let you enter the Competition?"

"Not just that. It took me years after that to realize I had been cheated. I left because all I wanted was a teacher who understood what I needed. Give me the right fingerings and bowings so I could have a chance to win something. He kept saying, 'There's no such thing as a right or wrong fingering' and 'Do what the music tells you to do.' I could have learned twice as many pieces if he hadn't made me think so much about what I was doing. Look, I was paying for lessons, wasn't I? I might as well have paid myself for all the help I was getting. It wasn't fair."

"And was it better when you went to Miss Jablonski?" asked Yumi. Perhaps I'll stay in New York and study with Jablonski, she thought. Then I'll definitely be rid of Jacobus and his suspicions, and might have a better chance for a career in the bargain. Perhaps he isn't as perceptive as I once thought.

"Yes. At first," said Rachel. "In one master class I played the Paganini Concerto. Victoria said it was 'note perfect.' 'Note perfect!' I'll never forget that."

"Yes? Then what happened?" Yumi asked.

Rachel stared at the screen saver on her computer monitor, a balloon bursting in slow motion into an infinite number of jagged shards.

"Rachel?" repeated Yumi.

"Victoria told me I wasn't 'soloist material.' "

Tears suddenly gathered in Rachel's eyes. Her pale complexion turned an ugly blotchy red. Her voice was choked.

"She told me I should switch to *viola!*"

Yumi was not particularly sympathetic. Though at the moment she was reluctant to agree with Jacobus on anything, she shared his view that music meant a great deal more than personal advancement.

Rachel regained her composure almost immediately, her voice again under control.

"All those eight-year-old brats were playing the same music the same way I was, but I was ten years older. She had made me sound just like they did. It wasn't fair. I was a second-class citizen. That's when she offered me a job. She said she needed someone to be with her, her number-one assistant. Then MAP gave me this. I do what I'm told. At least it pays better than one of those crummy orchestra jobs Jake wanted me to try out for."

"Rachel," said Jacobus. "You *are* a talented violinist, and believe it or not you're still a talented *young* violinist. You don't always find what you're looking for the first or even the second time around. But if you decide you want to find a new teacher and get a new start . . ." His voice trailed off.

"What? You'll be happy to help me find one? What violin teacher have you said a kind word to or about in the last ten years who'll even answer the phone when you call?"

Rachel gazed past Yumi and Jacobus. Yumi turned to see what Rachel was looking at from the tidy air-conditioned basement office—endless pairs of shoes walking by, all different, all going in different directions, the unordered energy of life passing by the soundproof glass door.

Rachel said to Jacobus, "I don't need your pity. I saw that little act you put on out there on the sidewalk."

Jacobus was silent. Yumi had no inclination to help him.

"I assume our little chat has come to an end," said Rachel, again staring intently at her hands, pallor returning to her cheeks.

Yumi stood up, eager to leave—to leave this office, this city, this country. Rachel's misery was infectious and she wanted no part of it.

"Well, yes, I suppose so. Thank you for your help, Rachel," said Jacobus.

"Another lie," she said.

"No. It isn't."

TWENTY-FOUR

Jacobus and Yumi arrived at Carnegie Hall in the midst of a Miss J master class. Victoria Jablonski was seated onstage, violin on knee, while a youth sawed his way through the Mendelssohn Violin Concerto. A dozen or so listless students sat in the audience, impatient at having to endure yet another meaningless rendition of what to them was just another hurdle in their march to fame and fortune. Though Jacobus and Yumi tried to enter discreetly, the students, seeking something of interest to while away the time, all turned their eyes to them, as did Jablonski. She interrupted the student in midphrase, excused him with a perfunctory "That will be all, Michael," and invited Jacobus up to the stage to join her. Jacobus gave his violin case to Yumi to put on a table in the wings along with hers.

Jacobus felt Victoria's strong grip on his arms tug him unwillingly toward her until their bodies were pressed together. He felt her strategically place her cheek against his, kissing the air, repeating the procedure on the other side of his face, as if she were European.

"I can't tell you what a pleasure it is to see you again, Daniel," said Victoria, releasing him.

"No, I suppose you can't," answered Jacobus, wishing he were anywhere but center stage of Carnegie Hall.

"You always change my meaning, don't you, Daniel?"

"Do I?"

"You're incorrigible, do you know that?"

Before Jacobus could manage a reply, Jablonski spoke again.

"Students, I would like to introduce to you Mr. Daniel Jacobus. The great Daniel Jacobus."

He heard tentative applause from various points in the front rows.

"Mr. Jacobus has come all the way from his little house in the country and has generously consented to listen to some of you play."

She couldn't care less what I think of her students, he thought. I couldn't care less either. Quite the manipulator, Victoria. Almost as good as me. Almost.

The next student, Noriko Watanabe, announced she would play the first movement of the Paganini Concerto in D Major.

"How nice," said Victoria. "Daniel, let me lead you to this chair over here where we can sit and listen. Students, isn't it laudible how Mr. Jacobus manages on his own?"

Jacobus heard Noriko Watanabe's high heels click their way onto the Carnegie Hall stage. The pianist plunked an A. Noriko tuned her violin and then managed to writhe through a passable rendition of the concerto, though it was not artistically interesting enough for Jacobus to pay much attention.

Midway through the recapitulation, Victoria said, "That will do for now, Noriko." However, in order to cut through the student's strident playing and oblivion-inducing concentration, she had to repeat herself, louder and louder, until she was actually shouting.

That's one thing she's good at, Jacobus thought. The girl finally stopped.

"Well, what do you think? Didn't you think that was wonderful?" Victoria asked Jacobus.

Victoria saved him from having to answer by not even waiting for one. She said to Noriko, "Next time a little faster. And try moving around some more."

Noriko said, "Thank you, Miss J," and quickly shuffled off the stage.

That's it? If that's a "Miss J lesson," Jacobus said to himself, I feel sorry for her current bed partner.

"May I comment?" asked Jacobus, immediately kicking himself because now he would have to say something constructive but not contradictory to the way Victoria taught.

"Certainly, Daniel," said Victoria. "You always have something clever to contribute. Nori, come back here, please."

"Just for starters," said Jacobus, "have you ever considered using warmer-sounding strings?"

Victoria intervened. "Are you still using those old fuddy-duddy strings of yours, Daniel? All my students use Megatones."

"Harmonium strings might give her a richer, more vocal sound."

"But Megatones have the power."

"Just as in life," said Jacobus, turning to Noriko, "there is more to music than power. Young lady, can you name me some of Paganini's contemporaries?"

"Ummm. Not really."

"Would it help you to know that Paganini was a contemporary of Rossini, Beethoven, even Haydn, and not Brahms or Tchaikovsky?"

"I guess."

"Well, without saying a word about technique, could you try the beginning again and imagine playing it in a more classical style, since that's what it really is?"

Noriko began again, and even though her playing was still strong, the phrases had a semblance of elegant profile that had been entirely lacking the first time around.

When she finished there was even a smattering of applause from the other students.

Victoria said, "Thank you, Nori. Students, isn't it wonderful to hear the old-fashioned way of playing once in a while. Who's next?"

They listened to a few more gifted but musically undeveloped students. Jacobus was getting antsy. Victoria interrupted his thoughts. "Did you know I'm the only teacher who's ever been given a private studio at Carnegie? Oh, of course you couldn't have known that. You're out there in the countryside. I find that so quaint."

"I do know that," said Jacobus. "You told me the last time we spoke."

"You always have had such a wonderful memory, haven't you?" She whispered to Jacobus, "Now, before we get down to business, let's play our little game."

"Let's not, Victoria," he whispered back. "Not here on the stage of Carnegie Hall." He started to get sick to his stomach. "Your students—"

"Oh, but it's our tradition. You used to enjoy it."

" 'Used to' is the operative phrase."

"But *I* still do. Do it for me, Daniel, and then we can talk about the Piccolino."

"Is this absolutely necessary, Victoria?"

"Absolutely. That is, if you expect me to answer any of your questions."

Jacobus threw his head back in disgust and frustration.

"Students," said Victoria, clapping her hands to recapture their waning attention, "the remarkable Mr. Jacobus has amazing powers of observation. You all saw how we briefly greeted each other a short while ago, onstage, in front of you all. Well, Mr. Jacobus will now tell us what he observed. Go ahead, Daniel."

Jacobus, head down, rattled off the list: "You've cut your hair. It's above your ears. You're wearing a double pearl necklace and long dangling earrings that undoubtedly match the necklace; French perfume—"

"Called Talon," Victoria prompted.

"Appropriately enough. A long, loose-fitting, fairly light green summer dress with no bra"—he heard some giggles—"and high-heeled shoes."

"Students, isn't Daniel something? A little naughty, perhaps, but he could tell all of that just from me greeting him! Please explain to us, how do you do it?"

Jesus! How did I get myself into this? This is so inappropriate, it's unbelievable. What is she up to?

"As I've told you every time you force me to do this—just like the sense of taste is ninety percent smell, sight is ninety percent other senses. The pace of your walk, the length of your stride, and sound of your footsteps— those tell me what kind of shoes you're wearing and the length of your dress. I felt and heard the clatter of your jewelry, smelled your perfume—"

"And felt that I have no bra?" There were now guffaws from the students, who sensed the intensifying atmosphere.

"Yes, Victoria's little secret," said Jacobus, eager for a chance to retaliate. "That was at your instigation. *You* hugged *me*, remember?"

"But how did you know my dress is light green? You must have had someone sending you secret messages."

"More of a guess. The *Times* fashion section. What the designers are calling 'forest hues'—what most humans call green—are in this summer. Knowing of your need to keep your wardrobe up-to-date but with better taste than to wear something bright green, I concluded it would be lighter."

"How very sweet. And is there anything else you can tell me about me, Daniel?" she asked.

So you want to get coy? he thought.

"You've gotten divorced since the last time we met."

"Who told you that?"

He congratulated himself on hearing the smirk wiped off her face.

"No one. When you held my hands, I noticed you were no longer wearing your wedding ring."

"How do you know I didn't just take it off a few minutes ago in order to play the violin?"

"Because you always used to wear the ring on your right hand, anyway, so it wouldn't interfere with your playing."

"Well, Daniel," said Victoria, "I don't want to waste any more of my students' valuable time with your banal games. Maybe you can tell us who this little girl in the audience is? She's not one of my students, so I deduce she must be one of yours. Would you be kind enough to introduce her to everyone?"

"Yumi Shinagawa," said Jacobus curtly. He sensed he was about to be lured into something even more unpleasant and rose from his chair in order to leave the stage.

Jacobus heard Yumi's steady voice from the audience.

"It is an honor to meet you, Miss Jablonski," said Yumi.

Victoria pulled him back down to his seat.

"Yes, dear, and what high school do you go to?"

"I'm actually from Kyushu, Japan, where I was a student at the university."

"Oh, I see. How interesting."

Apparently the interview was over. At least Jacobus hoped so.

But Victoria continued. "Daniel, you must be very busy, showing Yumi all around the big city. Yumi, did Daniel take you to Carnegie Deli for a pastrami sandwich yet?"

"Yes, how did you know?"

"Daniel's not the only one who understands things, dear. I also saw that you have your violin case with you. Using Daniel's logic, since you're new here I'm guessing that you just might like to play on the stage of Carnegie Hall. Am I right?"

Yumi paused. "I would like that very much," she said.

"See, Daniel, you're not the only genius. And I didn't even have to smell anything."

"Yumi," said Jacobus, "you don't have to play just to be polite. You must be tired. It's really up to you. I'm serious."

"Certainly, dear, I understand," said Jablonski to Yumi. "You must be very, very tired."

"No! I would like to play! Thank you. It would be very exciting."

"Isn't she sweet, Daniel? What will you play, dear?"

"I would like to play the Sarabanda from the Bach D-Minor Partita," said Yumi.

"That would be lovely, dear, unless you care to play something difficult."

Jacobus shook his head in dismay but didn't bother to respond. He might disagree with Strella on everything else, but he couldn't argue with the choice of the word "serpent" to describe Victoria Jablonski. He heard Yumi's footsteps echo in the resonance of Carnegie Hall, but it might as well have been a snake pit. She walked to the wings of the stage, where their violin cases lay side by side.

As she walked onto the stage with her violin, Victoria said, "Let's give Daniel's student a warm welcome," and started applauding loudly, followed by a sheeplike response from her disciples.

Jacobus took a deep breath. Even if Yumi's not intimidated by Victoria, he thought, she'll feel very alone standing on the stage of this cavernous hall. He recalled the sea of velvet seats rising as high as one could see, enveloped by imposing maroon and gold. No one, not even seasoned artists, could dispel the sensation that the spirit of every great violinist who had ever played in Carnegie Hall was listening with critical attention. The near emptiness of the hall made those spirits of violinists past seem even more present than when it was crowded with a live audience.

As soon as Yumi began to play the Sarabanda, Jacobus recognized a subtle but sublime change in Yumi's playing since he had so recently chastised her for lack of understanding of that same piece. Her tempo was not so slow as to be static, nor so fast as to be impersonal, nor so strict as to sound academic. The phrases were suggestively contoured without becoming obvious; the quality of sound, while appropriately dark, wove through an endless metamorphosis of color. The vibrato was alive without bringing attention to itself and was used as an expressive device as well, and the occasional chords and trills were elegantly executed within the context of the music. And of course it was immaculately in tune.

Jacobus, accustomed to having students progress quickly, was dumbfounded by such a compelling, polished personal performance. He was riveted, unaware of anything else but the music—his own definition of a great performance.

If this had been a real concert, the audience would not have applauded when Yumi finished. As the final note vanished seamlessly into silence, the audience would have been too spellbound. Indeed, it was several moments before anyone stirred.

"Very lovely, dear," said Victoria finally, clapping three times in mock applause, ringing hollow in the empty hall. "But don't you think it should be a little slower and louder? Students, what do you think?"

Jacobus heard a few mumbles of assent. He couldn't care less what they thought. He was still chagrined, euphorically so, at the performance.

Yumi responded in a clear voice, "I did consider that possibility, Miss Jablonski, and certainly the eighteenth-century sarabanda should feel dignified, especially one composed by Bach. But I think it is also important to remember that the sarabanda started out in Spain in the sixteenth century as a sensual love dance."

So she did some reading at Nathaniel's! thought Jacobus. A young lady of constant surprise and great resource. He would get her safely back to Japan even if it killed him.

Yumi continued. "The great author of *Don Quixote*, Miguel de Cervantes, attacked the sarabanda as immoral, and King Philip II even prohibited it. In the *Treatise Against Public Amusements*, Juan de Mariana called the sarabanda 'a dance and song, so lascivious in its words, so ugly in its movements, that it is enough to inflame even very honest people.'"

Don't push your luck, Yumi, thought Jacobus. Victoria's not terribly responsive to being shown up.

"So while I think this particular sarabanda is definitely not intended to be a fast dance, I do believe Bach wanted it to be flowing and . . . sensual. However, Miss Jablonski, I greatly appreciate your comments, and if I have the opportunity to perform it again in the future, I will of course seriously consider them in deciding what my interpretation will be, but I have learned that if a musician listens carefully enough, the fingers will find a way."

Now I'm in for it, Jacobus thought during the ensuing silence.

"Just who do you think you are, Daniel?" Victoria hissed.

I guess the game is over, he thought. Wonder who won.

"What do you mean?" he asked.

"You put her up to that."

"Up to what?"

"Trying to humiliate me, Mr. Professor."

"Hey, I had no idea you'd ask her to play. Anyway, why would I want to do that?"

"Because you're jealous."

"Jealous of what?"

"Isn't it obvious? You're jealous I studied with Malinkovsky when I was a kid and you only studied with that nut Krovney."

"Don't be—"

"You're jealous that even though I was once your student, your pride and joy, now *I* get the best students. Yes, *I* get them. You're jealous that they become famous, that I give them a better chance to get in front of the public, to get them a step ahead of the competition."

Jacobus had had enough. Why had he even attempted to be civil with her?

"Yes," he said, "you and your MAP friends dress them up and parade them around like Lipizzaner stallions doing their tricks. Only difference is the horses get to keep their balls."

"Ha! You hear that, students? Daniel, you're just jealous that I have a studio here and you don't. You're jealous that I make a lot more money than you do. Do you have any idea how much I'm paid per hour?"

"Yes."

"So you do know that I make a lot more than you do. Don't you?"

"No, you don't."

"How can you say that?"

"Because I make enough."

"Very witty, Mr. Professor. You're jealous because once you had a thing for me, and you can't stand it that other men like me."

So now we're mudslinging. The students must be having a ball out there. So be it.

"Like Dedubian, for instance?" asked Jacobus. He wasn't about to back down now.

"For instance."

"Like Strella, maybe?"

"What do you care?"

"I don't."

"Don't you! Because you're having a roll in the hay with sweet little Yumi?"

"That's enough," said Yumi.

Jacobus had almost forgotten she was there onstage with them. Now her voice was right next to them. Jacobus had let things spin out of control, and he knew it. Victoria's plan, no doubt.

"Well, how sweet," said Victoria. "The little concubine defending the honorable sensei."

Yumi continued. "You're an evil person, and if your students were intelligent they would look for a teacher more interested in them and in music than—"

Jacobus heard a sharp slap, then a gasp from the students. He felt powerless. He couldn't see Yumi's face flush red, or the trickle of blood on the corner of her swelling lip.

Jablonski said, "That's enough out of you, you young hussy. You need to learn your place. Class is over. Daniel, I'll be in my office."

"Yumi," said Jacobus, taking a deep breath. He couldn't allow her to feel she was alone, even if it meant changing his script, at least for the moment. "Are you okay? Why don't you wait by the box office until Nathaniel arrives? He should be here in a while. Don't worry about Victoria. I'll take care of her. I'll meet you there."

Jacobus followed Victoria's footsteps. She did not slow down for him. He preferred it that way.

She led the way off the stage, down the corridor, up the stairs, left turn, down the corridor, past the Green Rooms to her office. He didn't mind that she didn't say a word the whole way. It gave him time to concentrate on not walking into anything and on what he was going to say.

As soon as he crossed the threshold behind her, she slammed the door, startling him.

"You know, Daniel, I wouldn't be surprised if you stole that violin. I really wouldn't. You've always hated the Grimsley Competition. You've always hated my students, and you've hated me since I walked out on you."

"You are so full of shit," said Jacobus. That's what I was going to say? he thought. I could have done a little better than that.

"Am I?" said Victoria. "Then you tell me. Who had a better motive to steal the Piccolino? And who could pull the whole thing off, in a dark room, better than a blind man who knows every inch of this building? I saw you there. No one would have been surprised to see the great pedagogue Daniel Jacobus at Carnegie Hall."

Jacobus had heard this same song from Lilburn, Vander, Grimsley, Strella; MAP's orchestrated plan, setting him up as the thief, encouraging him to incriminate himself. To his ear, like Victoria's students, all their performances sounded rehearsed, artificial. That's the line they've all been tossing to take the heat off themselves while they rip off the system, he thought.

He started laughing. Well, I can't say I didn't help them along, he thought.

"What are you snickering about?" Jablonski asked.

"Well, I guess you've got it all figured out, Victoria. Oh, yes! You have figured it out. Perfectly. Sure I stole the Piccolino." But before he could say, "and you're the Virgin Mary," there was a knock at the door.

It was Harry Pizzi. "Miss J," he said through the door, "there's a Detective Malachi downstairs. Says he wants to talk to Daniel Jacobus."

Jablonski responded, "Thank you, Harry. Tell him Mr. Jacobus will be there momentarily."

As Pizzi went to do Jablonski's bidding, her voice echoed in the hallway. "Well, Daniel, I guess the party's over. It has been lovely seeing you again. I'm sure you can make your own way out." A more subdued, "Good-bye, Victoria," followed from Jacobus.

Halfway down the corridor to the elevator, Jacobus inhaled Victoria's familiar scent. Talon perfume. It must have infected either his clothes or his psyche.

A French word, "talon." "Claw." What the French call the frog, the ebony attachment at the base of the violin bow that holds the hair in place and where the bow is gripped by the right hand. Talon, claw, doubly appropriate for Victoria, Jacobus thought.

Jacobus met Nathaniel by the box office, as planned. Malachi was there also.

"Mr. Jacobus?" he asked.

He ignored the policeman. "Where's Yumi?" Jacobus asked Nathaniel.

"I don't know," Nathaniel said. "I thought she was with you."

"Mr. Jacobus," Malachi repeated.

"Yeah. Who are you?"

"Detective Al Malachi, NYPD. We've met once before, and I'm here to tell you that I would like nothing better than to arrest you for the theft of the Piccolino Strad and hope to do so as soon as possible."

"If there's nothing better you'd like to do than that," said Jacobus, "I feel sorry for your wife."

"Jake," said Nathaniel, pulling him aside, "tone it down, man. Tone it down. This business is difficult enough without the police breathing down our necks."

"Let go of me," said Jacobus. "After taking crap all day from the MAP bastards I don't need any more from this schmuck."

"Also," continued Malachi, "I have received reports from various members of MAP of harassment and intimidation—and I can see now that they were justified—so I am warning you to stay away from anyone associated with MAP or I will arrest you for stalking."

Nathaniel exploded. "Jake! How could you? I asked you nicely to lay off your personal agenda. I know you're a crusty old fart with everyone else, but I thought between the two of us . . ." He didn't bother to finish the sentence but threw up his hands in disgust.

"I'll let you boys have some alone time now," said Malachi as he left, "but if I get any more complaints I'll take you both in."

Jacobus tried to defend himself by relating how Jablonski had tried to humiliate him, had slapped Yumi in the face, and had, like the other MAP associates, accused him of stealing the Piccolino. The only thing he did, Jacobus said, was to "put her in her place."

Nathaniel was hardly assuaged.

"Jake, you've interviewed the last of the MAP people. I won't need you anymore for the investigation. You've done enough damage, especially with Jablonski. I suggest I drive you back home and we call it a day."

Jacobus was devastated. He knew this might happen but had taken the chance. He had lost. He tried to grab on to one last thread, not that it mattered anymore. He asked Nathaniel if he had brought the dossier on all the runners-up of the Grimsley Competition he had requested.

"It was one pain in the you know what, but I got it," said Nathaniel.

At that point Yumi arrived, carrying their violin cases.

"I'm sorry to take so long," Yumi said, slightly out of breath. "I had to wash my face."

"Forget about it, let's get out of here," said Jacobus.

The long drive back to Jacobus's home—they got stuck in a snarled mess of rush-hour traffic as they left the city—was notable only in that it had been fewer than forty-eight hours since they first arrived in New York.

They were distraught and exhausted, so there was little conversation. Even the vintage jazz on a nightly FM program brought little relief.

Jacobus said almost nothing. He spent some time thinking about the MAP situation, and along with mounds of expectedly extraneous information, Kate Padgett's scant résumé. It was almost blank. Alive? Dead? Who knows? Nathaniel couldn't find out for sure. No photos. No reviews. A few tidbits. A yellowed *New York Times* clipping of the 1931 Grimsley and a wordy but less than informative feature from the *Piddletown Herald* from the same year. A taped copy of an old 78 recording. One intriguing tidbit was the passport of a Mrs. Kate Desmond and a steamer booking to Japan in 1945 in the company of a Mr. Simon Desmond—could she be one and the same person as Yumi's grandmother? There was only that single tenuous connection between the name Kate and Japan, but Jacobus was banking on it. He had little else to go on.

Mainly, though, Jacobus was preoccupied with what he would say to Yumi when they got to his house.

He was not totally sure he had succeeded in prodding Yumi to return to Japan. He felt he had almost gotten there by the time they had left Rachel's office, but then Victoria! If he had stuck to his plan, he should have sided with Victoria after she slapped Yumi, but he just couldn't be that much of an ass. When the cop was there, he should have had Victoria arrested for hitting Yumi. Nathaniel had wanted to take her to a doctor, but Yumi said no and hadn't uttered a word of complaint since.

He wondered whether he should change his strategy. Should he tell Yumi what he knew? Should he explain to her that even though he sympathized with what she and the others had done, the violin still had to be returned? Could she be coaxed into cooperating without Granny's prior approval? What would be the right words to say to get her to tell him where the violin was? Certainly not his usual words. He would have to think of something face-saving for her. If he could accomplish that first, he would then figure out a way to return the violin without anyone else knowing—including Nathaniel—and without anyone ever being caught, or even suspected.

Jacobus woke with a start as he felt Nathaniel cautiously navigating the Rabbit around the graveled curve of his driveway. He had no idea how long he had slept.

"Jake, don't tell me you didn't lock the doors of your house."

"I never do," said Jacobus, rubbing his face in an effort to regain consciousness. "You know that. Why?"

"I think you've got trouble. There's a police car parked by the front door with the lights flashing."

"Shit. No one's ever broken in before."

"Someone's sitting on the doorstep, wearing a pair of old jeans and a stained work shirt."

"As big as you? Taller?"

"Yeah."

"That's Roy Miller, the town's entire police force. Part-time cop, full-time plumber."

Jacobus was fully awake now. Vandals? Or MAP? What could MAP want of his? Had they been planning to mug him here too? Mugging was only for cities, he thought.

They pulled up to the house. Jacobus got out of the Rabbit.

"Hey, Jake," said Miller. "These folks friends of yours?"

Jacobus quickly introduced them.

"What's the bad news, Roy? They take the fiddles?"

"Worse."

"Everything?"

"Worse, Jake."

Jacobus had played enough games with Victoria.

"Come on, Roy. Let's have it."

"Jake, I've gotta take you in for questioning."

"Questioning? For what?"

"For the theft of the Piccolino Strad."

"Roy, come on!"

Those MAP bastards are poison, Jacobus thought.

"That's not all, Jake."

Jacobus was silent.

"And for the murder of Victoria Jablonski."

DEVELOPMENT

TWENTY-FIVE

The Bullet Train hummed along Japan's southern coastline in the darkness, its rhythm quietly deceptive as it powered its way at 230 kilometers per hour. Nathaniel and Yumi slept. Jacobus was still deep in thought, reviewing the past, planning the future, the ashtray in the arm of his seat overflowing. When their plane had arrived at Nagoya airport, Nathaniel had bought a copy of the *International Herald Tribune*. Until he read Jacobus Lilburn's story that was carried from the *New York Times,* the two men had spoken very little to each other since leaving Jacobus's house.

Renowned Violin Teacher Brutally Slain
in Carnegie Hall Studio

By Martin Lilburn

NEW YORK: Victoria Jablonski, the most influential violin teacher in America and founding member of the powerful Musical Arts Project Group, was found brutally slain last evening in her Carnegie Hall studio, where she had taught for the past decade.

It is not known whether the killing was related to the recent disappearance of the so-called Piccolino Stradivarius violin. New York Police Department Detective Alan Malachi, who is in charge of the investigation, had no comment when asked if

Mr. Daniel Jacobus, a rival violin teacher who had once been her teacher and with whom he once reportedly had an amorous relationship, was a suspect in both the theft and the killing. However, a confidential source has reported that the Berkshire County, Massachusetts, sheriff's office has taken Mr. Jacobus into custody.

Mr. Jacobus had recently raised concerns that MAP was engaged in financial improprieties. According to a reliable source, evidence corroborating this claim is being brought to the attention of the fraud division of the Internal Revenue Service.

Members of MAP have expressed shock and horror over Ms. Jablonski's death and are planning a memorial service, details of which are still being determined. However, they had no comment in regard to the financial allegations. Anthony Strella, executive director of MAP, has requested that contributions be made in Ms. Jablonski's memory to MAP, a nonprofit corporation, in lieu of flowers.

The only thing that surprised Jacobus in the story was that it sounded like an investigation of MAP was being initiated. Why would Lilburn have written that if he could have avoided it? The rest of the story he could have written himself, though the one factual error was that he had been taken into custody. Clearly Lilburn wrote the story before learning that he had escaped.

It was still less than a week since the Piccolino Strad had been stolen. At the house about thirty hours ago—was it thirty? who could remember?—Roy Miller had remained the calmest.

Yumi had reacted even faster than he had, Jacobus recalled, when Miller had announced that Jacobus was wanted for questioning for murder. She had uttered something in Japanese and then thrown up. Jacobus quickly told Nathaniel to escort her inside the house and take care of her there.

"Give her a glass of water and have her lie down," Jacobus said. "I need to talk to Roy. Alone."

Roy had said, "Now, Jake, I know you didn't do either of those things, but this guy, this Detective Malachi, called me up from New York, all hot and bothered, and insisted I stay here until you arrived.

He said you were a desperate man and that I should take you in for questioning."

"Roy, how was Victoria killed?" asked Jacobus.

"Well, I'm not really at liberty to tell you, but you and me, we've known each other a long time now, so I suppose it'd be okay.

"Victoria Jablonski, or her body, I should say, was found in her studio at Carnegie Hall. She was sitting at her desk chair with a violin G-string wrapped real tight around her neck. Her neck was all scratched and bloody, probably from her trying to untie the string, because there was some blood under her fingernails. Her face was kind of blue and puffy with her tongue and eyes sticking out. It wasn't a pretty sight, as you may imagine."

Victoria would never approve of a blue face with her green dress, Jacobus thought. Shit, let it go.

"Signs of a struggle?" asked Jacobus.

"Nope. No cuts, no bruises—other than around her neck—no sexual assault. And nothing stolen. That's why they think whoever killed her was probably someone she knew, though the attack was so violent her carotid artery was collapsed internally and her windpipe crushed. Someone out there really didn't like her."

"And why does Malachi think I did it, Roy?"

"There you go again, Jake, asking questions I'm not supposed to answer. But if you don't mind, why don't we sit back down on your steps here so I can talk to you without my legs getting all achy. I had to install some baseboard heating today at this trophy home up on Pixley Road and it really takes it out on the old knees."

They sat in the dark of the muggy summer night. The only sound Jacobus heard was the distant rumble of thunder. Even the cicadas and crickets were oppressed into silence by the air's heavy torpor. He pulled from his memory the image of an approaching storm, the flashes of sheet lightning that provided fleeting illumination of random patches of ominous sky, of coalescing storm clouds you knew were there but could see only for an instant. Jacobus was deeply troubled at the direction his thoughts were leading, thoughts that were not about the weather. Thoughts about Yumi alone in Carnegie Hall, washing her face.

"That's better," Roy said as they sat down.

"Mind if I smoke?" asked Jacobus, who already had the pack out of his pocket.

"Go right ahead and dig your own grave if you want to," said Roy.

"Yeah, tell me about it."

"So, anyway, as I was saying, her body was discovered by this security guard named Pizzi. Said he had knocked on her door about fifteen minutes before to announce that our Detective Malachi was in the lobby and wanted to see you. Pizzi said that when he knocked the first time, you and the lady were having an argument, and he says he heard you bragging in a very loud voice something like, 'Yeah, I stole the Piccolino.' This Mr. Pizzi returned to her studio, as I said about fifteen minutes later, to tell her that Detective Malachi wanted to talk to her, and that's when he found her. So they have a pretty accurate time of death, somewhere between six and six fifteen."

Jacobus flicked his half-smoked cigarette into the night.

Miller continued. "There weren't many people in the building at that time and there wasn't any concert going on, as you probably know, so it wasn't hard for the police to interview everyone there. You were the only one who was seen going in or out of her studio during that time, which doesn't mean that someone else couldn't have, of course.

"My confreres in the NYPD eventually got around to the box office folks, where one of the young women who works there admitted to hearing you say, I guess it was to your friends here, 'Well, I guess I took care of her,' or something to that effect."

"More like, 'I've put her in her place,' " Jacobus corrected.

"Yeah, well, whatever. Anyway, that got this Malachi fellow interested in your whereabouts, as you can imagine. He called me about seven thirty and gave me instructions to wait here in case you should turn up. It's okay. I haven't been here too long and it's a nice night for sitting outside anyway. I always like watching lightning like this. Looks like we might finally get some rain and cool things off. We need it."

Jacobus lit another Camel and blew smoke into the air.

"While they were interviewing the box office people, a few of Jablonski's students and her secretary, Rachel something or other, showed up, so they questioned them too. The students said you and Jablonski really went at it during her class, and this Rachel admitted to having a fairly unpleasant conversation with you not long before. She also had a list of names supplied to her by your friend Mr. Williams, here, of people you had interviewed during the day regarding the missing violin. Malachi really got his boys off their butts because they called all those people . . . you know who I'm talking about, don't you, Jake? Most of them were saying you weren't the friendliest person they'd ever met, if you know what I mean, even to the point of you having suggested on a number of occasions that it wasn't such a bad idea that the violin was stolen."

"And exactly why do the police think I killed Victoria?" asked Jacobus.

He could smell prestorm ozone in the air. Calm now, he thought, but it's gonna come down in buckets pretty soon. He remembered there used to be lightning bugs in his yard. He wished he could see them and catch them, like he did when he was a kid. Put them in a jar and watch the whole thing glow. He rubbed the cigarette on the stoop, flicked it into the night, and lit another.

"Well, Jake, it's kind of a crazy theory, if you ask me. But the police down there are convinced of it. You know these New York cops. I used to be a big Kojak fan myself. Malachi thinks you could've stolen the violin the night of Kamryn Vander's recital from that little room in Carnegie Hall, but somehow you had an idea that Victoria Jablonski had seen you do it, so you set up an interview with the lady under the pretext of questioning her about trying to recover it. To throw everyone off, you know."

"If that were true, Roy, wouldn't I have avoided having a public argument with her?"

"*I* would say so, but the NYPD thinks that's just where you screwed up. You lost your cool, killed her, and got the heck out of Dodge."

Jacobus sat in silence for several moments, shoulder to shoulder with Roy. He had said enough for now. A cricket started chirping.

"They say Victoria Jablonski never performed," said Miller.

"That's right."

"Doesn't it seem kind of strange that someone who teaches people how to stand up there on a big stage and play in front of thousands of people never did it herself?"

Jacobus forced himself to choke up a phlegmy cough in order to avoid saying anything disparaging about Victoria—whatever truth there might be in his opinions would only help land him in jail at this point.

"The thought has occurred to me many times, Roy."

"You used to perform a lot, didn't you, Jake? Even after you lost your sight?"

"Yeah. Not so much recently, though. I've pretty much settled into teaching lately."

"Can you really teach someone how to perform, though? I don't mean just how to play, but how to perform. How you go up there onstage and not be nervous. You know my son, Roy Jr. He plays the trumpet. He's in school band, but he's always telling me how he screws up at concerts even though he sounded great at home. Is there anything I can tell him so he won't get so nervous?"

"When you walk onto the stage," Jacobus said, "even if there are only twenty people in the audience, you get this rush of adrenaline, you think about all the things you think you *can't* do, you say to yourself, 'What the hell am I doing here?' Only one shot to get it right or you get skewered by the critics. No way can you say to yourself, 'I'm just going to pretend that I'm at home in my nice comfy living room.'"

"Uh-huh."

"On the other hand, I tell my students, 'At the end of your daily practice session, practice performing.' Take a piece of music, even a scale, and try to get cranked up as much as possible, and under no circumstances stop. If the phone rings, if your music falls on the floor, if the dog pisses on your foot, keep going as best you can."

"Well, I certainly appreciate the advice, Jake, and I'm sure Roy Jr. will also, though getting him to play for the relatives will take some doing. So you're saying that when you perform, or performed, you didn't get nervous?"

"Not so much nervous—I really enjoyed performing, the challenge, you know—more of a sense of exhilaration, nervous energy. Lucky, I guess, because even though there was that sense of anxiety, even fear, it was a positive experience for me. In a way, one part of me, the thinking part, always stayed calm."

Jacobus thought for a moment and said with a sad, tired smile, "You are one smart cop, Roy. You just got me to describe a psychological profile of a murderer."

"Now Jake, as I was saying before, I know you didn't do it. That's why I knew I wouldn't find anything when they told me to search your house for that stolen violin."

"You searched my house?"

"No, Jake. You keep putting words in my mouth. I just said they told me to. I don't have any need to search your house. But you know, this whole business about missing violins makes me real curious. About violins themselves. Did you take your violin with you to New York?"

"Yeah. I wasn't sure how long I'd be there and figured I might need it to give Yumi a lesson . . . the girl who threw up. She's my student."

"Poor kid. Well, that sounds logical to me," said Roy Miller. "So your violin must still be in the car then."

"Yeah. That's right."

"Those violins. They say they all look a little bit different. Is that true?"

It's amazing how little most people know about violins, Jacobus thought. Sometimes he thought otherwise intelligent people were just pulling his leg.

Jacobus blew out some smoke. "Anything handmade like a violin is unique, but I personally am much more interested in how they sound."

"Sure, I can understand that, you being a musician. Nevertheless, I'd be curious to see a real good violin close up. Think I could take a look at yours, Jake?"

"Right now? In the dark?"

"It wouldn't take but a minute. I've got my flashlight. Come on, I'll help you over to the car to get it."

"Ah, what the hell. But Roy, if you think I've got the Piccolino, you're way off base."

"How many times do I have to tell you, Jake, I know you didn't steal that violin."

The two of them trudged over the gravel in the darkness. Roy gave Jacobus a hand opening the trunk of the hatchback, but he didn't help as Jacobus felt around the luggage and removed the violin case. Jacobus heard the hatchback click closed. They returned to the stoop, which was dimly illuminated by a moth-attracting porch light. Jacobus sat down again, setting the case on his lap.

"Now, Jake, if you wouldn't mind opening it up. I'd hate to pick up a violin the wrong way and break something."

Jacobus felt for zippers and the clasps, opened the case, and pulled out his violin.

"There," he said. "You can easily see this is not the Piccolino Stradivarius."

"As I said, I'm no expert, and I'm sure you're right. But I should tell you, Jake, your violin happens to be missing a string. I'm pretty sure it would be the G-string."

TWENTY-SIX

Jacobus had convinced Miller to let him spend the night in his own home. After all, he wasn't under arrest. They would meet the next morning, after a good night's sleep, when Jacobus would go to Roy's house for coffee and questioning.

As soon as Miller left, Jacobus called to Nathaniel.

Jacobus grabbed his shoulders.

"Nathaniel, I need to go to Japan. Now. And I need you and Yumi to go with me."

"Jake, you must be crazier than I gave you credit for! You know what it'll look like if you take off?"

"Goddammit, of course I know."

His cigarette breath was right in Nathaniel's face.

"Look at me! What do I look like, a fucking moron? It's the only chance I have. If I stay here, there is no chance. Can't you understand that?"

"And what do you expect to find in Japan? And why do *I* need to go?"

"The person responsible for the theft is there. I know it. If I can convince that person to return the violin, then I can come back and find Jablonski's killer. Hey, I know you've got damn good reasons not to want to go to Japan, but I need you to go, dammit, to tell them that I wasn't trying to escape justice. That I was trying to find the violin. They trust you."

If Nathaniel read Yumi into that equation, so be it, Jacobus thought. Time had run out far faster than he expected.

"Jake, I gotta tell you something. We've known each other a long time. I've always believed everything you've told me. But the way things look now, if you did have a reason to disappear in Japan there's no way

I could find you, and you damn well know that too. You'd be a ninja in the night. That's exactly what Jablonski's killer would do. So why don't we just report the name of the person you're so sure stole the violin and be done with it, man? Why drag the three of us to find a phantom in Japan, making me an accessory to something in the bargain? I don't like it."

"You don't like it! You don't like it!" said Jacobus in a venomous whisper. "You think *I* like it?"

"You haven't answered my question."

"All right, I'll answer your fucking question. Two things . . ."

"Jesus Christ, Jake!"

"Shut up. Number one, I'm not reporting the person's name because for me that person's a hero, not a criminal. And I'm not telling *you* the name in order to protect you as well. Number two, that person had nothing to do with Jablonski's murder. Now decide, Nathaniel. Now!"

Jacobus felt the sweat streaming down the crevices of his tired face. His hands were trembling on Nathaniel's shoulders. He couldn't tell Nathaniel the truth. He had to know for sure first. But he had no plan. He no longer had weeks to trace Yumi's path back to her home. He knew only that he had to get to Japan to buy precious time.

Finally he felt Nathaniel's hands on his own, gently removing them from his shoulders.

"I'll go get your passport," Nathaniel said. Jacobus heard him walk slowly over the gravel to the house. The screen door swung shut behind him.

The rain had started as a drizzle as they sped past Albany in Nathaniel's car on the way to Montreal. Suddenly, with one explosive clap of thunder, the oppressive heat wave that had been brooding for weeks erupted. Torrents of rain, searing bolts of lightning, rolling volleys of thunder rocked their car. Jacobus could hear the windshield wipers' frantic rhythmic pounding. Nathaniel had to slow to a crawl, unable to see, intensifying Jacobus's panic. Delay was disaster. Jacobus constantly exhorted Nathaniel to drive faster in the blinding deluge. Nathaniel did not respond.

One interminable hour passed. Two. Three. Waves of water blinded their way. Not until they had crossed the Canadian border at about three thirty in the morning—still long before Miller would discover Jacobus's disappearance and, with his tail between his legs, inform Detective Malachi—did the storm abandon its pursuit, grudgingly trudging off to the east. At Jacobus's instructions, Nathaniel had previously called the airport in Montreal from a pay phone to make three reservations, not using the phone in Jacobus's house, which would have left a record of the call and might already have been tapped. Leaving Nathaniel's dripping car in the airport parking lot, they boarded Air Canada flight 12, which departed at 5:48 A.M. for Vancouver and from there on JAL to Nagoya.

The Bullet Train propelled them through the night. Jacobus gathered it was night from the chorus of snoring around him, including Nathaniel's heldentenor from the seat in front of him. That man can sleep anywhere. It almost made him smile. He felt Yumi's head on his shoulder, gently bobbing to the rhythm of the train flying over the endless tracks.

Night? For me, always night. I don't know what it means anymore to sleep "when it's dark." What's a day? What's twenty-four hours? I can hardly remember. Meaningless. To see again! I'm so damn tired.

The rhythm of the train passing over the tracks, *bum*-buh-dum, *bum*-buh-dum, *bum*-buh-dum, relentless, monotonous, had etched itself in Jacobus's mind for hours now. Inexorable. Without conscious thought, Jacobus began tapping his fingers to the train's pulse, *bum*-buh-dum, *bum*-buh-dum, on the arm of his seat. His fingers became drumsticks. The rhythm quickened, transforming his fingers into the timpanist's thunderous hammering strokes that begin the fierce, fugal Scherzo of Beethoven's Ninth Symphony.

Since he became blind, in times of duress Jacobus's thoughts turned to Beethoven, music's most heroic genius—the closest thing to a god Jacobus had. For Jacobus, Beethoven, plagued by deafness most of his professional life, suffered a far more devastating blow for a musician than mere blindness.

Jacobus imagined himself at the packed Vienna premiere of Beethoven's Ninth Symphony, to hear what most knew would be the final symphony of the old, sick, totally deaf composer. What must the audience have thought to see on stage not just an orchestra but a chorus and four solo singers as well? It had never been done before. What was this eccentric visionary up to?

The monumental Allegro, the demonic Scherzo, with the inexorable rhythm Jacobus was still tapping, the sublime Adagio. But the chorus and soloists remained silent. The dissonant eruption that began the last movement. What followed was totally innovative in the history of music, a return to the themes of each previous movement interspersed with an operatic recitation of cellos and basses. Beethoven ruminating over his past. What next? How would he culminate his life's work? This symphony was already longer than any that had ever been written. Still no singing.

What's that? A march, a hymn? It lasted only a few seconds before Beethoven cut it off with yet another interruption of the cellos and basses. Yes, it *was* a hymn, an exquisite one, now being whispered by the cellos and basses.

Still the singers sat.

Then, variations on the hymn tune, growing into a march. What next? Suddenly, again the hellish blast that began the movement. The choir and soloists jumped to their feet. The baritone stepped forward. What would be the first words ever sung in a symphony?

"O friends, not *these* tones, but let us rather sing more pleasant and joyful ones." The hymn returns, sung first by the baritone, then by the entire chorus. The text, a plea for universal brotherhood. The symphony ended in triumph, joy, and hope.

"Not *these* tones!" What courage! thought Jacobus. Deaf Beethoven, of all composers, to be the one to offer the first words to be sung in the history of symphonic music! And that those words—"not *these* tones!"— were instructions from a deaf man to people who could hear! What strength to say, "I, *a deaf man,* prefer *other* sounds to the ones you have just listened to (even though those were the greatest that you or anyone has ever heard)!"

What power of will, to exist within a world of impenetrable and permanent silence, and yet be able to tell a hearing world that the sounds of harmony he has written are the very sounds of brotherhood! For Jacobus, Beethoven's Ninth Symphony was his bible, and its first words were the watchwords of his life. They gave him the strength to go on.

These were the watchwords for Jacobus that enabled him to survive the desolation he endured in his own world of darkness. And he would use them to complete the task now before him. Nothing else mattered.

The train's rhythmic monotony had lulled Jacobus into an uneasy sleep. His wizened cheek rested on Yumi's head. He briefly woke when the uniformed train employee rolled the snack cart down the aisle, asking politely in her high-pitched nasal voice if anyone wanted ice cream, beer, or dried squid snack. Jacobus went back to sleep and dreamed of sitting across an empty room from Beethoven—a blind man and a deaf man—desperately trying to communicate.

TWENTY-SEVEN

The Bullet Train slowed, its change in speed so smooth it was hardly perceptible. Jacobus awoke with a start, for a moment thinking he was back in the Rabbit arriving at his home. But then he quickly felt his jacket pocket for the cassette tape Nathaniel had given him, checking once again to make sure it was still there.

He now had his plan, such as it was.

He would have to gain access to Kate "Grandma" Padgett or Desmond—whatever her name was—through Max Furukawa, somehow coaxing him to obtain an invitation to Padgett but excluding Nathaniel. With the invitation from above, Yumi couldn't easily refuse to take him there.

There were two problems with the plan. One, he couldn't let Max know of his suspicions. If he was wrong he would be spreading indelible shame and mistrust. And there was his vow to have the Piccolino returned without revealing the perpetrator's—or, in his view, hero's—identity. The second problem was that he would have to do all his talking to Max through Yumi, who would undoubtedly be called upon to be his translator.

Why the hell didn't I learn Japanese? he asked himself. Lazy ass. How can I get what I need with Yumi assisting me? How can I get it *without* her?

Getting Yumi to hate him had served its purpose, maybe too well, and the sound of Victoria slapping her still echoed in his brain. Now, though, he had to try to reverse the process. He needed to ease her mind just enough to crawl together through yet one more sticky strand of the web, clinging to her as she pursued her escape. In order to get her to do that, he asked himself whether he had the ability to be something quite alien to him. The ability to be nice.

Yumi's head was still resting on his shoulder. Was she asleep or, like him, just pretending? He could tell if she were pretending, he thought. But he wasn't absolutely certain of that. She could be a good actor, another of her many talents. If she were acting, what was she thinking about now?

TWENTY-EIGHT

After crossing the bridge to Kyushu, the major southern island of Japan, the train arrived at the small town of Ochanomizu at 1:44 A.M., precisely on time, as always. The driver was waiting. Yumi, translating for Jacobus over the phone from Nagoya airport, had requested that Furukawa arrange for the taxi, and it was done. In keeping with the Japanese hierarchy of respect, Jacobus sat in front to the left of the driver—the driver's seat, as in England, on the right—with Nathaniel behind Jacobus and Yumi behind the driver. As Nathaniel had never been to Japan, Yumi had instructed him not to close the car door; the driver would do that automatically from his seat.

Nathaniel said, "This car reminds me of my grandmother's house— just as clean, and the seats have all these doily thingies on them. Covered in plastic too." Those were his first full sentences since reading the newspaper article at the Nagoya airport.

"Yeah, not the shit boxes they drive in New York," Jacobus replied, acknowledging reconciliation.

Nathaniel seemed calmer, the rebound from their confrontation.

He had every right to be uncomfortable being in Japan, Jacobus thought, even under the best of circumstances. Jacobus had never met Nathaniel's parents, nor Nathaniel his, whose lives had ended tragically in the war's European theater. That common experience had cemented their bond even more, but Jacobus had pushed Nathaniel's friendship to the breaking point. How much longer he could depend upon Nathaniel's faith in him was a constant dull ache.

The cab swung through the narrow, winding streets of Ochanomizu. The agricultural hamlet was deserted except for an occasional pedestrian or cyclist, and only a few dim lights from sidewalk vending machines or late-night taverns presumed themselves on the night. Two- and three-story houses and shops soon gave way to small, square rice paddies, barely distinguishable in the darkness. Nathaniel commented that this was not the image of teeming, neon Japan that he had gathered over the years. The road wound upward into the hillside, passing terraced fields, the moonlight reflecting off the water in the paddies, uniformly sized and right angled, rows of seedlings perfectly parallel.

Jacobus, who had taken this route when he could still see, rolled down the window to smell the sweet moisture of midnight air, helping him dust off cobwebbed images that had long been stored in the attic corners of his memory.

Only one life, he had said to Lilburn, but it was almost as if he was gleaning memories from another. Music had been his only concern the last time he was here. This time his life, Yumi's, and God knew who else's, were in the balance. Yet he felt that now, especially now, he needed music more than ever. He needed to connect this life to his past one.

Patterns, thought Jacobus. Rice paddies, for example. A signature of an unchanging human pattern, centuries old, etched into the earth. Patterns of human behavior. Usually so predictable, sometimes so confounding.

The taxi continued its slow progress, the hills awash in the sound of the crickets. The sluggish aroma of agriculture was replaced by the revitalizing scent of cedar, so Jacobus knew that the fields had disappeared and the cab was entering the forest, where the established patterns of human behavior, for better or worse, gave up trying to impose themselves on the landscape.

Patterns. Music and business, a double helix. A spiraling alchemy transforming art into avarice. Mozart, penniless genius, at one end; Anthony Strella, street-smart millionaire, at the other; endlessly intertwined, inextricable.

He had almost forgotten about MAP. Even with the cryptic comment in Lilburn's story he had little doubt his efforts there had failed. With his flight from the authorities, the focus of attention was no longer on MAP; quite possibly it had never been. He was reasonably certain that he had rattled them, but their day of reckoning would have to wait. With their battalion of accountants and lawyers, no doubt that day would dawn long after his sunset. The shame of it was that the model of their organization was being hailed as the salvation of the arts, and was replicating. A new pattern born, spawned from ambition, devouring the tender talent of youth to feed its unslaking hunger for dollars. He himself had brought Yumi to the edge of the abyss, and to his horror she had almost been sucked into it by Strella and Jablonski. It was a game he would never play again.

Yumi's patterns! So different—musically, behaviorally—from his other students. But so consistent. Until Victoria. That's what troubled Jacobus—the erratic changes in Yumi's behavior since. It made his own situation that much more precarious because it was only when he could not discern patterns that he truly felt his blindness.

The cab continued slowly for another fifteen, twenty minutes, winding slowly through the pungent cedar, their arrow-straight trunks like sentinels in the night. Then Jacobus heard the easygoing conversation of the stream that had carved the narrow valley through which the road had been built. They paralleled its path until they came upon a cluster of weather-beaten houses that couldn't even be called a village.

"*Aka-chochin,*" said Jacobus as the taxi slowed almost to a stop, veering sharply to the right as it left the paved road for an even narrower dirt lane hardly wider than the car itself.

"Ah, Mr. Jacobus," said Yumi, "you have a very good memory for directions."

Since their arrival at the train station Yumi's behavior had been opposite that of a fleeing fugitive. She had been polite and composed, if not cordial, leaving Jacobus pleased but perplexed. At the least it gave him some hope.

"Aka-what?" asked Nathaniel. "You're not talking in code now, are you, Jake?"

"*Aka-chochin,*" said Yumi, "are red paper lanterns that little neighborhood taverns traditionally display to show they are still open. Now the taverns themselves are called *aka-chochin.* Since we usually don't use street names in Japan, the *aka-chochin* on the corner here is used as a landmark for this lane that goes to Furukawa-sensei's house. The driver would have missed it had he not been staring into the night for it, and even then he almost passed it. Mr. Jacobus remembered it from when he worked with Furukawa-sensei."

The lane led them higher yet. Finally the driver turned off the lane onto a gravel path and came to a stop in front of Furukawa's tree-protected house. Diffuse light glowed through shoji screens from all four sides of the one-story unpainted wooden house. Though it was almost three in the morning, Makoto Furukawa was there to greet them at the entrance, standing with arms akimbo on the wear-polished wooden floor built just a few inches above the stone-paved alcove. About the same age as Jacobus, Furukawa radiated a sense of youth and energy, unlike Jacobus, who from youth conveyed a sense of age. Graying hair brushed straight back, smiling with his eyes as well as his mouth, Furukawa greeted them with relaxed but erect posture, bowing low from the waist with his hands on his thighs, displaying obvious comfort and ease wearing his blue-and-white cotton kimono, making his guests feel welcome. This was Makoto Furukawa's pattern, which Jacobus did not need to see in order to remember.

The driver pushed a button and the doors of the taxi opened automatically. Jacobus took money out of his wallet to pay the driver, but before he could pay he felt a touch, Yumi's, on his hand.

"Furukawa-sensei has already paid," said Yumi. "It is not necessary."

Jacobus listened for the swallows, descendants of the pair that decades ago had built a mud and straw nest above the polished wooden doorway—a traditional Japanese good-luck omen.

If I hear them, it's good luck, he thought. If I don't, then I'm not superstitious.

The birds, disturbed by the intrusion of strangers in the middle of the night, began to chirp pugnaciously, defending their nest.

Good luck. I'll take it, Jacobus concluded.

Furukawa's voice. Yumi quickly translated. "Furukawa-sensei says welcome to his home. He hopes you have had a comfortable trip."

At this cue, Jacobus bowed, knowing that he was reciprocating the gesture that Furukawa surely just made. Common courtesy.

Nathaniel didn't bow.

Yumi said, "Nathaniel, here in Japan it is an important custom to bow as a way of greeting."

Nathaniel replied, "Please tell Mr. Furukawa that with all due respect, my old grandpappy, who was the son of a slave, taught me not to bow to anybody. Not for a concert audience and certainly not in Japan." He turned to leave.

Jacobus thought, Jesus Christ, things are off to a great start. Damn swallows.

Even before Yumi had a chance to translate into Japanese, Furukawa responded.

Yumi translated Furukawa's words. "Please tell Jake's friend that I personally prefer the Western tradition of shaking hands, which shows respect among equals."

Nathaniel stopped. "In that case, I'm pleased to meet you." He extended his hand.

"Mr. Furukawa says you both must be very tired," said Yumi. "He will soon have food and drink waiting for you, but in the meantime first please take a bath."

"Do I smell that funky, Jake?" asked Nathaniel.

Yumi intervened, explaining that in Japan a bath is not so much for cleaning as it is for relaxation and pleasure, and that it's a custom for a host to invite a guest to bathe.

"You'll feel much better if you accept the invitation," she said.

Jacobus thought that for the first time since leaving New York he could hear confidence, if not a smile, in Yumi's voice.

"Well, what do you think, Jake?" asked Nathaniel.

"Why not, we could use a little tension relief. I'll show you the routine. And in response to your previous question, the answer is yes."

Yumi suddenly said, "Mr. Williams!"

"What now?" Nathaniel exploded. "Am I supposed to bow again?"

"No, no," said Yumi quickly. "Only that in Japan we always take off our shoes in a house. When you step onto the wooden floor, please wear these slippers; then, when you walk on the tatami mats, please take them off and walk in your bare feet."

"There's a custom I can live with. But next time remind me to wear shoes without laces."

"Now let's see if you can find slippers that'll actually fit your big hooves," said Jacobus.

"Nothing here more than half my size," said Nathaniel. "I feel like the ugly stepsister."

Yumi translated. Furukawa said something. Yumi suppressed a giggle.

"What did he say?" asked Nathaniel.

Yumi said she wasn't sure.

"Come on, honey, out with it."

"Furukawa-sensei said he knows the Cinderella story from the

Rossini opera, and that perhaps because it is after midnight is why you have already turned into a pumpkin."

"Is that supposed to be funny, Jake?" asked Nathaniel.

"Better than that, Nathaniel. It means he really likes you. He would never insult anyone he didn't consider a friend."

Furukawa, still laughing, led them down the wood-floored corridor that ran along the perimeter of the house.

Yumi said, "Mr. Jacobus, Furukawa-sensei wants me to tell you that nothing here has changed. This house that was your home one time is still the same."

Aided by the feel of wood polished by decades of stockinged feet and the barely perceptible pungent aroma of incense permeating the air, Jacobus tried to reconstruct his mental picture. He started with the large spaces and tried to fill in the details one by one, but it had been such a long time. He was certain that he was omitting a lot.

Reaching out, his hand brushed against the glossily smooth tree trunks that served as structural pillars. He recalled the one huge room in the middle of the house that was created when the sliding doors were all open, doors of wood frame and translucent paper that also served as walls. Floors that were finely woven straw tatami mats, smooth and accommodating to one's feet, each mat about three by six feet. Lacquered furniture that was sparse but elegant, constructed low to the ground. Yes, and in the far corner there was the alcove with the ornate pottery, a striking wall hanging with Japanese calligraphy, a beautiful flower arrangement, and a miniature ancestral shrine with a cracked Satsuma incense burner, the source of the scent that he was passing by right now. Simplicity. Elegance. Comfort. The opposite of his life.

The door to the bath slid open.

"O-furo," Furukawa said, patting Jacobus on his back. He laughed once more and left.

In the small antechamber leading to the main bathroom was a shelf with two bamboo trays. Each contained a fresh, folded yukata that would be their clothing after the bath.

"What now?" asked Nathaniel.

"We take our clothes off. What do you think?" said Jacobus.

They disrobed, placing the clothes they had been wearing for almost two days on the trays.

"Now open the door to the bath," said Jacobus.

Nathaniel slid open the inner door to the bathroom, the *o-furo* itself.

"This definitely ain't my bathroom in Manhattan," he said.

Though of similar dimensions, its design conveyed a feeling of space. The walls and floor were of cut but unpolished gray stone, with moss and hanging plants growing freely on the walls. There was one drain in the middle of the floor. Along one wall, about eighteen inches off the ground, were faucets. On the floor in front of the faucets were compartmentalized wooden trays containing washcloths, soap, and shampoo. Next to the trays were small wooden buckets and small wooden stools. In one corner was an inconspicuous wooden box, about three feet by four feet, rising just a few inches off the floor.

"Where's the bath?" asked Nathaniel.

"Over in the corner, if I remember correctly. It'll be covered with a wooden lid to keep the water hot."

"Looks kinda shallow to me, brother."

"Go take the top off. That should satisfy your curiosity."

Nathaniel did so and saw that the tub had been built deeply below floor level. Its sides were forest green tile, giving the impression of being bottomless. The water was level with the rim of the tub and steam was already forming into a small cloud.

"This is more like it," said Nathaniel as he began making sounds indicating he was getting into the tub.

"No!" shouted Jacobus.

"Say what?" asked Nathaniel. "What'd I do wrong now? The man said take a bath, so I'm takin' a bath."

"You have to wash first. The bath is just for soaking."

"Well, I'm lookin' around and I hope you don't expect me to sit on one of those stools to wash, because I can't even fit my left cheek on it!"

"You'll just have to do the best you can. Use two stools if you need to—cheek to cheek. Help me over to a stool and I'll show you."

Jacobus, sitting, felt for the faucet and turned it on. He found his tray and began washing. Covered with soap, he grabbed a loofah and scrubbed. Then he felt for the small bucket, filled it with hot water, and poured it over his head.

"Just do what I do."

After a while Nathaniel said, "Hey, this isn't so bad. When do we get to go into the tub?"

"When you're not funky. Since this tub isn't big enough for both of us, I'll go in first. By the time I'm finished, the water won't be too hot for you."

"What should I do in the meantime?"

"Keep washing."

Nathaniel helped Jacobus over the now slippery floor to the tub. Jacobus felt his way into it, quickly immersing himself in the water with a satisfied sigh. Within minutes he felt the tension draining. Like the pores of his skin, his mind opened. In the times he had spent in this bath, he had gained more revelatory insight about music than from any concert he had ever heard.

A fleeting image returned him to his home in the Berkshires, and to the state of near vagrancy of its current dilapidated condition. Maybe it was time to change. Whether he would have the chance was the bigger question.

"Your turn," he finally said to Nathaniel as he hauled himself out of the tub.

"Looks good," Nathaniel said, testing the water with a toe.

"Whoa!" he shouted.

"What's wrong?" asked Jacobus, concerned.

"I ain't no lobster."

"Don't worry. After about twenty seconds the pain will wear off."

Jacobus heard the plunge. Nathaniel gave a short "Huh!" with the shock of the heat, his bulk creating a minitsunami as waves flowing over the top of the tub noisily gurgled into the floor drain.

"Quite a performance," said Jacobus. He began drying himself with a towel, taunting Nathaniel by humming the melody of the "Trout" Quintet by Schubert.

There was no response from Nathaniel.

I guess he doesn't like my joke—or my singing—thought Jacobus.

After hearing nothing for two or three minutes, Jacobus became concerned.

"Nathaniel, are you all right?"

"Ahhhh," said Nathaniel. "Some of these customs aren't so bad."

"When you've been working on something for a thousand years," said Jacobus, "chances are you'll get it right."

"Maybe, but seems they didn't need so long for some things. Look what they've done here with classical music in just a few generations.

Pretty soon there'll be more Japanese playing the Mendelssohn Concerto than us folk."

Jacobus felt for his *yukata*, sliding his arms through elbow-length sleeves. He thought again about patterns—the historic pattern of Japanese adaptation of Western ideas and their notable ability to assimilate and transform them into something uniquely Japanese. Trade. Technology. Politics. Music?

Jacobus considered Yumi. When he first heard Yumi play, there was something about it that was unlike Furukawa's other students. Something about it that did not fit the pattern. A misty rice paddy with a bright thorny rosebush in the middle. At the time he couldn't put his finger on it. Two patterns intersecting.

Furukawa, the known quantity. One way of understanding music. One pattern. But there was another pattern. He now guessed it came from the other teacher, her first teacher.

"You're right," said Jacobus. "Let's go eat."

"Yeah," said Nathaniel. "I think I'm ready for that food and drink Furukawa was talking about. Is this the plug I pull to let the water out?"

The question rifled Jacobus's thoughts back to the present.

"No!" he shouted.

"Jesus H. Christ, what did I do now?" asked Nathaniel.

"Don't pull the plug. The water stays in for the rest of the night. Guests are always given dibs—I'm sure Furukawa and Yumi will be using it later. That's why you have to scrub so well before you get in. So just get your heinie out of the tub, put the cover back on, and don your *yukata*."

As Jacobus was about to leave the bathroom, he felt Nathaniel's mammoth hand on his shoulder, gently stopping him in his tracks.

"Yeah?" Jacobus said. "Sorry I shouted about the plug."

"No, not that," said Nathaniel. "Jake, ever since we left your house I've kept my big mouth shut. Okay, Japan has been a lot nicer than I expected, but you gotta realize I am one troubled black man. Intercontinental Insurance has no idea where I am or what I'm up to, which is the least of my worries, because if someone, like the police, is looking at this situation from the outside in, it sure could look like the two of us are just a pair of escaped felons, and that's not gonna do me a world of good when it comes to future employment. Now, I know you've told me the general idea here is to get the violin back and get you off

the hook for Victoria's death, but you haven't told me jack about
how."

"Yeah, I know."

"It's also obvious to me that somehow Yumi's involved with this
whole business, and that there was that girl who came in second in the
Grimsley Competition in 1931 who you figure went to Japan, though
you're not even sure if she's dead or alive. Now, I found out that stuff
before Victoria was killed, so are you saying they have something to do
with the theft?"

Jacobus considered his options.

"I'm not saying, Nathaniel. What I will tell you is that they may have
information that will be helpful . . . crucial . . . and that I hope to receive their assistance. Other than that, you'll have to trust me. But you
have my word, the violin will be returned."

They stood in silence. Jacobus wasn't going to show any more of his
hand than that. He knew it wasn't much, but now it was up to Nathaniel
whether he would throw in his cards.

"Jake," said Nathaniel, "I just want to tell you one thing."

"Not two?"

"Just one, you bastard. I just want you to know. I believe you."

"Thank you, Nathaniel. I appreciate that."

TWENTY-NINE

The two found their way back to Furukawa and Yumi in the main
room.

After they removed their slippers in order to walk on the tatami, Furukawa led Jacobus, followed by Yumi and Nathaniel, to the low black-
lacquered table in the center of the tatami room. Jacobus sat on floor
cushions, as cross-legged as he could manage, the other three taking
their own sides of the square. Jacobus placed his index fingers next to
each other directly in front of him on the edge of the table, then moved
them apart until his hands reached the corners. Having gauged the
table's size, he proceeded to nimbly feel around the setting in front of
him, first for chopsticks, then for the seemingly limitless array of small
dishes and glasses, all the while turning his head, listening, inhaling,

discerning, discovering. He was able to identify almost everything that was being served.

He found an abundance of traditional Japanese snacks in simple but elegant red-lacquered and blue-and-white porcelain bowls. There were rice crackers with bits of seaweed; various kinds of tiny dried and salted fish, eaten whole; sweet rice balls with toasted sesame seeds and wrapped in dried seaweed called nori; skewers of Japanese yakitori made from small pieces of chicken, chicken liver, and chicken skin; a large sliced squid broiled teriyaki style; colorful salty pickled vegetables; small cubes of fried tofu in a sweet soy sauce. All of these were complemented by an equally impressive array of drinks—large bottles of Sapporo beer; distinctive traditional carafes of sake, both hot and cold, to be drunk in small, square wooden sake cups; a local brew called *shochu*, a refreshing but potent combination of sake and fermented sweet potato liquor; a formidable assortment of Japanese whiskey; and a pitcher of cold wheat tea, especially refreshing for hot summer weather.

Nathaniel chose sake. In customary fashion, Yumi poured first for Nathaniel, then for herself. Furukawa poured a glass of whiskey for Jacobus and finally one for himself.

He stood up, and with Yumi translating, said, "I wish to officially welcome my old friend and my new friend to my home, and hope your stay will be a peaceful and successful one."

Amen to that, thought Jacobus, already planning how he would elicit his invitation to the Shinagawa household.

"*Campai!*" Furukawa shouted in full voice, downing his whiskey.

"*Campai!*" responded Jacobus and Yumi. Nathaniel, catching on, followed suit, and all downed their drink.

"Ah!" said Jacobus, smacking his lips. "Suntory. President's Special Blend, my favorite whiskey. You have a good memory too, Max."

Yumi, the intermediary, replied, "Furukawa-sensei says, 'How could he ever forget the first night he drank with you and Mr. Goldbloom.' That is why he has so many bottles on the table tonight."

Furukawa had first met Jacobus and Goldbloom when the Boston Symphony toured Japan in 1959. Furukawa had brought a few of his best students to their hotel room to play for both of them. When Jacobus and Goldbloom declined payment, Furukawa felt obligated to compensate them by other means. He took them from one elite geisha house to another, where they were wined and dined (costing Furukawa many times what the lessons would have cost) until the moment when Jacobus fell backward off his cushion and passed out. The night on the town cemented their friendship, and Jacobus returned regularly to Japan to work with Furukawa and his students, and to drink, until his blindness struck.

"Tell Max that he doesn't need to get me drunk again to impress me. I just came here to be with my old friend again."

"Furukawa-sensei is honored to have you visit but is sorry he didn't have more time to prepare better for your arrival."

"Tell Max that it has been a long year and I decided to reward myself. It is obvious from his hospitality that I have made the right decision."

"Furukawa-sensei says he hopes you will enjoy the food and drink he has put in front of you, even though at this late hour he is serving only this small snack. He remembers what you like. He also thanks you deeply for bringing Mr. Williams and me with you."

"Tell Max it would have been difficult to enjoy a conversation with him without your presence as a translator, and that I couldn't imagine a better introduction to Japan for my good friend Mr. Williams than by giving him an opportunity to experience Max's wonderful hospitality."

Nathaniel added, "I didn't expect to say this, but I have to admit I'm overwhelmed at your hospitality. But I do have one problem."

"What is the problem?" asked Yumi.

"I can't move my legs!" cried Nathaniel. "I wasn't made for sitting like this!"

Furukawa laughed. Yumi tried to help Nathaniel stand, but Jacobus could hear that her success was limited. Furukawa said something. Yumi laughed.

"What's so funny now?" asked Nathaniel.

"Furukawa-sensei says you look like the sumo wrestler who got kicked in the wrong place."

"Well, at least that's a step up from Cinderella."

Furukawa, still chuckling, continued.

Yumi translated, "And to you, Mr. Jacobus, he says he is so sorry that you will be in Japan only briefly, because it will surely take Mr. Williams longer than that to learn to sit in the Japanese style."

"Tell Max that I'd have to spend the rest of my life here if I had to wait for Mr. Williams to learn how to sit. Unfortunately I am obligated to return to the United States as soon as possible, but tell Max that one day with him is worth a week with anyone else."

Jacobus knew that it would not be long before the whereabouts of his unlikely trio—an unkempt blind man, a large bearded black man, and an attractive Japanese girl with green eyes—became pinpointed, even in this out-of-the-way place.

Furukawa was silent for a moment before replying. Jacobus heard him sip his whiskey.

"Furukawa-sensei says he understands and would like to know how you are enjoying teaching me." The slightest tremor, an almost undetectable waver of worry, bent Yumi's voice.

Jacobus chuckled. "Not easy to be a translator and the subject of discussion at the same time, is it?"

"No," said Yumi.

"Well, you can tell Max that if all his students play as well as you, he can send all of them to me."

"Furukawa-sensei says thank you but that will not be possible."

"Why not?" asked Jacobus, alarmed.

"Because," said Yumi, "I was sensei's final student. He has retired."

"Bullshit!"

"Furukawa-sensei says he is very happy to be retired. He believes he has accomplished his task as a teacher. He now devotes himself to many of the things he didn't have time for when he was teaching, like fishing and playing chess and singing with his karaoke machine. He hopes you will have time to play chess with him."

Real-life chess, thought Jacobus. And not just with you, my friend.

Furukawa suggested they refresh themselves with some garden air. Nathaniel declined, unaccustomed to the combined potency of sake, *shochu,* and Suntory drunk in copious quantities. "I haven't seen any beds in this house," he said. "But if there are any I wouldn't mind one bein' under me right now."

Yumi asked Nathaniel to wait while she retrieved bedding from a closet. By the time she returned with the futon and feather comforter, Nathaniel was already snoring on the tatami. Jacobus got out of the way as she unfolded the mattress and placed a traditional soybean-stuffed pillow at the head of the makeshift bed. Then, with great exertion, Jacobus, Furukawa, and Yumi rolled Nathaniel onto it.

"Furukawa-sensei says he hopes you will sleep comfortably." Yumi, still on her knees, slightly winded, bowed to the unconscious Nathaniel.

Outside, the mountain air was chilly, but the heat from the *furo* imbued Jacobus's body with lasting warmth under his *yukata.* In the darkness, their careful footsteps quietly followed the stone path of the garden as crickets chirped and frogs grunted contentedly. Furukawa was side by side with Jacobus; Yumi's light step, slightly out of his rhythm, was just behind them. The dim light emanating through the house's shoji screens did not reach Jacobus and Furukawa.

"There are fireflies here, just like at your home," Yumi said to Jacobus. "It is difficult to tell them apart from the stars. Furukawa-sensei's garden is not a typical Japanese formal garden. The trees and shrubs are not artistically sculpted or strategically placed."

Jacobus remembered all this from his earlier days here, but he did not interrupt Yumi. This was the first time she had spoken on her own. She spoke quietly, maybe so as not to disturb the tranquillity of the night, maybe because it was more a matter of will than of cordiality. What was the message she was trying to convey? Letting bygones be bygones? He didn't think so.

"It is more of an orchard. There are dozens of fruit trees and vines crowded together in this small space; they are carefully pruned for functional rather than aesthetic purposes."

Jacobus could smell the air, pungent with blossoms and of rotting fruit that lay on the moist, fertile ground.

Furukawa put his hand on Jacobus's arm, stopping him. Furukawa spoke.

Yumi translated. "This is a biwa tree. Please try the fruit."

He heard her tug at a branch, the leaves swishing as it recoiled.

"I don't think you have these in America. They are at the perfect stage of ripeness."

Furukawa spoke again, at greater length, and laughed.

"Furukawa-sensei asks me to tell you a story about this tree," Yumi said hesitantly.

"Go ahead. Don't be shy."

"When I first started to study the violin with Furukawa-sensei, I was very young, ten years old. I wanted to be a baseball player more than a violinist."

"Yeah? Red Sox or Yankees fan?"

"What? Yomiuri Giants, I suppose."

"Diplomatic answer."

"As you may know, I have no brothers or sisters, so my father, who I believe wanted a son to teach to play baseball, taught me instead. I loved to play nevertheless and at first did not want so much to study violin with Furukawa-sensei. So after my first lesson here, I came out to the garden and picked the biwa fruit from this tree. I then threw several of them through Furukawa-sensei's shoji screens."

"How far are we from the house?" asked Jacobus. "Thirty feet?"

"Maybe along the path. But a straight line? I think not so much. Maybe twenty feet."

"Still, pretty good throw for a ten-year-old. Furukawa-san must have been pissed off!"

"He never told me what he felt."

"Ask him!"

"I couldn't do that!"

"Hey, Miss Biwa Yomiuri Giants fan, this isn't you asking. It's me. Ask."

Yumi reluctantly complied. Furukawa's laughing response was equally brief and animated.

"Furukawa-sensei says that a little mischief is necessary to be successful in life. He calls this biwa tree 'Feelings Tree'—it's hard to translate—because this is where I expressed my true feelings. Of course, after time it became clear to me that I would not become a baseball player and that I loved the violin more."

"Ask Max if he has any other trees that he has named."

Jacobus waited for a reply.

"I don't hear him say anything."

"Furukawa-sensei made a hand gesture we Japanese understand, like a backhand flick of the wrist with fingers pointed down. To Americans it looks like 'go away'—I think you say 'shoo'—but in Japanese it means 'follow me.' Even if you had seen it, I would have had to translate anyway."

They walked along the path to what must have been the edge of Furukawa's garden. Jacobus felt Furukawa take one of his hands in his and place it on a tree. The bark felt coarse and deeply furrowed.

Sure as hell not a fruit tree, Jacobus thought.

He tried to run his hands around the circumference of the tree the same way he had felt the dimensions of the dinner table, but found that even with his arms outstretched he couldn't reach halfway. It was immense. He pressed his body against the tree and inched around to the other side. Suddenly he pitched forward. The whole side of the tree was gone! Jacobus literally stumbled into the center of the tree, still probing, feeling its rocklike hardness, finally emerging and creeping his way back to where he had begun. One last measurement, he put both hands on the tree and reached up as high as he could but felt no branches.

"This tree's ancient! Smells like cedar. But how does it survive? Most of it's missing."

After the translations, Yumi responded for Furukawa.

"This tree was planted by Furukawa-sensei's ancestors seventeen generations ago, more than four hundred years. His family has lived here ever since and has cared for this tree. That is why it is simply called 'Family Tree.' But Furukawa-sensei says what the tree means to him is that beauty comes in many forms and cannot be rushed."

When Yumi finished, Furukawa continued in a matter-of-fact tone.

"He says he does not like Japanese bonsai plants because they take new, healthy plants and try to make them look old and sick using wires and other unnatural means. Nor does he much prefer the American style of pruning old trees to make them look young, even though that might keep them living longer."

Furukawa had undoubtedly taken him to these trees for a reason. What he was explaining must have greater significance. So far, the biwa story reconfirmed his conclusions regarding Yumi's strong will. A damn good arm too. What else? Jacobus needed to explore further.

"Ask Max what's his ideal."

"Ideal?"

"Yeah. His way of caring for the trees. If he doesn't like the Japanese way or the American way, what does he like?"

"I see." She translated.

"Furukawa-sensei says a thing must be what it is. Sometimes the beauty of a plant is apparent almost immediately, like with annual flowers. Other times it takes years or even lifetimes before its beauty is perceived, as with this tree. When it was one hundred, two hundred, even three hundred years old it looked similar to many other trees. But a century ago lightning hit this tree. Nature has made it unique and has drawn out the tree's true character. Beauty is always inside things and if we just care for them rather than manipulate them, the beauty will always come out eventually."

"Does Max apply this philosophy to his teaching?"

Yumi translated his response.

"He feels his true job is to take small seedlings and nurture them until they are strong and healthy. He says he provides his students, these small seedlings, with . . . with fertilizer."

Yumi asked Furukawa what he meant by fertilizer.

"He means the skills and understanding necessary to begin their path to mature artistry."

Jacobus was still groping for his own understanding. *Is Furukawa just shoveling me another kind of fertilizer?*

"Then why has he given his students to me?"

"Furukawa-sensei says his students are like small tomato plants in a greenhouse. They get just the right amount of nourishment and attention so that they are all healthy. But he doesn't approve of forcing them to become something they're not ready to be. Unlike tomatoes, students take many years to ripen and must learn to live on the outside of the greenhouse. So he sends them to you because you can teach them to flourish—is that the word?—flourish in a world where they must be able to know how to use their skills and their artistry without the benefit of controlled conditions."

Jacobus had assumed the answer would be something like that, and he appreciated it, but he still didn't know in what direction Furukawa was trying to lead him. He knew he was being led, he just wasn't sure where. How was he going to get from Point A to Point Z? Where was Point Z? Hard to walk in a straight line in the dark. Jacobus was at a loss as to how he should continue.

It was very late. It must almost be dawn. No one was saying anything. Jacobus stood there listening to frogs and crickets, to Furukawa and Yumi breathing; he smelled the tree, smelled the soil and the sweetness of rotting fruit. What more was there? What had he not asked?

Furukawa spoke.

Yumi said, "Furukawa-sensei says that you should sleep, that perhaps tomorrow you will be busy."

Jacobus was about to agree when he suddenly realized that Furukawa had already told him what he needed to know. Yes, Max was trying to help.

Furukawa had said his job had been to *take* small seedlings. Nurture them. Not *plant* them. He didn't actually *plant* them. Maybe he did see the path Furukawa was showing him.

"Tell Max that I understand that he helps the seedlings grow and I help them develop into mature trees, but please ask where he gets the seedlings from. Who plants the seeds and helps them germinate?"

Yumi translated. Furukawa's answer came immediately.

"Furukawa-sensei says that in this area there are many such farmers even though the soil is thin and rocky. Many villages have teachers who begin toddlers on musical instruments. The talented ones are sent to him."

"Ask Max if he has gotten many seedlings from your village."

"Aren't you tired?" asked Yumi, a strain of desperation faintly audible.

"Please ask."

Yumi asked.

She said, "Furukawa-sensei says that many of his best students have come from my village. My mother, Keiko Shinagawa, is a violin teacher there, and Furukawa-sensei says she is one of the best such farmers he has known."

Jacobus spoke with renewed energy. Now he'd use his vestigial diplomatic skills.

"Tell Max that if all of Mrs. Shinagawa's students are such healthy seedlings, he has had a very easy job."

Yumi hesitated. Jacobus said, "Don't be shy. Remember, it's me talking. Go ahead."

Yumi translated.

Furukawa laughed. Jacobus knew that he needn't say more. Furukawa would lead the rest of the way.

"Furukawa-sensei says that even as we plant our own seeds, someone before us planted seeds for both you and him to grow. You learned from Dr. Krovney, and Krovney in turn studied with the great Romanian violinist Enesco."

Jacobus nodded.

"Furukawa-sensei says you might be interested to know that my mother was also taught by her mother." Yumi said this politely, without any trace of enthusiasm, like a soldier going through the formalities of surrender.

Jacobus said, "Please tell Max that you were kind enough to tell me at our second lesson that your grandmother played the violin, but I didn't realize she actually taught your mother."

"Furukawa-sensei says that she is a very special person, and even though she is old, she still occasionally helps my mother sow the good seeds."

Jacobus remained silent.

Furukawa said something. Jacobus thought he heard a name being repeated. Hashimoto. It made him frown.

Yumi was silent. Furukawa repeated his message to her, scolding her with sudden, forceful vehemence.

The name Hashimoto again! Who was this new player? He didn't know what it all meant, but he didn't need a translator to understand Furukawa's tone.

And I thought I could be a real schmuck! Jacobus said to himself.

The conversation had changed keys, a dissonant undertone, out of tune with the peaceful resonance of the garden, leaving Jacobus troubled and off balance.

Yumi choked out the message. "Furukawa-sensei says it would be very enlightening for you to meet such a wonderful teacher. It might help you with your own work."

"And what did you say to him?" asked Jacobus.

"I said that as I hadn't been able to contact my family when we left New York so suddenly, they don't even know I'm here. They will not be ready to prepare properly for our arrival."

"And what did Max say?"

Yumi paused. Jacobus was certain the translation he'd receive would be far from word-for-word.

"Furukawa-sensei said he will arrange everything. That my family will be honored by your visit."

"Please tell Max that neither he nor your family should go to any trouble."

Yumi repeated what Jacobus said and listened to Furukawa's reply.
"Furukawa-sensei says it is no trouble. He says, 'Now go to sleep.' "

In the darkness, in his blindness, Jacobus knew that Makoto Furukawa
was not smiling.

THIRTY

By the time Jacobus awoke after a few hours of jet-lagged, Suntory-
induced sleep, Furukawa had already made the arrangements. Yes,
Yumi's family would be delighted to have her new sensei visit. No, it
was no trouble. Yes, he will spend the night there. Would Jacobus-san's
friend, Williams-san, be joining them also? No, Furukawa-san decided
to take him fishing. Williams-san's own protests were futile. He will go
fishing. It is all arranged. Jacobus heard the anxiety in Yumi's voice
when she translated.

Later that morning, Furukawa was in his garden pruning his biwa
trees. It was a moist, balmy morning, sunlight filtering through the dap-
pled green foliage. Birds hopped along the ground, picking at the
apricot-sized biwa that had fallen. Furukawa was not surprised when
Inspector Kengo Taniguchi from the Sendai prefectural police department drove up.

Taniguchi had received the equivalent of an all points bulletin from
his central office, which had received the message from Tokyo that the
New York Police Department was searching for a murder suspect who
might be in Taneguchi's vicinity.

When Roy Miller found Jacobus's house empty the morning Jacobus
had promised to come down for questioning, he immediately phoned
Detective Malachi at the NYPD. Malachi slammed Miller with every
four-letter name he could think of, but it was only when he called him
a yokel that Miller responded, "Now hold on one minute." Malachi
wanted to chew out Miller even longer than he did, but he had to move
fast to find Jacobus. He ordered Miller to find out the license plate
number of Williams's red Rabbit and to put out an APB for any car
matching its description in case they changed the plates. Then he called
all international airports within a three-hour driving radius of the

Berkshires and told them who he was looking for. This was no small task in itself, as that area included Albany, Hartford, Boston, JFK, Newark, LaGuardia, and, as an afterthought, Montreal. He also contacted bus and train stations.

However, Malachi had no idea where Jacobus might be going. He could be hiding somewhere in his basement for all knew. He called each person at MAP and asked if they knew where Jacobus might be, assuming they would like nothing better than to see Jacobus behind bars, but they were no help at all. In fact, to his ear, they sounded confused, almost frightened. He didn't know what to make of it but put it in his back pocket for future consideration. Finally the call came in from Air Canada that Jacobus had ticketed a JAL flight to Nagoya, Japan, early that morning. He called the people at MAP again and asked whether they had any idea why Jacobus would be going to Japan. Again, they were of little help, but they mentioned the young student who was with him at his interviews. When Malachi asked her name, he received several different versions. He then called JAL and asked for the passenger manifest to ascertain the name. This was not so easy either, as many passengers on the full flight to Nagoya were Japanese. Having gone through the list and whittled her name down to three possibilities, he called the Customs and Immigration office at the Nagoya airport and waited impatiently on the line until an English speaker was found. He received addresses for the names and put in a request that they all be checked out.

How Malachi came upon Furukawa's address was a bit of luck. When he called Rachel Lewison and asked why Jacobus might have gone to Japan, she said that although she didn't know, Jacobus's friend, Sol Goldbloom, might, and that he had played a concert the night before in New York with the Boston Symphony. So Malachi called the Boston Symphony, found out that the orchestra was staying at the Wellington Hotel, and caught a break when someone pointed out Goldbloom just as he was checking out. Malachi asked Goldbloom if he knew of any contacts Jacobus had in Japan. He wouldn't explain why when Goldbloom asked the reason but just said it was important, and knowing that the two were old friends, stressed that it was for Jacobus's own good. Goldbloom told him about Furukawa. He didn't have the precise address but knew it was on Kyushu. Malachi went back to his notes, to see if one of the three women on his short list had an address on Kyushu.

Yumi Shinagawa's address was a match. That gave him another idea. He called Air Canada again and asked how Jacobus's and Shinagawa's tickets had been paid for. He then added a third name to the list—Nathaniel Williams—found out what he did for a living, and made several more calls, including one to Intercontinental Insurance Associates.

Inspector Taniguchi emerged from his spotless car wearing his spotless khaki police uniform. He bowed low to Furukawa, who was one of the most respected citizens of the prefecture. Furukawa invited Taniguchi in for tea. They entered the cool house, the exterior sliding doors open to admit a refreshing breeze. As Furukawa brewed and then poured the green tea, they patiently discussed the beautiful day, the state of Furukawa's garden, and the mixed blessing of the late arrival of the rainy season.

Taniguchi mentioned that earlier in the morning he had visited the Hashimoto home, which at a higher elevation than Furukawa's home was cooler and cloudier, and it looked like it might even rain. Furukawa asked whether he had a pleasant visit with the Hashimotos.

Taniguchi told him that he had tea there also, and that Mrs. Hashimoto and Mrs. Shinagawa were in good health, but that it had been his unpleasant task to inquire whether they knew the whereabouts of Mrs. Shinagawa's daughter, Yumi, or of two Americans traveling with her. The women had expressed surprise and concern, but no, they hadn't seen them nor knew where to find them. They said they would contact the inspector if they learned anything.

Furukawa shook his head and said he wished he could be helpful, especially as Mr. Jacobus was an old friend and Miss Shinagawa a former student. He regretted that he couldn't provide any constructive information.

Taniguchi bowed low, expressing his appreciation, and politely mentioning his admiration for the architecture of Furukawa's home. Furukawa understood this to be a request to have his house searched and offered to guide Taniguchi around the premises. Furukawa gave him a detailed tour, talking about the materials and craftsmanship of every nook and cranny. Of course he showed Taniguchi the *furo,* which was drained, dried, and spotless like every other inch of the house. Taniguchi patiently followed Furukawa throughout, frequently commenting with great sincerity about how someday he and his family might have a home even a fraction as beautiful.

Finally satisfied, Taniguchi bowed deeply to Furukawa, thanking him for his time and hospitality. Furukawa thanked him for having someone with whom to share his morning and told him he would call if he heard anything about Jacobus's whereabouts. Furukawa, like Mrs. Hashimoto, knew better than to ask the reason for Taniguchi's inquiry. First of all, to express any curiosity would have suggested they knew more than they were telling. Second, they knew Taniguchi would not have told them, anyway.

Furukawa waved good-bye as Inspector Taniguchi's car disappeared into the quiet morning. He then meandered along the garden path to the edge of his yard and knocked on the outside of "Family Tree." Nathaniel emerged and brushed some flaked-off bark from his shirt. Furukawa was smiling. Nathaniel bowed.

THIRTY-ONE

Furukawa had instructed the driver to take Jacobus and Yumi to Nishiyama the back way, which would avoid the main road that Taniguchi, who would be in a hurry, would be driving on to his house. Mrs. Hashimoto had called Furukawa the minute that Taniguchi had left her house.

Smells like the garbage on Fifty-fifth Street, thought Jacobus, inhaling. Worse. He required no imaginative speculation to appreciate the pungent aroma of cow manure and of sulfurous hot springs escaping from geothermal fissures. The cab continued upward along the winding road. Jacobus heard cattle lowing as they grazed in the moist pasture nestled in the shadow of precipitous, tree-covered mountains, gray in the distance, enshrouded by mist. The sharply curving route, and the car's complaining engine, indicated the steepness of the mountains. Odors permeated even the sealed environment of the car.

Smells like Hell, Jacobus thought.

The slow, rhythmic monotony of windshield wipers indicated a heavy drizzle. Not like the drive to Montreal, he thought. Thank God. Windshield wipers! That's all the driver needs to be able to see. He took a bitter last drag on his Camel, rolled open the window to flick away the butt, and almost gagged from the stinking fumes. He quickly closed the window.

He felt for the cassette. It was still in his pocket. He hoped to utilize it as planned but still wondered, Who exactly was this Hashimoto? He was worried she might not be his English English. What if she's a totally unknown Japanese Japanese? Jacobus was not like a jazz musician who could improvise on the spur of the moment. Not a scat singer, like Ella Fitzgerald. For Jacobus, improvising could be disastrous, whether in performance or in life. If all went well the violin would be returned by the end of the day. If not, the game would be over. He couldn't afford mistakes.

They arrived at Yumi's village of Nishiyama in early afternoon by Jacobus's reckoning, although with the thirteen-hour difference from New York his sense of time felt as accurate as a navigator on a cloudy night.

"So your house is between a rice paddy and vegetable garden," said Jacobus, emerging from the car into the mist.

"How do you know this?" asked Yumi.

"Smell of onions, cabbages, definitely compost here," he said, pointing to the left, "and here," pointing to the right, "flock of waterbirds. Use the paddies as their personal wetlands. Heard them take off when I closed the car door. The house being adjacent to the rice paddy, I'd also guess it's separated from the field by stone walls and built on a higher base of land. Traditional style."

"Yes, that is correct," said a new, unexpected voice in clear, if accented, English. "In fact, our house is even more old-fashioned than Furukawa-sensei's. We have the thatched roof, and the sliding doors along the side are made of wood planks."

"Shinagawa-san? *Konnichi-wa!*" said Jacobus, concealing his surprise.

Jesus, I hadn't heard her coming while I was talking to Yumi, he thought. Either I must be getting old, or she's light on her feet. Or both.

"Yes, I am Yumi's mother, Mr. Jacobus."

Jacobus felt his hand firmly grasped and shaken. Jacobus was encouraged by the Western greeting. It fit. So far.

"Oka-san," Yumi said to her mother, "please meet Jacobus-sensei."

"How do you do, sensei?" she said. "Welcome."

"Ah, now that I can speak in English," said Jacobus, "perhaps your daughter, whose translating had been invaluable, will be able to relax a little."

Mrs. Shinagawa chuckled politely, but Yumi did not respond.

"Come, Mr. Jacobus, Mother is waiting for you inside. Dinner is almost ready."

"Dinner?"

"Yes, the sun is just now setting. This is when we normally eat. Are you not hungry?"

"Well, I suppose I am. I guess my stomach is still on New York time," Jacobus said, covering his blunder.

Damn, he thought. He had made two mistakes in one minute.

"Yes," Keiko Shinagawa said, leading Jacobus into the house, "time is measured much differently here than in New York."

Arriving at the entrance, Jacobus could tell the house was indeed in the old farm style. Under his feet he could feel the unevenness of hard packed earth. From his right, where at one time animals had been stabled inside the house, wafted the irrefutable and ineradicable trace of hay and horse smell. There was the burly scent of creosote where once there had been a central fire pit for cooking and heating. With no chimney, it had sent its smoke up to the ceiling, making the beams and rafters hard and blackened over the decades.

Like me, Jacobus thought, immediately yearning for a cigarette.

"Mr. Jacobus," said a new voice, interrupting his analysis. This voice was not only speaking English but was clearly and gracefully English-accented. Mrs. English English?

Can't be Hashimoto. Must be Padgett. Or Desmond. All connected, somehow. All in one. It must be.

The voice came closer.

"How do you do, Mr. Jacobus? I have the distinct privilege of being Yumi's grandmother. It is indeed a pleasure to meet you, even on such short notice. Yumi has told us so many wonderful things about you. Yumi-chan, why don't you go and help your mother with dinner so Mr. Jacobus and I may chat for a bit. Then I'd like to hear all about your violin lessons, dear."

"Yes, Oba-san," Yumi said.

"Mrs. Hashimoto, I presume?" said Jacobus, extending his hand. His streaming adrenaline made it difficult to prevent his hand from trembling.

"Please call me Kate," she said, taking his hand in hers. "They call me Cato here. No one has called me Kate for a long time; we get so few Westerners visiting this region."

"In that case, you can call me Jake," he said, still holding her hand—longer than he should?—feeling in it her age but also confidence and vitality. Strength.

"Thank you, Jake, I will. We generally are a lot less formal than the folk in these parts. I think we're considered a bit odd on that account. Nevertheless, as you may know, we have had some success over the years teaching the local children to play the violin."

"If you've had other students like Yumi, it sounds like you're pulling that Japanese modesty stuff with me," said Jacobus as he removed a small wrapped package from his jacket pocket and handed it to Kate.

"A little something for you and your family," he said.

"How thoughtful!" said Kate. "Some Japanese traditions here *are* worth keeping, aren't they? A cassette. May I unwrap it?"

"Be my guest."

"Hmm . . . not labeled. Lovely! A surprise, and we'll listen to it right after tea," she said. "I'll just slip the cassette into the sleeve of my kimono, like those shady characters do in those hilarious samurai soap operas. Now, please allow me to escort you to our humble dining room."

Jacobus felt her arm entwine itself with his and judged from its angle that she was about his height, maybe a little taller. Through the fabric of the kimono he could feel her arm's musculature. Still firm. No flab hanging off bone. Not bad for an old broad, he thought.

She led him, at a speed neither too rushed to risk an accident nor too slow to be insulting, into a room that did not have a tatami floor.

Jacobus heard Yumi and Keiko in the adjacent kitchen, from which the flavorful smells suggested they were finishing preparations for the meal. Their coordinated movements, quiet and wordless, sounded practiced and efficient.

"This room is the one concession to England that my late husband, Mr. Hashimoto, was willing to make," said Kate. "Now that I'm getting on in years myself I'm glad he did. I don't know if I could enjoy my tea sitting on the floor anymore. Here we are, Jake. Here's your chair."

The dining table was old England but the meal pure Japanese. It started with sashimi, fillets of fresh raw fish from the local streams, served with spicy wasabi—which to Jacobus's palette tasted so fresh it must have been ground from leaves plucked from the same streams as the fish—pickled ginger, shredded daikon, and soy sauce. The mixture of flavors and textures aroused his taste buds.

"Isn't Mr. Shinagawa joining us?" Jacobus asked Keiko, his mouth still half full of a perch fillet.

"My husband," said Keiko, "works for the prefectural government. His office is in Kagoshima, which is several hours from here and makes it impossible to commute. So he has a flat there, and we go to visit him on occasion."

"Well, I'm sorry that I won't be able to meet him on this trip," said Jacobus, swallowing. Time to bait them like they baited this fish, he thought.

"Perhaps sometime in the future," said Keiko.

"I hope so. Could you please pass a little more wasabi? But that puts Yumi in a particularly uncomfortable position."

"How so, Jake?" asked Kate, with a hint of tension that anyone other than Jacobus would have missed.

Hooked her! I *am* on the right track, dammit.

"Well, here we are, three violin teachers and one student. It's not very fair, is it, three against one? I wouldn't want to be in her shoes!"

"Yes, we'll do our best not to gang up on you, Yumi-chan, won't we?" Kate laughed, relief evident. "After all, it's difficult enough studying with one teacher at a time. Mr. Jacobus, I see you have finished your sashimi. Lovely, isn't it? The next course will be served momentarily."

Without another word Jacobus heard Keiko slide her seat back and remove herself to the kitchen.

Efficient chain of command we have here, Jacobus thought. No question who the boss is either.

"You see, Jake," said Kate, "in a more traditional household it would be me in the kitchen while everyone else eats. But fortunately for me I'm a horrific chef—no doubt my English genes—and, frankly, some traditions just aren't worth a hoot."

Keiko brought in a huge tray of tempura served on rustic bamboo baskets. Thinly sliced vegetables from the family garden plot, shrimp, and fish had been dipped in a light batter and quickly deep-fried.

Jacobus dipped a tempura onion into the slightly sweet sauce. He smiled as he took his first bite, and Keiko commented, "Ah, Jacobus-sensei. I'm so glad it pleases you. Here we like good food."

"I have a friend who says the same thing," replied Jacobus, thinking about Sol's comment. Family. Music. Doing the right thing. Food.

"Then next time you visit us, you should definitely bring him with you," Kate said. "But in the meantime, we are happy to have you all to ourselves.

"Since all of us—or should I say three-quarters of us—are teachers, and since you're here for such a short time, Jake, would you mind terribly if we picked your brain? What a horrible saying, 'picking your brain,' but would you mind?"

"Well," said Jacobus, wiping off some tempura sauce dripping down his chin with his shirtsleeve, "if that food was intended as a bribe, you've succeeded. I've told Yumi that the key to understanding is asking questions. So go ahead, pick away."

And sooner or later the game'll begin. Now we're just setting up the chessboard.

"That is so kind of you, Jake. As you know, Keiko and I teach only beginners, but you've had advanced students brought to you by teachers like us from all over the world. What I'd like to know is, have you found any problems in violin playing that seem to be universal? After all, if music is truly the universal language, one must also reasonably expect that there will be universal speech impediments."

"You'd be surprised how many, but why that should be the case probably has more to do with the way one thinks about playing than about anything physiological," answered Jacobus.

"Hmm. Your pedagogical tone suits you well, Mr. Jacobus, but could you kindly provide an example?"

The two of them engaged a deep discussion of the difficulty students around the world have with the little finger of either hand—that finger being the weakest, thereby creating the tendency for the greatest tension, the result of which can bollix up one's whole technique. They were surprised and pleased that each had come up with similar solutions to solve the dilemma, and in addition how actually to use the fourth fingers to one's advantage to play in tune in the case of the left hand, and how to guide the bow with the right. What sounded like a purely technical symposium to most people was for Jacobus a Shakespeare sonnet.

"Kate," said Jacobus, "you're a mind reader."

Keiko brought in the final course, served on distinctive black lac-

quered trays. *Cha zaru soba,* a delicate noodle made of finely ground buck-
wheat and green tea, served cold and dipped in its own unique sauce,
was especially refreshing on a muggy summer evening.

"How did you know this is my favorite dish?" asked Jacobus, loudly
sucking up the noodles in the approved Japanese manner.

"As you say, we're mind readers here, Jake," said Kate, lighthearted.
"We also know why you are here in Japan."

Ah, the chess match begins.

"Do you?" asked Jacobus. He continued slurping.

"Certainly. Yumi has told us about your investigation of the theft
of the Piccolino Stradivarius, and you have come to seek Furukawa's
counsel to help you apprehend the thief."

"That is partly correct." Time to position my pawns.

"Oh? And which part is that?"

"I indeed came to seek Furukawa's counsel. However, please understand that capturing the thief is no concern of mine."

"No? If not that, then what is your concern?" asked Keiko, surprise
in her voice.

"Only to see that the violin is returned. That's all that my friend
Nathaniel Williams asked me to do. I have no desire to bring the thief to
justice, and who the thief may be is of no importance to me."

"But how can you expect to retrieve the violin without knowing who
the thief is?" asked Keiko quietly, as she poured chilled wheat tea into
four porcelain cups.

"Join me in a cigarette, Jake?" asked Kate.

"Thanks," said Jacobus. She inserted one, already lit, between his
lips.

Must've lit them both in her mouth. Cool customer, Granny.

"To answer your question, Keiko, I don't plan to retrieve the violin," said Jacobus, blowing out some smoke.

"Mr. Jacobus, you puzzle me," said Keiko. "I'm afraid you'll have to
explain."

"It is my belief," said Jacobus, "that whoever stole the violin will return it."

Taking another deep pull on the cigarette, he felt Kate's warm
smoky breath on his face. Must be leaning forward. Getting interested.

"Surely you can't be serious," continued Keiko. "If the thief had good reason to steal it in the first place, why do you think it would be returned?"

"I didn't say the thief had a good reason," said Jacobus, "but for argument's sake, why not assume for a moment the thief had good reasons. What would those reasons be?"

"Greed would not be a good reason," said Keiko.

"Clearly."

"Or profit."

"A good reason," said Yumi, "would be to do good."

"And how would stealing something be doing good?" asked Jacobus.

"You have said so yourself," said Yumi. "In your opinion the Grimsley Competition represents everything bad about music. Without the Piccolino, there would be no Competition, so by stealing it, the thief is making the world better."

"Yeah, that may have been the intent," said Jacobus. "And maybe it's even a good intent."

"So you agree, then," said Keiko, "that the violin should not be returned?"

"No."

"And why not, Jake?" asked Kate.

Jacobus heard her slowly rub out her cigarette butt in an ashtray, pick up her teacup, and take a long, slow sip.

Time to move out my knight.

"Has the world really become a better place? I don't think so. A young kid, the kid who won the Grimsley, who has the potential to become a fine violinist, is distraught. She's suffering potentially debilitating pain from playing on an inferior instrument, and her budding career may be ruined. Otherwise honorable people have been corrupted by its lure. I'm the chief suspect in this theft business, which I don't care for very much. And finally, the police have accused me of murdering Victoria Jablonski."

THIRTY-TWO

Kate's porcelain teacup shattered on the wood floor. Jacobus instinctively lurched his head away, protecting his face from splintered shards and scalding tea.

"Murder! I have heard nothing of murder!" cried Kate.

"I am sorry, Oba-san!" cried Yumi, jumping up. "I have not had a chance to tell you. Please don't harm us, Mr. Jacobus!"

"What?" Jacobus was astounded. "Why should I harm you?"

"Because of what you did to Miss Jablonski!" said Yumi. "At first, I thought you did it because of what she did to me. When she slapped me the humiliation was worse than the pain. When I heard she was dead I almost forgave you. But then you were so wild and angry and desperate, and you forced me to return here. I thought, is my family in danger now? What could I have done? If I had refused, you would still have come here. I had no choice. I had to go with you. I had to protect my family. I decided I would continue to play the role of student, but I tried to keep you away from here. And now I have failed."

"My God!" said Jacobus. He had indeed brought Yumi to this place because of the murder, but not because *he* had done it. He had thought Yumi killed Victoria after Victoria's humiliation of her, during that brief disappearance in Carnegie Hall after which she had brought him his violin with the missing G-string. There had been her violent reaction to Miller's announcement of Victoria's death and her erratic behavior, all of which had made him increasingly sure of her guilt. That's why he insisted on her coming with him, to get her out of harm's way, at least temporarily. But now he realized from Yumi's reaction that his own scenario had been equally wrong.

"And I am also sorry," said Jacobus, rising from his chair. "I've shocked you unnecessarily."

"Indeed you have, Jake," said Kate. "You've made my hands tremble. Not even the Paganini Concerto could do that." She tried, unsuccessfully, to conjure up a laugh.

Jacobus explained what had happened the day they went to Carnegie

Hall and how his suspicions of Yumi forced him to take her with him for her protection.

"You must believe me that when I left Victoria Jablonski's office the only injury I left her with were her bruised feelings."

Jacobus heard Yumi already mopping up the tea and the splintered cup, Keiko consoling Kate in Japanese.

"I'll be all right. I'll be all right," said Kate. "That poor, poor woman! What will become of all her students? And what is going to happen to you? Oh, my God!"

"Don't worry about me," said Jacobus. "Neither the thief, nor I, had anything to do with the murder. I'll just need to convince the police of that when I go back to New York. Justice will eventually prevail, I'm sure," he said with a smile he was fairly certain wasn't convincing.

"Well, where do we go from here?" asked Kate.

Her words were rapid-fire, their pitch elevated.

"Where?" asked Keiko.

"Yes, we don't want to spoil a lovely dinner, do we? Could I have another cigarette? Yumi, light one for me please. My hands are not quite settled yet."

Jacobus heard the deep intake of tobacco smoke and then the slow exhalation.

"Let's talk about the weather," Kate said. "Yes. Tell me about the weather. Shall I tell you about the weather? It has been a bit dreary today, don't you think?"

The conversation came to a halt as they listened to the drizzle outside turn into a steady shower. Jacobus let the silence continue.

Gathering her defenses. Give her time. It won't make a difference.

"Why don't we listen to Sensei's gift?" asked Keiko in a quiet, soothing voice.

The endgame begins.

"Yes, let's. Splendid idea, Keiko," said Kate.

"Oba-san," said Yumi to Kate, "I will clear the table."

"Good. And Keiko, would you please go fetch the tape recorder? My dears, Mr. Jacobus has presented us with yet another mystery—I hope a more pleasant one. I've got it somewhere in my sleeve. Here. A tape recording with no title. Would you care to give us any clues, Mr. Jacobus?"

Moving out my rooks to capture the queen.

"I'll tell you a little bit about the music. Your job is to guess the performer. The piece, for violin and piano, is called "Sicilienne" and is only about three minutes long. The composer was a woman, Maria Theresia von Paradis. She was a contemporary of Mozart and much admired by him as a skillful pianist as well as a composer. What is especially noteworthy about her to many people, though not to me, is that from the age of five she was blind."

"Is it not also remarkable," said Keiko as she inserted the tape, "for a woman to have achieved success as a composer long ago, as until recently it has been so difficult to do even as a performer?"

Keiko pushed Play.

Jacobus heard someone inhale slowly. He was fairly sure it was Kate. Resigning? Or just getting ready?

This particular Sicilienne was not nearly as dramatic or technically difficult as the one that begins Tartini's "Devil's Trill" Sonata. Rather, it had an extreme simplicity and poignancy hovering undecidedly between happiness and sadness, transformed by degree from moment to moment. It was the angel compared to Tartini's devil. Jacobus had once read a description of such music as "smiling through tears." That the composer had suffered through the obstacles of blindness, and of being a female composer in a man's world, heightened one's appreciation of the sublime resignation of the music.

Though the tape had obviously been duplicated from a scratchy old 78 recording, it came through clearly that the violinist, the accompanying pianist, and the composer spoke as one. Every sighing nuance, every shift, the expressive use of vibrato, told the wordless story.

The listeners were entranced, and when the final, fading note was lovingly abandoned to silence, the listeners remained motionless.

Keiko spoke first. "Sensei, you have brought us a beautiful treasure that we will never be able to repay. From what you have told us about the composer's blindness, I can only guess that it is you yourself on the recording."

"You flatter me, Keiko, but I must admit that it is not me. Nor, I am sorry to say, do I believe I have ever been able to play so beautifully."

Yumi said, "Then it must be Fritz Kreisler. Or Mischa Elman. Perhaps Nathan Milstein. Oh, I don't know.

"Grandmother, are you crying? You have not moved."

"You are an extraordinary man, Mr. Jacobus," said Kate.

"And you are a remarkable woman," he said quietly.

Checkmate.

No one spoke.

He now knew he had been right. And now Kate also knew that he knew. He knew that Yumi had suspected he had known, and shortly he would confirm that with her and Keiko. He had prepared for this moment since leaving New York. He would now prepare them for the return of the violin, for which he needed Kate's help. She would help because she already understood.

"Recently, Yumi asked me about perfection," Jacobus continued softly.

"Obviously, dear," Kate said to Yumi, regaining her matriarchal tone, "there is no such thing. To search for perfection is futility itself."

Yumi asked, "But playing the violin, isn't it important to try to play perfectly? Like the recording?"

"It's important to try, perhaps, but one must acknowledge it's physically impossible, even if there was an aesthetic definition of perfection, which there isn't."

"What about playing in tune?" asked Keiko. "Certainly something is either in tune or out of tune."

"One would think so," said Jacobus. "But that's not necessarily the case either."

Jacobus went on to explain in great detail how playing a note in tune with one open string of the violin might make it out of tune with another because of distinct overtone series. "And that's why it's problematic for a violinist to play with a pianist, because of the fundamentally different way half steps on the piano are calibrated. It's all compromise," he concluded. "No perfection there."

"So what can a violinist do when playing with a pianist?" asked Yumi.

"Make decisions. Human, musical decisions. Does that disturb you?"

"If there is no perfection, what is the goal of practicing?"

Kate intervened. "The goal, dear, is to search for beauty, an essential element of which is *im*perfection. That may seem contradictory, but for something to be perfect, it must contain imperfection, for that is what makes it human and enables us to appreciate its beauty. But then, of course, it is no longer perfect. A paradox. Sad but true."

"Oba-san," said Yumi, "this is very confusing."

Jacobus interrupted. "Your grandmother's exactly right. Take the Beethoven Violin Concerto, maybe the most 'perfect' concerto ever written. Even so, Beethoven knew there must be a flaw, if you can call it that, incorporated into the music."

"What flaw?" asked Keiko.

"For example, when the cadenza of the last movement ends up in the totally wrong key of A-flat Major, harmonically the most distantly related from the 'correct' key of D Major. And why? If Beethoven had wanted to be 'perfect' it would have been less interesting. By including an imperfection, he gives the music unpredictability, humor, mystery, making the resolution of all this musical 'confusion' more fulfilling, more powerful. He gives it a unique beauty, and that is what we, as musicians, must strive for."

Yumi asked, "Then is there nothing in music that's perfect?"

Jacobus responded, "Maybe your grandmother can answer that."

Kate said, "Yes, Yumi. The Piccolino Stradivarius. It is perfect. And that's why whoever stole it did so."

For the first time since he had arrived in Japan, Jacobus was unable to restrain the snarl in his voice. "But is it perfection? No! It's a piece of wood, at most a symbol. Not real. And look at the tragedy it's caused. And how many more tragedies if those who have it continue to conceal it?"

"Of course, you are precisely correct once again, Mr. Jacobus." Jacobus heard Kate shift her weight—leaning back?—and after a brief pause, she sighed. "And that is why whoever stole the violin will see that it is immediately returned to Miss Vander."

Keiko burst out in frantic Japanese but immediately silenced herself.

Yumi, younger and less reserved, cried, "Oba-san! How can you say this?"

"It's all right, dear," said Kate gently, almost with a smile. "Mr. Jacobus knows everything."

"How can he? How do you know?"

"The recording we just listened to," Kate said.

"Yes?" asked Yumi. "I don't understand."

"That was your grandmother playing," said Jacobus.

THIRTY-THREE

Jacobus understood the way that sound could affect one's psyche. What he marveled at at this moment, though, was how his own mood itself seemed to alter the very sounds he was hearing. Somehow, the quality of the sound of the rain falling on the rice paddies had changed. No longer was it dismal and remorseful. Now it seemed serenely revitalizing, refreshing, at peace.

Kate spoke. "It appears our clairvoyant Mr. Jacobus has unraveled our scheme, and that's all there is to it. Yumi, please go fetch the violin for Mr. Jacobus. I'm sure at some point he'll be kind enough to explain how he managed such a prodigious feat. Keiko, please bring me another cup and pour us all some more tea.

"Well," Kate continued lightly when Yumi returned, "it seems we have two choices. Either we can allow our good Mr. Jacobus to return to New York with that violin, or we can kill him, though I don't recommend the latter as it would deprive Yumi of a perfectly fine violin teacher."

The only response was the sound of the rain.

Kate cleared her throat. "Obviously my humor was not appropriate for the moment. Of course Mr. Jacobus will take the violin to its rightful owner, and we can only hope that he will be understanding of our motives for removing it in the first place."

"More than understanding," responded Jacobus. "Totally sympathetic. Be assured that the mystery of the stolen Stradivarius will remain a mystery to all but the four of us."

"For that, Mr. Jacobus, we bow our heads in eternal gratitude. Our fates are totally in your hands and at this point all we can ask of you is to please tell us how we ended up there."

"How?" asked Jacobus. "How would take a very long time to explain, so for now let me just say that if not for the unlikely coincidence of Max sending Yumi to me to study, and me being asked by my friend Mr. Williams to find the violin, *how* would never have been possible. On the other hand, I would like to tell you *what* I believe happened, and please correct me if I'm wrong.

"Kamryn Vander had a recital at Carnegie Hall. Keiko, you attended both the performance and the reception, absolutely inconspicuous, one of many elegant Asian women who so frequently attend concerts in New York. Then the security guard, Harry Pizzi, received the message to go to the stage door because Yumi, the accomplice, having climbed the fire escape to the top of the Patelson building—I'm guessing dressed in black to be invisible against the night sky—had just hurled baseball-sized rocks through the stage-door window. It was timed for just about when the celebrants at the reception would be getting restless to leave, with their minds more on traffic and bed, not violins. That was your signal, Keiko, and it was also the diversion you needed. You waited to see which security guard would take the bait and quickly but smoothly made your move while Yumi hightailed it out of there. Am I right so far?"

"Go on, Mr. Jacobus."

"You then entered Green Room B from the corridor before Robison had a chance to switch places. Here's a question for you. What if the door had been locked?"

"I would have picked it easily, Mr. Jacobus," said Keiko. "I have been practicing. And after all, it was not a door to a bank vault."

"No doubt your dexterity from playing the violin would have been helpful as well," said Jacobus. "Once you were in the room, if someone had caught you there, you would have apologized in rapid Japanese and backed out of the room, and no one would have given it a second thought. But so far so good.

"Now the question is, how to get the violin (a) out of the case, and (b) out of the room. My guess is that if the violin were locked in the case you would have brought a bigger case with the insides cut out so you could just put the three-quarter-size violin, case and all, right inside it. No one would have questioned someone carrying an instrument case in Carnegie Hall."

"Yes, it was a viola case," Keiko said quietly.

"There you go. But, in fact, the Piccolino's case had not been locked, which we know because it was left there, and since there were no unexpected fingerprints on the case you were no doubt wearing white gloves, which would have fit in just fine with most of the other ladies in the audience."

"Yes."

"So anyway, you had gone into the room from the corridor door, but with Robison now sitting at that post, which you knew because you heard him talking to me, you exited through the door to Green Room A and left Carnegie Hall with the rest of the throng. And like the others you hailed a cab on Fifty-seventh Street. The cab took you to JFK, and you were on the plane to Japan well before the police alert to the airports went out.

"Congratulations, and thank you for saving me the trouble."

"What trouble was that, Mr. Jacobus?"

"A minute after you stole that violin, I tried to crush it myself, and if it had been in the case like it was supposed to be, I'd be in the slammer right now."

"I'm glad we could be of service," said Kate. "But if you know all of this, why doesn't anyone else? Why not the police?"

"Because, Kate, you and I, we think alike."

"Well, Jake, would you be interested in inspecting the mystery violin?" Kate offered. "After all, you've gone to all this trouble to find it."

"Why the hell not? I wouldn't mind knowing what the big deal's been all about."

Jacobus heard Yumi remove the Stradivarius from its case. Her hand was on his, tentatively, preparing him to accept the instrument that had been the source of endless misfortune.

It was in his hands. With its neck nestled in his left hand, he gauged the flawless, albeit reduced, dimensions of the instrument with his right. He rolled his fingertips over the scroll's demonic dragon head, maple-hard and intimidating. Slowly his fingers slid lower along the delicate neck of the violin, the rounded contours of its shoulders, the graceful inward curves of its ribs, the roundness of its bottom.

Jesus! he thought. He had never held an instrument like this.

He placed his palm on the Piccolino's back to gauge its proportions and its gentle arching. The instrument accepted the warmth of his touch almost as if the violin were breathing in response.

It must be *me* breathing, he thought, or my pulse coursing through my fingers. That must be it.

Turning the violin over, he put his fingers on the belly of the instrument, seeking the openings of its f-holes—the most elegant and yet the most challenging carving of the craftsman—forming a visual image in his mind. Aroused by the violin's unique beauty and power, his hand began to perspire. He could understand being unable to part with it. He almost wanted it to be his.

Jacobus brought the violin to his ear, to pluck the strings, to hear and to feel the Piccolino's vibrations. To submit to the Siren. G-string, D-string, A-string, E-string.

Jacobus was puzzled. He plucked them again: G, D, A, E.

Frowning, he muttered something under his breath.

"Excuse me, Jake," said Kate. "What is that you said?"

Louder, but still to himself, he said, in long, drawn-out vowels, "No. No."

He plucked the strings more harshly. G, D, A, E.

"No what, Jake?"

Jacobus did not like being toyed with. Ever. But the implications of what was happening strained his already frayed nerves beyond a tolerable point.

"Give me a bow."

"Well, since you put it so politely, here."

Jacobus pulled the bow along the open strings, gauging the quality and duration of their resonance. He tried to prevent his arm from trembling, with limited success. He quickly adapted his left hand to the instrument's shorter string length and played a few slow three-octave scales from the very bottom of the violin's register up to its highest frequencies.

He stopped and held the violin out at arm's length, an Inquisitor, madly and incorruptibly certain of his Truth, brandishing a cross before a heretic.

"No, this is not a Stradivarius, Mrs. Padgett," snarled Jacobus. "This violin is not a Stradivarius, Mrs. Padgett! Where is the Piccolino Stradivarius, Mrs. Padgett?"

"I don't know what you mean, Jake," said Kate. "It's impossible! I am equally certain that the violin we have before us is the same one I saw in the Grimsley as I am that this young lady is my granddaughter."

Jacobus was fed up with the world. He didn't give a damn anymore.

"You know perfectly well what I'm talking about. Make a copy, keep the original, send me back with a fake holding my cock in my hands. Very clever. Fool the blind man, huh? Your lovely granddaughter already tried that on me once. Send me to prison while you sit here sipping your tea.

"It is no secret, Mrs. Padgett, that the violins made in Cremona in the seventeenth and eighteenth centuries—the violins made by the Amatis, the Guarneris, and Stradivari—have a unique sound. The Cremona sound. A smoothness, a richness. Where the E string sounds as warm as the G. Where the instrument sings with the sound of every great opera singer, soprano to bass, rolled into one. And that within the Cremona sound, the sound of a Stradivarius, especially one in pristine condition, is itself unique. A Guarnerius may have more power, but a Stradivarius has a warmth, a tone that gives it a soul. A unique soul. An *unmistakable* soul.

"This violin is not a Stradivarius, Mrs. Padgett. It is not even Cremonese. It is a good fake—like you. And I had been stupid enough to have thought better of you."

"Mr. Jacobus!"

Yumi's voice. Louder than usual. What the hell did she want?

"Mr. Jacobus, just two things. First of all, don't you dare talk to Grandmother like that. I will not permit it!"

She will not permit it, thought Jacobus. She will not permit it! Pretty brazen for a little thief. How he had mistaken her. For a while she had actually touched him with her playing. With her dedication. She had almost renewed his faith in himself. But now. He really should have given up teaching.

"Yeah?" said Jacobus. "And second?"

"Second," continued Yumi. She paused for a moment. Jacobus waited. What polite little excuse can she come up with now?

"Why the hell," she hollered, "would we be so silly to risk exposure, to risk everything, by having a copy of the Piccolino Strad made *just in case we would be caught,* when we believed we were totally successful with the theft? And we *were* totally successful. If we hadn't been, I would have returned to Japan with Mother. But no, I stayed to learn music from the great Daniel Jacobus, Furukawa-sensei's highly esteemed friend and colleague. I would become a violinist. I would be happy. I asked for no more.

"How could we have known?" she said, more to herself than to anyone in the room. "How could anyone have known you would be the one person in the world asked to find the Piccolino?"

"It's all right, dear," said Kate. "No one could have predicted it. No one could have known."

There was a moment of quiet, a light patter of gentle rain falling on the rice paddy outside. Jacobus hoped that Yumi had finished. Everything she said had been painfully true.

"What had I done to make you suspect me?" Yumi cried out, her eyes fixed on Jacobus. "With every question you asked, with every glance—even with your blind eyes—I sensed you knew something more about me no matter how I answered. You were an animal trainer with a whip, backing me into a corner. What could I do? Go home and never return, which would make you suspect me even more and end my hopes of playing the violin? If I stayed, what then? You would wear me down, little by little, with your questions.

"Why didn't I leave after our second lesson, when you threw me out? I've asked myself that question over and over. It would have been the perfect opportunity. If I had, you wouldn't be here now. On our drive back to your house from New York, do you know what I thought?"

Jacobus shrugged, his head down.

"I *thought* I finally understood why you had taken me to New York. I thought it was a test. That you were testing my will by exposing me to the ugly realities of being a musician. That these people—these agents, these dealers, these competitions, even these teachers—were like the Eta of Japan. Do you know who the Eta are, Mr. Jacobus?" asked Yumi.

"Yumi!" exclaimed Keiko.

"See?" said Yumi. "We don't even talk about them here. They're the hidden undercaste of Japan who work with corpses—butchers, leatherworkers, gravediggers who live in the poor dark fringes of our cities. Do you know what is Eta in English? 'Full of filth.'

"*I had thought* that perhaps you had been trying to make the tunnel dark so that the light at its end would be brighter. Those meetings with Dedubian, Vander, Grimsley, Rachel, Strella, Jablonski—especially Jablonski—had opened my eyes, showed me how idealism, devotion to the beauty of music could be compromised in so many ways. Dedubian, a man who makes money by holding hostage the instruments musicians must have, who in so many words called *me* a thief! Those people aren't Eta. They are *worse* than Eta!

"*I had thought* you were trying to open my eyes. *I had thought* you were trying to make the profession look as grotesque as possible so that I would cling to my integrity with ever more strength. *I had thought* I no longer hated you on that ride home. *I had thought* I was indebted to you. But no, you were just trying to catch me!

"And, Mr. Jacobus, even if we *were* so silly as to try to make a copy of the Piccolino that looks and sounds exactly like the original, how could we have done that in a matter of days? That makes no sense at all. And since you were correct in all your assumptions about us, and give yourself credit for being such an analytical genius, why now do you believe all those assumptions were wrong? That would be damned stupid, if you ask me."

Jacobus thought for a moment, in silence. Then he burst out in a wheezing laugh.

"I knew I was right," he said, in between efforts to inhale.

"What's so funny, Jake?" said Kate. "Right about what?"

"I told Yumi at her first lesson that by the end of the year she'd be arguing with me and I'd be learning something from her. It happened sooner than I thought."

THIRTY-FOUR

Jake's bones were tired. Tired from the last six days. Tired of the tension and tired of the effort. Tired of dishonesty and of death. His was not the tired of 'I need a good night's sleep' or 'I need to get away for some R and R.' His was the exhaustion of a ruined soul, with just enough strength to recall, perhaps for one last time, the happier moments of one's life. Of thinking that not breathing might be easier than breathing. Sitting neck-deep in the Shinagawas' cedar-lined *furo*, a half-empty bottle of Suntory his sole companion, he had little expectation that the intense heat would penetrate his bones to provide him some temporary resuscitation, because he knew his trials had only just begun.

It had been a bitter triumph, and he did not rejoice in having tracked down Kate Padgett. The mystery of the *real* missing Piccolino had not been solved—Kate, Keiko, and Yumi were unanimous in their insistence that they had no idea the violin in their possession was a forgery, and he believed them. And soon he would be in police custody for the murder of Victoria Jablonski. It was clear that Yumi had not killed Victoria. Or was it? He would almost prefer to be unjustly convicted than to see her justly accused. When she had sobbingly confessed that *she* had suspected *him* in Victoria's murder she had been so remorseful that he was convinced. It couldn't have been an act. Or could it?

One thing he knew for sure. Someone had outwitted all of them. For the first and maybe last time in his life, Jacobus felt his age.

Some chess game! he thought. Me, the great Grandmaster. I wasn't even playing with the right person.

He took what little comfort he could from the surrounding silence and, for once, in his darkness. He leaned back, pressing hard on his useless eyes with his tired wet hands.

Then there was a sound.

He strained to hear, motionless, allowing the drops of water to trickle off his elbows and blip into the *furo*.

It was the sound of the wooden door of the bathroom sliding open with a soft reptilian hiss. Silently. *Almost* silently. Closing slowly, carefully. He listened for the light switch to be turned on. He didn't hear it. It would be dark also for the intruder, Jacobus's only advantage. Bare feet slid carefully on the wet tile floor, seeking a secure foothold in the darkness.

Jacobus remained fixed, his head cocked, listening as he had never before listened, and with a cautious sniff in the air like a sightless mole that has detected the presence of a rattlesnake, scouted for information with his nose.

The faucet on the wall was turned on—diversionary white noise?— scalding water spattering on the tile floor, giving Jacobus a moment to think.

I'm a naked old blind man in a bathtub, is what he thought.

The faucet was turned off. The intruder approached with near-silent tread. Closer, coming toward him. A delicate clink of porcelain. He had neither the means nor the desire to resist. His nemesis slid into the hot water, opposite him.

"Ah, Miss Padgett," Jacobus whispered, "you've brought sake with you."

"May I join you?" whispered Kate.

"It's your tub," said Jacobus.

"Then I shall. Was I that obvious, sneaking in here? I thought I was being quite devious," Kate whispered back.

"Who else could it have been?"

"Perhaps a ninja assassin, come to do you in for having solved the mystery of the Piccolino Strad? Here, have some sake."

"Would a ninja assassin have scrubbed himself clean before doing his dirty work?"

He drained the small glass in one gulp, as he had before with the Suntory number one through whatever. The warm, lightly sweet rice wine went down smoothly. She poured him another.

"Good point. You have to admit, though, I was exceedingly quiet. And I did remove my perfume so you wouldn't smell me."

"Not bad. And you remembered not to switch on the light. Yumi and Keiko will never know you were here."

"Quite right. Part of my plan. But then again, you seem to have had no trouble solving the perfect crime either."

"Except that it's the wrong violin."

"Minor detail. Jake, I have to ask you, how did you catch on in the first place?"

The compact size of the *furo* made it impossible for Jacobus's ankles to avoid contact with Kate's. A small surge of heat made Jacobus's body tingle. Must be the hot water, he thought.

"Catch on?" he asked. His mind had wandered to other matters. Does Kate mind hairy legs?

"Yes. We thought we had everyone totally baffled."

"Oh, the theft. Well, when I first heard about it on the news I concluded that whoever did it had extraordinary reasons. That the thief was someone very much like . . . me."

"By that I gather you mean extremely intelligent, highly moral, sensitive, shrewd. Musical."

"Precisely." Jacobus was beginning to revive. He took another sip of sake, savoring its freshness. He began to sweat freely.

"Well, that's a lovely start, but there must be more people than me in this world who fit that flattering description."

"Not as many as you may think, but yes, that was the challenge. I asked myself—assuming that the thief's reasons were similar to mine for abhorring that Competition and its mascot violin—what person, or group of persons, might be involved?"

He explained his revelation after hearing Henry Lee Higginson's quote in the Matthilda Grimsley diary about finishing second as his inspiration to search for Grimsley runners-up.

"Genius!" exclaimed Kate. Pride glowed in her voice.

"Common sense," said Jacobus, "but maybe you should keep your voice down."

"Yes, of course," she whispered. "But Jake, there must have been so many. After all these years."

"Surprisingly few, actually, when you consider that the first Grimsley was in 1905 and they're only every thirteen years. So if my theory was correct—and if it had been wrong I had others to try—there would be only seven violinists to check out. And I was helped by a variety of sources."

"Such as?"

"First, the obituaries. I'm afraid that you have the honor of being the oldest remaining Grimsley second-place finisher, Kate."

"Quite an honor. I think I'll pour myself another sake. And you were in the Grimsley too," Kate continued. Jacobus felt her eyes on him. "You were that pale, skinny boy who got sick the day of the group photo."

Jacobus froze. He had never told anyone and couldn't even now. Later. Maybe. He forced his mouth to form words.

"Neither here nor there. What about *your* experience?" he asked. "I haven't been able to fill that gap, except for a couple newspaper clippings Nathaniel found."

"You mean the ones that stated how well all the children played, how difficult it was for the judges to determine a winner, and how without doubt all the finalists would go on to glorious careers?"

"You've seen them, then?" he asked.

"No, never. That's just what they all say. But to answer your question," Kate continued, "it was hell. I was only nine years old, the younger of the young, but for months before the Competition I was put through the paces. Whenever I wasn't in school I was practicing. Practice, practice, practice. Practice scales, practice études, practice concerti. If it was written, I practiced it. But not because it was beautiful or stimulating. Because, as they say, it was there. Make one mistake and you're out, even if the child who won was as musical as a . . . as a . . . fish." She made little ripples in the water with her hand.

"And 'Required Repertoire'! Now there was the rub. Even at that tender age I had an inkling that the true purpose of music was more than just to show you can jump through a flaming hoop better than the next toddler."

"But that wasn't the worst of it. There was the wardrobe selection, the bowing rehearsal, the smiling practice, if you can believe it. Trying to get us to simultaneously play like old men and look like infants. As you well know, for the entire two weeks of the competition it was against the rules to leave our rooms in some dingy hotel because they were afraid we would receive assistance in our preparations! Can you believe that? 'Can't allow these deceitful eight-year-old buggers to receive assistance. Not proper.'

"You may laugh, Mr. Jacobus, but it wasn't very funny at the time, especially an experience I had with the great Malinkovsky, which some-day before I die I may be able to talk about."

"Sounds like you need another drink." He handed Kate his whiskey bottle. They had even more in common than he imagined. Perhaps.

"Thank you. After the Grimsley I packed my bags and went back to England with Mum and Dad. You can't imagine how relieved I felt to be going back home, where I thought I had friends. Unfortunately, I turned out not to be the celebrity the UK had banked on. No engagements with the BBC. There was an article in our local paper. 'Dorchester Deb Doesn't Deliver.' Page eight, under the unemployment figures. So there. That's my story."

"Perverse, the whole business. Isn't it?" said Jacobus.

Kate's leg rubbed against his. Intentional? Should he rub back? What would she think? Maybe not.

"To say the least," she said. "I hated it and vowed somehow I would make the world a better place."

"By stealing the Piccolino?"

"Well, somehow, anyway."

"You did record the 'Sicilienne.'"

"What a lovely thing for you to say, Jake. It really is. And I'm amazed your Mr. Williams was able to find it. You see, we only made a hundred copies. I was ten years old. Intended for friends and family. And my pi-anist was so wonderful. About my age too. So sensitive. Lilburn, I think his name was."

"Lilburn? *Martin* Lilburn?"

"Yes. I believe that was his name. You remember him?"

"I know Martin Lilburn. Now! He's the music critic for the *New York Times*."

Am I being jealous? Jacobus asked himself. They were only toddlers at the time. Hardly a rival. And now we're all just old farts.

"How amazing! I have been so out of touch here. You must please tell him how much his collaboration meant to me. You see, it was the only recording I ever made."

"That's a loss to the rest of the world, but makes it all the more special."

"What made it special was that after the Grimsley I hated music. Absolutely hated it. But recording that piece, thinking about Paradis, made me realize that musicians far greater than myself have overcome far greater obstacles in life than losing ridiculous little competitions.

"But now I'm getting maudlin. Tell me what other aids you had in tracking me down."

"Well, I must admit that Yumi helped me quite a bit."

"Yumi? She told you?"

"Calm down. You're making waves. She did her best to act innocent, but remember, she's still a child herself. It's really what she didn't tell me."

"What didn't she tell you?"

Jacobus explained his observations of Yumi's curious behavior during her lessons and her response—"Oh?"—to his first mention of the Piccolino's theft.

"But surely, Jake, you couldn't conclude an old lady in Japan had stolen a Stradivarius violin just because a young girl in Massachusetts said 'Oh.' "

"Of course not. It was simply a signal for me to keep my ears open."

"You know, Jake, I'm beginning to be happy I had Keiko and Yumi steal the violin if for no other reason than for you and me to be here like this tonight. Are you happy to be here too?"

"Well, I hadn't actually thought about it like that." He paused. Unaccustomed to the idea of happiness, or the discussion of it, Jacobus was at a loss how to proceed. He was fairly certain, though, that he was not feeling as miserable as he thought he should be.

"Do you want to hear more about how I tracked you down?" he said, changing the subject.

"Mmm, by all means."

Jacobus cleared his throat, seeking security by assuming a professorial tone.

"It was simply a matter of analyzing Yumi's behavior after the initial 'Oh.' Every time the subject of the Piccolino came up, her reaction was always evasive. Either she'd just clam up or change the subject. That's why I decided to take her to all those interviews with me. I made it hell for her, but I had no choice."

"How distinctly Machiavellian of you."

"You and I are two peas in a pod, aren't we?" asked Jacobus.

"More like two peas in a pot at the moment," said Kate, gently wiping the perspiration from Jake's forehead, the washcloth lingering on his cheek. "Tell me what other things Yumi said that gave us away."

Jacobus felt the weight of her elbows on his submerged knees, as she propped her chin with her hands.

"The biggest thing was her touching tale of Noda-san as an allegorical defense of the Piccolino thief."

"Noda-san the wood-carver?"

"Yes, the wood-carver. I had never heard that tale."

"For good reason," said Kate.

"Oh?"

"There never was a Noda-san."

"You mean she made that up?"

"She didn't. *I* did. When she was a child, I used to make up didactic 'legends' for bedtime stories. You know, to build moral fiber without the toddlers realizing it. That's what grandmas are for, isn't it? I'm sure you do it in your teaching all the time. I had no idea she would remember that one."

"Next time be careful what you tell your grandchildren."

"I'm chastened. Cheers," she said, pouring them both another glass of sake.

"Interesting, though," said Jacobus. "Your mythical Noda-san reminds me of Martin Lilburn, in fact. Or what Lilburn's become, anyway. Thinking they're helping humanity when what they're really doing is trying to predict human nature. Bottoms up."

That should take care of any fond memories she has for Lilburn.

"Poor Martin. He was such a dear."

Damn.

"But one is always bound to fail at that in the end," she concluded.

"Hmm. Anyway, getting back to Yumi, I still had nothing to go on. Just suspicion. And the why was still gnawing at me," continued Jacobus, realizing he was grateful for finally being able to unburden himself.

"That's when I asked my friend Nathaniel Williams to research the lives of all the second-place finishers. Yours was the hardest trail, and we almost gave up."

"I tried to leave no trace. I wanted to disappear from the face of the earth."

"Kate Padgett, child prodigy. After the Grimsley you went back to England. And then what?"

"It was the Depression, then the War. Any career I might have gleaned from finishing second was trod on by those two heavy boots. I tried a few concerts here and there, then simply gave up."

"After making the recording," said Jacobus.

"Yes, and you found it."

"Actually, Nathaniel did."

"Remarkable."

"Still, there was nothing definite to go on, more of a . . ."

"Nagging suspicion?"

"Yeah. A nagging suspicion, bolstered by something a friend of mine, Solomon Goldbloom, said."

"Solomon Goldbloom?"

"That old friend Yumi and I bumped into at Dedubian's. I was trying to find a thread in my search . . . give me direction. So out of the blue I asked him what he thought were the most important things in life."

"And?"

"He said, 'Family, music. Doing the right thing. Good food.' "

"In that order?"

" 'It depends on what's on the menu,' he said. Helped clear my vision . . . so to speak . . . about a possible motive."

"Ah! The Wisdom of Solomon. I like your friend already. His list fits mine to a T. But it didn't do me any good, did it?"

"I'm afraid not. Especially after Nathaniel finally traced your odyssey to Japan after the war, starting with a call to the *Piddletown Herald.* Passport records, ship manifests. Little things like that."

"Yes, those little brushstrokes paint quite a picture. I came here with my first husband."

"Mr. Desmond?"

"Yes. He was in business and thought he could 'open up markets' here. Businesspeople are always trying to 'open up markets,' aren't they?"

"He died shortly after coming here?"

"Yes. He wasn't very strong. Dysentery took him. Poor man. He was lovely."

"But you stayed."

"Yes. I had no good reason to go back. And the people here were so considerate. And forgiving."

"Forgiving? What had you done?"

"Not me, specifically. But the War, you know. There was no animosity. It surprised me. It also surprised me that I married again. Never thought it would happen. Frankly, I was more fascinated by what he did than who he was."

"So from being Kate Padgett Desmond you became Cato Hashimoto."

"That must have thrown a monkey into your wrench."

"It didn't help. What did he do?"

"Mr. Hashimoto? He was a traditional papermaker. He made paper by hand, from scratch. Cutting down the saplings, mashing the pulp, soaking it, sieving it through the wire screens to get the water out. *Washi.*"

"Thank you, I already did."

"No. That's what the papermaking is called. *Washi.*"

"Aha. Could you pour me a little more sake? So what did he do with the paper? Write music for you?"

"No no. Nothing like that. It was for shoji screens. They're actually quite beautiful, and durable too."

"Except when biwa are thrown through them."

"You heard about that."

"Yeah. When I heard about Yumi's baseball exploits with the biwa it became obvious who threw the rocks through the Carnegie Hall window. So those shoji screens were Mr. Hashimoto's?"

"His were the screens that went in *after* the incident. No charge, of course. Mr. Hashimoto was like that. A very kind man, though he didn't open many markets either. He died two years ago."

Jacobus gave this fact some thought, though through his thickening haze it seemed to be taking him more time to than usual to digest its implications.

"You waited for him to die before stealing the violin!"

"He was quite old. But yes. I waited."

"Just a minute! I don't mean to bring up sad memories, but that was only the last piece of the puzzle. You raised a daughter and taught her the violin, and she had a daughter who you also taught to play the violin and who also learned to throw a fastball at the same time. Then you found her the best violin teacher in Japan. Was this all part of the plan too, Kate? Did you plan this vendetta fifty years ago and indoctrinate two more generations to go along with it?"

"Hmm, it's all fitting together, isn't it?" said Kate after a pause, with amazing calm. "But no, even though it sounds like it, I truly did wait until my second husband passed away before putting my thoughts into a plan. Plan or no plan, there always would have been music in our lives. But one thing I don't understand, Jake. Of all the stories, why did Yumi have to tell you that one about the biwa, I wonder? It is a bit incriminating."

"She didn't do it intentionally. Furukawa led her through it without her knowing why. I gave him hints I was in Japan to make contact with her family but didn't want her to know why. She suspected, no doubt, but had no idea how much I knew. Max caught on and planned a conversation so that even with Yumi translating, it would become reasonable for *him* to innocently suggest I meet you. If *I* had suggested it to Yumi, she would have found a way to prevent it. So Furukawa took advantage of being at the biwa tree when Yumi joined us, and then at his ancient family tree. I only had to ask the right questions."

"Why didn't you want Yumi to know you suspected?"

"Well, at first, when we were in New York, I did want her to suspect, but then I had to change my strategy. But that's a long story. Once we got here, though, I had two reasons. First, if Yumi was sure what I knew and made a scene, Furukawa would no doubt have discovered what was up, and I didn't want anyone ever to know who stole the violin."

"How considerate of you. But doesn't your friend Mr. Williams know?"

"I told him that I knew the culprit was in Japan, and I also told him that I was meeting you, but only for consultation and assistance, just like with Furukawa, that you're doing for me simply what I've done for Nathaniel, which is to assist an investigation.".

"And second?"

"Second? Oh, yeah. Second, if for some reason I had been wrong—and it looks like I was, doesn't it?—well, I wouldn't have wanted to scandalize your name out of error, or Max's name either. Y'know, when he told me that Yumi was his last student, for a moment I thought there might have been a reason for that which I really didn't want to know. That he might have been involved also. I hadn't considered that possibility, and it shocked me for a while."

"How did you determine he wasn't involved?"

"If he had been, he never would have led me to you, right? He would have sent me on a wild-goose chase to protect you.

"You know, Kate, that violin has ruined too damn many lives. You were concerned enough about the repercussions to wait through two husbands before trying to make the world a better place. What good would it have done for me to tell Furukawa that the whole Hashimoto-Shinagawa clan stole the Piccolino Strad? The least I could do was respect your desire for anonymity."

"Jake, you've obviously spent a lot of time thinking about *me*. But what's to become of *you*? You've got to go back and face the music for something I've done. Couldn't you give them your cooperation from here?"

Suddenly he felt hotter than the water. There was an exquisite ache between his legs that he refrained from defining, though he knew he hadn't felt it for a long time. He drained the sake in his cup.

"Are you propositioning me, Kate?"

"We're a little too old for that, aren't we? Let's simply call it an open invitation."

Jacobus sat in silence, for once not knowing how to break it.

"Jake," Kate said. Her voice had changed; it was lower, even in its whisper. Was she making an effort to stay in control of it? "I saw how you touched that violin earlier this evening."

He was ashamed of himself for that display and had hoped it would never be brought up. Was she going to rub it in now?

Kate continued. "I have to admit, it made me horrifically jealous." She paused. "Do I get my turn?"

Suddenly Jacobus felt momentarily sober. He said hoarsely, "You know, my old teacher, Dr. Krovney, used to say—"

"No violin lessons now, Professor Jacobus. Please answer my question. Would you care to know what I look like?"

" 'Care'? Would I 'care'? Why would I 'care'?" asked Jacobus.

"I'll take that as a yes. That's part of the invitation." Kate took Jacobus's hands in hers and placed them on her face.

With the fingertips, uncharacteristically reluctant and fumbling, that had taught him how to see, Jacobus explored her face. As his fingers moved, gradually more and more analytically, by fractions of an inch, Jacobus's inner turmoil threatened to tear him apart. There was no way that Kate, immobile, could comprehend the full force of his will to continue, to keep his trembling hands from recoiling. He touched her skin, her eyes (green, no doubt), her eyebrows, her eyelashes, her cheeks, her nose, her ears, her lips, her chin, her jaw, her hair, her forehead, her temples, back to her eyes for a moment, interpreting every feature, picturing her in his mind's eye, assimilating this new data with the composite image he had based only upon her voice, her handshake, and her story. He put his hands around her neck and traced the line of her collarbone. He halted at her shoulders, indecisive. Kate remained motionless, breathing slowly. He finally withdrew his hands, placing them on his own thighs in the steaming water.

"Huh," he muttered.

"That's all?" asked Kate.

"Okay, so you're more beautiful than I thought," stammered Jacobus.

"That's quite flattering for an old lady to hear, though from the way you say it I can't tell whether it really is a compliment or whether you're just peeved you might have been mistaken," teased Kate.

"The former, I suppose."

It was Jake's turn to pause.

"There was a tear on your cheek," he said.

Kate suddenly lunged forward, sobbing. She put her arms around Jacobus's neck, pressing her forehead against his. Jacobus felt her breasts cling to his chest, wet from perspiration and the steamy mist rising from the *furo*. He tried to ignore the sensation, and though he knew he should, he could not put his arms around her to console her.

"What have I done, Jake?" Kate cried. "What have I done? I've spent my life raising and training a daughter and a granddaughter to satisfy my revenge. I've taught them to steal. I've poisoned them. I've made you suspect your closest friends and they suspect you of theft and murder. I've—"

"Nonsense! I can't think of anything better that's happened to me . . . Yumi . . . and you. Nonsense!"

"But how can I ever forgive myself?"

"Hey, honey, don't give yourself too much credit. It's me you should forgive. All your plans would have worked out if it wasn't for me being such a royal pain in the ass."

Kate sniffed. "Jake, thank you for making me smile."

What am I supposed to say now? he thought.

Her hands were still around his neck. He could feel her tears on his cheek, her warm breath on his skin. Hope her nose isn't running. Ah, who gives a shit?

Kate pulled herself closer to Jacobus. Her mouth was next to his ear. The pace of her breathing changed.

"May I ask you another question?" Kate said.

Jacobus swallowed.

"Could I tell you what _you_ look like? The same way?" asked Kate.

Jake felt Kate's fingers on his face. He sat very still.

Her fingers began to move.

"Stop," said Jacobus abruptly.

"But Jake," said Kate.

"I said stop."

Kate remained motionless, then moved away.

"You are a sweet man, Mr. Jacobus, and I owe you a great deal. But now I should leave. You have taken advantage of an elderly woman quite enough. Good night."

"Good night, Miss Padgett."

Jacobus remained in the _furo_ for . . . he didn't know how long, though the Suntory bottle was now empty. It was so quiet. His life had come full circle. A completed pattern? Why go back and be imprisoned? MAP would continue—or not. The true thief would be found—or not. The killer would be found—or not. It didn't really matter. He had found Kate Padgett, yes, but with that he had confronted himself. There was nothing left for him to know.

Slowly he let himself slide down into the water until his entire body, head and all, was submerged. He held his breath. The warmth enveloped him. Whether he came up again or not did not concern him.

The ivy embraced him, pulling him down, as the eye watched impassively. This time he didn't resist. With his abused lungs, he knew it wouldn't take long. Even when, as if seeing something in front of him that had been there all along, he understood with clarity who Victoria's killer was, he let the ivy have its way. All he needed to do now was open his mouth. Let the air out. Let the water in. He had struggled all his life. This would be easy. He opened his mouth.

The ivy, abruptly entangling in his hair, painfully yanked Jacobus upward. With an unrelenting grip, it pulled and pulled and he spun around like a small fish on a large hook. He was being lurched in odd directions. Still he did not resist though the pain on his scalp was intense. He was on his back and the ivy pressed with immense weight upon his chest, like a python, over and over again, constricting and releasing. Suddenly, out of his open mouth spewed a torrent of vomit, whiskey, and water. He coughed out some more of it and then wheezed in a rush of air.

"If this is another of your Japanese traditions," said Nathaniel, easing the pressure of his hands off Jacobus's chest, "you can count me out."

RECAPITULATION

THIRTY-FIVE

Sitting at his desk, a CD of Bruckner's Fourth Symphony playing in the background at low volume, Lilburn read Rachel's notes from yesterday's MAP meeting one more time. He had asked for the meeting after he found out his initial information about Jacobus's arrest was incorrect, or as the *Times* later informed its readers in its retraction, "premature." Rachel's notes, more a litany of questions and doubts, reflected the palpable swirl of confusion that engulfed them.

1. Jacobus killed Victoria? (General inclination to assume.)
2. J. alive?
3. If not, did someone kill both V. and him?
4. If alive, where? And if so, plotting to kill other MAP members?
5. Where are Williams and Japanese girl?
6. Did he kill them too? Or are they accomplices?
7. What about Piccolino? J. runs off with it?
8. How does all reflect on MAP? Deeper trouble? No trouble at all?

Lilburn then reread his own brief reflections: "Not going well. Not at all. Failed to make them see light."

It had been Strella's idea for Lilburn to write the last-minute story about MAP's shock over the murder and to mention the "memorial fund" set up in Victoria's memory. Strella pointed out the opportunity to obtain positive media spin and contributions—tax-deductible, of course.

What Strella had not bargained on, though, was Lilburn's insinuation of MAP's financial impropriety in the story. Lilburn had added that tidbit right before it went to press, making any retraction impossible. This issue had become the main subject of the meeting's agenda.

"I think it was a big mistake, Martin," Strella had said. His tone implied, "I am now about to cut your balls off." What Lilburn kept in his back pocket, figuratively and literally, was a tape recording addressed to him that he had found sitting on his desk the day of Victoria's murder, a tape recording about Victoria and Cynthia Vander, as told by Anthony Strella to Daniel Jacobus.

This tape was the lit fuse that could cause MAP to implode. The implications of this conversation in regard to Victoria's murder, whether founded or not, had ramifications that would reduce MAP's deceitful financial foundations to rubble. And Lilburn had no doubt that Jacobus, wherever he was, would make that tape available to the authorities even if they were strapping him into the electric chair. Seeing the inevitability of this outcome, Lilburn had chosen to make his first step toward exoneration by putting himself on record in the *Times* before he could be dissuaded by anyone.

In his notes, Lilburn had written: "Boris terribly shaken. Shrunken? Ill? More by Piccolino than Victoria? Possible? 'Oh, to mourn the theft more than mere mortal's death!' "

Lilburn retrieved the key under his desk blotter and unlocked the bottom drawer, from which he removed a locked diary. His wallet was in the inside pocket of his suit jacket. In the wallet, behind his social security card, was another, smaller key, with which he opened the diary. He reviewed his latest entry:

Jacobus, of course, had been right. I suppose I had known that all along. That was the essence of it. How had it been possible for me to have lost my

way so badly? What was the point at which my intentions became corrupted? Was there any one point? Even if it hadn't been for money, my
opinions would still have been unethical, wouldn't they? Have I used my
position, glibly dispensing life-affecting judgment upon true musicians, simply to provide fodder for my egotism? Have I been crucifying others to as-
suage my own failure as a musician?

He began writing.

> I feel like one of New York's magnificent old stone buildings—Carnegie
> Hall, perhaps—which, over generations, accumulated layer upon layer of
> grime, of soot, of pigeon excrement, which, heedless of the rock's hardness,
> seeped into its very pores, changing its color from sun-warmed umber to
> dripping funereal black. There was no single moment of transformation
> when the stone was clean and then not clean, but it became covered in filth
> for so long that that is what people thought the building was supposed to
> look like. Only when the building was sandblasted—as I had been sand-
> blasted by Jacobus—did the vibrant stone return to life.
>
> But that isn't always the case. Sometimes the stone is marred irrepara-
> bly by the corrosive chemistry of acid and mineral, an intermingling so
> debasing and destabilizing that no amount of restoration can return the
> building to structural health. Sometimes the building, in the interest of safety,
> has to be razed to the ground, leaving a gaping emptiness in the horizon
> where a glorious monument to human achievement once stood.
>
> Is it too late for me to extricate the filth from my soul?

After the second MAP meeting, Lilburn had made a stealthy incursion
into MAP's computer banks, obtaining financial data reserved for the
accountants and lawyers. He had pored over the numbers, summarized
them, translated them into comprehensible form. "Scrutinized them
up the ass," as Goldbloom had said. He had not slept.

His presentation at yesterday's meeting, painstakingly prepared,
diplomatically worded, had moved only Dedubian. Grimsley, trembling
from anxiety and drink, morbidly concerned with being assassinated by
Jacobus, still didn't seem to comprehend. Rachel was cold, unrespon-
sive, predictable.

Strella understood immediately. He hadn't needed Lilburn's numbers. He knew them all by heart. Strella's initial advice "to play it by ear

until this all blows over" was accepted by the others but rejected by Lilburn and, haltingly, by Dedubian.

That's when Strella's threat came, calmly delivered.

"If you pursue this, Martin, you'll wish you got off as easy as Victoria."

Lilburn turned up the volume on the Bruckner symphony, whose plodding predictability had always facilitated his ability to concentrate on meaningful things without distraction. His story—his most important story—was almost finished and he did not want the errant noises of the office surrounding his cubicle to deflect his concentration. He had commanded the receptionist to block any calls from getting through to him. It was essential that he get the wording exactly right.

The phone rang.

"Dammit," he said, growling into the receiver. "What do you want?"

Silence.

"I repeat, what do you want?"

A voice at the other end said, "Bruckner Fourth?"

"Jacobus!" Lilburn's story immediately left his thoughts.

Jacobus said, "What do you listen to that shit for? I thought you had taste."

"Wait! Wait! Let me turn it down. I can hardly hear you."

Lilburn spun on his swivel chair and lunged for the volume control, the centrifugal force almost causing him to be boomeranged out of the office. Adjusting the volume, he returned to the phone with greater caution.

"Where are you, Jacobus? The entire NYPD is after you," Lilburn said as he rummaged frantically for a clean pad and a sharpened pencil.

"I need some information," said Jacobus.

"Why?" asked Lilburn. "I'm the reporter. I should be getting information from you." He got his pencil ready.

"Is there going to be a reception after Vander's concert on Sunday?"

"You don't know? It's in all the papers. Where are you?"

"Just tell me."

"Yes, of course. There was a big story in—"

"MAP bastards going?" interrupted Jacobus.

"Really! Shall we go around the mulberry bush once again?"

"Yes or no?" Jacobus shouted at him.

"Yes."

"All of them? All?"

"What's this about? Mr. Jacobus, you need to give me something. If you don't, I'm going to hang up immediately."

There was a brief silence on the line.

"I know who the murderer is," said Jacobus.

Lilburn's lips tightened.

"Hold on a minute. Let me turn the music up so no one can hear me talking about this."

Lilburn carefully adjusted the volume so that the Bruckner was loud enough to allow him to talk without being overheard but not so loud that he couldn't hear Jacobus.

"Jacobus, you're the one they're after."

"Don't you think I fucking know that?" hollered Jacobus. Then calm again. "Lilburn, I want you to write a story, play up the return of the Piccolino."

"What are you saying?"

"You wanted me to give you something. I've giving, schmuck. Now listen. Play up the return of the Piccolino. Vander's performing Paganini, right? Make sure you mention Paganini. And that she loves playing the Paganini on the Piccolino."

"Considering that you've only recently accused me of journalistic prevarication, that you would make such a request fills me with chagrin. How do I know for a fact what you're telling me is true? I'm not going to make that up," said Lilburn.

"Why not? That wouldn't be anything new for you," Jacobus snarled.

Lilburn almost hung up. Instead, he pressed the phone to his forehead, not saying anything.

"Sorry, Lilburn," said Jacobus. "Write what you can. I don't give a shit. Just be at the reception and make sure they're all there—all—and you'll get the biggest story you've ever had."

Suddenly the door to his office swung open. It was Jack Redmond, a third-string sports writer, whose gut was threatening to rend the seams of his ten-year-old New York Giants T-shirt. Lilburn, frowning, placed his hand over the phone receiver.

Redmond said, "Hey, Lilburn, turn down that racket you call music. We're trying to work here."

"Get out of my office right now," Lilburn bellowed, "or, damn you, I'll have you reassigned to the Pro Bowlers Tour!"

Redmond's eyes opened wide in surprise, and he sheepishly retreated. Lilburn, no less surprised, forced himself not to smile.

He picked up the receiver and said, "Tell me, Jacobus. Who is the murderer?"

But the only response he heard was the dial tone.

THIRTY-SIX

There was more than the usual preconcert effervescence among the packed crowd in the Carnegie Hall lobby. The sudden reappearance of the Piccolino Strad the previous day had created almost as much sensation as its disappearance. Kamryn Vander's concerto performance with the Grimsley Competition Symphony Orchestra, which had been on hold, was now on go.

In the midst of the swirling crowd, Jacobus's jet-lagged mind was on overload. Just a day before, the Japanese immigration officials at Nagoya airport had politely but firmly requested that he, Nathaniel, and Yumi enter a private room. Waiting for them was Detective Al Malachi of the New York Police Department, who had been contacted at his prior request by Intercontinental Insurance Associates immediately after Nathaniel had called them that the Piccolino had been found. Malachi placed Jacobus under arrest and read him his rights.

When Jacobus handed him the violin, Malachi said, "This doesn't prove you didn't steal the Piccolino Stradivarius, Jacobus. All it proves is that you have just handed me a violin."

Jacobus said, "Up yours."

On their long flight back to the United States, the three of them were grilled individually by Malachi. Each told him his or her part of the story, leaving Malachi to piece together the mosaic. Malachi tried to use his rudimentary knowledge of classiscal music to break through Jacobus's defenses but made a big mistake when he commented that he thought Tchaikovsky's *1812 Overture* was a great piece of music.

"In that case, schmuck," said Jacobus, "*you* should be the one going to jail."

When Malachi finished his questioning, Jacobus asked if he would in return provide him with one bit of information.

"You ask what you want, and I'll decide if I'll give it to you," said Malachi.

"The G-string that was used to kill Victoria Jablonski. What was the color of the wrapping at the end of the string?"

"I'll think about it."

Though Jacobus, Nathaniel, and Yumi didn't say everything they knew, everything they did say was true and was sufficient to bring Malachi around to the conclusion that MAP had indeed tried to pin the theft on Jacobus. There simply had been no hard evidence to conclude otherwise. Malachi had checked with Air Canada and JAL, the two carriers that the fleeing trio had used, and they both confirmed that neither Jacobus, Yumi, nor Nathaniel had either checked or carried on any baggage. Thus it appeared to be true that Jacobus had not stolen the violin but had fled in order to retrieve it and clear himself. Indeed, one of the reasons Yumi returned to the United States with Jacobus and Nathaniel—over Jacobus's vociferous objections that were quietly but definitively overruled by Kate—was to demonstrate that there was no reason for them to fear justice. Nevertheless, Malachi still had sufficient doubt about Jacobus's flight to Japan that, upon their arrival at JFK, Jacobus was immediately taken into custody as the one and only suspect in the murder of Victoria Jablonski. He was fingerprinted, handcuffed, had his passport confiscated, and jailed. However, in consideration of his efforts to secure the return of the Piccolino, he was freed on one million dollars bail, paid by Intercontinental Insurance Associates at the behest of Nathaniel Williams as an advance on his commission. Roy Miller, who wanted to prove that his previous trust in Jacobus wasn't entirely mislaid, also made an effort to persuade the judge to agree to bail, arguing that as long as Nathaniel remained with Jacobus there would be no danger of him fleeing again. The judge was not wholly convinced and required Jacobus to wear a remote-controlled tracking device around his ankle before granting his liberty. Jacobus thought, *This anklet's not nearly as bad as this goddam tie Nathaniel made me wear.*

The violin situation had been resolved. Dedubian, the recipient of

Jacobus's second phone call from Japan after the one he made to Lil-burn, had ultimately, though grudgingly, agreed to his plan. Malachi had turned the violin over to the court. A representative of Intercon-tinental, who verified the authenticity and condition of the instru-ment, was present at the exchange. The violin was then immediately transferred to Boris Dedubian, its legal custodian, for safekeeping. Within hours of taking the instrument into his possession, Dedubian sent a box of souvenirs to a strange address in Japan. He then called the Vanders, who arrived at his studio minutes later, at which point he placed the Piccolino Strad back into Kamryn Vander's hands.

Now Jacobus was back at Carnegie Hall, and he couldn't stand wait-ing in the lobby like this. Nothing to do now until after the concert when they would apprehend the killer. Jostled by a throng as unseeing as he was, Jacobus wandered aimlessly, a useless concert program in his hand. No one was talking to him, notoriety notwithstanding. He was being ignored.

Hell, they all think I'm a goddamn killer, he thought. Why *would* they talk to me? "Hello, Mr. Jacobus. Good to see you again. Murder any-one lately?"

On sensory overload, a barrage of perceptions inundated his brain. Usually he could block out the extraneous stuff, but now in his hyperac-tive, overstressed anxiety he couldn't filter it. Street noise—buses, cars, horns, engines, brakes—alternately amplified or muted when the doors of the Hall opened and closed. Shoes shuffling—it was too crowded to actually walk—the clatter of jewelry. Voices—hundreds of voices in the lobby, at the box office, at the concession stand, murmuring, laughing, conversing, disconnected bits of gossip about the concert, the Grims-ley, the violin, business. Deafening.

He felt the low rumbling vibrations of the New York subway under his feet, the hum of electricity. He smelled perfume, cologne, hair spray, aftershave, deodorant, body odor. He noted with a conspiratorial chuckle that some silently embarrassed patron of the arts had stepped in dog shit.

Jacobus was going mad with apprehension and anticipation.

What a contrast to a quiet village in Japan. He promised himself to return for a vacation—for Kate—if he wasn't in prison.

If all went as he had planned, he needn't worry. Justice was imminent. He'd wait until after the performance—let everything proceed as scheduled. Let the Infanta have her moment in the sun with the violin. Why not? It was because of him that she was now able to perform on it.

He would confront the killer at the reception. The police hadn't cooperated when he requested their presence. They said he was their one and only suspect, that he should count his blessings he wasn't in jail, that even their most minute concession toward his possible innocence would damage their case against him, and if he caused any more trouble they'd lock him up and throw away the key.

Pizzi and Robison, the security guards, though, would be there. They were employees of Carnegie Hall, and because their bumbling had opened the door—literally—to the theft of the Piccolino, Jacobus had no doubt they'd be glued like epoxy to their stations.

The cops wouldn't have believed who had done it, anyway, even if he had told them. He hadn't told anyone. After all, he didn't have a scrap of evidence. But everything pointed to it. He was certain he was right. Jacobus knew what he had to say to get a confession. That was the key. The rest of the MAP bastards would be there as witnesses. Lilburn would be there to get the story. Jacobus had faith in his journalistic skills, if not his integrity, to get the facts straight.

Jacobus forced himself to think about the performance while his mind raced. Kamryn Vander would be playing the Paganini First Violin Concerto—in how many minutes? fifteen? twenty?—on the instrument everyone believed was once owned by Paganini himself. Have I thought of everything? The damned instrument I had wanted to disappear, why the hell did I have to find it? Damn, still at least thirty minutes; they haven't even opened the doors to the seats yet. Why can't I get myself to think about music? Ironic.

So, Jacobus thought, tonight's the final chapter—Kamryn Vander, a talented but immature kid, becomes the heir of Piccolino and Paganini. Talk about irony. Victoria Jablonski's murderer is apprehended. By me. And I ride off into the fucking sunset, whatever that looks like. Great story. And it will end tonight, after the concert.

"Jake! Jake!" said Nathaniel.

"Yeah?"

"You daydreaming or what? Here's Lilburn."

"Mr. Jacobus," said Lilburn, panting.

"What took you so long?"

"Getting through this crowd was just impossible. Your fault. There wouldn't be a soul here tonight but for your not insignificant efforts."

"You check on Pizzi and Robison?" said Jacobus.

"Yes. They're firmly ensconced right outside the door to Kamryn's Green Room and promised they won't budge."

"They'll escort her to the stage?"

"And back."

"They won't let anyone into the Green Room?"

A hand grabbed Jacobus's shoulder from behind. He whipped himself around, knocking a lady's purse from her hand.

"Hey, Jake. Take it easy."

"Sol."

Jacobus had asked Goldbloom to stick with Yumi, just in case she needed protection too.

"Yumi there?" asked Jacobus.

"Yes, I'm here, Mr. Jacobus."

"Good. Just wanted to make sure you were safe."

"So what's not to be safe?" said Sol. "Ah! They're opening the doors."

Jacobus heard the familiar change in the crowd's buzz as they started to herd themselves to their seats. But almost immediately there was another change. Something wasn't right. He could feel it.

"What the hell?" said Sol.

"Sol, what's happening?"

Lilburn answered. "It's pitch-black in here, Jacobus. The lights must have gone out. Can't see a thing!"

People started pushing. Hollering. Screaming.

"Imbecile!" Jacobus yelled. "Imbecile! Imbecile! Imbecile!"

Lilburn shouted back, "It's not my fault, I couldn't—"

"Not you! *Me!*" said Jacobus.

He tried to think. Someone tried to yell for calm but was drowned out by other voices more strident. The crowd was panicking.

"Nathaniel! Are you here?"

"Yeah, Jake. I'm here."

"To the Green Room. *Now!*"

"Jake, I can't see my hand in front of my face. How am I gonna get you to the Green Room?"

Jacobus felt the surging pressure of bodies against him, throwing him off balance. He knew what he had to do, and he had to do it before the stampede began.

"Hey," he said, "if a blind man doesn't know how to goddam walk in the dark, what else is he good for? Grab on to me."

He yelled at Lilburn to call the police, but before Lilburn could answer, Jacobus heard a voice.

"I'm right behind you, Jacobus," said Detective Al Malachi of the NYPD.

"Son of a bitch," said Jacobus. "You've been tailing me all this time?"

"Hey, aren't I allowed to go to a concert?" asked Malachi.

Under normal circumstances, Jacobus could have made his way to the side corridor in seconds. Now, pushed and shoved by by a mob made increasingly hysterical by the pitch blackness, with Nathaniel's stumbling bulk clinging to him, and with Malachi holding on to Nathaniel, he had to continuously reconsider his direction.

No time to spare. He made a decision and headed unswervingly to the point he concluded led to the corridor, grabbing and pushing people out of his way, hoping he was right.

"Hey, fella, who d'you think you're shoving?" said someone with a Midwestern twang.

Jacobus said, "Sorry, I'm a New Yorker."

They made it to the corridor. Next, the stairway.

"Faster," said Jacobus.

"How can you walk without seein' where you're goin'?"

"Two things," said Jacobus, panting. "Left foot. Then right."

Jacobus hauled Nathaniel up the stairs, telling him his plan along the way.

Left turn. Race along the corridor.

"We're almost there."

Jacobus suddenly tripped over something and went sprawling, Nathaniel and Malachi on top of him. Jacobus braced himself for a crushing impact against the hard floor but was momentarily relieved to land on something soft, cushioning his fall. That relief quickly turned to anxiety as he groped for tactile information.

A heavy metal music stand lying across the corridor. A body. Two bodies. One fat. One skinny. Two badges.

Pizzi and Robison. Unconscious. Bloody. But alive.

Jesus! The Vanders!

No sound from the Green Room.

Jacobus struggled to his feet, feeling the wall as much for support as a guide to the door. He found it. Turned the knob.

Locked. Thank God. Hope.

He knocked. No answer. Banged the door.

Called out, "Open the door. It's me, Jacobus."

No answer. Banged again.

Malachi spoke softly. "Mrs. Vander. This is Detective Malachi of the New York Police Department. If you're in there, let us know. We're here to make sure Kamryn's safe. We'll protect you. Please trust us."

A moment of silence.

Then a voice. Muffled crying.

"We can't see in here. We heard yelling. Fighting."

Jacobus whispered to Malachi, "Why didn't the bitch answer when *I* called them?"

"It's okay, Mrs. Vander," said Malachi, ignoring Jacobus. "Please open the door so we can take you to safety."

Tentative steps to the door. Bolt unlocked.

Jacobus barged through.

"No time to explain!" said Jacobus. "The two of you, leave with the cop! Immediately! Leave the violin with me!"

"For you to steal again?" said Cynthia Vander, hysterically. "You must be out of your mind! I'm not letting go of this violin."

Before Jacobus could argue, Nathaniel interrupted, panting and sweating. "Jake, I can't leave you here with a killer!"

"It's the only way. If we don't catch the killer now—not to be too melodramatic—I'll be in prison for the rest of my life. Now hurry! Get the hell out of here. All of you."

"What's going on?" shouted Cynthia Vander. "What killer?"

Jacobus heard Kamryn on the other side of the room, sobbing softly.

Jesus, what's the rest of this kid's life going to be like? Short, if her mother doesn't hurry up.

"Mrs. Vander, your daughter's life is in danger," said Malachi. "We have reason to believe Victoria Jablonski's killer will return to this room. For Kamryn and for the Piccolino. Please let Nathaniel take the child to safety. Stay here with Jacobus and me if you must."

"You're leaving too, Malachi," said Jacobus. "As we both know, I don't have a shred of evidence yet, and I can only get a confession if you're out of smelling distance. Get out of here."

"You better be right," said Malachi. "I'll get the medics to take care of Pizzi and Robison. Then I'll be back."

"Mrs. Vander, Kamryn needs to go now," said Nathaniel.

She said, "Princess, go with Mr. Williams. It'll be all right."

Jacobus said to Nathaniel, "You stand here where you won't get lost. I'll get the kid."

In the blackness, Jacobus easily found the source of the whimpering.

"Stick your hand out, Kamryn."

Jacobus waved around, found it, and held it in his as he led her cautiously back to Nathaniel.

"Don't worry, kid," said Jacobus as he transferred the girl's hand to Nathaniel's. "You're okay."

"Good luck, Jake," said Nathaniel.

"Get the hell out of here," said Jacobus.

Jacobus closed the door and found a chair facing it on the far side of the room.

He sat down and said to Cynthia, "Hand me the violin."

"How dare you talk to me like—"

"Hand me the fucking violin! Now!"

She handed him the violin.

"Sit here next to me."

"What?" A little fear returned to her voice.

The room was dark and silent.

"What do you need the violin for?" Vander asked quietly.

"Have to lure the killer back."

"Why?"

"To make sure the killer will strike again."

"I'm sorry I asked."

He lifted the violin to his shoulder. He tried to be calm, but he was trembling. Frustrated, flustered, fuming at himself for his vain confidence, adrenaline rushing, he couldn't think of anything to play. He couldn't remember anything.

Ah, what the hell.

He started playing the Siciliano from the "Devil's Trill" Sonata.

Sounds like shit, he thought.

He switched to the Paradis "Sicilienne." He tried to play it the way he heard it on Kate's recording. It helped calm him down.

Vander was quiet.

Jacobus thought, well, at least that shut her up.

Wait! Imbecile again! Don't play like Kate! Don't play like Kate! Play like Kamryn!

Now he started playing Paganini, playing the way Kamryn played—the way Victoria had taught her—faster vibrato, louder, more accents. Fool the killer. Fool the poor, disillusioned killer.

Jacobus heard the footsteps. He kept playing. He heard the key inserted into the lock. He heard the heavy doorknob slowly, quietly turn. He heard Cynthia Vander whisper something to herself.

Yeah. Say your prayers, babes. He kept playing.

The door opened.

He smelled the perfume. Talon. The perfume that, unlike Kate Padgett, she had forgotten to remove.

"Hello, Rachel," he said quietly. He felt defeated, as if his life was a failure. He had failed Rachel. All the other successes, such as they were, didn't make up for this. "May I please have my G-string back?"

"Jacobus! You? Again?" Her voice was confused but spouted venom. "No!"

"Rachel," asked Jacobus. "Why?"

"I already told you once. That violin belongs to *me*, not to you or that little twit, Kamryn. She's just one of those little twits."

"But Victoria. Why Victoria?"

"Be-cause-I-hate-ed her!"

Her piercing, high monotone tore through Jake's soul. In the most profoundly sorrowful sense, her voice was devoid of music. Nor was he comforted by the sound of Rachel locking the door behind her.

She cackled. She was talking fast now. It wasn't her voice.

"She didn't like it that I slept with Strella and Dedubian," Rachel said. "She kept telling me not to. But there was nothing she could do about it."

"She was doing that for your own good, Rachel."

"You old fool, you think you know everything. She didn't like it because she was jealous they weren't fucking *her* anymore!"

"Rachel!"

"And you know what? You know what?" She was laughing uncontrollably. "You know who she ended up sleeping with?"

Jacobus was silent.

"Me! She was having sex with the booby prize!

"Both of you ruined my life. Both of you thought you were God. But you're not. I proved that with Victoria, didn't I? And *you* stole the violin. Pizzi wasn't the only one who heard you tell Victoria! You stole the violin for your little honey, Yumi, just so I wouldn't have it. But now it's going to be mine."

"Mr. Jacobus, Mr. Jacobus," Cynthia whispered. "The lights are back on."

Shit, there goes my advantage.

"And she's holding a music stand. With blood on it."

"Thanks."

"How did you know I have your string?" asked Rachel.

I better keep her talking, Jacobus thought. Only chance now.

He said, "At first I thought you took the G-string off my violin and returned to Victoria's office to kill her with it. But that couldn't have been right, could it, because if you had planned on killing Victoria there was no way of knowing for sure that my violin would be left alone, and you couldn't have known when, where, or even if she and I would have a confrontation."

"But I set it up pretty well, didn't I, Jake? I even had that cop show up at the right time."

"You certainly did, Rachel. You had your own G-string ready in advance. And when you heard Victoria and me arguing in her office, you waited in the hallway until I left Victoria's room."

"And you walked right past me!" Rachel chuckled grotesquely, deep in her throat. "All I had to do was stand still. I know how careful I have to be around you, the great Daniel Jacobus. But it was so easy. So easy. I just stood still. I'm good at standing still, aren't I? My whole life has been one long standing still. Until now. You never knew it was me, did you?"

"No, not at first. At first I actually suspected Yumi, after Victoria humiliated her. That might have been a motive. And Yumi knew where my violin was and could have easily taken my string without anyone knowing. I thought maybe she was trying to frame me for some reason.

"But then it occurred to me that you too knew which was my violin.

You figured, why not kill two birds with one stone. So *after* you killed Victoria, you sneaked backstage and took the G-string off my violin to make it look like I did it. Only problem is I use Harmonium strings and you use Megatones, like all of Victoria's students. The wrapping on Megatones is red and white, and the wrapping on Harmoniums is blue. Malachi confirmed to me that the string used to kill Victoria was red and white."

"You can't prove that just because it was a Megatone it was mine and not yours."

"You don't think so? I think so," said Jacobus. "When the crime lab compares the kind of rosin found on the string with the rosin on our violins, they'll figure out who the string belongs to. When they measure the distance of the rosin residue from the end of the string and compare it to the distances on the strings still on our violins they'll see that you, like all of Victoria's students, play closer to the bridge than I do because all she cared about was power, not quality.

"And maybe I didn't know your exact motive, Rachel, but I realized what sent you over the edge."

"What do you mean?"

"You remember when you were telling me that Victoria had told you that you had played the Paganini Concerto 'note perfect'?"

"So?"

"Well, for you to have been surrounded by young students like that student . . . what was her name?"

"Noriko Watanabe. One of the twits," Rachel hissed.

"Yes. One of the twits. For you to have been around students like that and then she goes and plays the thing a lot less than 'note perfect,' well, that must've been very humiliating for someone of your skills."

"You don't know what humiliation is, Jake. Did it ever occur to you that I've known all along that there's something in the music I wasn't getting? How do you think that feels, that no matter how hard you try, how hard you work, how hard you try to understand, you know you'll never feel what you're supposed to feel? Isn't that bad enough? Isn't that torture enough? And then to be demeaned by people like you. Like Victoria. After that stage show the two of you put on that was called a master class? That charade? And then to hear the sniggers behind your back by twits half your age because of the judgments descending from on high by god almighties like you and her? To be made to feel like you're subhuman?"

"But I do know humiliation, Rachel." Jacobus choked back tears. "More than you can know. And I also know why you're here tonight. Kamryn's going to play the Paganini Concerto too. Another twit. And on the Piccolino, no less. But I made a mistake."

"You, the great Daniel Jacobus, made a mistake?" Rachel spat.

"Yeah, even I can make a mistake. I thought you'd wait until after the performance. Isn't that stupid of me? See, I thought you'd return to the scene of the first crime, when the Piccolino was stolen, where there'd be a crowd, commotion, distractions. More chance of fading into the woodwork. More chance of framing the original suspects. That's why you've got my own Harmonium G-string with you right now, isn't it? Because you were planning to frame me for yet another murder. But I guess I was just being too poetic thinking about the timing. You really couldn't stand to hear Kamryn play tonight, could you?"

"No," said Rachel. "I couldn't."

What else? Have to keep this going. She's getting restless.

"And then, you know, if Yumi had wanted to find Victoria's room in order to go and kill her, she would've had to ask someone, anyone, for directions. She doesn't know Carnegie Hall. That would have been dangerous for her, you know, to ask directions, if she was going to kill someone. But you . . . you know your way around the building as well as anyone. Well enough to know where the main light switch is. Well enough to go get a key to this door when you found it locked."

Rachel laughed. "Those security guards never knew what hit them. And with a music stand! How poetic! I do pretty well in the dark, like you, don't I, Jake?"

Jacobus forced himself to laugh.

"And what better moment for you to strike at Victoria than when both Yumi and I would have motive, means, and opportunity? Very clever, Rachel. Very clever. I must admit."

"But how did you know your little sweetheart Yumi *didn't* kill . . . ? Didn't kill . . . ?"

Jacobus didn't know whether to thank God she was taking the bait as he stalled for his life, or to deny His existence, for how could a God permit this girl, unable even to say the name of the person she killed, to endure such wretched misery? What would Father McCawley say to that?

How long do I have to stall until those assholes get here? he asked himself.

"Well, if Yumi had gone into Victoria's room at that point, knowing Victoria, she would have confronted Yumi. If Yumi had wanted to kill her, there would have been a huge struggle. I'm not even sure who would've won. As it was there were no signs of violence, except of course the G-string.

"So you went into Victoria's room," prodded Jacobus. "She had no reason to fear you, even with the Megatone string in your hand. She trusted you, Rachel. You waited until her back was turned and then wrapped it around her neck. Isn't that what happened, Rachel?"

"And framed you in the process. I told you I was a winner, Jake."

Jacobus heard footsteps running down the hall. Several pairs of welcome footsteps.

"Then the final clue. It's been puzzling me. I just have one question, Rachel."

"Not two?"

"Just one."

"So what is it this time, Mr. Genius?"

"If you hated Victoria so much, why do you still wear her perfume?"

Rachel uttered an inhuman, groaning animal sound.

Jacobus heard the sudden clang of the music stand as Rachel hoisted it up above her head, base up. Cynthia Vander screamed. Jacobus, sensing Rachel's onrush, raised the fabled Piccolino Stradivarius in front of him for protection.

A familiar grunt. The door shattering on its hinges as it slammed open, rebounding against the wall.

"Nathaniel, turn off the lights!" shouted Jacobus.

"Yumi . . ."

Then, the impact of the music stand against the violin. Jacobus heard its neck snap with a nauseating crack, causing the tailpiece to rip off, protesting strings twanging angrily. The bridge collapsed with a bang like a gunshot and the sound post burst through the top. The shuddering blow glancing off the violin shattered his glasses. Then, the stunning pain in his temple.

Jacobus opened his eyes. He looked up. The light blinded him. He closed his eyes but still couldn't keep it out.

Where am I? he asked himself. On the floor? No, not the floor. Someone's lap.

He opened his eyes again. Someone holding my head. With bloody hands.

Others here. Outlines. The light's so bright.

"Nathaniel. My old friend Nathaniel." Jacobus tried to talk but managed only a hoarse croaking sound. "What I do for a pastrami sandwich, huh?"

"Don't talk, Jake."

Damn light killing my eyes. Who else?

"We got her, Jacobus," said Detective Malachi. "Thanks to you."

"Lilburn, is that you?" asked Jacobus.

"Yes, Mr. Jacobus."

"Figured. You look as pompous as you sound. So you got your big story."

"Yes. Thank you. I got it."

The pain in his head was intolerable.

"Yeah, my obituary."

He tried to laugh but only choked. Who's holding me? he wondered.

He twisted around, craning his neck, to see the face that belonged to the hands that cradled his head.

"Yumi . . . Yumi," he said. There was light behind her. She was glowing.

"Jake," Yumi said, trying to smile through tears.

He smiled back. She called me Jake, he thought.

"Beautiful as your grandmother . . . almost," he whispered hoarsely, just before he was engulfed by a wave of darkness even deeper than that to which he was accustomed.

CODA

THIRTY-SEVEN

On the seventh day, Jacobus awoke. He lay there for some time and simply listened, unable to move. It took him a great deal of effort to translate thought into the mechanics of speech, especially with a tube down his throat.

"So, Padre," he finally said in a whisper, "you have a cigarette?"

Father McCawley almost dropped his book, clutching at it just before it hit the ground.

"My God, Mr. Jacobus," said McCawley, "you almost startled me to death. How did you know I was here?"

"Who else would sit so patiently at the bedside of a dying man, turning page after page. What else could it be but a Bible? You've come to read me my last rites?"

"Only at your request, Mr. Jacobus."

With supreme effort Jacobus raised his head an inch from the pillow.

"Then get the hell out of here!" he said with as much force as he could muster.

Father McCawley's laughter faded as Jacobus fell back to the bed. From what seemed like a great distance, the last thing he heard was the priest saying, "Mr. Jacobus, there's something I need to talk to you about," before he returned to a deep sleep.

———

Nathaniel had been by his side since day one in the hospital, refusing to leave except when people like Yumi or Father McCawley came to visit and insist he get some rest. Mostly he sat with his arms folded. Occasionally his head slumped to his chest and he joined Jacobus in sleep. He was determined to protect his friend even if he didn't know from what. Sylvia brought a gallon of chicken soup from the Carnegie Deli for Jacobus. The doctor on call told her it wouldn't help. "Well, it wouldn't hurt" was her reply, and she left it there.

Nathaniel had brought his reel-to-reel tape recorder to play dusted-off tapes from their old Dumky Trio days, hoping that the music's rays of light would somehow penetrate the dark depths of Jacobus's slumber. Mozart, Haydn, Beethoven, Schubert, Mendelssohn, Brahms, Dvořák were his chicken soup for Jake.

When Jacobus woke again, a week later, he felt much better.

There was the music. There was the soup. There was also a large bottle of Suntory whiskey, President's Special Blend, from Max. That would definitely help with his recovery. Salvador came by to see how Jacobus was doing.

There was a simple but elegant porcelain vase of purple irises from Kate, which he didn't remove from his sill even though the blooms, which he could still smell, had no doubt faded. The note with them, read by his nurse, said, "Thank you for the lovely souvenirs. The invitation to visit is still, and always will be, open." The nurse also read the terse note from Father McCawley. "Please call," and the phone number. Those Catholics, thought Jacobus, never give up.

Though Jacobus now had only a small bandage left to show for his wound, Yumi insisted on coming daily to tend to him whether he wanted her to or not. She was trying to convince Jacobus to allow her to help him finish his book as payment for her violin lessons.

Detective Al Malachi visited and succinctly filled Jacobus in on what had transpired.

"That night in Carnegie Hall, in the Green Room, Nathaniel Williams bursts in, Yumi Shinagawa right behind him. Just before he shuts off the lights, she reaches for the first thing she can throw—a desk bust of Holbrooke Grimsley—and hurls it at the perp, Rachel Lewison. The statuette hits the perp's arm, and, combined with the lights being out, causes her to panic and misdirect her swing of the music stand, saving your life.

"The perp was ultimately subdued by the combined efforts of Williams, Shinagawa, and myself, and taken into custody, where she is at present awaiting trial for the murder of Victoria Jablonski. Security guards Pizzi and Robison have recovered from head wounds and concussions. Pizzi has decided to retire. Robison is on paid sick leave."

Jacobus did not press any charges from his own encounter with Rachel. In fact, he planned to cooperate with her defense lawyer to testify on her behalf. Temporary insanity would be the plea, no doubt. Jacobus hoped, but was not confident, that "temporary" was an accurate diagnosis. Malachi couldn't understand why Jacobus wouldn't assist the prosecution of someone who had tried to kill him, but they parted on friendly terms nevertheless. Kamryn Vander's Paganini performance, of course, had been canceled and all future Grimsley Competitions as well, thereby providing Trevor Grimsley ample time to concentrate on plea bargaining with the IRS attorneys.

The *New York Times,* encouraged that the arts world for once could produce news that would actually help its circulation, covered the MAP story thoroughly. Lilburn had submitted the taped conversation between Jacobus and Anthony Strella to the news bureau, and an investigation had been opened. With both the *Times* and the IRS breathing down his neck, Strella had little choice but to take his final bow from concert management. He was known to be seeking employment, as yet unsuccessfully, in the investment field.

Nathaniel reluctantly declined his $1.6 million commission from Intercontinental Insurance Associates with the excuse that in the long run the goodwill was more important for his business. It had not been an easy decision. Even Jacobus had urged him to take the money. "Don't be a schmuck. Think of all the doughnuts!" But Nathaniel explained why, and Jacobus couldn't disagree.

Intercontinental Insurance, perplexed but overjoyed at its unexpected windfall, was quite content to pay the substantial claim to repair the significant, but not lethal, damage that the violin had suffered. However, any claims that might have been staked regarding the violin's "perfection" were clearly no longer applicable.

Dedubian himself did the restoration. When the work was finished, the Piccolino looked as astonishingly beautiful as ever, but nevertheless the damage it had received made its value only a fraction of what it had been in its virgin condition.

Grimsley, his ardor for the world of classical music grown cold and in need of a considerable amount of cash, arranged a Russian Tea Room luncheon with Solomon Goldbloom. He agreed to sell the Piccolino at an exceedingly low price to the delighted Goldbloom, who had little difficulty convincing Grimsley that he would get a much better rate of return from the cash he was offering than from the modest annual appreciation of a broken three-quarter-size violin. Goldbloom was so tickled by his good fortune he even paid for the lunch.

Gradually Jacobus's head began to feel better, and they removed the tubes. One day he received a *New York Times* article in Braille and a gift from Martin Lilburn. Nathaniel told him the gift was Alfred Brendel's recording of the complete Beethoven piano works, and he read Lilburn's inscription on the record jacket. "Have decided to play the piano again. Only one lifetime!" Jacobus waited until night, when the hospital was quiet and the well-wishers were all gone, before reading the article, in order to savor the moment. His fingers felt along the embossed text, reading and rereading it, regretting and relishing its content.

Martin Lilburn to Resign from *Times* Staff

By Martin Lilburn

It is not standard practice for a journalist to report in the first person. I have never done so until now. As I am the subject of this story, however, it does not seem inappropriate.

I have been a major player in a long-standing and cruel charade. Acting as a member of the Musical Arts Project Group simultaneous with my responsibilities as a reporter—a clear conflict of interest—I have disseminated tainted opinions about musicians whose performances I have attended. These opinions, appearing as they have in this distinguished newspaper, have molded, if not actually created, public perception of the abilities of these artists, and so have affected their careers and their lives; sometimes for the better, sometimes for the worse, but in many cases falsely.

Furthermore, I have profited financially from my dalliance with cultural king- and queen-building. While MAP is in appearance a nonprofit corporation, its members went far beyond exploiting legal loopholes in enriching themselves on public funds and private supporters, whom they have misled. To rectify this injustice, Mr. Boris Dedubian, the well-known violin dealer, and I have made a detailed presentation to the Internal Revenue Service regarding our financial situation. Mr. Anthony Strella, former president of Zenith Concert Artists, and Mr. Trevor Grimsley, president of the now-defunct Grimsley Violin Competition, have chosen to seek legal counsel, as is their legitimate right.

Mr. Daniel Jacobus, who in previous articles has been maligned and demonized, should be recognized for being an unwavering beacon of artistic and moral integrity. He has focused the glaring light of honesty upon MAP, and we have withered under it. His admirable efforts in retrieving the stolen Piccolino Stradivarius violin and in apprehending Victoria Jablonski's alleged killer must be duly noted.

Regardless of my intent to promote great music and musicians, I have betrayed the trust of the readers and the publishers of the *New York Times,* and whatever credibility I may have had as a critic is now nonexistent. As a result, I have no option other than to immediately resign from my position at the *Times.*

So Lilburn does have balls, after all, Jacobus thought. He could have had the scoop of a lifetime that night at Carnegie Hall and didn't even mention it. Jacobus carelessly tossed the newspaper article on the floor.

He tried to sleep, but the patient in the next ward decided to start watching reruns of *The Brady Bunch* on the wall-mounted TV. After all these years, Jacobus mused, finally an advantage to being blind. He picked up the phone and dialed the number he had memorized.

"Good evening, Father McCawley speaking."

"Padre. Jacobus."

"Ah! Mr. Jacobus. How are you feeling?"

"Peachy. They're letting me out of this hellhole in two days. What's up?"

"Well, Mr. Jacobus. It's a little hard to say."

"You can speak freely with me, my son."

"Very funny. You learn quickly. Well, let me spit it out. When I came to visit you in the hospital the first time, when you were in the coma, nevertheless you were talking in your sleep. Actually, you were talking quite a bit."

"How much is quite a bit?"

"Well, I know you have friends named Kate and Max."

"Is that it?"

"No, Mr. Jacobus." Father McCawley paused. "There's more. You struggled with some ivy, I believe it was."

Jacobus squirmed.

"Eh, so what?" he said.

"You also spoke of a second Piccolino Stradivarius."

"Who else heard?" asked Jacobus in a sudden panic. This could undo everything.

"No one else while I was there. But I thought—"

"What is it you want?"

"Oh, Mr. Jacobus! I would never! . . . I just thought, if you wanted to tell me all about it, get it off your chest, maybe you wouldn't talk about it by accident anymore."

Jacobus thought. What were the risks? Could he trust the priest? What were the chances of someone hearing him reveal his secrets in his sleep? Would his "confession" really help him rest in peace, as McCawley was suggesting?

"Mr. Jacobus. Are you there?"

"It would be confidential?"

"I would never tell a soul. It would be between you, me, and God."

"Okay, Padre. Here's the deal. I don't know what good it'll do, but I'm willing to play the odds. Come here tomorrow night when it's quiet, with a pack of Camels, and I'll tell you all about it."

"But Mr. Jacobus, they don't allow cigarettes there. After all, it's a hospital."

"Well, Padre, I guess this presents you with what you'd call a moral dilemma. Maybe you should pray for a solution."

"All right, Mr. Jacobus. I'll pray. But just to help my prayers along, do you smoke filtered or unfiltered?"

———

The next night, his last in the hospital, Jacobus tossed about in his bed. Where's the damn priest? he asked himself as he fidgeted with the name tag on his wrist, the levers of the bed, and anything else he could get his hands on. Finally, close to midnight, the door opened.

"Sorry I'm so late," said Father McCawley. "There was a death."

"You got my Camels?" asked Jacobus.

"I'm disappointed in you, Mr. Jacobus. I thought you'd have some sympathy."

"Yeah? Well, some things never change."

"I see. Well, here are your cigarettes. I'll see you later."

Jacobus felt the pack land on the bed.

"Wait!" said Jacobus.

"For what, Mr. Jacobus?"

"Look, I was good as dead the first time we met and you helped me out. So maybe I owe you one. Have a seat."

"All right, I'll do that."

"Now, where do I start?" said Jacobus.

"You said in your sleep that you made a deal with the devil for the second Strad. You sounded amazingly cogent."

"For once!" Jacobus laughed. "And while I'm unconscious."

Jacobus gave Father McCawley a concise summary of how he got to Japan and found the false Piccolino. He mentioned all the names and places, omitting only that Nathaniel had saved him from suicide.

"When I was at Padgett's on my wild-goose chase and Nathaniel was at Furukawa's, Nathaniel suddenly had an epiphany, as he calls it. A seemingly insignificant detail of our investigation jumped out and he knew he needed to see me before Inspector Taniguchi figured out where we were. So he called Dedubian for confirmation, which he got, but didn't know how he would explain everything to Max. But when Max saw the look in his eye, nothing needed to be said. He immediately arranged for a driver, and Nathaniel, bowing and shaking hands extra-vigorously, took off."

"That sounds like a preamble, Mr. Jacobus," said Father McCawley. "I take it we're getting to the epiphany."

"Getting there," said Jacobus, and he described the night at the Carnegie Deli when Nathaniel read Matthilda Grimsley's diary.

"Well, it appears that Grimsley, old Holbrooke Grimsley, was a more astute businessman than Nathaniel and I gave him credit for.

When he bought what turned out to be the Piccolino Strad—totally by accident—he took it to Aram Dedubian, Boris's grandfather, in Rome. There he had Aram certify that the violin was indeed the Piccolino Strad and had the shop's chief restorer, Valerio Bartolini, clean up the fiddle. It apparently was in remarkably good condition and required no repair to speak of. But Grimsley didn't just have the violin cleaned up. Matthilda wrote in her diary that he left it there for several weeks. Several weeks! Now why the hell would he have left the violin in the shop for such a long time if all it needed was a damn simple polish? A day would have been enough for that. Take a guess, Padre."

"I wouldn't have a clue. Did he try to sell it?"

"Nah! Grimsley left the violin there for several weeks so that Bartolini could make a copy! A damned copy. That was Nathaniel's epiphany. I should have realized it myself after Yumi gave me hell for being stupid enough to think that you could have a fake made in a few days."

"But why make a copy?" McCawley asked.

"Because he worried about the very thing that happened," Jacobus said. "He was worried about it being stolen."

"So he had a copy made . . ." said McCawley.

"And left Aram Dedubian's shop with the fake," said Jacobus, "leaving the original Piccolino Strad in Dedubian's vault, where it remained, ending up in the hands of grandson Boris. So you see, Padre, Mrs. Padgett was correct. The violin she saw so many years ago and the one she held in her hands in her home were one and the same. Unfortunately, neither was the real thing. That's why Nathaniel couldn't find it in him to claim his reward. Because the violin we found was pure unadulterated phony baloney. It would've gnawed at him the rest of his life."

Jacobus added, "So the violin I heard Kamryn Vander perform on was not the real Piccolino, and it bugged the shit out of me why it didn't sound right when she played it."

"That's certainly astonishing," said McCawley. "But how do we know this to be true? Boris Dedubian's word? I don't mean to be uncharitable, but after all, he *is* a violin dealer. It could be an old wives' tale. And who's to say Boris didn't make a fake himself and has presented that as the original? He's certainly had his hands on the real thing enough to have the time to do it."

"Good thinking, Padre. Mrs. Padgett asked the same questions. And so did Nathaniel to Boris, and Boris had all the right answers.

"As I said, Grimsley was smarter than I would have guessed. When he had the fake made, he had Aram Dedubian write two copies of a very detailed document stating what had been done. It was signed by both of them and by Bartolini in the presence of a judge in Rome, who gave both copies the stamp of his official seal."

"So Boris Dedubian has one copy and Trevor Grimsley the other? It sounds like a conspiracy to me."

"Not exactly. Boris does have one of the documents. It was given to him by his father, Ashot, which was given to him by Aram himself, who had been sworn to secrecy by Holbrooke Grimsley. Boris took the same oath. But Holbrooke didn't trust his own family, including offspring who didn't even exist yet, to keep the same oath."

"So exactly where is the other copy of the document?"

Jacobus pressed his thumb and forefinger to the bridge of his nose and shook his head, still almost doubting the plausibility of it all.

"In the Vatican."

"Well, I'll be blessed!" said McCawley. "But that still doesn't tell us which is the original Piccolino Strad and which is the copy, does it?"

"Well, that's the interesting part," said Jacobus. "When Bartolini made the copy, he made it exact in every detail. Even the grain of the wood matches up, though that wouldn't really have mattered, anyway, since no one had seen the original for such a long time. But there was one detail that was shown to the judge he intentionally left out of the copy, so that there is no question as to which is original."

"And that would be . . . ?"

"Would you believe a drop of blood?"

"A drop of blood!" repeated McCawley. "This is astonishing! Of course, I suppose what else would one expect with such a violin? Wear and tear? A crack? That would be way too mundane. And whose blood was this, may I ask? Was the oath of secrecy solemnized by a group bloodletting? This doesn't seem to fit the profile of this supposedly astute businessman you've been talking about."

"They're not totally sure who the drop of blood belonged to," Jacobus said, "but it seems possible it was the blood of Piccolino himself, assuming he actually existed. It looks like it dripped in through the left f-hole and landed next to his name on the label Stradivari had inserted into the violin. It then seeped across the label and into the wood, in a way creating its own seal of authenticity, certifying that the label and the violin truly did belong to each other. And you can tell by the way the drop of blood seeped into the grain that it happened when the wood was newly cut. According to Dedubian there's no question. Maybe there *is* some truth to Pallottelli's book about Piccolino. Maybe the horny little runt really did exist. Maybe he *was* stabbed by the cuckold husband."

Jacobus was suddenly stabbed himself, not by a sword but by an intense emotion it took him a moment to define. Not so much that Piccolino might have been murdered, but rather that he might actually have truly existed! To reach across an unbroken chain of music through the centuries and rediscover a genius, a kindred spirit, perhaps. Damn, I'm getting sentimental, he thought.

"But why didn't he say anything?" asked McCawley, interrupting Jacobus's reverie.

"Why didn't who say anything?" responded Jacobus.

"Mr. Dedubian. After all, you were accused of a crime you didn't commit. If Mr. Dedubian knew Padgett's family had taken a fake, why didn't he tell anyone what he knew all along?"

"Good question, Padre. Holbrooke Grimsley was what we often call a man of his times. He believed in the supremacy of business, the manifest destiny of capitalism, particularly American capitalism, and of his place in it. At the same time, he also believed in a very basic, almost naive turn-of-the-century American notion of right and wrong. So in his agreement with Aram Dedubian he stipulated that if someone were to steal the fake—the *fake*, mind you—Dedubian or his descendants had to wait one year before presenting the original."

"But why? The fake's almost worthless."

"Simple, my dear Watson," said Jacobus. "In order to give the authorities time to catch the gonif who stole it. Even though the copy's only worth a small fraction of the original, the thief doesn't know it's a copy, right? Grimsley felt that a thief should be tracked down and brought to justice on principle alone. A crook's a crook, and chances are, if the original's immediately returned, a thief who takes a mere copy would get off a lot easier, or even escape justice entirely. Holbrooke Grimsley didn't envision the possibility of a good person doing the stealing."

The two men sat in the late-night quiet of the hospital, accompanied only by the soft whirring of unfathomable medical machinery.

"Well, that's an absolutely amazing story, Mr. Jacobus. But you'll have to forgive me for asking yet another question."

"I knew you'd get to it sooner or later, Padre."

"Yes. Well, why is it, then, that you didn't have to wait for an entire year before showing your face again?"

"Bingo. You see, that's what I took care of when I called Boris from Japan. All I needed to do was return with the fake."

"That sounds very simple, but there must be more to it than that."

"Yes. Well. Since no one in memory—other than Boris Dedubian—had ever seen the real Piccolino, I figured from now on there must only be one Piccolino. And so I persuaded Boris to take a new vow. He will never mention there was ever another Piccolino. No one will know there ever was a copy. No one will ever be able to tie Kate, Keiko, or Yumi to the theft."

"But someday, someone will no doubt discover there is a second one," said McCawley. "Won't they?"

"I think not," Jacobus said with a chuckle. "From now on, there will be, in fact, only one Piccolino Stradivarius. You see, when I called Boris and made the deal with him, his end of the bargain was to send Kate a few 'souvenirs' from his shop. A scroll, a peg, that sort of thing. I thought it would be nice for Kate to hand them out to some of her students . . . as a reward for practicing hard, of course. I think of it as collateral, sort of."

"Mr. Jacobus! I'm speechless. But collateral for what, may I ask?"

"Well, collateral against my pledge not to testify against Boris and Lilburn in that MAP scandal. Even better, I'm going to testify on their behalf. Boris was very appreciative. I suspect he has a good chance of retiring to his condo in Montreux very soon."

"Well, I'll be damned," said Father McCawley.

"Don't get carried away, Padre. Now, can you give me a match for my cigarette?"

"Who said anything about matches?"

When Jacobus was ready to leave the hospital, Nathaniel, not a penny richer, nevertheless had his '74 Rabbit waxed and ready to drive him home, where Roy Miller was waiting to greet them. Whether Jacobus saw—or only thought he saw—Nathaniel, Yumi, and the others while lying wounded, he couldn't really remember. In any event, his sight had not come back. The violin might have saved his life, but it didn't perform miracles.

The hesitation in his new student's approaching footsteps, almost at the door now, amused Jacobus. He took a final drag of his half-smoked Camel and coughed up some phlegm. He tried to take a deep breath, not for fresh air but to inhale the lingering wafts of cigarette smoke from the butt he had just crushed into his new favorite ashtray, the actual back of an old three-quarter-size, finely formed violin, inverted and already black-hardened with the scars of innumerable cigarette burns, all recent. Late summer heat had returned and he was starting to feel crotchety again. He immediately lit another cigarette.

The doctors had ordered Nathaniel to remove the toby jug ashtray from Jacobus's home while he was still bedridden at the hospital. They had said that if he continued to smoke, it would kill him. He had replied, "If you make me stop, I'll kill *you!*" Then he almost coughed himself to death in a fit of hacking laughter.

The new student walked into the room and began to tune.

"Good morning, Kamryn," said Jacobus. "Just one thing before we start."

"Yeah? What?"

"Please bow when you come into my studio."

Do I regret having had such a fine fiddle dismantled? Jacobus asked himself. Was I too rash in seeing justice done? Maybe. Maybe not. What the hell. He extinguished his Camel, pressing the butt into the wood with an extra twist, obliterating the final trace of the violin's label so that no one could ever tell whether it may have been one that had a drop of blood on it.

ACKNOWLEDGMENTS

When I first started writing *Devil's Trill* more than ten years ago, it was called *Violin Lessons* and bore little resemblance to the finished product. I had no idea how to get a book published, and so when I read the jacket to Katharine Weber's eminently enjoyable novel *The Music Lesson* and saw that she, like I, had a connection to Yale University, I figured "what the hell?" and wrote her a letter asking for guidance.

Katharine, who didn't know me from Adam, was not only kind enough to read my book but somehow saw through all its flaws. Buoyed by her moral and technical support, and by her invaluable assistance finding the perfect agent, I just kept plugging away. To Katharine, I am eternally indebted.

That agent turned out to be Simon Lipskar of Writers House. Simon not only has an abundance of expertise in the literary field, he had a career in music that paralleled mine to an uncanny degree, so it was not difficult for me to accede to his suggestions to rewrite, rewrite, and rewrite yet again. When he shared my book with fellow agent and mystery specialist Josh Getzler, who had me rewrite yet again, I always had the sense that the book was not just changing, it was getting better. To Simon and Josh, my deepest gratitude.

My thanks also to St. Martin's Press and my wonderful editor, Michael Homler, who have enabled me to realize one of my fondest dreams by publishing my first book and allowing me to write a second.

It would be remiss of me not to express my limitless appreciation of Johann Sebastian Bach, Maria Theresia von Paradis, Niccolo Paganini, Ludwig van Beethoven, Felix Mendelssohn, and—it goes without saying—Giuseppe Tartini, without whose assistance this book would have been impossible. I would urge all readers of *Devil's Trill* to listen to the music discussed and performed in the book to enhance their enjoyment of the story and of life in general.

Many of the characters in *Devil's Trill* are composites of people I have known in my forty-plus years in the classical music world—musicians, teachers, concert agents and managers, violin dealers—people from whom I've learned much about music, ethics, integrity, and, not the least important, humor. To them I owe a debt of gratitude for providing me with enough wealth of insight and stories to last a lifetime.

Then, of course, there are my toughest critics—my family. My wife, Cecily, and my children, Kate and Jake, have remained positive and supportive while enduring having to read yet another rewrite and have provided both encouragement and, at times, painfully frank criticism. To them, my thanks and my love.